SILENT PREY

SILENT PREY

JOHN SANDFORD

G. P. PUTNAM'S SONS
New York

G. P. Putnam's Sons
Publishers Since 1838
200 Madison Avenue
New York, NY 10016

Library of Congress Cataloging-in-Publication Data

Sandford, John, date.
Silent Prey / John Sandford.
p.   cm.
ISBN 0-399-13742-4 (alk. paper)
I. Title.
PS3569.A516S55   1992   91-43696 CIP
813'.54—dc20

Printed in the United States of America
1   2   3   4   5   6   7   8   9   10

This book is printed on acid-free paper.

SILENT PREY

CHAPTER

1

A thought sparked in the chaos of Bekker's mind.

The jury.

He caught it, mentally, like a quick hand snatching a fly from midair.

Bekker slumped at the defense table, the center of the circus. His vacant blue eyes rolled back, pale and wide as a plastic baby-doll's, wandering around the interior of the courtroom, snagging on a light fixture, catching on an electrical outlet, sliding past the staring faces. His hair had been cut jailhouse short, but they had let him keep the wild blond beard. An act of mercy: the beard disguised the tangled mass of pink scar tissue that crisscrossed his face. In the middle of the beard, his pink rosebud lips opened and closed, like an eel's, damp and glistening.

Bekker looked at the thought he'd caught: *The jury.* Housewives, retirees, welfare trash. His *peers,* they called them. A ridiculous concept: he was a doctor of medicine. He stood at the top of his profession. He was *respected.* Bekker shook his head.

Understand . . . ?

The word tumbled from the judge-crow's mouth and echoed in his mind. "Do you understand, Mr. Bekker?"

What . . . ?

The idiot flat-faced attorney pulled at Bekker's sleeve: "Stand up."

What . . . ?

The prosecutor turned to stare at him, hate in her eyes. The hate touched him, reached him, and he opened his mind and let it flow back. *I'd like to have you for five minutes, good sharp scalpel would open you up like a goddamn oyster: zip, zip. Like a goddamn clam.*

The prosecutor felt Bekker's interest. She was a hard woman; she'd put six hundred men and women behind bars. Their petty threats and silly pleas no longer interested her. But she flinched and turned away from Bekker.

What? Standing? Time now?

Bekker struggled back. It was so hard. He'd let himself go during the trial. He had no interest in it. Refused to testify. The outcome was fixed, and he had more serious problems to deal with. Like survival in the cages of the Hennepin County Jail, survival without his medicine.

But now the time had come.

His blood still moved too slowly, oozing through his arteries like strawberry jam. He fought, and simultaneously fought to hide his struggle.

Focus.

And he started, so slowly it was like walking through paste, trudging back to the courtroom. The trial had lasted for twenty-one days, had dominated the papers and the television newscasts. The cameras had ambushed him, morning and night, hitting him in the face with their intolerable lights, the cameramen scuttling backward as they transferred him, in chains, between the jail and the courtroom.

The courtroom was done in blond laminated wood, with the elevated judge's bench at the head of the room, the jury box to the right, tables for the prosecution and defense in front of the judge. Behind the tables, a long rail divided the room in two. Forty uncomfortable spectator's chairs were screwed to the floor behind the rail. The chairs were occupied an hour before arguments began, half of them allotted to the press, the other half given out on a first-come basis. All during the trial, he could hear his name passing through the ranks of spectators: *Bekker Bekker Bekker.*

The jury filed out. None of them looked at him. They'd be secluded, his *peers,* and after chatting for a decent interval, they'd come back and report him guilty of multiple counts of first-degree murder. The verdict was inevitable. When it was in, the crow would put him away.

The black asshole in the next cell had said it, in his phony street dialect: "They gon slam yo' nasty ass into Oak Park, m'man. You live in a motherfuckin' cage the size of a motherfuckin' refrigerator wit a TV watching you every move. You wanta take a shit, they watchin' every move, they makin' movies of it. Nobody ever git outa Oak Park. It is a true motherfucker."

But Bekker wasn't going. The thought set him off again, and he shook, fought to control it.

Focus . . .

He focused on the small parts: The gym shorts biting into the flesh at his waist. The razor head pressed against the back of his balls. The Sox cap, obtained in a trade for cigarettes, tucked under his belt. His feet sweating in the ridiculous running shoes. Running shoes and white socks with his doctor's pinstripes—he looked a fool and he knew it, hated it. Only a moron would wear white socks with pinstripes, but white socks *and* running shoes . . . no. People would be laughing at him.

He could have worn his wing tips, one last time—a man is innocent until proven guilty—but he refused. They didn't understand that. They thought it was another eccentricity, the plastic shoes with the seven-hundred-dollar suit. They didn't know.

Focus.

Everyone was standing now, the crow-suit staring, the attorney pulling at his sleeve. And here was Raymond Shaltie . . .

"On your feet," Shaltie said sharply, leaning over him. Shaltie was a sheriff's deputy, an overweight time-server in an ill-fitting gray uniform.

"How long?" Bekker asked the attorney, looking up, struggling to get the words out, his tongue thick in his mouth.

"Shhh . . ."

The judge was talking, looking at them: ". . . standing by, and if you leave your numbers with my office, we'll get in touch as soon as we get word from the jury . . ."

The attorney nodded, looking straight ahead. He wouldn't meet Bekker's eyes. Bekker had no chance. In his heart, the attorney didn't want him to have a chance. Bekker was nuts. Bekker *needed* prison. Prison forever and several days more.

"How long?" Bekker asked again. The judge had disappeared into her chambers. *Like to get her, too.*

"Can't tell. They'll have to consider the separate counts," the attorney said. He was court-appointed, needed the money. "We'll come get you . . ."

Pig's eye, they would.

"Let's go," said Shaltie. He took Bekker's elbow, dug his fingertips into the nexus of nerves above Bekker's elbow, an old jailer's trick to establish dominance. Unknowingly, Shaltie did Bekker a favor. With the sudden sharp pulse of pain, Bekker snapped all the way back, quick and hard, like a handclap.

His eyes flicked once around the room, his mind cold, its usual chaos squeezed into a high-pressure corner, wild thoughts raging like rats in a cage. Calculating. He put pain in his voice, a childlike plea: "I need to go. . . ."

"Okay." Shaltie nodded. Ray Shaltie wasn't a bad man. He'd worked the courts for two decades, and the experience had mellowed him—allowed him to see the human side of even the worst of men. And Bekker was the worst of men.

But Bekker was nevertheless human, Shaltie believed: *He that is without sin among you, let him cast the first stone. . . .* Bekker was a man gone wrong, but still a man. And in words that bubbled from his mouth in a whiny singsong, Bekker told Shaltie about his hemorrhoids. Jail food was bad for them, Bekker said. All cheese and bread and pasta. Not enough roughage. He had to go. . . .

He always used the bathroom at noon, all through the ten days of the trial. Raymond Shaltie sympathized: he'd had them himself. Shaltie took Bekker by the arm and led him past the now empty jury box, Bekker shuffling, childlike, eyes unfocused. At the door, Shaltie turned him—docile, quiet, apparently gone to another world—and put on the handcuffs and then the leg chains. Another deputy watched the process, and when Bekker was locked up, drifted away, thinking of lunch.

"Gotta go," Bekker said. His eyes turned up to Ray Shaltie.

"You'll be okay, you'll be okay," Shaltie said. Shaltie's tie had soup stains on it, and flakes of dandruff spotted his shoulders: an oaf, Bekker thought. Shaltie led Bekker out of the courtroom, Bekker doing the jailhouse shuffle, his legs restricted to a thirty-inch stride. Behind the courtroom, a narrow hallway led to an internal stairway, and from there, to a holding cell. But to the left, through a service door, was a tiny employees-only men's room, with a sink, a urinal, a single stall.

Shaltie followed Bekker into the men's room. "Now, you're okay . . ." A warning in his voice. Ray Shaltie was too old to fight.

"Yes," Bekker said, his pale-blue eyes wandering in their sockets. Behind the wandering eyes, his mind was moving easily now, the adrenaline acting on his brain like a dose of the purest amphetamine. He turned, lifted his arms up and back, thrusting his wrists at Shaltie. Shaltie fitted the key, uncuffed the prisoner: Shaltie was breaking the rules, but a man can't wipe himself if he's wearing handcuffs. Besides, where would Bekker go, high up here in the government building, with the leg chains? He couldn't run. And his wildly bearded face was, for the moment at least, the most recognizable face in the Cities.

Bekker shuffled into the stall, shut the door, dropped his trousers, sat down. Eyes sharp now, focused. They used disposable safety razors in the jail, Bics. He'd broken the handle off one, leaving only the head and a stub, easy to hide during the shakedowns. When he'd had a chance, he'd burned the stub with a match, rounding the edges, to make it more comfortable to wear.

This morning he'd taped it under his balls, fixed with the end of a Band-Aid. Now he peeled the razor off himself, pulled the remaining tape off the razor, and began hacking at his beard.

He'd grown the beard to cover his furrowed face. Bekker, once so beautiful, the possessor of a classic Nordic face, a pale, uninflected oval with rose lips, had been beaten into a grotesque gnome, torn to pieces and only poorly repaired. *Davenport. Get Davenport.* The fantasy seized him: opening Davenport, using the knife to peel the face, lifting the skin off inch by inch. . . .

He fought it: fantasies were for the lockup. He forced Davenport out of his mind and continued shaving, quickly, raggedly, the razor scraping over his dry skin. The pain prompted a groan. Outside the stall, Shaltie winced.

" 'Bout done in there?" Shaltie called. The bathroom smelled of ammonia, chlorine, urine, and wet mops.

"Yes, Ray." Bekker dropped the razor in his jacket pocket, then worked on the toilet-paper holder. Originally, it had been held in place with four screws. He'd removed and flushed two of them during the first three days of the trial, and had worked the other two loose. He'd actually had them out the day before, to make sure the holder would pull free. It had. Now he removed the screws one last time, dropped them in the toilet and eased the paper-holder free from the wall. When he grasped it by the roller, it fit his hand like a steel boxing glove.

"Okay now, Ray." Bekker stood, pulled his pants up, pulled off his jacket, dropped the coat over the iron fist, flushed the toilet. Took a breath. Put his head down, as though he were looking at his fly. Opened the door. Shuffled forward.

Shaltie was waiting with the cuffs: jowly, freckled, slow on the uptake. "Turn around. . . ."

Seeing Bekker's face, realizing: "Hey . . ."

Bekker was half-turned, wound up. He dropped the jacket, his right hand whipping like a lash, his mouth open, his white teeth flashing in the fluorescence. Shaltie lurched back, tried to cover with a hand. Too late, too late. The stainless-steel club hit him above the ear: Shaltie went down, cracking the back of his head on the porcelain sink as he fell.

And then Bekker was on him, lifting the steel fist, smashing it down, lifting it, feeling Sheltie's skull crack, the blood spatter. *Hit hit hit hit . . .*

The synapses of Bekker's brain lit with the static sparks. He fought it, fought for control, but it was hard, the smell of fresh blood in his nose. He stopped swinging, found his left hand on Shaltie's throat. Pulled the hand away, half stood, brain not quite right: He said aloud, shushing himself, "Shhh. Shhhhhh," finger to his lips.

He straightened. His blood was running like water now, like steam, filling him. Now what? Door. He hobbled to the door, flipped the catch. Locked. Good. He went back to Shaltie, who was supine on the tile floor, blowing blood bubbles through his torn nose. Bekker had watched the deputy handle his keys, and the keys had gone in Shaltie's right pocket. . . . He found them, popped the locks on the leg chains. Free. *Free.*

Stop. He brought himself back, looked in the mirror. His face was a mess. He retrieved the razor from his jacket pocket, splashed water and liquid soap on his face and raked the razor across it. Listened to Shaltie, breathing, a gargling moan. Shaltie's head lay in a puddle of blood, and Bekker could smell it.

Bekker threw the razor in a trash basket, turned, stooped, caught Shaltie under the shoulders, dragged him to the toilet stall, sat him on the toilet and propped him against the wall. Shaltie made a snoring sound and more blood bubbled from his nose. Bekker ignored him. Not much time.

He stripped off his suit pants, put the Sox hat on his head, and used the pants to wipe up the blood on the floor. When he finished, he threw the pants, jacket, shirt and tie over Shaltie's body. Checked himself in the mirror: green tank top, red shorts, gym shoes, hat. A jogger. The face was bad, but nobody had seen him close up, without a beard, for weeks. A few of the cops would know him, a couple of lawyers. But with any luck, they wouldn't be looking at joggers.

Davenport. The thought stopped him. If Davenport was out there, had come to see the verdict, Bekker was a dead man.

No help for that. He threw off the thought, took a breath. Ready. He stepped inside the stall with Shaltie, locked it, dropped to his back, slid under the door, stood up again.

"Motherfucker." He said it out loud, had learned it in jail: the standard, all-purpose curse. He dropped back on the floor, slid halfway under the stall, groped for Shaltie's wallet. Found it, checked it. Twelve dollars. One credit card, a Visa. Not good. Money could be a problem. . . . He slipped the wallet into his underpants, went to the door, listened.

Could hear Shaltie breathing, bubbling. Bekker thought about going back into the stall, strangling him with his belt. All the humiliations of the past week, the torture when they took away his chemicals . . . Not enough time. Time was hurting him now. Had to move.

He left Shaltie, living, turned the lock knob, peered into the hallway. The internal corridor was empty. Went to the next door—public hall. Half-dozen people, all down at the public end, near the elevators, talking. He wouldn't have to walk past them. The stairs were the other way: he could see the exit sign, just beyond the fire hose.

Another breath. And move. He stepped out into the hall, head down. A lunchtime bureaucrat-jogger on his way outside. He walked confidently down the hall to the stairs, away from the elevators. Waiting for a shout. For someone to point a finger. For running feet.

He was in the stairway. Nobody took the stairs, not from this high up. . . .

He ran down, counting the floors. As he passed six, a door slammed somewhere below and he heard somebody walking down ahead of him. He padded softly behind, heard another door open and shut, and stepped up the pace again. At the main level, he stopped and looked out. Dozens of people milled through the reception area. Okay. This was the second floor. He needed one more. He went down another level, and found an unmarked steel door. He pushed it open. He was outside, standing on the plaza. The summer sun was brilliant, the breeze smelled of popcorn and pigeons. A woman sitting on a bench, a kid next to her. She was cutting an apple with a penknife, her kid waiting for the apple.

Head down, Bekker jogged past her. Just another lunchtime fitness freak, weaving through the traffic, knees up, sweating in the sunshine.

Running like a maniac.

CHAPTER

2

Lucas whipped down the asphalt backroads of Wisconsin, one hand on the wheel, one on the shifter, heel-and-toe on the corners, sunlight bouncing off the Porsche's dusty windshield. He slow-footed across the St. Croix bridge at Taylor's Falls into Minnesota, looking for cops, then dropped the hammer again, headed south into the sun and the Cities.

He caught Highway 36 west of Stillwater, the midday traffic sparse and torpid, pickups and station wagons clunking past the cow pastures, barns and cattail sloughs. Eight miles east of Interstate 694, he blew the doors off a red Taurus SHO. Clear road, except for the occasional crows picking at roadkill.

His eyes dropped to the speedometer. One hundred and seven. *What the fuck are you doing?*

He wasn't quite sure. The day before, he'd rolled out of his lake cabin late in the afternoon and driven eighty miles north to Duluth. To buy books, he thought: there were no real bookstores in his corner of Wisconsin. He'd bought books, all right, but he'd wound up drinking beer in a place called the Wee Blue Inn at eight o'clock in the evening. He'd been wearing a dark-blue dress shirt under a silk jacket, khaki slacks, and brown loafers, no socks. A laid-off ore-boatman, drunk, had taken exception to the bare feet, and for one happy instant, before the barkeeps arrived, it had looked like the boatman would take a swing.

He needed a bar fight, Lucas thought. But he didn't need what would come afterward, the cops. He took his books back to the cabin, tried to fish the next day, then gave it up and headed back to the Cities, driving as fast as he knew how.

A few miles after blowing off the SHO, he passed the first of the exurban ramblers, outriders for the 'burbs. He groped in the glove box, found the radar detector, clipped it to the visor and plugged it into the cigarette-lighter socket as the Porsche screamed down the cracked pavement. He let his foot settle further; punched up the radio, Cities-97. Little Feat was playing hard hot boogie, "Shake Me Up," the perfect sound to accompany a gross violation of the speed limit.

The interstate overpass flicked past and the traffic got thicker. A hundred and eighteen. Hundred and nineteen. A stoplight he'd forgotten about, looming suddenly, with a blue sedan edging into a right-on-red turn. Lucas went left, right, left, heel-and-toe, blowing past the sedan; and past a station wagon, for a split second catching at the periphery of his vision the surprised and frightened face of a blonde matron with a car full of blond kids.

The image fixed in his mind. Scared. He sighed and eased off the gas pedal, coasting. Dropped through a hundred, ninety, eighty. Across the northern suburbs of St. Paul, onto the exit to Highway 280. When he'd been a cop, he'd always been sneaking off to the lake. Now that he wasn't, now that he had time sitting on him like an endless pile of computer printout, he found the solace of the lake less compelling. . . .

The day was warm, sunshine dappling the roadway, playing games with cloud-shadows on the glass towers of Minneapolis to the west. And then the cop car.

He caught it in the rearview mirror, nosing out of Broadway. No siren. His eyes dropped to the speedometer again. Sixty. The limit was fifty-five, so sixty should be fine. Still, cops picked on Porsches. He eased off a bit more. The cop car closed until it was on his bumper, and in the rearview mirror he could see the cop talking into his microphone: running the Porsche's tags. Then the light bar came up and the cop tapped his siren.

Lucas groaned and rolled to the side, the cop fifteen feet off his bumper. He recognized him, a St. Paul cop, once worked with the Southwest Team. He used to come into the deli near Lucas' house. What was his name? Lucas dug through his memory. Kelly . . . Larsen? Larsen was out of the car, heavy face, sunglasses, empty-handed. No ticket, then. And he was jogging. . . .

Lucas shifted into neutral, pulled the brake, popped the door and swiveled in the seat, letting his feet fall on the shoulder of the road.

"Davenport, God damn it, I *thought* this was your piece of shit," Larsen said, thumping the Porsche's roof. "Everybody's looking for your ass. . . ."

"What . . . ?"

"Fuckin' Bekker blew out of the government center. He's knocked down two people so far."

"What?" Lucas Davenport: deep summer tan, jagged white scar crossing his eyebrow, khaki short-sleeved shirt, jeans, gym shoes. A surge of adrenaline almost took his breath away.

"Two of your buddies are laying up at your place. They think he might be coming for you," Larsen said. He was a large man who kept hitching up his belt, and peering around, as though he might spot Bekker sneaking through a roadside ditch.

Lucas: "I better get my ass down there. . . ."

"Go." Larsen thumped the top of the car again.

Back on the highway, Lucas picked up the car phone and poked in the direct-dial number for the Minneapolis cops. He was vaguely pleased with himself: he didn't need the phone, rarely used it. He'd installed it the week after he'd bought the gold-and-steel Rolex that circled his wrist—two useless symbols of his freedom from the Minneapolis Police Department. Symbols that he was doing what every cop supposedly wanted to do, to go out on his own, to *make* it. And now the business was snaking off in new directions, away from games, into computer

simulations of police tactical problems. Davenport Games &
Simulations. With the growing sales, he might have to rent an
office.

The switchboard operator said, "Minneapolis."

"Gimme Harmon Anderson," Lucas said.

"Is that you, Lucas?" the operator asked. Melissa Yellow
Bear.

"Yeah." He grinned. Somebody remembered.

"Harmon's been waiting. Are you at home?"

"No, I'm in my car."

"You heard what happened?" Yellow Bear was breathless.

"Yes."

"You take care, honey. I'll switch you over. . . ."

A moment later, Anderson came on, and said without preamble, "Del and Sloan are at your place. Sloan got the key from
your neighbor, but they're wasting their time. He won't be coming after this long. It's been three hours."

"How about Del's place? He and Bekker are relatives of some
kind."

"We've got a couple of guys there, too, but he's hiding somewhere. He won't be out, not now."

"How did he—"

"Go on home and Sloan can fill you in," Anderson said,
interrupting. "I gotta go. This goddamn place is a madhouse."

And he was gone. *Police work to do, no time for civilians.* Lucas
got off at University Avenue, took it to Vandalia, across I-94 and
down Cretin, then over to the tree-shaded river road. Brooding.
No time for Davenport.

Feeling sorry for himself, knowing it.

Two blocks before he got to the house, he slowed, watching,
then turned a block early. The neighborhood offered few places
to hide, other than inside the houses. The yards were open,
tree-filled, burning with color: crabapple blossoms and lines of
tulips, banks of iris, pink peonies and brilliant yellow daffodils,
and the odd patch of buttery dandelions that had somehow
escaped the yard-service sprayers. The day was warm, and peo-

ple were working in their yards or on their houses; a couple of
kids in shorts shot baskets at a garage-mounted hoop. Bekker
couldn't hide in the open yards, and breaking into a house would
be tough. Too many people around. He turned a corner and
idled down toward his house.

Lucas lived in what a real estate woman had once called a soft
rambler: stone and clapboard, a fireplace, big trees, two-car garage. At the end of the asphalt drive, he slowed, punched the
garage-door opener, and waited at the end of the driveway until
the door was all the way up. A curtain moved in the front room.

When Lucas pulled into the garage, Sloan was waiting in the
door between the house and the garage, hand in his jacket
pocket. He was a thin man with high cheekbones and deep-set
eyes. As Lucas got out of the car, Del drifted up behind Sloan,
the butt of a compact 9mm pistol sticking out of his waistband.
Del was older, with a face like sandpaper, a street burnout.

"What the hell happened?" Lucas asked as the garage door
rolled down.

"An old-fuck deputy uncuffed him so he could take a shit,"
Sloan said. "Bekker'd been telling everybody that he had hemorrhoids and he always went to the can at the noon recess."

"Setting them up," Lucas said.

Del nodded. "Looks like it."

"Anyway, the jury went out and the deputy took him to the
bathroom before hauling him down to the holding cell," Sloan
continued. "Bekker unscrewed a steel toilet-paper holder from
the wall of the stall. Came out of the stall and beat the shit out
of the old guy."

"Dead?"

"Not yet, but he's leaking brains. He's probably paralyzed."

"I heard he hit two guys?"

"Yeah, but the other was later . . ." Del said, and explained.
Witnesses waiting outside a courtroom had seen Bekker leave,
without knowing until later who he was. Others saw him cross
the government-center plaza, running past the lunchtime brown-

baggers, through the rafts of pigeons, heading down the street in his shorts. "He went about ten blocks, to a warehouse by the tracks, picked up a piece of concrete-reinforcement rod, went in the warehouse and whacked a guy working at the dispatch desk. A clerk. Took his clothes and his wallet. That's where we lost him."

"The clerk?"

"He's fucked up."

"I'm surprised Bekker didn't kill him."

"I don't think he had time," Del said. "He's in a hurry, like he knows where he's going. That's why we came here. But it don't feel right anymore, the longer I think about it. You scare the shit out of him. I don't think he'd take you on."

"He's nuts," said Lucas. "Maybe he would."

"Whatever, you got a carry permit?" asked Sloan.

"No."

"We'll have to fix you up if we don't get him. . . ."

They didn't get him.

Lucas spent the next forty-eight hours checking old sources, but nobody seemed much inclined to talk to him, not even the cops. Too busy.

He brought a Colt Gold Cup .45 up from the basement gun safe, cleaned it, loaded it, kept it under the bed on a book. During the day, he carried it hidden in the Porsche. He enjoyed the weight of the gun in his hand and the headache-making smell of the gun-cleaning solvent. He spent an hour in a Wisconsin gravel pit, shooting two boxes of semi-wadcutters into man-sized silhouettes.

Then, two days after Bekker broke out of the courthouse, neighbors found the body of Katherine McCain. She'd been an antiques dealer and a friend of Bekker's wife, and she'd had the Bekkers to a party six or eight weeks before Bekker's wife had been murdered. Bekker knew the house and knew she lived alone. He'd been waiting when she came home, and killed her with a hammer. Before he left in her car, he'd used a knife to slash her eyes, so her ghost couldn't watch him from the other world.

And then he disappeared.

McCain's car was eventually found in an airport parking lot in Cleveland, Bekker long gone. On the day the car was found, Lucas put the .45 back in the gun safe. He never got the carry permit. Sloan forgot, and then after a while, it didn't seem important.

Lucas had temporarily gone off women, and found it hard to focus on the idea of a date. He tried fishing, played golf every day for a week. No good. His life, he thought with little amusement, was like his refrigerator—and his refrigerator contained a six-pack of light beer, three cans of diet caffeine-free Coke, and a slowly fossilizing jar of mustard.

At night, unable to sleep, he couldn't get Bekker out of his head. Couldn't forget the taste of the hunt, of closing in, of cornering him . . .

He missed it. He didn't miss the police department, with its meetings and its brutal politics. Just the hunt. And the pressure.

Sloan called twice from Minneapolis, said it looked like Bekker was gone. Del called once, said they'd have to get a beer sometime.

Lucas said *yeah.*

And waited.

Bekker was a bad penny.

Bekker would turn up.

CHAPTER

3

Louis Cortese was dying.

A brilliant floodlight lit his waxy face and the blood on his cheeks, and emphasized the yellow tint in his eyes. His lips were twisted, like those of an imp in a medieval painting.

Bekker watched. Touched a switch, heard the camera shutter fire. He could feel death swooping down on them, in the little room, in the lights, as Louis Cortese's life drained into a plastic jug.

Bekker's brain was a calculator, an empty vessel, a tangle of energy, a word processor, and an expert anatomist. But never more than one thing at a time.

Three months in the Hennepin County Jail had changed him forever. The jailers had taken away his chemicals, boiled his brain, and broken forever the thin electrochemical bonds that held his mind together.

In jail, lying in his cell in his rational-planner mode, he'd visualized his brain as an old-fashioned Lions Club gumball machine. When he put in a penny, he got back a gumball—but he never knew in advance what color he'd get.

The memory of Ray Shaltie, of the escape, was one color, a

favorite flavor, rattling down the payoff chute of his psyche.
When he got it, it was like a wide-screen movie with overpower-
ing stereo sound, a movie that froze him in his tracks, wherever
he was. He was *back there* with Ray Shaltie, with the steel fist,
smashing. . . .

Bekker, real time.

He sat in a chromed-steel chair and watched Cortese's death
throes, his eyes moving between the monitor screens and the
dying subject's face. A clear plastic tube was sewn into Cortese's
neck, piping the blood from his carotid artery to an oversized
water jug on the floor. The blood was purple, the color of cooked
beets, and Bekker could smell it, his fine nostrils twitching with
the scent. On the EKG, Cortese's heart rate soared. Bekker
trembled. Cortese's consciousness was moving outward, expanding, joining with . . . what?

Well. Nothing, maybe.

Cortese's . . . essence . . . might be nothing more than a bubble
reaching the top of a cosmic glass of soda water, expanding only
to burst into oblivion. The pressure of the thought made Bekker's eyebrow jump uncontrollably, twitching, until he put a
hand to his forehead to stop it.

There *had to be* something beyond. That he himself might just
blink out . . . No. The thought was insupportable.

Cortese convulsed, a full-body rictus throwing him against the
nylon restraining straps, his head cranking forward, his eyes
bulging. Air squeezed from his lungs, past the elaborate gag, a
hoarse bubbling release. He was looking at nothing: nothing at
all. He was beyond vision. . . .

The alarm tone sounded on the blood-pressure monitor, then
on the EKG, twin tones merging into one. With his left hand
still clapped to his forehead, restraining the unruly eyebrow,
Bekker turned toward the monitors. Cortese's heart had
stopped, blood pressure was plummeting toward zero. Bekker
felt the large muscles of his own back and buttocks tighten with
the anticipation.

He looked at the EEG, the brain-wave monitor. A jagged, jangled line just seconds before, it began flattening, flattening . . .

He felt Cortese go: could feel the *essence* go. He couldn't measure it—not yet—but he could feel it. He bathed in the feeling, clutched at it; fired a half-dozen photos, the motor drives going *bzz-whit, bzz-whit* behind his head. And finally the magic *something* slipped away. Bekker jumped to his feet, frantic to hold on. He leaned over Cortese, his eyes four inches from the other's. There was something about death and the eyes. . . .

And then Cortese was gone, beyond Bekker's reach. His body, the shell of his personality, went slack beneath Bekker's hands.

The power of the moment spun Bekker around. Breathing hard, he stared at a reflection of himself in a polished stainless-steel cabinet. He saw himself there a dozen times a day, as he worked: the raw face, the sin face, he called it, the cornrows of reddened flesh where the gunsights had ripped through him. He said in a small, high voice: "Gone."

But not quite. Bekker felt the pressure on his back; his spine stiffened, and a finger of fear touched him. He turned, and the dead man's eyes caught him and held him. They were open, of course. Bekker had carefully trimmed away the eyelids to ensure they would remain that way.

"Don't," he said sharply. Cortese was mute, but the eyes were watching.

"Don't," Bekker said again, louder, his voice cracking. Cortese was watching him.

Bekker snatched a scalpel from a stainless-steel tray, stepped to the head of the table, leaned over the body and slashed at the eyes. He was expert: it only took a second. He carved the eyes like boiled eggs, and the vitreous aqua leaked down Cortese's dead cheeks like jellied tears.

"Good-bye," Bekker said dreamily. The ruined eyes were no longer threatening. A gumball dropped, and Bekker went away. . . .

* * *

Thick stopped at the curb, rocking on his heels, waiting patiently for the light. Thin snapped a cigarette into the street, where it exploded in a shower of sparks. The cars went by in a torrent, battered Toyotas and clunking Fords, fender-bent Dodges, pickups and vans blocking the view ahead, trucks covered with graffiti, buses stinking up the streets with noxious diesel fumes, all rolling past like iron salmon headed upstream to spawn. Through all of it, the taxis jockeyed for position, signaling their moves with quick taps on their horns, an amber warp to the woof of the street. New York was noise: an underground rumble of trains and steam pipes, a street-level clash of gears and motors and bad mufflers, a million people talking at once, uncounted air conditioners buzzing above it all.

All of it congealed in the heat.

"Too fuckin' hot," Thick said. And it was; he could feel it on his neck, in his armpits, on the soles of his feet. He glanced at Thin, who'd stopped at the curb beside him. Thin nodded but didn't answer. They were both wearing long-sleeved shirts with the sleeves rolled down to their wrists. Thin was a problem, and Thick didn't quite know what to do about it. Hadn't really known, he thought wryly, for almost forty years now. . . .

The walk sign flashed on and he and Thin crossed the street. A traffic-light pole, splattered with pigeon shit and encrusted with the grime of decades, sat on the corner. At the bottom, and up as high as a hand could reach, it was covered with fading posters. Above that, two street signs were mounted at right angles to each other, a bus-stop sign faced the street, and a temporary traffic-diversion sign pointed an arrow to the left. Above all that, a spar went out to the traffic signal, and another supported a streetlight.

Oughta put one in a fuckin' museum someplace, just like that. Our own fuckin' totem poles . . .

"Dollar . . ." The woman on the sidewalk reached up at him, holding a dirty hand-lettered card: "Help me feed my children." Thick walked past, thinking that it was impossible that the woman had children. In her forties, perhaps, she was withered as a week-old carrot, her emaciated legs sprawled beneath her, her bare feet covered with open sores. Her eyes had a foggy-white glaze, not cataracts, but something else. She had no teeth at all, only dimples in gray gums, like the vacant spots left by corn kernels popped from a cob.

"I read this book about Shanghai once, the way it was before World War Two," Thick said as they passed on. Thin looked straight ahead, not responding. "The thing was, begging was a profession, you know? But an ordinary guy couldn't get any alms. You needed to be special. So they'd take kids and burn their eyes out or smash their arms and legs with hammers. They had to make them pitiful enough to get money in a whole city full of beggars. . . ."

Thin looked up at him, still saying nothing.

"So we're getting there, too," Thick said, looking back at the woman on the street. "Who's gonna give money to your average panhandler when you walk by something like that every day?" He half turned to look back at the woman.

"Dollar," the woman wailed, "Dollar . . ."

Thick was worried. Thin was talking about running out. He glanced at his partner. Thin's eyes were angry, fixed straight ahead. Thinking . . .

Thick was carrying a large, flat, cardboard box. It wasn't particularly heavy, but the shape was awkward, and he slowed to hitch it up under his arm.

"I wouldn't mind . . ." Thick started, then let it go. He reached up to scratch his face, but he was wearing thin, flesh-colored surgeon's gloves, and he couldn't effectively scratch. They moved along, quickly, to an apartment building across the street from the steak house. Thick had the key in his free hand and opened the door.

Thin said, "I can't do it."

"We gotta. Jesus Christ, if we don't we're fuckin' dead, all of us. . . ."

"Listen . . ."

"Off the street, off the street . . ."

Inside the door, the hall and landing were dimly lit by a yellow sixty-watt bulb. The stairs were immediately to the right, and Thick started up. Thin, undecided, looked back out at the street, then, reluctantly, because Thick was already moving, followed. At the top of the stairs, they stopped in the hallway for a moment and listened, then went to the front apartment and opened the door with a key. The only light in the apartment came through the yellowed shades on the front windows, from the street. The place smelled of dead air, old coffee grounds, and dry plants. The owners had been in Rome for a week, to see the Pope. They'd go to the Holy Land afterward. The Holy Land in July. They'd burn their brains out, if they had any, which they probably didn't, if they were going to the Holy Land in July.

Thin shut the door behind them and said, "Listen . . ."

"If you weren't going to do it, why'd you come this far?"

"Because you got us into it. I don't want you to get fucked up."

"Jesus . . ." Thick shook his head and stepped carefully through the dark room to the windows and lifted a shade. "Get the rifle."

"I'm not . . ."

"All right, I'll do it. Jesus, if that's the way you feel about it, go. Get the fuck out," Thick said, anger riding his voice. He was older than Thin by twenty-three years and two days, his face stamped with the cuts and gullies of a life on the street. He picked up the box he'd carried in. "Go."

Thin hesitated, watching. The box was five feet long by three wide, but only eight inches deep. It might have held a mirror, or even a painting, but it didn't—it held a Colt AR-15 with a flash suppressor, a twenty-shot magazine, a two-power light-gathering scope, and a laser sight. The weapon, manufactured as a semiautomatic, had been converted to selectible fire, semiauto or full auto, by a machinist in Providence.

Thick had spent an afternoon in the Adirondacks shooting plastic milk jugs from a perch high on the bank of a gully. The gallon-sized jugs closely simulated the kill zone of a man's chest from any angle. Thick used hand-loaded cartridges, and he was a very good shot. When hit by one of Thick's hot loads, the milk jugs literally exploded.

Thick used a penknife to cut the twine that held the box shut, stripped off a couple of pieces of tape, opened it, and took the weapon out of the sponge-rubber packing. New scope mounts weren't as delicate as those he'd grown up with, but there was no point in taking chances. He hadn't. A fully loaded magazine was packed with the weapon. Each cartridge had been polished with a chamois to eliminate fingerprints. Thick slapped the magazine home with his rubber-gloved hands.

"Get the couch," Thick said. "Hurry it up."

"No: he's a cop. If he wasn't a cop . . ."

"Bullshit." Thick went to the windows, looked out on the empty street, then unlocked one of them and carefully raised it until it was fully open. Then he turned, glanced at Thin, and picked up the rifle.

"You never had this problem before. . . ."

"The guy hasn't done anything. The others were scumbags. . . . This is a cop. . . ."

"He's a goddamn computer asshole cockroach and he's gonna put good guys in jail for doing what had to be done. And you know what happens if we get sent up? We're fuckin' dead, that's what. I personally doubt that I'd last a fuckin' week; if they come for me, I'm stickin' my goddamn pistol in my mouth, because I ain't goin'. . . ."

"Jesus . . ."

Thick, standing well back from the window, looked at the restaurant across the street through the low-powered scope. A Visa emblem was stuck to the window on the door, under the script of the restaurant's name and logo. Looking at the logo, the theme song from an old television show trickled through his head: *"Have gun, will travel" is the card of a man* . . .

He picked up the Visa sign in the scope, touched the laser switch with his thumb. A red dot bloomed on the sign. Thick had a head the size of a gasoline can, with small ears that in the semidark looked like dried apricots. "He's worse than the shoo-flies."

"He . . ." Thin's eyes went to the street, and Thick followed them. The restaurant door was opening.

"Wrong guy," Thin blurted.

"I know. . . ."

A man in a white tennis shirt and white shoes stood there, probing his gums with a plastic toothpick. The toothpicks were shaped like swords, Thin knew. They'd made a recon trip to the steak house the night before, to figure times and placements. The target always came in for the Friday special, New York strip with sour-cream baked potato and choice of draft beer. The man in the tennis shirt ambled down the street.

"Fuckin' faggot," said Thick. He flicked the switch on the laser sight and the red dot bloomed on the Visa sign.

Bekker sighed.

All done.

He turned away from Cortese's body, his mind like a coil of concertina wire, tense, sharp, dangerous. He touched his shirt pocket: the pocket was empty. He stepped out of his room, with a touch of anxiety, and went to the old dresser where he kept his clothes. A half-handful of pills were scattered across the top of it, and he relaxed. Enough. He picked up several, developing a combo rush as he went, popped them into his mouth, savored the acrid bite, and swallowed. So good; but so few. He looked at the top of the dresser, at the pills there. Enough for another day, no more. He'd have to think about it—but later.

He went back into the workroom, killed the monitors, their green screens blanking out. Nothing to see anyway, just horizontal lines. Bekker ignored the body. Cortese was simply garbage, a matter of disposal.

But before the death . . . A new gumball dropped, and Bekker froze beside the worktable, his mind sliding away.

Louis Cortese had been dark-haired, seventy-one and one-half inches tall, one hundred and eighty-six pounds, and thirty-seven years old—all of it carefully recorded in Bekker's notebooks. He'd been a graduate in electrical engineering from Purdue University. Before Bekker'd cut off his eyelids, when Cortese had still been trying to ingratiate himself, still fending off the idea that he was about to die, he'd told Bekker that he was a Pisces. Bekker had only a vague idea what that meant, and he wasn't interested.

Cortese's body lay on a stainless-steel countertop, which had cost six hundred and fifty dollars at a restaurant-supply shop in Queens. The countertop, in turn, was fixed to an old wooden library table; Bekker'd had to cut down the legs to get the proper working height. Overhead, a rank of three shop lamps threw a flat, cold light on the table.

Because his research subjects would be alive, Bekker had fixed restraining rings to the table. A brown nylon strap was clipped to a ring just below Cortese's right armpit, and ran diagonally from the armpit across the chest between the nipple and the shoulder, to another ring behind the neck, then from behind the neck, back across the opposite side of the chest to another ring below the left armpit; it held Cortese like a full nelson. Additional straps crossed the body at the waist and knees and bound the wrists and ankles.

One of the hands was taped as well as bound: Bekker monitored blood pressure through a catheter placed in the radial artery, and the wrist had to be totally immobilized. Cortese's jaws were spread wide, held open by a hard-rubber cone: the subject could breathe through the nose, but not through the mouth. His screams, when he tried to scream, sounded like a species of humming, though not quite humming.

Mostly, he'd been as silent as a book.

At the head of the table, Bekker had stacked his monitoring equipment in what a discount stereo store had called a home entertainment center. The arrangement was pleasingly professional. The monitors measured body temperature, blood pressure, heartbeat, and brain-wave activity. He also had a neuro-intracranial pressure monitor, but hadn't used it.

The room around the equipment was also carefully finished:

he'd worked on it for a week before he was satisfied. Scrubbed it with disinfectant. Installed an acoustic-tile ceiling and Formica wall panels in a smooth oyster-white finish. Put down the royal-blue carpet. Brought in the equipment. The monitors had been the hard part. He'd finally gotten them from Whitechurch, a dealer at Bellevue. For two thousand in cash, Whitechurch had taken them out of a repair shop, first making sure they'd been fixed. . . .

Sigh.

One of the monitors was telling him something.

What was it? Hard to concentrate . . .

Body temperature, eighty-four degrees.

Eighty-four?

That was too low. He glanced at the clock. 9:07 . . .

He'd been gone again.

Bekker rubbed the back of his neck, disturbed. He would go away, sometimes for an hour. It never seemed to happen at critical times, but still: he should have recognized it, the sigh when he came back. When he went away, he always came back with a sigh. . . .

He stepped to the tape recorders, looked at the counters. They were slightly out of sync, one of them at 504, the other at 509. He rewound them to 200 and listened to the first.

"*. . . direct stimulus brings only a slight reaction, no more than one millimeter . . .*"

His own voice, hoarse with excitement. He turned off the first recorder, turned on the second. "*. . . no more than one-millimeter reflex in the iris followed by immediate release of . . .*"

He turned off the second one. The recorders were working fine. Identical Sonys, with battery backup in case of power failure, they were better than the ones he'd used at the University of Minnesota.

Bekker sighed, caught himself, looked quickly at the clock, afraid that he'd been away again. No. 9:09. He had to clean up, had to get rid of Cortese's body, had to process the Polaroid color-slide film in the cameras. And he had some ideas about the taking of the specimens, and those ideas should be noted. Many things to do. But he couldn't, not at just this moment. The PCP hadn't arrived, and he felt . . . serene. The session had been a good one.

Sigh.

He glanced at the clock, felt a tiny thrill of fear. Nine twenty-five. He'd been gone again, frozen in one place; his knees ached from the unmoving stance. It was happening too much. He needed more medication. Street cocaine was good, but not precise enough. . . .

Then: *Dink.*

Bekker turned his head. The intrusive sound came from a corner of his basement apartment. Almost a bell, but not quite. Instead of ringing, it simply struck once each time the old woman pushed the button.

Dink.

Bekker frowned, walked to the intercom, cleared his throat, and pressed the talk button. "Mrs. Lacey?"

"My hands hurt." Her voice was shrill and ragged. Old. She was eighty-three, hard of hearing, nearly blind in one eye. Her arthritis was bad and growing worse. "My hands hurt so much," she complained.

"I'll bring a pill . . . in a few minutes," Bekker said. "But there are only three left. I'll have to go out again tomorrow. . . ."

"How much?" she asked.

"Three hundred dollars . . ."

"My golly . . ." She seemed taken aback.

"It's very difficult to find these days, Mrs. Lacey," Bekker said. And it had been for decades. She knew that. Morphine had never been street-legal in her lifetime. Neither had her marijuana.

A few days after he'd taken the job as a live-in helper—the old woman's word, she didn't need bathroom assistance—he'd shown her a *Wall Street Journal* story about bank failures. She'd read it, nearly whimpering. She had her Social Security, she had her savings, some $370,000, and she had her building. If any of them broke down . . .

Edith Lacey had watched the old street women as they went by, pushing their shopping carts along the broken pavement, guarding their bundles of rags. She knew them, she said, although Bekker didn't believe her. She'd look out and make up stories about them. "Now that one, *she* once owned a grocery on Greenwich . . ."

Bekker suggested that she spread her cash among three or four unrelated banks, so more would be insured by the Federal Deposit Insurance Corporation.

"Uncertain times," he told her in his careful voice.

She'd talked to her only ambulatory friend about it. Bridget Land, who didn't like Bekker, had thought that spreading the money among banks would be a good idea. And she'd volunteered to go with them: "To make sure everything is on the up-and-up," she'd said, her eyes moving almost involuntarily toward Bekker. "At the banks, I mean."

They'd moved the money in a single day, the two old women nervously guarding the cashier's checks like mother hens. Edith Lacey carrying one inside her blouse, Bridget Land the other in a buttoned pocket, *just in case*. They'd focused so closely on the checks that neither had paid much attention to Bekker as he reviewed Edith's applications for new accounts. Bekker had simply checked the "yes" box that asked if the applicants wanted automatic-teller cards. He picked up the mail each afternoon; a week after they'd moved the money to the banks, he'd intercepted the automatic-teller codes, and a week after that, the cards themselves. The cards were each good for five hundred dollars a day. During the first month, Bekker worked the accounts almost daily, until he had twenty thousand in cash.

"Get fruit," the old woman ordered.

"I'll stop at MacGuire's," he said on the intercom.

"Apricots."

"Okay." He started to turn away.

"Be sure to get apricots. . . ."

"Yes," he snapped.

"You didn't get them last time. . . ."

He was seized by a sudden urge to go up and choke her: not the urge that took him to his subjects, but an almost human desire to choke the shit out of a common nag. "I'm sorry," he said, abjectly, hiding the sudden fury. "And I'll *try* to get your pills."

That would shut her up. . . .

Bekker turned away from the intercom and, through the dark living quarters, saw Cortese's body in the bright light flowing from the operating room. *Might as well do it now.*

From the kitchen, he brought a long roll of black polyethylene, sold as painter's dropcloth. He unrolled it beside the dissection table, used a scalpel to cut it to the right length, then unfolded it. Unstrapped the body. Pulled the catheter from the wrist, pulled the temperature probe. The temperature was down to seventy-nine. Cooling quickly.

Bodies are hard to manipulate, and Bekker, with much experience, didn't even try. He simply walked to the far side of the table and pushed. The body rolled out of the tray and fell on the plastic sheet with a meaty thwack. He walked back around the table, wrapped it, folded the extra length, tied it with clothesline. He took two extra loops at the waist, to use as a handle. He hauled the body through the living quarters and up the steps to the building's reinforced back door, struggling with it. Even when you didn't care if they were damaged, bodies were difficult. And Cortese had been hefty. He should go after smaller people. . . .

The back door of the Lacey building was hidden from the street by a lean-to structure, designed as a car shelter. He popped open the door, chain still on, and checked the lean-to. In the past, bums had sheltered there. Nothing but the Volkswagen, undisturbed. He dragged the body outside, and, with some difficulty, stuffed it into the passenger seat. When it was in, he stepped to the edge of the lean-to and peeked toward the street. Nobody. He went back inside, closed the door, and hurried down the stairs.

Bekker showered, shaved carefully, dressed, and put on his makeup. The process was intricate: The heavy base makeup covered his ruined face, but had to be carefully shaded into the clear skin at his temples without obvious lines. He took half an hour, working at it. He'd just finished when Mrs. Lacey rang again.

"What?" *Old hag . . .*

"My hands," she whined.

"I'm coming now," he said. Maybe he should kill her, he thought. He allowed himself to feel the pleasure of the idea. But then he'd have to explain her absence to Bridget Land. Though he *could* eliminate Land . . . But that led into a maze of unresolvable questions and dangers: Did Land have other friends, and did they know she came to see Edith Lacey? If Land disappeared, would others come looking for her?

Killing her would be dangerous. . . . No, he would kill neither of them. Not yet. Lacey was the perfect front and Land was, so far, only a modest inconvenience. Bekker, thinking about them, got a bottle of pills from his bureau, shook one into the palm of his hand, went to the bottom of the stairs, flicked a light switch, and went up.

The stairs emerged into the back part of the first floor, then curled and went up to the second and third floors. The first floor had once been a plumbing-parts supply business, but had been vacant for years. During the day, a murky green light filtered through from the street. At night, the grille-covered windows were simply dark panels on either side of the street door.

The old woman huddled on the second floor, where she'd lived with her two cats since her husband's death. The second floor reeked of the three of them: cooked carrots, dope, and cat piss. Bekker hated the cats. They knew what he was and watched him from shelves, their eyes glittering in the gloom, as the old woman huddled in front of the television, wrapped in her tie-dyed shawl.

The third floor had once been part of the living quarters, when Mrs. Lacey's husband was living, but now, like the first, was vacant.

Bekker climbed to the second floor, the smell of carrots and marijuana closing around him. "Mrs. Lacey?"

"In here." She was a small woman, with thick glasses that enlarged her rheumy blue eyes. Her hair, wiry and gray, clung close to her head. She had a small button nose and tiny round lips. She was wrapped in a housecoat. She had four of them, quilted, in different pastel colors. She was waiting in the big chair in the living room, facing the television. Bekker went to the kitchen, ran a glass of water and carried the pill out to her. A cat ran from under her chair and hid in the next room, looking back at Bekker with cruel eyes.

"This'll help. I'll get more tomorrow."

"Thank you." She took the pill and drank greedily from the glass.

"You have your pipe and lighter?"

"Yes."

"You have enough of your tea?"

"Yes, thank you kindly." She cackled. She'd washed out of the bohemian life of the forties, but she still had her tea.

"I'm going out for a while," he said.

"Be careful, it's dangerous this late. . . ."

Bekker left her in her chair and went back down the stairs and carefully checked the lean-to again. Nobody.

The Lacey building fronted on Greene Street. The buildings on either side ran all the way back to Mercer, but the Lacey building filled only half the lot. The back lot, overgrown weeds and volunteer sumac, was closed off with a ten-foot chain-link fence. Before Bekker had arrived, vandals and bums had been over and through it and had broken the lock on the gate. After Bekker had bought the Volkswagen, he'd had the fence fixed and a long twisty strand of razor wire laid along the top.

Now he backed the Volkswagen out of the lean-to, wheeled it to the fence, hopped out, opened the gate, drove through, stopped once more, and locked the gate again.

New York, he thought.

Bagels and lox / Razor wire and locks.

Bekker giggled.

"Door," said Thick. He was standing by the window, the M-15 at his shoulder.

On the street below, an old-fashioned Volkswagen, a Bug, zipped past. Thick, looking through the scope, ignored it. A man had stepped out on the street and paused. He had light hair, slightly mussed, and gold-rimmed glasses. Narrow shoulders. He was smiling, his lips moving, talking to himself. He was wearing a blue short-sleeved shirt, and jeans that were too long for his legs. He used his index fingers to push his glasses up on his nose.

"Yes," Thick grunted, his finger tightening on the trigger.

"No . . ." said Thin, taking two steps toward the window.

But a red dot bloomed on the target's chest. He may have had an instant to think about it; again, maybe not. The blast of the gun was deafening, the muzzle flash brighter than Thin had expected. The target seemed to jump back, and then began a herky-jerky dance. Thin had once seen a film showing Hitler dancing a jig after the fall of France. The man on the street looked like that for just a second or two: as though he were dancing a jig. The thunder rolled on, six shots, eight, twelve, quick, evenly spaced, the lightning flickering off their faces.

A little more than halfway through the magazine, Thick flicked the selector switch and unloaded the remaining cartridges in a single burst. The target was now flat on the sidewalk, and the burst of bullets splattered about his head like copper-jacketed raindrops.

Thin stood by the window, unspeaking.

"Go," said Thick. He dropped the rifle on the floor. "Hands."

With their gloved hands pressed to their faces, they walked down the hall to the back of the building, ran down a flight of stairs, along another hallway, then out a side door into an alley. The alley led away from the shooting.

"Don't run," said Thick as they emerged onto the street.

"Watch it," said Thin.

A Volkswagen lurched past, a Bug, catching them in its lights, their pale faces like street lamps in the night. It was the same car that had driven past the restaurant just before the computer fag came out on the sidewalk. . . .

With the body beside him, Bekker was tense, cranked, watching for cop cars, watching everything that went by. He had a small pistol by his side, a double-barreled derringer .38 Special, but if he had to use it, he'd probably be finished.

But so far, so good.

SoHo streets were quiet at night. Once out of the neighborhood, things would get more complicated. He didn't want anything high beside him, a van or a truck. He didn't want a driver looking down into the Volkswagen, even though he probably wouldn't see much. The body, wrapped in dark plastic, looked more like a butterfly's chrysalis than anything, a cocoon. What you might expect from a Bug.

Bekker almost laughed. Not quite; he was too crazy to have a genuine sense of humor. Instead he said, "Motherfucker."

He needed a wall, or an unguarded building with a niche in the wall. Some place where nobody would look out and see him unloading the body. He hadn't thought much about disposal: he'd have to think more. He'd need a random dispersal pattern, nothing they could use to focus on his particular block. He'd have to decide the optimum distance—far enough not to point at SoHo, but not so far that the drive itself became risky.

He drove past the Manhattan Caballero, a Village steak house, a couple of bright beer signs in the small barred windows. The door opened as he went by and he saw a slender man come out, caught just for a moment by the light inside the doorway; and behind him, a cigarette machine.

The gunshots sounded like popcorn. Or like a woman ripping a piece of dress material. Bekker looked in the mirror, saw the lightning. Bekker had been in Vietnam; he'd heard this noise from a distance, this snickering popcorn thunder. He'd seen this flickering light. The man he'd seen in the doorway was flopping on the sidewalk as the bullets tore through him.

"Motherfucker . . ." Teeth bared, mouth wide, Bekker screamed the word: he was innocent, he had nothing to do with it, and he could get caught, right here. Half panicked, afraid that neighbors would take the number of every car they saw, Bekker floored the accelerator and raced to the end of the long block. The gunfire lasted for only two or three seconds. It took another five before he could turn left, out of sight, onto a one-way street. The adrenaline surged through him, the PCP panic. And up ahead, yellow lights flashed in the street.

What?

The panic jumped him. He jammed on the brake, forgetting the clutch, and the Volkswagen stalled. The body crinkled its plastic coat as it swayed in the seat toward him. He pushed it back with one hand, fighting the fist in his throat, trying to breathe, trying to get some air, and stabbed at the gas pedal. Finally realizing what had happened, he dropped the clutch and turned the key again, got started, shifting into second.

He jerked the car to the left, still dazzled, before he realized that the yellow lights were road-construction warnings. No reason to turn—but he already had, and he sped on. Near the end of the block, two figures stepped out of an alley. His headlights swept them, and he saw their hands come up. They were hiding their faces, but before they'd covered them, they'd been as clear as the face of the moon.

Bekker swerved, kept going.

Had they seen his plates? No way to tell. He peered into the rearview mirror, but they were already lost in the dark. He was okay. He tried to choke down the fear. The back plates were old and dirty.

But the gunfire.

Had to think. Jesus, he needed help. He felt for the matchbox. No, that wouldn't be right. He needed speed. Uppers, to help him think.

Sirens.

Somewhere behind him. He wasn't sure quite where he was anymore, took a left, moving away, coming up to a major intersection. He looked up at the street signs. Broadway. What was the other? He rolled forward a few feet. Bleecker. Okay. Good. Straight ahead, along Bleecker. Had to get the body out. A darker block, a deep-red building with niches, but no place to pull over. Another fifty feet . . . there.

He pulled to the curb, hopped out, and looked around. Nobody. He could hear somebody talking, loud, but it sounded like a drunk. He hurried around the car, shifted the body out and dropped it in a doorway. Looked up: the ceiling in the deep doorway was decorated with intricate designs in white terracotta; the designs caught his mind, dragged it into the maze of curves. . . .

Another siren brought him back. It was somewhere down Bleecker, but he couldn't see the lights. He hurried back to the car, sweating, climbed inside, and looked back through the open door at the mortal remains of Louis Cortese. From any more than a few feet, the body looked like a bum sleeping on the sidewalk. And there were hundreds of bums in the area.

He risked a last look at the terra-cotta, felt the pull, then tore his eyes away and slammed the door. Hunched over the steering wheel, he headed for home.

Thick picked up the pay phone and dialed the number scrawled on a scrap of paper. He let the phone ring twice, hung up, waited a few seconds, dialed again, let it ring twice more, hung up again.

Thin was waiting in the car, didn't speak.

"It'll be okay," Thick said.

After a very long time, Thin said, "No, it won't."

"It's fine," the big man said. "You did good."

* * *

When Bekker got to the Lacey building, he parked the car, went down into the basement, stripped off his clothes, scrubbed his face, changed into a sweat suit. And thought about the killing he'd seen. New York was a dangerous place—someone really ought to do something about it. . . . There was some cleanup to do in the operating theater. He worked at it for ten minutes, with a sponge and paper towels and a can of universal cleaner. When he was done, he wrapped all the paper and put it in the garbage. He remembered the blood just as he was about to turn out the lights. He picked up the bottle and tipped it into a drain, the blood as purple and thick as antifreeze.

Again he reached for the lights, and saw the four small nubbins of skin sitting on top of an anesthetic tank. Of course, he'd put them there, just a convenient place at the time.

He picked them up. Shriveled, with the long shiny lashes, they looked like a new species of arachnid, a new one-sided spider. They were, of course, something much more mundane: Cortese's eyelids. He peered at them in the palm of his hand. He'd never seen them like this, so separate, so disembodied.

Ha. Another one. Another joke. He looked in the stainless-steel cabinet, laughed and held his belly, and pointed a finger at himself. *Disembodied* . . .

He went back to them, the eyelids. Fascinating.

CHAPTER

4

Lucas was lying on the roof of his house, the shingles warm against his shoulder blades, eyes closed, not quite snoozing. He'd put down one full flat of green fiberglass shingles and didn't feel like starting another. A breeze ruffled the fine black hair on his forearms; the humid air was pregnant with an afternoon storm and pink-and-gray thunderheads were popping up to the west.

With his eyes closed, Lucas could hear the after-work joggers padding along the sidewalk across the street, the rattle of roller blades, radios from passing cars. If he opened his eyes and looked straight up, he might see an eagle soaring on the thermals above the river bluffs. If he looked down, the Mississippi was there, across the street and below the bluff, like a fat brown snake curling in the sunshine. A catsup-colored buoy bobbed in the muddy water, directing boat traffic into the Ford lock.

It all felt fine, like it could go on forever, up on the roof.

When the taxi pulled into the driveway, he thought about it instead of looking to see who it was. Nobody he knew was likely to come calling unexpectedly. His life had come to that: no surprises.

The car door slammed, and her high heels rapped down the sidewalk.

Lily.

Her name popped into his head.

Something about the way she walked. Like a cop, maybe, or maybe just a New Yorker. Somebody who knew about dog shit and cracked sidewalks, who watched where she put her feet. He lay unmoving, with his eyes closed.

"What are you doing up there?" Her voice was exactly as he remembered, deep for a woman, with a carefully suppressed touch of Brooklyn.

"Maintaining my property." A smile crept across his face.

"You could have fooled me," she said. "You look like you're asleep."

"Resting between bouts of vigorous activity," he said. He sat up, opened his eyes and looked down at her. She'd lost weight, he thought. Her face was narrower, with more bone. And she'd cut her hair: it had been full, to the shoulders. Now it was short, not punk, but asymmetrical, with the hair above her ears cut almost to the skin. Strangely sexy.

Her hair had changed, but her smile had not: her teeth were white as pearls against her olive skin. "You're absolutely gorgeous," he said.

"Don't start, Lucas, I'm already up to my knees in bullshit," she answered. But she smiled, and one of her upper incisors caught on her lower lip. His heart jumped. "This is a business trip."

"Mmmm." Bekker. The papers were full of it. Six already dead. Bodies without eyelids. Cut up, in various ways—not mutilated. Bekker did very professional work, as befitted a certified pathologist. And he wrote papers on the killings: strange, contorted, quasiscientific ramblings about the dying subjects and their predeath experiences, which he sent off to scientific journals. "Are you running the case?"

"No, but I'm . . . involved," she said. She was peering up at him with the comic helplessness with which people on the ground regard people on roofs. "I'm getting a crick in my neck. Come down."

"Who'll maintain my property?" he teased.

"Fuck your property," she said.

He took his time coming down the ladder, aware of the special care: *Five years ago, I'd of run down . . . hell, three years ago . . . getting older. Forty-five coming up. Fifty still below the horizon, but you could see the shadow of it . . .*

He'd been stretching, doing roadwork, hitting a heavy bag until he hurt. He worked on the Nautilus machines three nights a week at the Athletic Club, and tried to swim on the nights he didn't do Nautilus. Forty-four, coming onto forty-five. Hair shot through with gray, and the vertical lines between his eyes weren't gone in the mornings.

He could see the two extra years in Lily as well. She looked tougher, as though she'd been through hard weather. And she looked hurt, her eyes wary.

"Let's go inside," he said as he bent to let her kiss him on the cheek. He didn't have to bend very far; she was nearly as tall as he was. Chanel No. 5, like a whiff of distant farm flowers. He caught her by the arm. "Jesus, you look good. Smell good. Why don't you call?"

"Why don't you?"

"Yeah, yeah . . ." He led the way through the front door to the kitchen. The kitchen had been scorched in a gunfight and fire two years past, a case he'd worked with Lily. He'd repainted and put in a new floor.

"You've lost some weight," he said as they went, groping for something personal.

"Twelve pounds, as of this morning," she said. She dropped her purse on the breakfast bar, looked around, said, "Looks nice," pulled out a stool and sat down. "I'm starving to death."

"I've got two cold beers," Lucas said. He stuck his head in the refrigerator. "And I'm willing to split a deli roast beef sandwich, heavy on the salad, no mayonnaise."

"Just a minute," Lily said, waving him off. He shut the refrigerator door and leaned against it as she took a small brown spiral notebook from her purse. She did a series of quick calculations, her lips moving. "Airline food can't be much," she said, more to herself than Lucas.

"Not much," he agreed.

"Is it light beer?"

"No . . . but hell, it's a celebration."

"Right." She was very serious, noting the calories in the brown notebook. Lucas tried not to laugh.

"You're trying not to laugh," she said, looking up suddenly, catching him at it. She was wearing gold hoop earrings, and when she tipped her head to the side, the gold stroked her olive skin with a butterfly's touch.

"And succeeding," he said. He tried to grin, but his breathing had gone wrong; the dangling earring was hypnotic, like something out of a magician's show.

"Christ, I hate people with fast metabolisms," she said. She went back to the notebook, unaware of his breathing problems. *Maybe.*

"That's all bullshit, the fast-metabolism excuse," Lucas said. "I read it in the *Times.*"

"Another sign of decline, the *Times* printing obvious bullshit," Lily said. She stuffed the notebook back in her purse, put the purse aside and crossed her legs, clasping her hands on her knees. "Okay, a beer and half a sandwich."

They ate at the breakfast bar, facing each other, making small talk, checking each other. Lucas was off the police force and missed the action. Lily had moved up, off the street, and was doing political work with a deputy commissioner. Lily asked, "How's Jennifer? And Sarah?"

Lucas shook his head, finishing the sandwich. "Jen and I—we're all done. We tried, and it didn't work. Too much bad history. We're still friends. She's seeing a guy from the station. They'll probably get married."

"He's okay?"

"Yeah, I guess," Lucas said.

But he was unconsciously shaking his head as he said it.

Lily considered the tone: "So you think he's an asshole?"

"Hell . . . No. Not really." Lucas, finished with his half of the sandwich, stepped over to the sink, squirted Ivory Liquid into the palm of one hand, turned on the water and washed off the traces of the sandwich's olive oil. His hands were large and square, boxer's hands. "And he likes Sarah and he's got a kid of his own, about seven months older than Sarah. They get along. . . ."

"Like a family . . ." Lily said. Lucas turned away and shook the water off his hands and she quickly said, "Sorry."

"Yeah, well, what the fuck," Lucas said. He went back to the refrigerator, took out another bottle of Leinenkugel's and twisted the top off. "Actually, I've been feeling pretty good. Ending it. I'm making some money and I've been out on the road, looking at the world. I was at Little Bighorn a couple of weeks ago. Freaked me out. You can stand by Custer's stone and see the whole fucking fight. . . ."

"Yeah?"

He was marking time, waiting for her to tell him why she'd come to the Cities. But she was better at waiting than he was, and finally he asked, "What're you here for?"

She licked a chip of roast beef from the corner of her mouth, her long tongue catching it expertly. Then: "I want you to come to New York."

"For Bekker?" he asked skeptically. "Bullshit. You guys can handle Bekker. And if I was a New York cop, I'd get pissed off if somebody came in from the outside. A small-town guy."

She was nodding. "Yeah, we can handle Bekker. We've got guys saying all kinds of things: that we'll have him in a week, in ten days. . . . It's been six weeks, Lucas. We'll get him, but the politics are getting ugly."

"Still . . ."

"We want you to jawbone the media. You're good at that, talking to reporters. We want to tell them that we're doing everything we can, that we're even importing the guy who caught him the first time. We want to emphasize that we're pulling out all the stops. Our guys'll understand that, they'll appreciate it—they'll know we're trying to take the heat off."

"That's it? A public-relations trick?" He grimaced, began to shake his head. He didn't want to talk to reporters. He wanted to get somebody by the throat. . . .

"No, no. You'll work the case, all right," she said. She finished the sandwich and held her hands out, fingers spread, looking for a napkin, and he handed her a paper towel. "Right down on the street with the rest of them. And high priority, too. I *do* value your abilities."

Lucas caught something in her voice. "But?"

"But . . . all of that aside, there's something else."

He laughed. "A third layer? A Lily Rothenburg layer? What're you doing?"

"The thing is, we've got serious trouble. Even bigger than Bekker, if you can imagine it." She hesitated, searching his eyes, intent, then balled up the paper napkin and did a sitting jump shot into a wastebasket before continuing. "This can't come out anywhere."

Irritated, he wordlessly backhanded the comment away, like a bothersome gnat. She nodded, slipped off the stool, took a quick turn around the kitchen, picked up an enamel coffee cup, turned it in her hands, put it down.

"We're looking at thirteen murders," she said finally. "Not Bekker's. Someone else's. These are all . . . hits. Maybe. Of the thirteen—those are the ones we're sure of, we think there are more, as many as forty—ten were out-and-out assholes. Two of them were pretty big: a wholesaler for the Cali cartel and an up-and-coming Mafia guy. The other eight were miscellaneous small-timers."

"Number eleven?"

"A lawyer," Lily said. "A criminal defense lawyer who represented a lot of big dopers. He was good. He put a lot of people back on the street that shouldn't have been there. But most people thought he was straight."

"Hard to be straight, with that job," Lucas said.

"But we think he was. The investigation hasn't turned up anything that'd change our mind. We've been combing his bank records, along with the IRS and the state tax people. There's not a goddamned thing. In fact, there wouldn't have been any point in his being crooked: he was pulling in so much money he didn't need any more. Three million bucks was a slow year."

"Okay. Who was twelve?"

"Number twelve was a professional black . . . spokesman," she said. "A community leader, a loudmouth, a rabble-rouser, whatever you want to call him. But he wasn't a crook. He was a neighborhood politician trying to climb the pole. He was shot in a drive-by, supposedly a couple of gang-bangers. But it was very slick for gang-bangers, good weapons, a stolen car."

"Thirteen?"

"Thirteen was a cop."

"Crooked?"

"Straight. He was investigating the possibility that we've got a rogue group inside the police department, inside intelligence, systematically killing people."

There was a moment of silence as Lucas digested it. "Sonofabitch," he said finally. "They've killed thirteen people for sure, and maybe forty?"

"The cop who was killed—his name was Walter Petty—claimed there were twelve, for sure. He's the thirteenth. We think. He said there could be thirty or forty more."

"Jesus Christ." Lucas pulled at his lip, turned away from her, blankly staring at the microwave. Forty? "You should've picked it up. . . ."

"Not necessarily," Lily said, shaking her head. The short hair whipped around her ears, like a television advertisement, and he caught a smile and suppressed it. This was *business,* she said. "For one thing, they were killed over a long time. Five years, anyway. And most of them died like you'd have expected, knowing their records. Except more efficiently. That's what you notice when you decide you've got a pattern: the efficiency of it. Bang, bang, they're dead. Never any cops close by—once or twice, they were actually decoyed out. There are never any good witnesses. The getaways are preplanned. No collateral damage, no mushrooms getting knocked down."

"So you've got a pattern of small-time assholes killed by big-time shooters," Lucas said.

"Right. Like this one guy, I met him myself, years ago, when I was just coming off patrol. Arvin Davies." She lifted her eyes to the ceiling and wet her lips, remembering the file. "He was forty-two when he was killed. He was a doper, a drunk. A brawler. He had twenty priors going back to age twelve, and he'd been picked up for one thing or another maybe twenty more times. All small stuff. Street muggings, burglaries, car thefts, rip-offs, possession. He'd get his nose clogged up with angel dust and beat his victims. He killed one five or six years ago, but we could never prove it. He spent twenty years inside, all short time. The last time he got out, he did a couple of muggings and then somebody put him on a wall. Shot him twice in the heart and once in the head. The head shot came when he was already down, a coup de grace. The shooter walked away," she said, hopping back up on the breakfast-bar stool across from him.

"A pro," Lucas said.

"Yeah. And there just wasn't any reason a pro would go after Arvin Davies. He was small-time, chickenshit. But whoever killed him took a real asshole off the streets for good. Maybe forty or fifty nasty crimes a year."

"All the miscellaneous hits are like that?"

"Yup. I mean the techniques are different, but they're all cold, efficient, researched."

Lucas nodded, studying her. "All very enlightening—but where do I come in?"

She looked straight into him, fixing him. "A couple of guys in intelligence spotted the pattern. They got nervous about it. All of the victims, or whatever you'd call them, were heavy in intelligence files. Like the files had been used to choose them. Once they made the report, a secret working group of six ranking officers was set up to monitor it. Petty was eventually brought in to do the dog work."

Lucas interrupted. "He was a shoofly, or whatever you guys call them?"

She shook her head. "He was a crime-scene guy for most of his career, and later on a computer specialist. He was officially a detective second. In this case, he was reporting to the working group under the direct supervision of my boss, John O'Dell. John chairs the working group."

"So there was no past internal-affairs work that might have left a grudge," Lucas said.

"No. And just before he was shot, there was an odd break on the case. . . ." Lily put a hand on top of her head as if she were patting herself, a gesture of thought. "The black guy who was killed, the loudmouth, was named Waites. The file is still open, we still have people digging into it. As a matter of routine, Walt got all the reports coming out of the active cases. He found a report that said a supposed witness to the Waites killing had recognized one of the shooters as a cop. The witness was named Cornell, last name probably Reed. The trouble is, when Walt went looking for him, Cornell Reed had disappeared. Maybe left town. But Walt found him, somehow. He tried to get in touch with us that afternoon, he came by the offices, and when he couldn't, he left a note on voice mail. He said he knew where Reed went."

"Where?"

"We don't know. And Walt was killed that night."

"Jesus—somebody got the voice mail?"

"Unlikely; it's coded," Lily said. "And the shooting was too well set up. They'd planned it ahead of time. If finding the witness had anything to do with it, it was just the trigger that made them go ahead with the shooting."

"Huh. How about Petty's records? Notes?"

"Nothing in his office, but he wasn't keeping anything there, anyway, because of the sensitivity," she said. "He was working

out of his apartment, mostly. And that's another thing: somebody got to his apartment before we did. All of his computer
disks were gone, and the internal drive—hard drive, is that it?—
had been wiped somehow. I don't know how you do it, but there
was nothing recoverable."

"Another computer freak?"

"Not necessarily. Whatever they did wasn't fancy. A couple of
short commands apparently took care of it. Something like a
reformat with a write-over? Does that make sense?"

"Yeah, yeah. Petty must've talked to somebody. It's hard to
believe he'd get a break and coincidentally be hit that same
night. . . . Who'd he tell about the witness?" Lucas asked.

"We don't know," Lily said. "We *do* know he came up to our
office, after hours, looking for us. O'Dell and I spend a lot of time
in a car, going around, putting out political brush fires. We were
talking to some people in one of the projects that night. Walt
didn't try the car—our driver was waiting in it, and nobody
called. The thing is, when Walt came up to the office, he might've
bumped into somebody from the working group, there in the
hallway. He really wouldn't talk to anybody else, not on this
topic."

"So he accidentally bumps into another member of the working group and that guy leaks?"

Lily frowned. "Well . . . the shooting was too quick for a
careless leak. Whoever tipped the rogue group did it directly. A
phone call. In other words, whoever leaked knows the killers.
Maybe he even runs them."

"Sonofabitch. But if you know it's one of the six working-
group guys . . ."

Lily shook her head and smiled. "Nothing's ever that easy.
For one thing, every one of those six reports to somebody, and
they did. And every one of the six has assistants, and some of the
assistants know what the working group is doing."

"Doesn't sound very secret," Lucas said.

"Maybe fifteen people know details, and twenty-five know

about the problem," Lily said. "That's pretty secret for the department . . . but you see where that leaves us. If one of the working group tipped the killers, he's in a position to know everything. So we're paralyzed. The working group appointed a new lead investigator, an unassigned captain, but he's not doing anything. He's just there to cover our asses, in case something leaks. You know, so we can say we've got an active case under investigation by a ranking officer."

"And you want *me* to look into it," Lucas said.

Lily nodded. "My boss and I talked it over. We need the work done off the books. Nobody will know but the two of us. It's the only way. And because of Bekker, you're a perfect fit. The goddamn media's going nuts about Bekker, of course, the TV and the *Post* and *News,* Doctor Death and all that. You can't get in a cab without hearing a radio talk show about him. So we bring you in, the guy who caught him last time. A consultant. But while you're looking, we're going to put you close to a couple of people Walt was looking at."

"Huh." Lucas sat and thought for a long moment, then he looked up. "This guy who got shot," he said. "You called him Walt, like . . . he wasn't just another guy. Is there something I should know?"

She looked at his face, but not into his eyes: her eyes seemed suddenly blank, as though she were seeing another face. "Walt was my oldest friend," she said.

And she told him about the dream. . . .

The dream had started the night Petty was killed; it began not with a vision, but with an odor, the smell of ozone, as if electrical circuits were burning somewhere. Then she saw herself, through a haze, but with increasing clarity, seated on a simple marble bench, the kind found in cemeteries, with Petty's bleeding, shattered body stretched across her lap. A pietà. *She did nothing at all, but simply sat there, looking into his face. In the dream, the point-of-view closed on the face, like a camera creeping forward, and at the last moment, focused not on an image of Christ-like peace, but on a face that had been shredded by high-velocity slugs, at yellow molars slick with drying blood. . . .*

A ludicrous image, but one that came, night after night.

But that wasn't the way it had been, the night Petty was killed.

Petty's seventy-one-year-old mother had called, confused, incoherent. Her only child had been killed, she said, her voice an ancient moan. Walt was dead, dead . . . Lily could see the old woman in her mind's eye, the narrow gray face bent over the black telephone, body shaking, twitching, the withered hand with the handkerchief, the doilies on the TV behind her, the Sacred Heart on the wall. Lily could even smell it, cabbage and bread dough. . . .

The old woman said that Lily had to go to Bellevue to identify Walter. Was there a cop there, Lily asked? Yes, right here, and Father Gomez. And the mayor was coming.

Lily spoke to the cop. Take care of Gloria Petty, she said, the wife of a cop, the mother of a cop. The last one alive in this family. Then, trembling with fear and grief, she'd gone to Bellevue.

No pietà *at Bellevue.*

Just a body, waxlike, dead, sprawled on a blood-soaked gurney, raw from the pickup. The body was wrapped in layers of plastic, like beef being moved. She noted professionally that one of the slugs had ripped off Petty's cheek, exposing his molars; a preview of Petty as a naked skull, a reminder of Petty's naive, happy smile. The smile that flashed every time he saw her, delighted with her presence.

She recalled a day from their Brooklyn childhood, when the two of them were seven or eight. Late fall, blue skies, crisp weather, a hint of Halloween. There were maple trees on the block, turning red. She'd been sick and had been kept home from school, but her mother let her out in the afternoon to sit on the stoop.

And here was Walter, running down the street, a paper held overhead, flapping, joy in his eyes. Her spelling test from the day before. A perfect score. Common enough for Lily, but Walter, so generously pleased for her, that smile, that young blond hair slicked down with Vaseline . . .

Come to this, the bloody teeth.

"That's Walter Petty," she told a tired assistant M.E.

At home again, changing clothes, preparing herself to see Petty's mother, she thought of her school yearbook. She went into the living room, pulled a box from a built-in cupboard, and found three of them. And his senior picture: his hair never quite right, his face too slender, the slightly dazed smile.

Lily broke and began to weep. The spasm was uncontrollable, unlike anything she'd experienced before, a storm that ended with dumb exhaustion. Wearily, she finished dressing, started for the door.

And smelled Petty: Petty in the morgue, the stink of the blood and the body in her nose. She ran back to the bathroom, washed her face and her hands, over and over.

Early the next morning, after the nightmare interlude with Gloria Petty, as she fought for an hour or two of sleep, she dreamed and saw herself on the marble bench, Walter Petty draped on her lap, broken, torn, his bloody teeth leering from the side of his face. . . .

Petty was gone.

"Jesus." Lucas was staring at her. "I didn't know you had . . ."

"What?" She tried to smile. "That kind of depth?"

"That kind of old-time relationship. You know about me and Elle Kruger . . ."

"The nun, yes. What would you do if somebody murdered her?" Lily asked.

"Find whoever did it and kill him," Lucas said quietly.

"Yes," Lily said, nodding, looking straight at him. "That's what I want."

The late-afternoon sun had gone red, then a sullen orange. A heavy atmospheric hush, accompanied by a distant rumbling, announced the line of thunderstorms that Lucas had seen from the roof. When Lily first arrived, Lucas, sitting on the roof, had said, "You're absolutely gorgeous." She'd cooled the sense of contact with a quick, "Don't start, Davenport." But there was an underlying tension between them, and now it sprang up again, riding with them as they moved out of the kitchen, into the living room.

Lily perched on a couch, knees together, fumbled through her purse, found a roll of Certs, tipped a couple of them into her hand, then popped them into her mouth. "You've changed things," she said, looking around the house.

"After Shadow Love, the place was pretty shot up," Lucas said. He dropped onto a leather recliner, sitting on the edge of it, leaning toward her. "Some wiring got wrecked and I needed a new floor. Plaster work. He was shooting that goddamn M-15, it was a mess."

Lily looked away: "That's what they used on Walt. An M-15. A full clip: they emptied a full clip into him. They found pieces of him all over the block."

"Jesus . . ." Lucas groped for something else to say, but all he could find was, "How about you? Are you okay?"

"Oh, sure," she said, and fell silent.

"The last time I saw you, you were on a guilt trip about your old man and the kids. . . ."

"That's not over. The guilt trip. Sometimes I feel so bad I get nauseous," she said.

"Do you see the kids?"

"Not so much," she said sadly, looking away from him. "I tried, but it was wrecking all of us. David was always . . . peering at me. And the boys blame me for leaving."

"Do you want to go back?"

"I don't love him," she said, shaking her head. "I don't even like him very much. I look at him now, and it all seems like bullshit, the stuff that comes out of his mouth. And that's weird, because it used to seem so smart. We'd go to parties and he'd spin up these post-Jungian theories of racism and class struggle, and these phonies would stand around with their heads going up and down like they were bobbing for apples. Then I'd go to work and see a report on some twelve-year-old who shot his mom because he wanted to sell the TV to buy crack, and she wouldn't let him. Then I'd go back home and . . . shit. I couldn't stand listening to him anymore. How can you live with somebody you can't stand listening to?"

"It's hard," he said. "Being a cop makes it worse. I think that's why I spent so much time with Jennifer. She was a professional bullshit artist, but basically, she knew what was what. She spent the time on the streets."

"Yeah . . ."

"So where're you at?" he asked again.

She looked at him unsteadily, not quite nervous, but apprehensive somehow. "I didn't want to get into that right away—I wanted to get you committed first. Will you come?"

"Somebody new?" he asked, his voice light.

"Will you come?"

"Maybe . . . so you've got someone."

"Sort of."

"Sort of? What's that?" He hopped off the chair and took a turn around the room. He wasn't angry, he thought, but he looked angry. He reached down and turned on the TV and a tinny, distant voice instantly cried, "Kirrrbeee Puck-it." He snapped it off again. "What does 'sort of' mean? One foot on the floor at all times? Nothing below the waist?"

Lily laughed and said, "You cheer me up, Davenport. You're so fucking crass. . . ."

"So . . . ?" He went to the window and looked out; the thunderheads were gray, with soaring pink tops, and were bearing down on the line of the river.

She shrugged, looked out the window past him. "So, I was seeing a guy. I still am. We hadn't started looking for an apartment together, but the possibility was out there."

"What happened?"

"He had a heart attack."

Lucas looked at her for a minute, then said, "Why does that make perfect sense?"

She forced a smile. "It's really not very funny, I'm afraid. He's in terrible shape."

"He's a cop?"

"Yeah." The smile faded. "He's like you, in some ways. Not physically—he's tall and thin and white-haired. But he is—was—in intelligence and he loves the streets. He writes articles for the *Times* op-ed page about the street life. He has the best network of spies in the city. And he has a taste for, mmm . . ." She groped for the right phrase.

"Dark-eyed married women?" Lucas suggested, moving closer.

"Well, that," she said, the tentative smile returning. "But the thing is, he likes to fight . . . did like to fight. Like you. Now he can't walk two dozen steps without stopping for a breath."

"Jesus." Lucas ran a hand through his hair. He'd had nightmares of being crippled. "What's the prognosis?"

"Not so good." Tears glistened at the corners of her dark eyes. At the same moment, she smiled and said, "Shit. I wish I didn't do this." She wiped the tears away with the heel and knuckles of her hand. "This was his third attack. The first one was five years ago. That was bad. The second one was a couple months after the first, and wasn't so bad. Then he was coming back. He'd almost forgotten about them, he was working. . . . Then this third one, this was the worst of all. He's got extensive damage to the heart muscle. And he won't stop working. The doctors tell him to spend a year doing graded exercise, to stay away from work, from the stress. He won't do it. And he's still smoking, I think. He's sneaking them. I can smell them on his clothes . . . in his hair."

"So he's going to die," Lucas said.

"Probably."

"That's not so bad," Lucas said, leaning back, looking at her, his voice flat. "You just say fuck it. You do what you want, and if you go, you go."

"That's what you'd do, isn't it?"

"I hope so," he said.

"Men are such goddamn assholes," Lily said.

SILENT PREY · 59

After another long silence, Lucas asked, "So what are you doing for sex?"

She started to laugh, but it caught in her throat, and she stood up and picked up her purse. "I better get going. Tell me you'll come to New York."

"Answer the question," Lucas said. Without thinking about it, he moved closer. She noticed it, felt the pressure.

"We're . . . very careful," she said. "He can't get too carried away."

Lucas' chest felt curiously thick, a combination of anger and expectation. The electricity between them crackled, and his voice was suddenly husky. "You never really liked being careful."

"Ah, Jesus, Lucas," she said.

He stepped up to her until he was only inches away. "Push me away," he whispered.

"Lucas . . ."

"Push me away," he said, "I'll go."

She stepped back, dropped her purse. Outside, the first heavy drops of rain careened off the sidewalk, and a woman with a dog on a leash dashed past the house.

She rocked back on her heels, looked down at her purse, then grabbed his shirt sleeve to balance herself, lifted one foot, then the other, pulled off her shoes, and stepped into the hallway that led to the bedroom. Lucas, standing in the living room, watched her go, until halfway down the hallway she turned her head, her dark eyes looking at him, and began to unbutton her blouse.

Their lovemaking, she said later, sometimes resembled a fight, had an edge of violence, a tone of aggression. They might begin with an effort at tenderness, but that would slip and they would be bucking, wrenching, twisting. . . .

That night, as the last of the storm cells rumbled off into Wisconsin, with the room smelling of sweat and sex, she sat on the edge of the bed. She seemed weary, but there was a smile at the corner of her lips.

"I'm such a goddammned slut," she said.

"Oh, God . . ." He laughed.

"Well, it's true," she said, "I can't believe it. I was such a nice girl for so long. But I just *need.* It's not intimacy. You're about as intimate as a fuckin' bear. I need the *sex.* I need to get *jammed.* I really can't believe it."

"Did you know you were going to sleep with me?" Lucas asked. "When you got here?"

She sat unmoving for a moment, then said, "I thought it might happen. So I went to the hotel first, and checked in. In case anyone called."

He ran a fingernail down the bumps of her spine, and she shivered. She was going back to the hotel in case "anyone" called. . . .

"This guy you're sleeping with? 'Anyone'?" Lucas said.

"Yes?"

"What are you going to tell him?"

"Nothing. He doesn't need to know." She turned toward him. "And don't you tell him anything, either, Davenport."

"Why?" Lucas said. "Why would I ever see him?"

"His name's Dick Kennett." In the half-light of the bedroom he could see a tiny, rueful smile lift the corner of her mouth again. "He's running the Bekker case," she said.

CHAPTER

5

Early morning.

Lucas strolled along Thirty-fifth Street, sucking on half of an orange, taking in the city: looking at faces and display windows, at sleeping bums wrapped in blankets like thrown-away cigars, at the men hustling racks of new-made clothing through the streets.

The citric acid was sharp on his tongue, an antidote for the staleness of a poor night's sleep. Halfway down the block, he stopped in front of a parking garage, stripped out the last of the pulp with his teeth, and dropped the rind into a battered trash barrel.

Midtown South squatted across the street, looking vaguely like a midwestern schoolhouse from the 1950s: blocky, functional, a little tired. Six squad cars were parked diagonally in front of the building, along with a Cushman scooter. Four more squads were double-parked farther up the street. As Lucas paused at the trash basket, disposing of the orange, a gray Plymouth stopped in the street. A lanky white-haired man climbed out of the passenger side, said something to the driver, laughed and pushed the door shut.

He didn't slam the door, Lucas noticed: he gave it a careful push. His eyes came up, checked Lucas, checked him again, and then he turned carefully toward the station. The fingers of his left hand slipped under a brilliant-colored tie, and he unconsciously scratched himself over his heart.

Lucas, dodging traffic, crossed the street and followed the man toward the front doors. Lily had said Kennett was tall and white-haired, and the hand over the heart, the unconscious gesture. . . .

"Are you Dick Kennett?" Lucas asked.

The man turned, eyes cool and watchful. "Yes?" He looked more closely. "Davenport? I thought it might be you. . . . Yeah, Kennett," he said, sticking out his hand.

Kennett was two inches taller than Lucas, but twenty pounds lighter. His hair was slightly long for a cop's, and his beige cotton summer suit fit too well. With his blue eyes, brilliant white teeth against what looked like a lifetime tan, crisp blue-striped oxford-cloth shirt and the outrageous necktie, he looked like a doctor who played scratch golf or good club tennis: thin, intent, serious. But a gray pallor lay beneath the tan, and his eye sockets, normally deep, showed bony knife ridges under paper-thin skin. There were scars below the eyes, the remnants of the short painful cuts a boxer gets in the ring, or a cop picks up in the street—a cop who likes to fight.

"Lily's been telling me about you," Lucas said, as they shook hands.

"All lies," Kennett said, grinning.

"Christ, I hope so," Lucas said. Lucas took in Kennett's tie, a bare-breasted Polynesian woman with another woman in the background. "Nice tie."

"Gauguin," Kennett said, looking down at it, pleased.

"What?"

"Paul Gauguin, the French painter?"

"I didn't know he did neckties," Lucas said uncertainly.

"Yeah, him and Christian Dior, they're like brothers," Kennett said, flashing the grin. Lucas nodded and they went on toward the door, Lucas holding it open. "I fuckin' hate this, people holding doors," Kennett grumbled as he went through.

"Yeah, but when you croak, how'd you like it to say on the stone, 'Died opening a door'?" Lucas asked. Kennett laughed, an easy extroverted laugh, and Lucas liked him for it, and thought: *Watch* it. Some people could *make* you like them. It was a talent.

"I could die pulling the tab on a beer can, if they let me drink beer, which they don't," Kennett was saying, suddenly sober. "Hope the fuck it never happens to you. Eat aspirin. Stop eating steak and eggs. Pray for a brain hemorrhage. This heart shit—it turns you into a coward. You walk around listening to it tick, waiting for it to stop. And you're weak. If some asshole mugged me, I'd have to take it."

"I don't want to hear about it," Lucas said.

"I don't want to talk about it, but I do, all the time," Kennett said. "Ready to meet the group?"

"Yeah, yeah . . ."

Lucas followed Kennett through the entrance lobby, waited with him until the reception sergeant buzzed them through to the back. Kennett led the way to a conference room with a piece of notebook paper Scotch-taped to the door: "Kennett Group." The room had four corkboards hung from the walls, covered with notes and call slips, maps of Manhattan, telephones, a couple of long tables and a dozen plastic chairs. In the center of it, a burly, sunburned cop in a white shirt and a thin dog-faced detective in a sport coat were facing each other, both with Styrofoam coffee cups in their hands, voices raised.

". . . your people'd get off their fuckin' asses, we could get somewhere. That's what's fuckin' us up, nobody wants to go outside because it's too goddamn hot. We know he's using the shit and he's got to get it somewhere."

"Yeah, well I'm not the asshole who told everybody we'd have him in a week, am I? That was fuckin' crazy, Jack. As far as we know, he's buying whatever shit he's using in Jersey, or down in fuckin' Philly. So don't give me no shit. . . ."

A half-dozen more plainclothes cops, in thin short-sleeved shirts and wash pants, weapons clipped to their belts, watched the argument from the plastic chairs spread around the institutional carpet. Four of the six held Styrofoam coffee cups, and two or three were smoking cigarettes, snubbing them out in shallow aluminum ashtrays. One unattended cigarette continued to burn, the foul odor like a fingernail scratch on a blackboard.

"What's going on?" Kennett asked quietly, moving to the front of the room. The argument stopped.

"Discussing strategy," the sunburned cop said shortly.

"Any conclusions?" Kennett asked. He was polite, but pushing. Taking over.

The cop shook his head and turned away. "No."

Lucas found a seat halfway back, the other cops looking at him, openly, carefully, with some distance.

"That's Lucas Davenport, the guy from Minneapolis," Kennett said, almost absently, as Lucas sat down. He'd picked up a manila file with his name on it, and was flipping through memos and call slips. "He's gonna talk to the press this morning, then go out on the street this afternoon. With Fell."

"How come you let this motherfucker Bekker get out?" the sunburned cop asked.

"Wasn't me," Lucas said mildly.

"Should of killed him when you could," dog-face said. Dog-face's two top-middle teeth pointed in slightly different directions and were notably orange.

"I thought about it," Lucas said, staring lazily at dog-face until the other broke his eyes away.

Somebody laughed, and somebody else said, "Shoulda."

Kennett said, "You won't remember this, Davenport, but let me introduce Lieutenants Kuhn, Huerta, White, Diaz, Blake, and Carter, and detectives Annelli and Case, our serial-killer specialists. You can get the first names sorted out later. . . ."

The cops lifted hands or nodded at him as their names were called out. They looked like Minneapolis cops, Lucas thought. Different names, but the attitude was the same, like a gathering of paranoid shoe salesmen: too little pay, too many years of burgers and fries and Butterfingers, too many people with big feet trying to get into small shoes.

A red-haired woman walked into the room carrying a stack of files, and Kennett added, "And this is Barb Fell. . . . Barb, that's Lucas Davenport in what appears to be a five-hundred-dollar silk-blend jacket and two-hundred-dollar shoes. . . ."

Fell was in her mid-thirties, slender, her red hair just touched with gray. An old scar, shaped like a new moon, cupped one side of her long mouth, a dead-white punctuation mark on a pale oval Welsh face. She sat next to him, perching, shook hands quickly and turned back to the front of the room.

"John O'Dell's coming over, he's going to sit in," one of the cops was telling Kennett. Kennett nodded, dragged a chair around to face the others and said, "Somebody tell me we've got something new."

After a moment of silence, Diaz, a tall, gaunt detective, one of the lieutenants, said, "About the time Bekker would've got here, a cab disappeared. Three months old. One of them new, round Caprices. Poof. Gone. Stolen while the driver was taking a leak. Supposedly."

Kennett's eyebrows went up. "Never seen again?"

"Not as far as we can tell. But, ah . . ."

"What?"

"One of the guys checked around. The driver doesn't know anything from anything. Went into a bar to take a leak, comes out, and it's gone. But the thing had been in two accidents, and the driver says it was a piece of shit. Says the transmission was shot, there was something wrong with the suspension, the front passenger-side door was so tight you could barely open it. I'd bet the sonofabitch is in a river someplace. For the insurance."

Kennett nodded but said, "Push it. We've got nothing else, right?" He looked around. "Nothing from the Laski surveillance . . . ?"

"No. Not a thing," said another of the lieutenants.

"Um . . ." Lucas lifted a finger, and Kennett nodded at him.

"Lily told me about the Laski scam, and I've been thinking about it."

The cops at the front of the room turned in their chairs to look at him. "Like what?" asked Kennett.

"I don't think Bekker'll go for it. He'd think of Laski as a wrong-headed colleague, not somebody he'd hit. Maybe somebody he'd debate. He's an equal, not a subject."

"We got nothing else going for us," snapped Carter, the sunburned cop. "And it's cheap."

"Hey, it's a smart idea," Lucas said. Laski was a Columbia pathologist who had agreed to analyze Bekker's medical papers for the media. He had condemned them, attacked their morality and science, attacked Bekker as a sadist and a psychotic and a scientific moron—all of it calculated to bring Bekker in. Laski, his apartment and his office were covered by a web of plainclothes cops. So far, Bekker hadn't touched any of the trip wires. "That's why I was thinking about it. About variations."

"Like what?" prompted Kennett.

"Back in the Cities, Bekker subscribed to the *Times,* and I bet he reads it here. If we could set somebody up to give a lecture, some kind of professional speech that would pull him in . . ."

"Don't tease me, darlin'," Kennett said.

"We have some guy lecture on the medical experiments done by Dr. Mengele," Lucas said. "You know, the Nazi dude . . ."

"We know . . ."

"So he lectures on the ethics of using Mengele's studies in research and the ethics of using Bekker's stuff," Lucas said. "And what might come out of their so-called research that's valuable. And we make an announcement in the *Times.*"

The cops all looked at each other, and then Huerta said, "Jesus Christ, man, half the fuckin' town is Jewish. They'd go batshit. . . ."

"Hey, I don't mean any goddamn anti-Semite fruitcake lecture," Lucas said. "I mean some kind of, you know, soft, intellectual, theory thing. I read about this Mengele ethics debate somewhere, so there's something to talk about. I mean, legit.

Maybe we get somebody Jewish to front it, so nobody gets pissed off. Somebody with credentials."

"You think that'd do it?" Kennett said. He was interested.

"Bekker couldn't resist, if he heard about it. He's nuts about the topic. Maybe we could arrange for this guy, whoever we get, to have a controversy with Laski. Something that would get in the papers."

Kennett looked at the others. "What do you think?"

Carter tipped his head, grudgingly nodded. "Could you fix it?"

Kennett nodded. "Somebody could. O'Dell, maybe. We could get somebody at the New School. We know Bekker's around there."

"Sounds okay," said Huerta. "But it'll take a while to set up."

"Two or three days," said Kennett. "A week."

"We oughta have him by then. . . ."

"So we cancel. It's like Laski: I don't see any downside, frankly, and it's cheap," Kennett said. He nodded at Lucas. "I'll get it started."

"Quick."

"Yeah," Kennett said. He looked around the room. "All right, so let's go over it. John, what'd we have from Narcotics?"

"We're hassling everybody, but nothing sounds good," said Blake. "Lotsa bullshit, we're chasing it . . ."

As they reviewed the status of the case, and routine assignments, Fell whispered to Lucas, "Your interviews are all set up. A couple of reporters are already here, and three or four more are coming."

Lucas nodded, but as she was about to add something, her eyes shifted away from him toward the door. A fat man walked in, his body swaying side to side, bumping the door frame, small dark eyes poking into the corners of the room, checking off the detectives, pausing at Lucas, pausing at Fell. He looked like H. L. Mencken in the later years. Spidery veins crisscrossed the gray cheeks; his thinning reddish hair was combed straight back with some kind of oil. His jowls were emphasized by a brooding, liverish underlip that seemed fixed in a permanent pout. He wore a three-piece suit in a color that might have been called oxblood, if anyone made oxblood suits.

"O'Dell," Fell said under her breath, at his ear. "Deputy commissioner in charge of cutting throats."

Lily followed O'Dell into the room, picked out Lucas, tipped her head and lifted her eyebrows. She wore a tailored navy-blue suit and a long, mannish red necktie knotted with a loose Windsor. She carried a heavy leather cop's purse over her shoulder, her hand lying casually on the strap at the back of the purse. If she moved her hand four inches, she'd be gripping the butt of a .45. Lucas had seen her use it once, had seen her shove the .45 in a man's face and pull the trigger, the man's face smearing as though he'd been struck with a hammer, all in the space of a tenth of a second. . . .

Lily touched O'Dell's elbow, guided him toward a chair, then moved around where she could sit next to Lucas. "Get a chance to talk to Dick?" she whispered.

"Yeah. He seems like a pretty good guy. . . ."

She looked at him, as though checking to see if he was serious, then nodded and looked away.

O'Dell was up-to-date on the case's progress, and had no particular ideas about what to do next, he told the cops. He just wanted to sit in, to get a feel for the movement. "What about decoys?" he asked. "Somebody downtown suggested that we might put a few people on the street. . . ."

They argued about decoys for a while, a last-resort effort, but Kennett shook his head. "The area's too big," he said. He wandered over to a bulletin board–sized map of Manhattan, ran a finger from Central Park to the financial district. "If he was hitting a specific group, like hookers or gays, then maybe. But there's no connection between the victims. Except some negatives. He doesn't take street people, who'd probably be the easiest. . . ."

"He may specifically pick victims who look healthy," said Case, one of the serial-killer specialists. "This science thing he has—Danny and I think he rules out anybody who's too odd, or diseased or infirm. They'd mess up his findings. The medical examiner reports are all pretty much the same: these people are healthy."

"All right," said Kennett. "So he takes seven people, five female, two male, one black, six white. Two of the whites are Hispanic, but that doesn't seem to mean anything."

"They're all noticeably small, except the first one," Kuhn said. "The second guy was only five-six and skinny."

"Disposal," Huerta grunted.

They all nodded, and there was another long moment of silence, everybody in the room staring at the map of Manhattan.

"It's gotta be a cab," somebody said. "If he can't let anybody see him, and he's gotta have money for drugs, and he's gotta have someplace to gas these people. . . ." One of the cops looked at Lucas: "What are the chances that he had some money stashed? He was pretty well-off, right? Could he have ditched . . . ?"

Lucas was shaking his head. "When we took him, we blindsided him. He thought he was home free. When his wife's estate got into court, all their money was accounted for."

"Okay, that was pretty thin."

"It seems to me that somebody's protecting him," Lucas said. "An old friend or a new friend, but somebody."

Kennett was nodding. "I've worried about that, but if that's right, there isn't much we can do about it."

"We can try pushing his friend, using the media again," Lucas said. "If he depends on somebody else . . ."

O'Dell, seated heavily on a shaky folding chair, interrupted. "Wait, wait. You guys are getting ahead of me. How do we think this, that he has a friend?"

"We've papered the goddamn town with his picture and with simulations of what he'd look like if he dyed his hair or grew a beard or if he shaved his head," said Kennett. "These aren't identikit mock-ups, these are based on good-quality photographs. . . ."

"Yeah, yeah . . ." O'Dell said impatiently.

"So unless he's invisible or living in the sewers, he's probably being protected," Lucas said, picking up the thread from Kennett. "He can't be a regular tenant somewhere. He'd have to pay rent and people'd see him on a regular basis. He can't risk landlords or nosy neighbors."

"And that means he's living with somebody or he's on the street," Kennett said.

"He's not on the street," Lucas said positively. "I can't see him living like that. He just wouldn't do it. He's . . . fastidious. Besides, he's got to have a vehicle. He didn't call a cab to haul these bodies around."

"Unless he drives a cab himself," said Huerta.

"Not much there," said Diaz, shaking his head. "We'll push the stolen one. . . ."

"And it'd still be pretty risky," Lucas said.

"Yeah, but it answers a lot of questions: how he gets transportation, how he makes money and still keeps his face hidden," Kennett said. "If he worked a couple of hours a night, late, and picked his spots . . . maybe concentrated on the tourist and convention areas, you know, the Javits Center, places like that. He'd mostly be dealing with out-of-towners, which would explain Cortese. People trust cabbies. Like if he pretended he had a parcel, gets out and asks somebody where an address was . . ."

"I don't know," said Lucas.

They all stared at the map some more. Too much city; single buildings that would hold the populations of two or three small towns.

"But I still think you might be right, that he's living with somebody," Kennett said finally. "How he gets his money . . ."

"He's got skills," Lucas said. "He's got an M.D., he knows chemistry. A good chemist on the run . . ."

"Methedrine," said White, a bald man in gray knit slacks. "Ecstasy. LSD. It's all back, almost like the old days."

"Be a good reason to protect him, too," said Kuhn. "He'd be a cash cow."

"Assuming this isn't just bullshit, what does it get us?" O'Dell asked impatiently.

"We start looking for ways to put pressure on whoever he's living with or who's covering for him," Lucas said. "We need some heavy-duty contact with the media."

"Why?" said O'Dell.

"Because we have to move them around. Get them to do a little propaganda for us. We need to talk about how anybody who's hiding Bekker is an accessory to mass murder. We need some headlines to that effect. That their only hope is to roll over on him, plead ignorance, get immunity. We've got to chase him out in the open."

"I could call somebody," O'Dell said.

"We need the right emphasis . . ."

"We can figure something out," O'Dell said. "Are you still talking to the reporters this morning?"

"Yeah."

"Throw something in, then. . . ."

When the meeting broke up, O'Dell lurched ponderously out of his chair, leaned toward Lucas, and said, "We'd like to sit in on the press thing. Me and Lily."

Lucas nodded. "Sure." O'Dell nodded and headed toward the front of the room, and Lucas turned to Fell. "We're going out this afternoon?"

"Yeah. They've got us looking for fences," she said. She had gray eyes that matched the touch of gray in her hair; she was five-six or so, with a slightly injured smile and nicotine-stained fingers.

"Could I get copies or printouts of all the Bekker files, or borrow what I can't copy?"

"Right here," she said, patting the stack of manila folders in her lap.

From the front of the room, where he was talking to Kennett, O'Dell called, "Davenport." Lucas stood up and walked over, and O'Dell said, "Dick has been telling me about your idea, the lecture thing, the Mengele. I'll call around this afternoon and set it up. Like for next week. We'll play it like it's been set for a while."

Lucas nodded. "Good."

"I'll see you in the hall," O'Dell said, breaking away. Out of the corner of his eye, as O'Dell spoke to him, Lucas could see Kennett's mouth tic. Disgust? "I've gotta pee."

When he was gone, Lucas looked at Kennett and asked, "Why don't you like him?"

The distaste that had flicked across Kennett's face had been covered in an instant. He looked at Davenport for a long, measured beat and then said, "Because he never does anything but words. Maneuvers. Manipulations. He looks like a pig, but he's not. He's a goddamn spider. If he had a choice between lying and telling the truth, he'd lie because it'd be more interesting. That's why."

"Sounds like a good reason," Lucas said, looking after O'Dell. "Lily seems to like him."

"I can't figure that," Kennett said. They both glanced down the room at Lily, who was talking with Fell. "That pig-spider business, by the way . . . I put my ass in your hands. If he knew I thought that, my next job'd be directing traffic out of a parking garage."

"Not really," said Lucas. Power equations weren't that simple.

Kennett looked at him, amused. "No. Not really. But the asshole could be trouble."

They were both looking toward Lily, and when she tipped her head toward the hall, Lucas started for the door. "You coming?" he asked Fell.

She looked up from one of her files. "Am I invited?"

"Sure. Gotta be careful, though. . . ."

Reporters from three papers and two television stations were waiting, along with two TV cameras. The reporters were in a good mood, joking with him, chatting with each other about problems at the papers. They didn't think much of the story: the interviews were easy and loose, focused on a trap that Lucas had built for Bekker in Minneapolis, and on Bekker himself.

"Really quick," one of the television reporters said to Lucas as the talk was wrapping up, " 'cause we're not going to have much time. . . . You know Michael Bekker. You even visited with him in his home. How would you characterize him? From your personal acquaintance? He's been called an animal . . ."

"To call Bekker an animal is an insult to animals," Lucas said. "Bekker's a monster. That's the only word I can think of that's even close to what he is. He's a real, live horror-show freak."

"Far out," said the reporter, a harried blonde in a uniform blue blazer. She asked her cameraman, "How'd that look?"

"Looked good, that's what they'll use. Let's get a reverse shot on you, reacting . . ."

When the reporters were gone, O'Dell, sitting spread-legged on a folding chair, the way fat men do, nodded approvingly. "That was good. You say Bekker's smart and hard to catch and that everything is being done." His heavy lips moved in and out a couple of times. "Like the blonde broad said, 'Far out.' "

CHAPTER
6

The Tropic of Sixth Avenue.

The sky was pink from the pollution haze boiling off the asphalt, and heat mirages made the light poles shimmy like belly dancers. Fell pushed the beat-up Plymouth through the cab traffic, one arm out the window, an unfiltered cigarette between her fingers, old-gold rock 'n' roll playing from a personal boom-box in the backseat. The Doors, "Light My Fire."

". . . don't have enough money to fix the air conditioner," she was saying, "but we get three computer terminals so we can do more paperwork, and they're not even new terminals, they're rehabs . . ."

Black and brown arms hung from the driver's windows of the amber taxis beside them, while the paler passengers slumped in back, simmering in their own juices.

"Why fences?" Lucas asked. They were looking for fences. Fell, he'd been told, specialized in burglary and industrial theft, down through the manufacturing district of Manhattan.

"Because Kennett was reading one of these nut-case medical papers Bekker is writing, and figured out that Bekker was taking measurements that you can only take with medical monitoring gear. One of the papers mentions blood pressure taken from a catheter at the radial artery. You gotta have the right stuff. . . ."

"Check the medical-supply houses?"

"Yup, everywhere in North America and the major Japanese and European suppliers. Nothing. Checked the hospitals for stolen stuff and came up empty, but he had to get it somewhere. . . . There are a couple of other guys checking secondary sources. . . ."

They stopped at a traffic light. On the sidewalk, a fruit vendor sat in a plastic lawn chair with a wet rag on his forehead and took a continuous long peel off a red apple, using a thin-bladed stiletto with a pearl handle. A slow-moving, ratty-furred tiger-striped cat walked past him, stopped to look at the dangling peel, then hopped down into the gutter, took a last look around at the daylight world, and dropped into the sewer. Anything to get out of the heat.

". . . some kind of heat inversion and the temperature never goes down at night, see. That's when things get weird," Fell said, gunning the car through the intersection. "I got a call once where this PR stuck his old lady's head . . ."

"A what?"

"Puerto Rican. Where this Puerto Rican dude stuffed his old lady's head in the toilet and she drowned, and he said he did it because it was so fuckin' hot and she wouldn't shut up. . . ."

They rolled past the Checks Cashed and the Mexican and Indian restaurants, past the delis and the stink of a dog-'n'-kraut stand, past people with red dots on their foreheads and yarmulkes and witty T-shirts that said "No Farting," past bums and sunglassed Mafia wannabees in nine-hundred-dollar loose-kneed suits with shiny lapels.

Past a large woman wearing a T-shirt with a silhouette of a .45 on the front. A newspaper-style map arrow pointed at the gun's muzzle and said, "Official Map of New York City: You Are Here."

"There's Lonnie," Fell said, easing the car to the curb. A taxi behind them honked, but Fell ignored it and got out.

"Hey, whaddafuck . . ."

Fell made a pistol of her thumb and index finger and pointed it at the cabby and pulled the trigger and continued on around the car. Lonnie was sitting on an upturned plastic bottle crate, a Walkman plugged into his ear, head bobbing to whatever sound he was getting. He was looking the other way when Fell walked up and tapped the crate with her toe. Lonnie reared back and looked up, then pulled the plug out of his ear.

"Hey . . ." Lucas turned in front of him, on the other side. Nowhere to run.

"You sold three hundred hypodermic syringes to Al Kunsler on Monday," Fell said. "We want to know where you got them and what else you got. Medical stuff."

"I don't know nothing about that," Lonnie said. He had scars around his eyebrows, and his nose didn't quite line up with the center of his mouth.

"Come on, Lonnie. We know about it, and I don't much give a shit," Fell said impatiently. Her forehead was damp with the heat. "You fuck with us, we take you down. You tell us, we drive away. And believe me, this is something you don't want to get involved in."

"Yeah? What's going on?" He looked like he was about to stand up, but Lucas put his hand on his shoulder, and he settled back on the crate.

"We're looking for this fruitcake Bekker, okay? He's getting medical gear. We're looking for suppliers. You know at least one. . . ."

"I don't know from this Bekker dude," Lonnie said.

"So just tell us where you got them," Lucas said.

Lonnie looked around, as if to see who was watching. "Atlantic City. From some guy in a motel."

"Where'd he get them?" Lucas asked.

"How the fuck would I know? Maybe off the beach."

"Lonnie, Lonnie . . ." said Fell.

"Look, I went to Atlantic City for a little straight action. You know you can't get straight action around here anymore. . . ."

"Yeah, yeah . . ."

". . . And I meet this guy at the motel and he says he's got some merchandise, and I say, 'Whatcha got?' And he says, 'All sortsa shit.' And he did. He had, like, a million sets of Snap-On tools and some computer TV things and leather flight bags and belts and suits and shit, and these needles."

"What was he driving?" Lucas asked.

"Cadillac."

"New?"

"Naw. Old. Great big fuckin' green one, color of Key Lime pie, with the white roof."

"Think he's still there?"

Lonnie shrugged. "Could be. Looked like he'd been there awhile. I know there was some girls down the way, he was partying with them, they acted like they knew him. . . ."

They touched a half-dozen other fences, small-time hustlers. At half-hour intervals, Fell would find a pay phone and make a call.

"Nobody home?"

"Nobody home," she said, and they went looking for more fences.

Fell was a cowgirl, Lucas thought, watching her drive. She'd been born out of place, out of time, in the Bronx. She'd fit in the Dakotas or Montana: bony, with wide shoulders and high cheekbones, that frizzy red hair held back from her face with bobby pins. With the scar at the end of her mouth . . .

She'd been jabbed with the broken neck of a beer bottle, she said, back when she was on patrol. "That's what you get when you try to keep assholes from killing each other."

Babe Zalacki might have been a babe once, before her teeth fell out. She shook her head and smiled her toothless pink smile at Lucas: "I don't know from medical shit," she said. "The closest I got to it was, I got three hundred cases of Huggies a couple of weeks ago. Now Huggies, you can sell Huggies. You take them up to Harlem and sell them on the street corners like that. . . ." She snapped her fingers. "But medical shit . . . who knows?"

Back on the street, Fell said, "Sun's going down."

Lucas looked up at the sky, where a dusty sun hung over the west side. "Still hot."

"Wait'll August. August is hot. This is nothin'. . . . Better make a call."

Up the street, a bald man in a jean jacket turned to face a building, braced a hand against it, and began urinating. Lucas watched as he finished, got himself together, and continued down the street. No problem.

Fell came back and said, "He's home. Phone's busy."

They took a half hour, cutting crosstown as the light began to fail, through a warehouse section not far from the water. Fell finally slowed, did a U-turn, and bumped the right-side wheels over the curb. She killed the engine, put her radio on the floor in the backseat, fished a sign out from under the seat and tossed it on the dashboard: "No radio inside."

"Even a cop car?"

"Especially a cop car—cop cars got all kinds of goodies. At least, that's what they think."

Lucas climbed out, stretched, yawned, and ran his thumb along his beltline, under his jacket, until it hit the leather of the Bianchi holster. The street was in deep shadow, with doorway niches and shuttered carports in brick walls. A red brick cube, unmarked by any visible sign or number, loomed overhead like a Looney Tune. Rows of dark windows started three stories up; they were tall and narrow, and from the third to the eleventh floor, dark as onyx. Half of the top floor was lit.

"Lights are on," Fell said.

"Weird place to live," Lucas said, looking around. Scrap paper sidled lazily down the street, borne on a hot humid river breeze. The breeze smelled like the breath of an old man with bad teeth. They were close to the Hudson, somewhere in the twenties.

"Jackie Smith is a weird guy," Fell said. Lucas stepped toward the door, but she caught his arm. "Slow down. Give me a minute." She dug into her purse and came up with a pack of Luckys.

"You've got it bad," Lucas said, watching her. "The habit."

"Yeah, but at least I don't need an alarm clock."

"What?" He stepped into it.

"Every morning at seven o'clock sharp, I wake myself up coughing." When Lucas didn't smile, she peered at him and said, "That was a joke, Davenport."

"Yeah. Inside, I'm laughing myself sick," he said. Then he smiled.

Fell tapped a Lucky on the back of a pack of matches, stuck it in her mouth with a two-finger flipping motion, cupped it with her hands and lit it.

"You're not going to fuck me up, are you?" she asked, her eyes flicking up at him.

"I don't know what that means," Lucas said. He stuck a finger between his collar and his neck. His neck felt like sandpaper. If ring around the collar were a terminal disease, they'd be burying him.

"I saw the pictures of Bekker, after the arrest," Fell said. "He looked like somebody stuck his face in a blender. If you do that in New York, with somebody connected downtown, like Jackie is, your fuckin' *career* goes in the blender."

"I don't have a career," Lucas said.

"I do," said Fell. "Four more years and I'm out. I'd like to make it."

"What're you going to do when you get out?" Lucas asked, making talk while she smoked. He tipped his head back and looked up again. He seemed to do that in New York, even with buildings only twelve stories tall.

"I'm gonna move to Hollywood, Florida, and get a job as a topless waitress," Fell said.

"What?" She brought him down, startled him.

"Joke, Davenport," she said.

"Right." He looked back up, turning in the street. "Who is this guy?"

She took a drag, coughed, covered her mouth with a rolled fist. "Jackie? He's fairly big. The others we've talked to, they were middle-sized or small-timers. Jackie's a wholesaler. There are three or four of them here in midtown. When somebody hijacks a truck full of Sonys, one of the wholesalers'll get it and parcel it out to the small-timers. If Jackie feels like it, he could put out the word on Bekker to fifty or sixty or a hundred guys. If he feels like it. And those guys could probably talk to a million junkies and thieves. *If* they feel like it."

"If you know all this . . . ?" He looked at her with a cool curiosity. A man turned the corner behind them, saw them standing on the sidewalk, and went back around the corner out of sight.

"He's got his own business, remaindering stuff," Fell continued. "If somebody has six zillion nuts and no bolts to go with them, he calls up Jackie. Jackie buys them and finds somebody who needs them. That's all legal. If you tag him, you'll find him going in and out of warehouses all day, ten or twenty a day, different ones every day of the week. Talks to all kinds of people. Hundreds of them. Somewhere in the mess, he's got eight or ten people working for him, running the fencing business out the back door of these legit warehouses. . . . It's tough, man. I know he's doing it, but I can't find his dumps."

"He knows you?"

"He knows who I am," she said. "I once sat outside this place for three days, watching who came and went. Running license numbers. It was colder than shit. You know how it gets when it's too cold to snow?"

"Yeah. I'm from . . ."

"Minnesota. Like that," she said, looking down the street, remembering. "So the third night, this guy comes out of the building, knocks on our window, my partner and me, and hands us a Thermos of hot coffee and a couple of turkey sandwiches, courtesy of Jackie Smith."

"Hmph." He looked at her. "You take it?"

"I poured the coffee on the guy's shoes," Fell said. She was talking through her teeth. She took a last drag, grinned at him and flicked the cigarette into the street, where it bounced in a shower of sparks. "The silly shit thought he could buy me with a fuckin' turkey sandwich. . . . C'mon, let's do it."

The warehouse door was built of inch-thick glass poured around stainless-steel rods, with an identical second door six feet farther in. A video camera was mounted on the wall between the two doors. Fell pushed a doorbell marked "Top." A moment later, an electronic voice said, "Yes?"

Fell leaned close to the speaker plate. "Detectives Fell and Davenport to see Jackie Smith."

After a short pause, the voice said, "Step inside and hold your badges in front of the camera."

The door lock buzzed and Fell pulled the door open, and they went inside. Now between the two doors, they held their badges in front of the camera. A second later, the lock on the second door buzzed. "Take the elevator to twelve. It's on the way down," the voice said.

A sterile lobby of yellow-painted concrete block waited behind the second door. There were no windows, only the elevator doors and a steel fire door at the far end of the lobby. The elevators were to the left, and another video camera, mounted in a wire cage near the ceiling, watched them.

"Interesting," Lucas said. "We're in a vault."

"Yeah. You'd have a hell of a time getting this far if Jackie didn't want you in. You'd probably need plastique to do it in a hurry. Then you'd have to get through the fire door, to find the stairs, assuming that the elevator was up and locked. By that time, Jackie'd be gone, of course. I'm sure he's got a bolthole somewhere. . . ."

"And he's probably recording all of this," Lucas said.

Fell shrugged. "I'd like to get him, and I've thought about it—that ain't no secret." Halfway up, she said, "You got a thing with Rothenburg?"

He looked down at her. "Why?"

"Just curious," she said. They watched numbers flickering off the floor counter, and then she said, "When she came in, the way she looked at you, I thought you had a thing."

"Nah . . ."

She shook her head; she didn't believe him. Then the elevator doors opened and they stepped into a lobby identical to the one on the bottom floor: yellow-painted concrete block with a gray steel door set in one wall. Another video camera was mounted in a corner.

"Come in," the disembodied voice said.

The steel door opened on Wonderland.

Lucas followed Fell onto a raised hardwood deck, shaped like a half-moon, overlooking an enormous room. Ten or twelve thousand square feet, Lucas thought, most of it open. Different activity areas were defined by furniture, lights and carpet, instead of walls. The kitchen was to the right; a blond man was peering into a stove, and the odor of fresh hot bread suffused the room. To the left, halfway back, a dark-haired man stood on a square of artificial turf with a golf club.

"Over here," said the voice from the hallway, and the man with the golf club waved at them. Fell led the way, a weaving route through what seemed like an acre of furniture.

A jumble of furniture, with no specific style, Lucas thought: it looked as though it had fallen off the back of a truck. Or trucks— different trucks, from different factories. A king-sized English four-poster bed sat on a huge Oriental carpet, and was covered with an American crazy quilt. A six-foot projection TV faced the bed, and three tripod-mounted video cameras pointed at it.

Behind the TV, a semicircular wall of shoulder-high speakers flanked a conversation pit; a marble-topped table in the center held an array of CD and tape equipment, along with a library of a thousand or more compact discs. The floor beneath the stereo area was hardwood, covered with animal skins: tiger and jaguar, stitched beaver, a buffalo robe, a sleek dark square of what might have been mink. Erroll Garner bubbled out of the speakers, working through "Mambo Carmel."

Beyond the bed, and between the bed and the sports area, a glass shower stall stood out of the floor like an oversized phone booth. Two toilets sat next to it, facing each other, and on the other side, a huge tub.

Smith waited in the sports area, two thirds of the way to the back wall. The wall was pierced by three or four doors. So there were more rooms, Lucas thought. . . .

Smith, his back to them, waggled a driver, drove a golf ball into a net, shook his head, and put the club in a bag that hung from a wall peg. Behind him, a rank of unlit lights waited over what appeared to be a real grass putting green, built on a raised surface. Beyond the green, a stained-glass lamp hung over an antique pool table; and at the back of the room, a basketball net hung from a wall. Below it, a court was complete out to the top of the free-throw circle.

"Can't keep my head down," Smith said. He strode toward them, his golf shoes scuffing over the artificial turf. Smith was a short, barrel-chested, barrel-gutted man with a fuzzy mustache and kinky black hair. He wore a black golf shirt tucked into black pleated slacks, with a woven leather belt circling his waist. A gold chain dangled from his neck, with what looked like a St. Christopher medal. He smiled at Fell and stuck his hand out. "You're the cop who was watching me last year . . ."

Fell ignored the hand. "We need to talk to you about this Bekker guy," she said bluntly. "The guy who's chopping up these people . . ."

"The freak," Smith said. He took his hand back, couldn't find a place for it, and finally stuck it in his slacks pocket. He was puzzled, his mustache quivering. "Why talk to me?"

"He needs money and drugs, and he can't get them legitimately," Lucas said. He'd drifted past the driving area to the putting green. The green's surface was knee high, but dished, to provide a variety of contours. He reached down and pressed his fingers against it. Real grass, carefully groomed, cool and slightly damp to the touch.

"Now that's a hell of a project, right there," Smith said enthusiastically. He picked up a remote control, touched a series of buttons, and the lights over the putting green flickered and came on. "Those are special grow lights," he said, pointing up at the lighting fixture. "Same spectrum as the sun. Joe over there, he knows all about different grasses, he set it up. This is genuine bent grass. It took him a year to get it right."

Smith stepped up and onto the green, walked lightly across it, then turned to look at Lucas. Back to business: "So this guy needs money and drugs?"

"Yeah. And we want you to put the word out on your network. Somebody is dealing with him, and we want him. Now."

Smith picked up a putter that was leaning against the far end. Three balls waited in a rack, and he popped them out, lined up the first one, stroked and missed. The ball rolled past the cup and stopped two feet away.

"Twenty-two feet. Not bad," he said. "When you've got a long lag like that, you just try to get it within two feet of the cup. You pretend you're shooting for a manhole cover. That's the secret to single-bogey golf. Do cops play golf?"

"We need you to put out the word," Fell said.

"Talk into my belly button, said Little Red Riding Hood," Smith said. He lined up another putt, let it go. The ball rolled four feet past the cup. "Fuck it," he said. "Nerves. You guys are putting pressure on me."

"There's no wire," Lucas said quietly. "Neither one of us is wired. We're looking for a little help."

"What do I get out of it?" Smith asked.

"Civic pride," Lucas said. The pitch of his voice had dropped a bit, but Smith pretended not to notice, and lined up the last ball.

"Civic pride? In fuckin' New York?" He snorted, looked up

and said, "Excuse the language, Dr. Fell. . . . Anyway, I really don't know what you're talking about, this network."

He walked around the green, squinting at the short putt. The blond man approached with a china platter covered with steaming slices of bread. "Anybody for fresh bread? We've got straight and garlic butter. . . ."

"Fuck the bread," said Fell. She looked at Lucas. "We're not getting to him. Maybe we ought to have the fire department check his . . ."

"Nah, political shit doesn't work with a guy who's really connected," Lucas said. "Mr. Smith sounds like he's connected."

Smith squinted at him. "Who're you? I don't remember you. . . ."

"I've been hired as a consultant here," Lucas said. He wandered back to the driving net, speaking so softly that the others could barely pick up the words. He pulled a three iron out of the golf bag and looked at it. "I used to work in Minneapolis, until I got thrown off the force. I caught Bekker the first time, but not before he killed a good friend of mine. Cut her throat. He let her see it coming. Made her wait for it. Then he sawed right through her neck. . . . She was tied up, couldn't fight back. So later, when I caught Bekker . . ."

"His face got all fucked up," Smith said suddenly.

"That's right," said Lucas. He'd come back, carrying the iron. "His face got all fucked up."

"Wait a minute," said Fell.

Lucas ignored her, hopped up on the putting green, and walked toward Smith. Out of the corner of his eye, he saw Fell's hand sliding into the fold of her shoulder bag. "And I didn't worry about fucking him up. You know why? Because I've got a lot of money of my own and I didn't need the job. I don't need any job."

"What the fuck are you talking . . ." Smith backed away, looked quickly at the blond.

". . . And Bekker got me really pissed," Lucas said to Smith, his voice riding over the other man's. His eyes were wide, the tendons in his neck straining at his shirt collar. "I mean *really fuckin' pissed.* And I had this pistol, with this big sharp front sight on it, and when I caught him, I pounded his face with the sight until you couldn't tell it was a face. Before that, Bekker'd been really pretty, just like this fuckin' green. . . ."

Lucas pivoted and swung the three iron, a long sweeping swing into the perfect turf. A two-pound divot of dirt and grass sprayed off the platform across the pool table.

"Wait, wait . . ." Smith was waving his hands, trying to stop it.

The blond had set the china tray aside and his hand went toward the small of his back and Fell had a pistol out, pointed at his head, and she was yelling, "No, no, no . . ."

Lucas rolled on, swinging the club like a scythe, screaming, walking around Smith, saliva spraying on Smith's black shirt. "Pounded his face, pounded his motherfuckin' face, you believe the way we pounded his fuckin' face."

When he stopped, breathing hard, a dozen ragged furrows slashed the surface of the green. Lucas turned and looked at the blond man. Hopped down off the platform, walked toward him.

"You were going to pull out a gun," he said.

The blond man shrugged. He had heavy shoulders, like a weight lifter, and he shifted, setting his feet.

"That really pisses me off," Lucas shouted at him.

"Hold it, for Christ's sake," said Fell, her voice low and urgent.

Lucas swung the iron again, quickly, violently, overhead, then down. The blond flinched, but the iron smashed through the freshly baked bread and the platter beneath it. Pieces of china skittered across the floor, and he shouted, "And tried to fuckin' bribe us . . ."

Then he ran down, staggered, turned back to Smith and pointed the club like a saber.

"I don't want to be your friend. I don't want to deal. You're a goddamned dirtbag, and it makes me feel nasty to be here. What I'm telling you is, I want you to put the word out on your network. And I want you to call me. Lucas Davenport. Midtown South. If you don't, I will fuck you up six different ways. I'll talk to the *New York Times* and I'll talk to the *News* and I'll talk to *EyeWitness News* and I'll give them pictures of you and tell them you're working with Bekker. How'd that help business? And I might just come back and fuck you up personally, because this is a serious matter with me, this Bekker thing."

He turned in a half-circle, his breath slowing, took a step toward the door, then suddenly whipped the club into the kitchen like a helicopter blade. It knocked a copper tureen off a wall peg, bounced off the stove, and clattered to the floor with the tureen. "Never was any fucking good with the long irons," he said.

On the way out of the building, Fell watched him until Lucas began to grin.

"Nuttier'n shit, huh?" he said, glancing at her.

"I believed it," she said seriously.

"Thanks for the backup. I don't think blondie would've done much. . . ."

She shook her head. "That was funny; I mean, funny-strange. I didn't know Jackie Smith was gay until I saw this guy. That's like dealing with spouses, only worse. You whack one and the other's liable to come after you with a knife. . . ."

"Are you sure they're gay?"

"Does Raggedy Ann have a cotton crotch?"

"I don't know what that means," Lucas said, laughing.

"It means yes, I'm sure they're gay," she said.

"How come he called you Dr. Fell?" Lucas asked. "Are you a doctor?"

"No. It's from the nursery rhyme: 'I do not love thee, Dr. Fell; the reason why I cannot tell; but this I know, and know full well: I do not love thee, Dr. Fell.' "

"Huh. I'm impressed," Lucas said.

"I know several nursery rhymes," Fell said, digging in her purse for the pack of Luckys. "Want to hear 'Old King Cole' ?"

"I mean with Smith. Knowing the rhyme."

"I don't impress you, huh?" She flipped the cigarette into her mouth, her eyes slanting up at him.

"Don't know yet," he said. "Maybe . . ."

Barbara Fell lived on the Upper West Side. They dropped her city car at Midtown South, found a cab, and she said, "I've got a decent neighborhood bar. Why don't you come up and get a drink, chill out, and you can catch a cab from there."

"All right." He nodded. He need some more time with her.

They went north on Sixth, the sidewalk traffic picking up as they got closer to Central Park, tourists walking arm in arm along the sidewalks.

"It's too big," Lucas said, finally, watching through the window as the city went by. "In the Twin Cities, you can pretty much get a line on every asshole in town. Here . . ." He looked out and shook his head. "Here, you'd never know where it was coming from. You got assholes like other places got raindrops. This is the armpit of the universe."

"Yeah, but it can be pretty nice," she said. "Got the theaters, the art museums . . ."

"When was the last time you went to a theater?"

"I don't know—I really can't afford it. But I mean, if I could."

"Right."

In the front seat, the taxi driver was humming to himself. There was no tune, only variations in volume and intensity as the driver stared blank-eyed through the windshield, bobbing his head to some unheard rhythm. His hands gripped the wheel so tightly that his knuckles were white. Lucas looked at the driver, looked at Fell and shook his head. She laughed, and he grinned and went back to the window.

The bar was small, carefully lit, convivial. The bartender called Fell by her first name, pointed her at a back booth. Lucas took the seat facing the entrance. A waitress came over, looked at him, looked at Fell, said, "Ooo."

Fell said, "Strictly business."

"Ain't it always," the waitress said. "Didja hear Louise had her kid, baby girl, six pounds four ounces?"

Lucas watched Fell as she chatted with the waitress. She looked a little tired, a little lonesome, with that uncertain smile.

"So," she said, coming back to Lucas. "Do you really freeze your ass off in Minnesota? Or is that just . . ."

Small talk, bar talk. A second drink. Lucas waiting for a break, waiting. . . .

Getting it. A slender man walked in, touched a woman on the cheek, got a quick peck in return. He was blond, carefully dressed, and after a moment, looked at the back of Fell's head, said something to the woman he'd touched, then looked carefully at Lucas.

"There's a guy," Lucas said, leaning across the table, talking in a low voice. "And I think he's looking at you. By the bar . . ."

She turned her head and lit up. "Mica," she called. To Lucas she said, "He used to be my hairdresser. He's, like, moved downtown." She slid out of the booth, walked up to the bar. "When did you get back . . . ?"

"I thought that was you . . ." Mica said.

Mica had been to Europe; he started a story. Lucas sipped the beer, lifted his feet to the opposite seat, caught Fell's purse between his ankles, pulled it in. Fumbled with it, out of sight, watching. The waitress glanced his way, lifted her eyebrows. He shook his head. If she came over, if Mica's story ended too soon, if Fell hurried back to get a cigarette . . .

There. Keys. He'd been waiting all day for a shot at them. . . .

He glanced at the key ring in his hand, six keys. Three good candidates. He had a flat plastic box in his pocket that had once held push pins. He'd dumped the pins and filled both the bottom and the lid with a thin layer of modeling clay. He pressed the first key in the clay, turned it, pressed again. Then the second key. The third key he did in the lid; if he made the impressions too close together, the clay tended to distort. . . . He glanced into the box. Good, clean, impressions, six of them.

Fell was still talking. He slipped the keys back into her purse, gripped it with his ankles, lifted it back to her seat. . . .

Pulse pounding like an amateur shoplifter's.

Jesus.

Got them.

CHAPTER

7

Lily called the next morning, "Got them," she said. "We're going to breakfast. . . ."

Lucas called Fell, catching her just before she left her apartment.

"O'Dell called," he said. "He wants me to have breakfast with him. I probably won't make it down until ten o'clock or so."

"All right. I'll run the guy Lonnie told us about, the guy with the Cadillac in Atlantic City. It won't be much. . . ."

"Unless the guy's into medical supplies. Maybe the syringes weren't his only item."

"Yeah . . ." She knew that was bullshit, and Lucas grinned at the telephone.

"Hey, we're driving nails. I'll buy you lunch later on."

The Lakota Hotel was old, but well-kept for New York. It was close to the publishing company that produced Lucas' board games, convenient to restaurants, and had beds that his feet didn't hang off of. From this particular room, he had a view over the roof below into the windows of a glass-sided office building. Not wonderful, but not bad, either. He had two nightstands, a writing table, a chest of drawers, a window seat, a color television with a working remote, and a closet with a light that came on automatically when he opened it.

He went to the closet, pulled out a briefcase and opened it on the bed. Inside was a monocular, a cassette recorder with a phone clip, and a Polaroid Spectra camera with a half-dozen rolls of film. Excellent. He closed the briefcase, made a quick trip to the bathroom, and rode back down to the street. A bellhop, loitering in the phone-booth-sized lobby, said "Cab, Mr. Davenport?"

"No. I've got a car coming," he said. Outside, he hurried down the street to a breakfast bar, got a pint of orange juice in a wax carton, and went back outside.

After leaving Fell the night before, he'd gone to Lily's apartment and given her the key impressions. Lily knew an intelligence officer who could get them made overnight, discreetly.

"Old friend?" Lucas asked.

"Go home, Lucas," she'd said, pushing him out the door.

And now she called his name again: a black town car slid to the curb, a cluster of antennas sticking out of the trunk lid, and when the back window slid down, he saw her face. "Lucas . . ."

O'Dell's driver was a broad man with a Korean War crew cut, his hair the color of rolled steel. A hatchet nose split basalt eyes, and his lips were dry and thick; a Gila monster's. Lucas got in the passenger seat.

"Avery's?" the driver asked. The front seat was separated from the back by an electric window, which had been run down.

"Yeah," O'Dell said. He was reading the *Times* editorial page. A pristine copy of the *Wall Street Journal* lay between his right leg and Lily's left. As he looked over the paper, he asked Lucas, "Did you eat yet?"

"A carton of orange juice."

"We'll get you something solid," O'Dell said. He'd not stopped reading the paper, and the question and comment were perfunctory. After a moment, he muttered, "Morons."

Lily said to the driver, "This is Lucas Davenport next to you, Aaron—Lucas, that's Aaron Copland driving."

"Not the fuckin' piano player, either," Copland said. His eyes went to Lucas. "How are ya?"

"Nice to meet you," Lucas said.

At Avery's, Copland got out first and held the door for O'Dell. Copland had a wide, solid gut, but the easy moves of an athlete. He wore a pistol clipped to his belt, just to the left of his navel, and though his golf shirt covered it, he made no particular attempt to conceal it.

A heavy automatic, Lucas thought. Most of the New York cops he'd seen were carrying ancient .38 Specials, revolvers that looked as though they'd been issued at the turn of the century. Copland, whatever else he might be, was living in the present. He never looked directly at Lucas or Lily or O'Dell as they were getting out of the car, but around them, into the corners and doorways and window wells.

In the closest doorway was a solid oak door with a narrow window at eye height, and below that, a gleaming brass plaque that said AVERY'S. Behind the door was a restaurant full of politicians: they had places like this in Minneapolis and St. Paul, but Lucas had never seen one in New York. It was twenty feet wide, a hundred feet deep, with a long dark mahogany bar to the right side of the entrance. Overhead, wooden racks held hundreds of baseball bats, lying side by side, all of them autographed. A dozen flat Plexiglas cases marched down the left-hand wall opposite the bar, like stations of the cross, and each case held a half-dozen more bats, autographed. Lucas knew most of the names—Ruth, Gehrig, DiMaggio, Maris, Mays, Snider, Mantle. Others, like Nick Etten, Bill Terry, George Stirnweiss, Monte Irvin, rang only faint bells in his memory. At the end of the bar, a double row of booths extended to the back of the restaurant; almost all of the booths were occupied.

"I'll be at the bar," Copland said. He'd looked over the occupants of the restaurant, decided that none of them was a candidate for shooting.

O'Dell led the way back: he was an actor, Lucas realized, rolling slowly down the restaurant like a German tank, nodding into some booths, pointedly ignoring others, the rolled copy of the *Wall Street Journal* whacking his leg.

"Goddamn town," O'Dell said when he was seated at the booth. He dropped the papers on the seat by his leg. Lily sat opposite him, with Lucas. He peered at Lucas across the table and said, "You know what's happening out there, Davenport? People are stringing razor wire—you see it everywhere now. And broken glass on the tops of walls. Like some goddamned Third World city. New York. Like fuckin' Bangkok." He lowered his voice: "Like these cops, if they're out there. A death squad, like Brazil or Argentina."

A balding waiter with a pickle face came to the table. He wore a neck-to-knees white apron that seemed too neatly blotched with mustard.

"Usual," O'Dell grunted.

Lily glanced at Lucas and said, "Two coffees, two Danish."

The waiter nodded sourly and left.

"You got a reputation as a shooter," O'Dell said.

"I've shot some people," Lucas said. "So has Lily."

"We don't want you to shoot anybody," O'Dell said.

"I'm not an assassin."

"I just wanted you to know," O'Dell said. He groped in his pocket and pulled out a strip of paper and unfolded it. The *Times* story. "You did a good job yesterday. Modest, you give credit to everyone, you stress how smart Bekker can be. Not bad. They bought it. Have you read the files? On this other thing?"

"I'm starting tonight, at Lily's."

"Any thoughts so far? From what you've seen?" O'Dell pressed.

"I don't see Fell in it."

"Oh?" O'Dell's eyebrows went up. "I can assure you that she is, somehow. Why would you think otherwise?"

"She's just not right. How did you find her?"

"Computer. We ran the dead guys against the cops who busted them. She came up several times. Repeatedly, in a couple of cases. Too many times for it to be a coincidence," O'Dell said.

"Okay. I can see her nominating somebody. I just can't see her setting up a hit. She's not real devious."

"Do you like her?" asked Lily.

"Yeah."

"Will that get in the way?" O'Dell asked.

"No."

O'Dell glanced at Lily and she said, "I don't think it will. Lucas fucks over both men and women impartially."

"Hey, you know I get a little tired . . ." Lucas said irritably.

"Fell looks like another Davenport kill," Lily said. She tried for humor, but there was an edge to it.

"Hey, hey . . ." O'Dell said.

"Look, Lily, you know goddamned well . . ." Lucas said.

"Stop, stop, not in a restaurant," O'Dell said. "Jesus . . ."

"Okay," said Lily. She and Lucas had locked up, and now she broke her eyes away.

The waiter returned with a plate piled with French toast and a small tureen of hot maple syrup. A pat of butter floated on the syrup. He unloaded the French toast in front of O'Dell, and coffee cups in front of Lucas and Lily. O'Dell tucked a napkin into his collar and started on the toast.

"There's something more going on here," O'Dell said, when the waiter had gone. "These three hits we're most worried about, the lawyer, the activist, and Petty himself—I believe these guys may be coming out. The shooters."

"What?" Lucas glanced at Lily, who stared impassively at O'Dell.

"That's my sense, my political sense," O'Dell said. He popped a dripping square of toast into his mouth, chewed, leaned back and watched Lucas with his small eyes. "They're deliberately letting us know that they're out there and that they aren't to be fooled with. The word is getting around. Has been for a couple of months. You hear this shit, 'Robin Hood and his Merry Men,' or 'Batman Strikes Again,' whenever some asshole is taken off.

There are a lot of people who'd like the idea that they're out there. Doing what's necessary. Half the people in town would be cheering them on, if they knew."

"And the other half would be in the streets, tearing the place apart," Lily said to Lucas. She turned her head to O'Dell. "There's the other thing, too, with Bekker."

"What?" asked Lucas, looking between them.

"We're told that this is real," she said. She fished in her purse, took out a folded square of paper and handed it to him. A Xerox copy of a letter, addressed to the editor of the *New York Times.*

Lucas glanced down at the signature: Bekker. One word, an aristocratic conceit and scrawl.

> . . . taken to task for what I consider absolutely essential experiments into the transcendental nature of Man, and accused of crimes; so be it. I will stand on my intellectual record, and though accused of crimes, as Galileo was, I will, like him, be vindicated by a future generation.
>
> Though accused of crimes, I am innocent, and I will have no truck with criminals. It is in that spirit that I write. On Friday night last, I witnessed an apparent gang-land shooting. . . .

"Jesus Christ," Lucas said, looking at Lily. "Was this one of the killings you were talking about?"

"Walt," she said.

Lucas went back to the letter. Bekker had seen the two killers clearly.

> . . . would describe him as white, thick, square-faced with a gray, well-trimmed mustache extending the full length of his upper lip, weighing two hundred and twenty pounds, six feet, two inches tall, sixty-one years old. As a trained forensic pathologist, I would wager than I am not wrong by more than five pounds either way, or by more than an inch in height, or two years in age.
>
> The description of the other one, the one I have called Thin, I will hold to myself, for my own reasons. . . .

"This never ran in the paper?" Lucas asked, looking at O'Dell.

"No. They've agreed to hold it at our request, but they've reserved the right to print it if it seems relevant."

"Do you have any idea who it is? This Thick guy?"

He shook his head: "One of four or five hundred cops—if it's a cop at all."

"You could probably narrow it more than that," Lucas said.

"Not without going public," Lily said. "If we started checking out five hundred cops . . . Christ, the papers would be all over us. But the main thing is, you see . . ."

Lucas picked up her thought: "Bekker can identify two cop killers and he's willing to do it. . . ."

"And for that reason, we think these guys'll make a run at Bekker."

"To shut him up."

"Among other things."

"If they are coming out, they're more likely to go for Bekker," O'Dell said. "They might have to go for him anyway, if they think he can identify two of them. But there's more than that: Killing Bekker would be one way to make their point, that some people have to be killed. Bekker's a nightmare. Who can object to killing him? He's made to order for them, if they can find him."

"This is getting complicated," Lucas said. "I worry about Lily. She's close to this thing, funneling stuff around. What happens if they come after her?"

"They won't," O'Dell said confidently. "Two dead cops would be unacceptable. . . ."

"I'd think one dead cop would be unacceptable."

"One dead cop can be finessed. Denied. Two is a pattern," O'Dell said.

"Besides, I'm not exactly a pushover," Lily said, patting the purse where she kept her .45.

"That'll get your ass killed," Lucas said, anger in his voice. They locked up again. "Anyone's a pushover when the shooters are using a fuckin' machine gun from ambush. You're good, but you ain't bulletproof."

"All right, all right . . ." She rolled her eyes away.

"And there's always Copland," O'Dell said. "When Lily's outside working, she's usually with me in the car. Copland's more than a driver. He's tough as a nail and he knows how to use his gun. I'll have him take her home at night."

"Okay." Lucas looked at Lily again, just for a second, then shifted back to O'Dell. "How'd you get onto Fell? Exactly?"

"Exactly." O'Dell mopped up a river of syrup with a crust of the toast, looked at it for a minute, then popped it in his mouth and chewed, his small eyes nearly closing with the pleasure of it. He swallowed, opened his eyes. Like a frog, Lucas thought. "This is it, exactly. Once or twice a semester I go up to Columbia and lecture on Real Politics, for a friend of mine. Professor. This goes way back. So a few years ago—hell, what am I saying, it was fifteen years ago—he introduced me to a graduate student who was using computerized statistical techniques to analyze voting patterns. Fascinating stuff. I wound up taking classes in statistics, and a couple in computers. I don't look like it"—he spread his arms, as if to display his entire corpulent body—"but I'm a computer jock. When these guys in intelligence found what they thought was a problem, I sorted the killings. There *was* a pattern. No mistake about it. I called in Petty, who specialized in computer searches and relational work. We turned up almost two hundred possibles. For one reason or another, we eliminated a lot of them and got it down to maybe forty. And twelve of those, we were just about sure of. I think Lily told you that . . ."

"Yeah. Forty. That's a pretty unbelievable number."

O'Dell shrugged. "Some of the killings are probably just what they seem to be—thugs getting killed on the street by other thugs. But not all of them. And I'm sure we missed some. So balancing everything out, I think forty, fifty aren't bad numbers."

"How does Fell fit in?" Lucas asked.

"Petty ran the bad guys against cops who'd know them—a lot of complicated name sorts here, but I've got total access."

"And Fell's name came up. . . ."

"Way too much."

"I hate statistics," Lucas said. "The newspapers were always fuckin' with them back in Minneapolis, drawing stupid conclusions from bad data."

"That's a problem, the data," O'Dell agreed. "We'd certainly never get Fell in court, based on my numbers."

"Mmmph." Lucas looked at Lily and then O'Dell. "I need some heavy time to dig through this. . . ."

"Don't," said O'Dell. He pointed a fork at Lucas' nose. "Your first priority is to find Bekker and to provide a diversion for the media. We need a little air. You've got to do that for real. If this gang is out there, these killers, they won't be easily fooled. Bringing you to New York was supposed to be like bringing in a psychic from Boise: to keep the Boises in the newsroom happy. Everybody's buying it so far. They've got to keep buying it. This other thing has to be way, way in the background."

"What happens if we catch Bekker too soon?" Lucas asked. "Before we identify these guys?"

Lily shrugged. "Then you go home and we find some other way to do it."

"Mmm."

"So. We're in a position where we're hopin' a goddamn psycho holds out for another few weeks and maybe butchers somebody else's kid, so we can run down our own guys," O'Dell mumbled, half talking to himself, staring into the half-eaten sludge pile of toast and syrup. He turned to Lily. "We're really fucked, you know that, Lily? We're really and truly fucked."

"Hey, this is New York," Lucas said.

O'Dell slogged through the rest of the French toast, filling in background on Petty's computer search for the killers.

"Is there any possibility that he turned up something unexpected with the computer?" Lucas asked.

"Not really. Things don't work that way—with a computer, you grind things out, you inch forward. You don't get a printout that says 'Joe Blow Did It.' I think something must have happened with this witness."

When they left the restaurant, O'Dell walked ahead, again nodding into some booths, pointedly ignoring others. Lily grabbed Lucas' sleeve and held him back a step.

"Here." She handed him three keys on a ring.

"That was quick," Lucas said.

"This is New York," she said.

Lucas took a cab from Avery's to Fell's apartment building. The cabdriver was a small man with a white beard, and as soon as Lucas settled in the backseat, he asked, "See *Misérables*?"

"What?"

"Let me tell you, you're missing something," the driver said. He smelled like a raw onion and was soaked with sweat. "Where're you going? Okay—Listen, you gotta see *Misérables*, I mean why d'ya come to New York if you ain't gonna see a show, you know what I mean? Look at the crazy motherfucker over there, you should excuse the language, you think they should let a jerk like that on the streets? Jesus Christ, where'd he learn to drive?" The driver stuck his head out the window, leaning on the horn. "Hey, buddy, where'd you learn to drive, huh? Iowa? Huh? Hey, buddy." Back inside, he said, "I tell you, if the mayor wasn't black . . ."

Lucas called Fell at the office from a pay phone mounted on the outside wall of a parking garage. The garage paint, covered with indecipherable graffiti, was peeling off, to reveal another layer of graffiti. "Barb? Lucas. I gotta run back to my place, just for a minute. Are we still on for lunch?"

"Sure."

"Great. See you in a few minutes," Lucas said. He hung up and looked across the street at Fell's apartment building. A thousand apartments, he thought. Maybe more. Ranks of identical balconies, each with a couple of plants, most with bicycles.

Yuppie-cycles, the mountain bikes, in case the riders encountered an off-trail situation in Central Park. Some of them, as high as he could see, were chained to the balcony railings.

The lobby of her building was a glass cage surrounding a guard. At the back were two ranks of stainless-steel mailboxes. The guard, in an ill-fitting gray uniform, was stupidly watchful.

"Where's the sales office?" Lucas asked. A light flickered in the guard's eyes. This situation was specifically covered in his orders. "Second floor, sir, take a right."

"Thanks." Apartment security; it was wonderful, if you had it. Lucas walked back to the elevators, punched two. The second floor had several offices, all down to the right. Lucas ignored them, took a left. Found the stairs, walked up a floor, went back to the elevators and punched sixteen.

The telephone call assured him that Fell was still at Midtown; he didn't have to worry that she'd slipped back home for a snack or to pay bills, or whatever. She lived alone, she'd said. He'd gotten her apartment and home phone numbers from an office roster sheet.

He rode up alone, got out in an empty corridor, took a left, got lost, retraced his steps past the elevators. Her door was green; the others were blue, a tomato-red and beige. Other than that, they were identical. He knocked. No answer. Looked around, knocked again. No answer. He tried a key, hit it the first time, popped the door. The silence inside seemed laced with tension.

Gotta move, move, move . . .

The apartment smelled lightly, inoffensively, of tobacco. The living room had a sliding glass door that led out to the balcony; the doors were covered by off-white curtains, half-drawn. She had a view of a similar building, but if he looked sideways, across the street, Lucas could see another rank of buildings across a gap. The gap was probably the Hudson, with Jersey on the other side.

The apartment was neat, but not compulsively so. Most of the furniture was good, purchased as matched sets. Two green overstuffed La-Z-Boy chairs faced a big color television. A low table sat between the chairs, stacked with magazines. *Elle, Vogue, Guns & Ammo.* More magazines lay on the table, and under it he found a pile of novels. Beside the television was a cabinet with a CD player, a tuner, a tape deck and a VCR. A second table held more magazines, four remote controls, an oversize brandy snifter full of matchbooks—Windows on the World, the Russian Tea Room, the Oak Room, The Four Seasons. They were pristine, and looked as though they'd come from a souvenir packet. Other matchbooks were more worn, half-used—several from the bar they'd visited the night before, one with a crown, one with a chess knight, one with an artist's palette. An ashtray held four cigarette butts.

On the walls around the television were photo portraits: a woman standing on a pier with two older people who might have been her parents, and another picture of the same woman in a wedding veil; a square-shouldered young man on a hillside with a collie and a .22, and another of the young man, grown older, dressed in an army uniform, standing under a sign that said, "I know I'm going to heaven, because I served my time in Hell: Korea, 1952." Something wrong with the young man . . . Lucas looked closer. His upper lip was twisted slightly, as though he'd had a harelip surgically repaired.

Her parents? Almost certainly.

A hallway broke to the left out of the living room. He checked it, found a bathroom and two bedrooms. One bedroom was used as an office and for storage; a small wooden desk and two file cabinets were pushed against one wall, while most of the rest of the space was occupied by cardboard boxes, some open, some taped shut. The other bedroom had a queen-sized bed, unmade, with a sheet tangled by its foot, and two chests of drawers, one with a mirror. An oval braided rug lay underfoot, just at the side of the bed, and a pair of underpants lay in the middle of the rug. A thigh-high woven-bamboo basket with a lid half-hid behind one of the chests. He opened it. Soiled clothes: a hamper.

He could see it. *She sleeps in her underpants, sits up, still tired, yawns, gets out of beds, drops her pants for a shower, figures to toss them in the hamper when she gets back, forgets. . . .*

He went back through the living room to the kitchen, which looked almost unused—a half-dozen water glasses sat in a drying rack in the sink, along with a couple of forks, but no dishes. A Weight Watchers lasagna package lay inside a wastebasket. A bottle of Tanqueray gin sat on the cupboard, two-thirds full. He looked in the refrigerator, found bottles of lime-flavored Perrier and Diet Pepsi, a six-pack of Coors, a bottle of reconstituted lime juice and four bottles of Schweppe's Diet Tonic Water. A sack of nectarines lay on top of the fruit drawer. He touched the stove-top. Dust. A freestanding microwave took up half the counter space. No dust. She didn't cook much.

He did the kitchen first: women hide things in the kitchen or the bedroom. He found a set of dishes, inexpensive, functional. Rudimentary cooking equipment. A drawer full of paper, warranties for all the appliances and electronics in the place. He pulled the drawers out, looked under and behind them. Looked in tins: nothing, not even the flour and sugar that was supposed to be there.

In the bedroom, he looked under the bed and found a rowing machine and dust bunnies the size of wolverines; and in the bedstand drawer, where he found a Colt Lawman with a two-inch barrel, chambered for .38 Specials. Swung out the cylinder: six loaded chambers. He snapped the cylinder back, replaced the weapon as he'd found it.

Looked through the chest of drawers. Bundles of letters and postcards in the top drawer, with cheap jewelry and a sealed box of lubricated Trojans. He looked through the letters, hurrying.

Dear Barb, Just back from New Hampshire, and you should have come! We had the best time!

Dear Barb: Quick note. I'll be back the 23rd, if everything goes right. Tried to call, but couldn't get you, they said you were out, and I was afraid to wake you during the day. I really need to see you. I think about you all the time. I can't stop. Anyway, see you on the 23rd. Jack.

The letter was in an envelope, and he checked the postmark: four years old. He made a mental note: Jack.

Not much else. He pulled out the drawers. Ah. More paper. Polaroid photos. Barbara Fell, sitting on a man's lap, both holding up bottles of beer. They were naked. She was thin, with small breasts and dark nipples.

He was as thin as she, but muscular, dark-haired, and looked at the camera with a practiced lack of self-consciousness. Another shot: the two of them sitting on what looked like a zebra-skin rug, both nude, their eyes red pinpoints. In the background, a mirror, with a brilliant flash reflecting back at the camera. The camera in the mirror was on a tripod, unattended. No third person. The expression on her face . . . Fear? Excitement? Trepidation?

Another photo, the two of them clothed, standing outside what looked like a police station. A cop? He went back to his briefcase, got the Polaroid out, clipped on the close-up attachment, knelt, and duplicated the photos.

There was nothing else in the bedroom. The bathroom was odorless, freshly scrubbed, but the vanity countertop was a jumble of lipsticks, shampoos, soap, deodorant, a box of something called YeastGard, panty shields, a pack of needles, tweezers, a huge box of Band-Aids and a bottle of sesame body oil. The medicine cabinet held a small selection of over-the-counter items: aspirin, Mycitracin, Nuprin.

He headed for the office.

She was meticulous about her accounts, and everything seemed about right: she had one bank account, a safety-deposit box, and an account with Fidelity Investments, which turned out to be an IRA.

And where was her book? He shuffled through the desk drawers. She must have a personal phone book. She probably carried an annual one with her, but she should have some sort of book she kept at home, that she wouldn't be changing every year. He frowned. Nothing in the desk. He walked out to the front room and looked around the telephone. Nothing there. The phone had a long cord, and he walked over to the pile of magazines on the television table, stirred through them. The book was there, and he flipped it open. Names. Dozens of them. He got the Polaroid and began shooting. When he finished, he'd used all but two shots.

Enough. He looked around, checked the lights and back-tracked out of the apartment. The guard was staring stoically at a blank marble wall when Lucas left, and never looked up. The guard's job was to keep people out, not keep people in.

Kennett and another detective were looking at paper, while a third cop talked on a telephone.

"Barbara's down the hall," Kennett said, looking up when Lucas walked in. "We got you an empty office so you can have a little peace. . . ."

"Thanks," Lucas said.

Fell was sorting through a stack of manila files. He stopped in the doorway, watched her for a moment. She was focused, intent. Attractive. The nude photos popped up in his mind's eye: she looked smaller in the photos, more vulnerable, less vivid. She began paging through a file. After a moment, she felt him in the door, looked up, startled: "Jesus, I didn't hear you," she said.

He stepped inside, walked around the table. Picked up a file: "Robert Garber, 7/12." "Is this everything?"

"Yeah. I've been reading through it. A zillion details," she said. She brushed a lock of hair out of her eyes. "The problem is, we don't need any of it. We know who Bekker is and what he looks like, and he admits in these crazy medical papers that he did the killings. All we have to do is find him; we don't need all the usual shit."

"There must be something. . . ."

"I'll be goddamned if I can see it," Fell said. "The other guys made a list, like the stuff you were talking about at the meeting this morning. He needs an income. He needs a place to hide. He needs a vehicle. He needs to change his face. So they've put out the publicity to employers: watch who you're paying. They've contacted all the hotels and flophouses and anyplace else he might stay. They're talking with the taxi companies, thinking maybe he's moving around in the cab—that would explain how he gases them, using the back seat as a gas chamber. They've gone to all the stores that sell cover-up makeup for people who are disfigured, and every place that sells theatrical makeup. The narcotics guys are talking to dealers, and we're chasing fences. What else is there?"

"I don't know, but it's not enough," Lucas said. He flipped his hand at the stack of paper. "Let's look at the victims first. . . ."

They spent an hour at it. Bekker had killed six people in Manhattan, their bodies found scattered around Midtown, the Village, SoHo and Little Italy. Working on the theory he wouldn't take them far, he was probably south of Central Park, north of the financial district. The zip codes on the envelopes he'd mailed to the medical journals suggested the same thing: three papers, three different zips: 10002, 10003 and 10013.

"He uses halothane?"

"That's what they assume," Fell said, nodding. "They found traces in all three people when they were doing the blood chemistry. And that supposedly accounts for the lack of any sign of a struggle. The stuff is quick. Like one-two-three-gone."

"Where did he get it?"

"Don't know yet—we've run all the hospitals in Manhattan, northern Jersey, Connecticut. Nothing yet, but you know, nobody tracks exact amounts of the stuff. You could transfer some from one tank to another. If the tank wasn't gone, how can you tell?"

"Nnn. Okay. But how does he get close enough to whip it on them?" Lucas got up and went out into the hallway, came back with a cone-shaped throwaway water cup. "Stand up."

She stood up. "What?"

He thrust the cup at her face. "If I come at you like this, from the front, I can't get the leverage."

Fell stepped back and the cup came free.

"Even if they got some gas, they could get far enough back to scream," he said.

"We don't know that they didn't scream," said Fell.

"Nobody heard anything."

She nodded. "So if he hits them on the street, he must come up from the back."

"Yeah. He grabs them, pulls them in, claps it over their mouth . . ." He turned her around, clapped the cup over her mouth, his elbow in her spine, his hand hooked over her shoulder. "One, two, three . . . Gone."

"Do it again," she said.

He did it again, but this time, she grabbed his wrist and twisted. The paper cup crumbled and her mouth was open. "Scream," she said. He let go and she said, "That doesn't work too well, either."

"This woman . . . Ellen Foen." Lucas picked up the file, flipped it open. "Statements from her friends say she was very cautious. She'd had some trouble with street people—they hang out in the alley behind the place she worked, going through the dumpsters. She could look out through the glass port in the door while it was still locked, and she always checked before she went out. So if Bekker was there, she must have seen him."

"It was late."

"Nine o'clock. Not quite dark."

"Maybe he was dressed okay. He's not a real big guy—maybe she just wasn't worried."

"But with his face?"

"Makeup. Or . . . I don't know. It makes more sense to me that he's driving a cab. She gets in, he's got one of the security windows between himself and the backseat. He's got it sealed up somehow, and when she shuts the door, he turns on the gas. She passes out. I mean, I just can't see a woman, somebody supposedly cautious, letting a guy get that close to her. And even if he comes up from behind, she'd fight it. You're a hell of a lot bigger than Bekker, but you'd have a hard time holding a mask over my mouth, even from behind."

"Maybe that's why he picks small people, women," Lucas suggested.

"Even so, you just twist away. Even if he gets you, there'd be bruises—but the M.E. hasn't found any bruises. It's gotta be a cab, or something like it."

"But why did Foen take a cab? She was running across the street to get Cokes for everybody. Her boyfriend was supposed to pick her up at nine-thirty, when she got off."

"Maybe . . . fuck, I don't know."

"And look at Cortese. Cortese walks out of this club and across Sixth Avenue, down Fifty-ninth Street toward the Plaza. His friends saw him go in at the Sixth Avenue end. He apparently never arrived at the other end, because there was a phone message for him at the Plaza from nine o'clock on, and he never got it. So he gets picked up on Fifty-ninth between Fifth and Sixth. What happened in there? Why would he flag a cab? He only had to go a few hundred feet."

She shrugged. "I don't know. And it's dark in there, so maybe he got jumped. But you gotta be careful when you start looking for logic, man. . . ."

"I know, I know. . . ."

"It could be anything. Maybe Cortese left his friends because he was looking for a little action."

Lucas shook his head. "He sounds awful straight."

"So does Garber . . . I don't know."

"Keep reading," said Lucas.

She was watching him, he thought. Odd glances, wary. "Is there something wrong?" he asked finally.

After a moment, she asked, "Are you really here working on Bekker?"

"Well . . ." He spread his arms to the stack of paper on the table. "Yeah. Why?"

"Oh, the more I think about it, the odder it seems. We'll catch him, you know."

"Sure, I know," Lucas said. "I'm mostly here for the publicity thing. Take some heat off."

"That doesn't seem quite right either," Fell said. She studied him. "I don't know about you. You hang out with O'Dell. You're not Internal Affairs?"

"What?" He pulled back, surprised. "Jesus, Barbara. No. I'm not Internal Affairs."

"You're sure?"

"Hey. You know what happened to me in Minneapolis?"

"You supposedly beat up somebody. A kid."

"A pimp. He'd cut up a woman with a church key, one of my snitches. Everybody on the street knew about it and I had to do something. So I did. He turned out to be a juvenile—I guess I knew that—and I got hammered by Internal Affairs. There was nothing particularly fair about it. I was just doing what I had to do, and everybody knew it, I got fucked because fucking me was safer than not fucking me. But I'm not Internal Affairs. You can check, easy enough."

"No, no."

She went back to her papers, and Lucas to his, but a minute later he said, "Jesus, Internal Affairs."

"I'm sorry."

"Well . . ."

They took a break, walked two blocks down, bumping hips, and got a booth in a Slice-o'-Pie pizza joint, with gallon-sized paper cups of Diet Pepsi. She liked him; Lucas knew it and let the talk drift toward the personal. He told her about his onetime long-distance relationship with Lily; about the ambiguity now. About his kid.

"I wouldn't mind having a kid," Fell said. "My fuckin' biological alarm clock is banging like Big Ben."

"How old are you?" he asked.

"Thirty-six."

"Any fatherhood prospects on the horizon?"

"Not at the moment," she said. "All I meet are cops and crooks, and I don't want a cop or a crook."

"Hard to meet people?"

"Meeting them isn't the problem. The problem is, the guys I like, don't like me. Eventually. Like five years ago, I was going out with this lawyer dude. Not a big-time lawyer, just a guy. Divorced. Long hair, did a lot of pro bono. And pretty hip. You know."

"Yeah. Exactly. Nice neckties."

"Yeah. He was looking around to get remarried. I mighta. But then one day I was out decoying and this big asshole comes onto me really hard, gets me on a wall, whacks me—he's getting off on whacking me. And I go down and I've got this little hideout piece on my leg, this .25 auto, and he's just bending over to pick me up and I stick the piece in his teeth and his eyes get about the size of dishpans and I back him off, he's saying, 'Hold it, hold it . . .'"

"Where's your backup?"

"They're just running up. They put the guy on the wall and one of them says, 'Jesus, Fell, you're gonna have a mouse bigger'n Mickey'—the asshole'd whacked me right under the eye, right on the eye-socket bone, you know?" She rubbed her eye socket, and Lucas nodded. "Hurt like hell. And I say, 'Yeah?' And they got the guy leaning on the wall with his legs apart, and I say, 'Say good-bye to your nuts, shitbag,' and I punted the sonofabitch so hard his balls had to take a train back from Ohio."

"Yeah?" Lucas laughed. Cop stories were the best stories, and Fell looked positively merry.

"So I tell this story to my lawyer friend and he freaks out. And he's not worried about my eye," she said wryly.

"He's worried about the guy on the wall?"

"No, no. He knew that happened. He didn't mind if *somebody* did it, he just didn't want me to do it. And I think what really

bothered him was my quote: 'Say good-bye to your nuts, shitbag.' I shouldn't have told him that. It really bothered him. I
think he wanted to join a country club somewhere, and he could
see me sitting out on the flagstone terrace with a mint julep or
some fuckin' thing, telling the other country club ladies this, 'Say
good-bye to your nuts, shitbag.' "

Lucas shrugged. "You ever tried a cop?"

"Yeah, yeah." She nodded, with a small smile, eyes unfocusing. "A trouser snake. We were hot for a while, but . . . You want
a little peace and quiet when you're home. He wanted to go out
cruising for dopers."

Lucas took a bite out of a slice of pepperoni, chewed a minute
and then said, "A couple of years ago, Lily and I were involved.
This is between you and me?"

"Sure." The curiosity was wide on her face, unhidden.

"We were getting intense, this was back in Minneapolis, her
marriage was falling apart," Lucas said. "Then this Indian dude
shot her right in the chest. Goddamn near killed her."

"I know about that."

"I freaked out. Man. So then we saw each other a few times,
but I'm afraid to fly, and she was busy. . . ."

"Yeah, yeah . . ."

"Then last year . . ."

"The actress," Fell said. "The one that Bekker killed."

"I'm like a curse," Lucas said, staring past Fell's head, eyes
and voice gone dark. "If I'd been a little smarter, a little
quicker . . . Shit."

After lunch, they went back to the paper, working through it,
finding nothing. Fell, restless, wandered down to the team room
as Lucas continued to read. Kennett brought her back a half-
hour later.

"Bellevue," she said, plopping down in the chair across from
Lucas.

"What?" Lucas looked at Kennett, leaning in the door.

"Bellevue lost some monitoring equipment from one of its
repair shops. We never found out because it wasn't too obvi-

ous—everything was accounted for, on paper. But when the stuff didn't come back from repair, somebody checked, and it was gone. The repair people have receipts, they thought it was back on the floor. Anyway, it's been gone for more than a month, and probably more like six or seven weeks. From before the time Bekker killed the first one," Kennett said.

"They lost exactly what Bekker's been using in his papers," Fell said.

"He could've gotten the halothane there, too, and probably any amount of drugs," Lucas said. "All from one source, if it's a staffer."

"Sounds like him," Fell said.

"I'd bet on it," Kennett said. He ran a hand through his hair, straightened his tie. Pissed. "God damn it, we were slow pulling this in."

"What're you going to do?"

"Move very quietly: we don't want to scare anybody off," Kennett said. "We'll start processing Bellevue staffers against criminal records. And we'll touch all the dopers we know, see who knows who on the inside. Then we do interviews. It'll take a few days. Maybe you guys could get back to your fences? See if you could find somebody who handles Bellevue."

"Yeah." Lucas looked at his watch. Almost three. "Let's get back to Jackie Smith," he said to Fell.

Smith met them in Washington Square. The afternoon was oppressively hot, but Smith was cool: he arrived in a gray Mercedes, which he parked by a hydrant.

"I don't want to talk to you. You want to talk to somebody, talk to my lawyer," Smith said as Lucas and Fell walked up. They stood just off the boccie ball courts, under a gingko tree, hiding from the sun.

"Come on, Jackie," Lucas said. "I'm sorry about the goddamn putting green. I got a little overheated."

"Overheated, my ass," Smith snarled. "You know how long it'll take to fix it?"

"Jackie, we really need to make an arrangement, okay?" Lucas said. "Something new came up on this Bekker guy, and you're in a position to help. Like I said last night, it's personal with me. No bullshit. I just need a little information."

"I don't know fuckin' Bekker from any other asshole," Smith said impatiently.

"Hey, we believe you," Lucas said. "And I had to do the green. I had to get your attention—you were blowing us off. Isn't that right?"

Smith stared at him for a long beat, then said, "So what do you want? Exactly?"

"We need the names of guys who can get stuff out of Bellevue."

"That's all you want? Then you'll get off my back?"

"We can't promise," Lucas said. "I can't talk for Barbara—but *I'd* be a hell of a lot friendlier."

"Jesus Christ, I'm dealing with a fuckin' fruitcake," Smith said. Then: "I don't handle deals at that level. That's small-time."

"I know, I know, but we need a guy who does handle that kind of action. A couple of names, that's all."

"You gonna fuck them over?"

"Not if they talk to me. But if they fuck *me* over, I'll be back to you."

Fell jumped in with a sales pitch: "Jesus, Jackie, this'd be so easy if you just ride along. It's no skin off your ass. You're actually not helping the cops. You're helping some poor woman who's gonna get her heart cut out, or something."

"Yeah, you're the one who poured my coffee on the street," Smith said, apropos of nothing at all. He looked across the plaza, where a group of black kids were working through a dance routine to rap music from a boombox. "All right," he said. "Two guys. Well: a guy and a woman. They're not actually inside the hospital, but they can put you onto guys who are inside."

"That's all we were asking for. . . ."

"Yeah, yeah. Jesus, you're both full of shit. . . ." Then he started toward his car and said, "I'll be a minute."

"Making a call," Fell said as Smith disappeared into the Mercedes.

He was back in two minutes, with two names and addresses. Lucas wrote the names in his notebook. Smith, with a snort of disgust, turned back to his car, shaking his head.

"Angela Arnold and Thomas Leese," Lucas said to Fell. "Where're these addresses?"

Fell looked and said, "Lower East Side. Never heard of them, though. Want me to run them?"

"Yes. Or just drop them off, get them run overnight," Lucas said, looking at his watch. "Kennett wants to be careful, and I don't want to step on him. Let's not worry about talking to them until tomorrow."

Fell dropped him at the hotel, then went on to Midtown South. Lucas cleaned up, ate dinner in the hotel restaurant, went back to his room and watched the Twins and Yankees through the seventh inning, then caught a cab for Lily's apartment. She buzzed him up and came to the door in her bare feet.

"You're late," she said.

"Got hung up," Lucas said, stepping inside. He'd stayed in her apartment almost two years earlier, when she'd just moved in: the furniture then had a temporary, scrounged look. Boxes had been stacked in the living room, a television had sat on two short metal file cabinets. The kitchen wallpaper had been a bizarre bamboo design, with monkeys; the countertops a well-chipped plastic. Now the place had a careful, colored look: warm rugs over a beige carpet; bright hand-printed graphics on the walls; sparse, but carefully chosen chairs and a broad leather couch. The kitchen was a subtle gold with hardwood counters. He'd stopped by the night before to drop off the key impressions, but hadn't stayed long enough to look around. Now he took a few minutes. "The place looks good," he said finally. He felt a pressure: when he'd been there two years before, they'd spent a lot of time in bed, Lily intent on exploring, feeling, desperate for the intensity of the sex. Now they were polite.

"That's what happens when your marriage splits up. You work on the apartment," she said. She stood close to him, but not too close, one hand just touching the other at her waist, like a hostess. Polite and something else. Wary?

"Yeah, I know."

"I made the back bedroom into an office, everything's stacked up in there. Go on back. Want a beer?"

"Sure." He wandered back to the office, yawned, sat down at the desk, pushed the chair back far enough that he could get his heels on a half-open drawer, picked up the first file. He'd been reading files all day; a million facts floating around free-form.

"Kays, Martin." He flipped the file open. Kays had been arrested twice for rape. Served two years the first time, acquitted the second time. He was suspected in as many as thirty attacks on the Upper West Side. He had had it down to a science, attacking women at night in locked parking garages. He apparently entered when a car exited, ducking under the descending door, then waited until he caught a woman alone in the dark. Half-dozen busts on drug-possession charges, assault, theft, drunkenness.

"Kays," Lily said, looking over his shoulder. "He should've gotten it five years earlier."

"Wrong thinking, *mon capitaine,*" Lucas said, looking up at her. She handed him a Special Export.

"Yeah, but it's part of the problem: with the exception of the three killings I told you about, and Walt, which they can deny, most people in town would be rootin' for these guys if they knew about them. Especially when they're doing guys like Kays. I doubt we could find a jury that'd convict them."

"You mean it was all right, as long as they were hitting dirtbags?"

"No. Just that if you kill somebody who deserves to die, and will anyway, someday, but maybe fuck up a hundred people's lives before then . . . hurrying the due date along doesn't seem that terrible. Compared to killing innocent people. But these guys aren't hitting criminals anymore, they're attacking . . . freedom."

"I can't operate at that kind of rarefied theoretical level," Lucas said, grinning at her.

"It does sound like wimpy-ass bullshit, doesn't it?" she said.

"It does."

"But it isn't," she said.

"All right."

"If you don't feel it . . . why'd you sign on?" she asked.

He shrugged. " 'Cause you're a good friend of mine."

"Is that enough?"

"Sure. As far as I'm concerned, it's one of the few good reasons for doing anything. I'd hate to kill somebody out of patriotism or duty; I could never be a warden and throw the switch on somebody. But in hot blood, to protect family or friends . . . that's all right."

"Revenge?"

He thought for a minute, then nodded. "Yeah, revenge is in there. I like hunting Bekker. I'm gonna get him."

"You and Barb Fell."

"Yup. Speaking of whom . . ." He dug in his jacket shirt pocket. "Look at these. The guy looks like a cop and she's tight with him, or was." He handed her two of the Polaroids he'd taken at Fell's.

"Oh, Barbara," Lily muttered, looking at them, shaking her head. "I know this guy. Vaguely. He's a lieutenant in Traffic. We'll run him against the killings and see what we get."

"And I've got some names for you. Friends of hers. I don't know how many are cops, but if you could run them . . ."

"Sure."

Lucas stayed until two o'clock, taking notes on a yellow legal pad, when Lily came in and asked, "Find anything?"

"No. And you were right. These guys were the scum of the scum. How many people could put together a list like this?"

"Hundreds," she said. "But Barb Fell was at the intersection of a lot of possibilities."

Lucas nodded, ripped the sheets off the legal pad, folded them and stuck them in his jacket pocket. "I'll keep working her."

Lily's apartment was on the second floor of a converted townhouse. Lucas left at ten after two, the night just beginning to find the soft coolness that lay between the tropical days. He was a little tired, but still awake; at home he might have gone for a walk along the river, smoothing down for bedtime. In New York . . .

The street was reasonably well lit; a taxi loitered in the next block. He turned that way and started walking, hands in his pockets.

There were two of them.

They were big, quick, like professional linebackers.

The cars along the street were parked bumper-to-bumper. The guy behind the Citation got Lucas to turn toward him by dragging something metallic across the bumper, a chilling, ripping sound, like a knife dragged down a washboard.

Lucas instinctively stepped away and half-turned, pivoting toward the sound. Something was happening: a sound like that had to be intentional. His hand dropped to the small of his back, toward the weight of his .45.

And as he turned, the second guy, the guy who'd hidden behind the stoop, charged onto the walk, slashed at Lucas' elbow with a sap, hit him in the spine with a shoulder, and drove him into the Citation.

The pain from the sap was like an explosion, as clear as a star on a cold night, separate from the impact, standing by itself: a skillful, debilitating cop-pain. It began at his elbow and exploded up his arm to his shoulder, and Lucas screamed, thinking he might have been shot, his arm flopping uselessly as he was smashed into the car. He tried to swing the arm back, to clear out to the right, but it wouldn't move.

He saw the other man's hand coming down, and partially

blocked it with his left, then was hit in the cheekbone with a fist and rocked back against the car.

The second man, coming over the car's fender, hit him, leather gloves, the second punch in a quick one-two-three combo, and Lucas, back hunched, tried to cover.

Thought: *Clear out, clear out . . .*

He was hit again, across the ear, but this time it didn't hurt: it was stunning and he started down, rolling. A gloved hand struck at him and he grabbed it with his good left hand, pulled it under him, pinned it against his chest, let his weight fall on it. He heard what seemed to be a faraway screaming as they hit the concrete walk, felt a snap; he'd broken something. He felt a dim, distant satisfaction, because he was losing this, they were killing him. . . .

Heard glass breaking, registered it, didn't know what it was, but felt the pressure change.

Thought: *Clear out, clear out.* Let go of the gloved hand, felt it wrench away, and the other man screaming . . . Tried to roll under the car, but it was too close to the curb. Tried to cover his head with his good arm . . .

The .45 was like a thunderbolt.

The muzzle-flash broke over them like lightning, freezing everything in a strobe effect. The attackers wore nylon ski masks and gloves, long-sleeved shirts. The one who'd hit him from behind was pivoting, already running. A sap dangled from his hand, long, leather-bound, with a rounded bulge at the business end. The one whose arm Lucas had broken scrabbled to his feet and screamed, "Jesus . . ." and ran.

The .45 struck down again as Lucas sat down on the curb, his legs gone, trying to roll under the car and away from the lightning, not knowing where it came from, groping in the small of his back with his good arm, but the holster was too far around, trying to free his pistol as the attackers faded like ghosts, without a word, down the sidewalk. . . .

Then silence.

And Lily was there in a cotton nightgown, the .45 in her fist, a ludicrous combination, the soft white human cotton and the dark steel killer Colt.

"Lucas . . ." She maneuvered toward him, controlling the .45, not really looking at him, her eyes searching for targets. "Are you okay?"

"Fuck no," he said.

CHAPTER
8

Bekker was first astonished, then swept away. When he returned to the bookstore, he glanced at the counterman with a sigh.

"Are you okay?" The counterman was concerned. He had a long neck and a narrow head with small features, like an oversized thumb sticking out of his shoulders. His face was cocked to one side and the store lights glittered off the right lense of his spectacles, lending him a Strangelovian menace.

"I'm fine, I'm fine," Bekker squeaked. He shuffled his feet and looked away, down the store.

The store was fifteen feet wide and forty deep. Vinyl paneling sagged away from the walls behind rough shelving; the linoleum floor was cracked and holed. The narrow aisles smelled of moldy paper, disintegrating bookcovers and the traffic of the unwashed. An obese man stood at a sale table halfway back, under a round antishoplifting mirror, a hardcover Spiderman anthology propped on his gut, feeding a nut-covered ice cream bar into his face. Bekker hadn't even seen him come in.

He looked down at the book in his hands, the book that had taken him away. He'd dug it out of a pile of crap in the Medicine/Anthropology section. . . .

"You didn't move for so long, I thought maybe, I don't

know . . ." thumb-face said, his Adam's apple bobbing like a toy boat.

He's trying to pick me up, Bekker thought. The notion was flattering, but unwanted. Nobody was allowed too close. Before the Minneapolis cops had beaten him with their pistols, Bekker had been beautiful, but now Beauty was dead. And though he wore heavy Cover Mark makeup to hide the scars, they were visible in bright light. The *Post* had carried the pictures, with every cut and scar for the world to see. . . .

Bekker nodded, polite, not speaking, glanced at his watch. He'd been gone five minutes; he must have been an odd sight, a reader frozen, absolutely unmoving, unblinking, for five minutes or more.

Better leave. Bekker walked to the counter, head down, and pushed the book across. He'd trained himself to speak as little as possible. Speech could give him away.

"Sixteen-fifteen, with tax," the counterman said. He glanced at the book's cover. "Pretty rough stuff."

Bekker nodded, pushed seventeen dollars across the counter, accepted the change.

"Come back again," thumb-face called, as Bekker went out into the street. The bell above the door tinkled cheerily as he left.

Bekker hurried home, saw his name on the front of a newspaper, and slowed. A picture, a familiar face. What?

He picked up a half-brick that held the newspapers flat. Davenport? Christ, it *was* Davenport. He snatched up the paper, threw a dollar at the kiosk man and hurried away.

"Want yer change?" The dealer leaned out of the kiosk.

No. He had no time for change. Bekker scuttled down the street, his heels scratching and rapping, trying to read the paper in the dim ambient light. Finally, he stopped in the brilliantly lit doorway of an electronics store, the windows full of cameras, fax machines, tape recorders, calculators, disc players, portable telephones, miniature televisions and Japanese telescopes. He held the paper close to his nose.

. . . controversial former detective from Minneapolis who is generally credited with solving Bekker's first series of murders and identifying Bekker as the killer. In a fight at the time of the arrest, Bekker's face was badly torn . . .

. . . could have shot him," Davenport said, "but we were trying to take him alive. We knew he had an accomplice, and we believed that the accomplice was dead—but unless we took Bekker alive, we'd never know for sure . . .

Liar. Looking up from the paper, Bekker wanted to scream it: *Liar*. Bekker touched his face, hidden beneath the layers of special cosmetic. Davenport had ripped it. Davenport had destroyed Beauty. Bekker froze, was gone. . . .

A bum came up, saw him in the doorway.

"Hey," the bum said, blocking the sidewalk, and Bekker came back. The bum was not particularly large, but he looked as though he'd been hit often and wasn't afraid to be hit again. Bekker wasn't buying it.

"Fuck off," he bawled, his teeth showing. The bum stepped aside, suddenly afraid, and Bekker went by like a draft of Arctic air. Cursing to himself, Bekker turned the corner, waited for a moment, then stepped back to see if the bum was coming after him. He wasn't. Bekker went on to the Lacey building, muttering, growling, crying. He let himself in the front door, hurried down the basement, dropped into his reading chair.

Davenport in town. The fear gripped him for a moment and he flashed back to the trial, Davenport's testimony, the detective staring at him the whole time, challenging him. . . . Bekker lived through the testimony, mind caught, tangled in the random sparking of his mind. . . . And he came back, with a sigh.

What? He had a package on his lap. He looked at it in puzzlement, dumped it. The book. He'd forgotten. *Final Cuts: Torture Through the Ages*. The book was filled with illustrations of racks and stakes, of gibbets and iron maidens. Bekker wasn't interested. Torture was for freaks and perverts and clowns. But near the end of it . . .

Yes. A photo taken in the 1880s. A Chinese man, the caption said, had assassinated a prince, and had been condemned to the death of a thousand cuts. The executioners had been slicing him to pieces as the photo was taken.

The dying man's face was radiant.

This was what he'd sought in his own work, and here it was, in a century-old photo. This was the light, the luminance of death, pouring from the face of the Chinese man. It wasn't pain—pain was disfiguring: he knew that from his work. He'd been doing his own photography, but had never achieved anything like this. Perhaps it was the old black-and-white film, something special about it.

Bekker sat and gnawed his thumb, Davenport forgotten, obliterated by the importance of this discovery. Where did the aura come from? The knowledge of death? Of the imminence of it? Was that why old people, at the edge, were often described as radiant? Because they knew the end was there, they could see it, and understood there was no eluding it? Was the knowledge of impending death a critical point? Could that be it? An intellectual function, somehow, or an emotional release, rather than an autonomic one?

Too excited to sit, he dropped the book and took a turn around the room. The matchbox was there, in his pocket; three pills. He gobbled them, then looked at the now empty box. *Here* was a crisis. He'd have to go back out. He'd been putting it off, but now . . .

He glanced at his watch. Yes. Whitechurch would be working.

He stopped in the bathroom, clumsily fished himself out of the pants, peed, flushed, rearranged himself, then went to the telephone. He knew the number by heart and punched it in. A woman's voice answered.

"Dr. West, please," Bekker said.

"Just a moment, please, I'll page."

A moment later: "West." The voice was cool, New Jersey, and corroded. The voice of a fixer.

"I need some angels," Bekker breathed; he used a breathy voice with Whitechurch.

"Mmm, that's a problem. I'm short. I've got plenty of white, though, and I've got crosses. Almost none of the other," Whitechurch said. He sounded anxious. Bekker was an exceptional customer, white, careful, and paid in cash. A Connecticut schoolteacher maybe, peddling to the kids.

"That's difficult," Bekker said. "How much of the white?"

"I could give you three."

"Three would be good. How many crosses?"

"Thirty? I could do thirty."

"Good. When? Must be soon."

"Make it a half-hour."

"Excellent, half an hour," Bekker breathed, and hung up.

When he'd cleaned out the basement, he'd found a pile of discarded sports equipment—a couple of dried-out leather first baseman's mitts with spiderwebs in the pockets; a half-dozen bats, all badly marred, and one split; a deflated basketball; mold- and dirt-covered baseball shoes with rusted metal spikes; two pairs of sadly abused sneakers; and even a pair of shorts, a tank top and a jock. He'd thrown it all in a long box with a Frisbee, a croquet set and a couple of broken badminton racquets. He'd pushed the box into a dark corner. Anybody looking into it could see all the junk with a glance; nothing good; nothing you'd even want to touch.

Bekker had sliced a C-shaped hatch in the bottom of the basketball and stashed his cash inside. Now he picked up the ball, took out three thousand dollars and carefully put the ball back.

After a quick check in the mirror, he climbed the stairs to the ground floor and padded to the back. Just as he reached the back door, the old woman's voice floated down the stairs. "Alex . . . ?"

Bekker stopped, thought about it, then exhaled in exasperation and walked back across the darkened floor to the staircase. "Yes?"

"I need the special pills." Her voice was shadowy, tentative.

"I'll get them," Bekker said.

He went back down to his apartment, found the brown bottle of morphine, shook two into his hand, and climbed back up the stairs, talking to himself. Images of the deathly radiance played through his mind, and, preoccupied, he nearly stumbled into Bridget Land. Land was standing at the base of the stairs that led up to Edith Lacey's apartment.

"Ah," she said, "I was just leaving, Alex. . . . You have Edie's medicine?"

"Yes, yes . . ." Bekker kept his face turned away, head down, tried to brush past.

"Are the pills illegal? Are they illegal drugs?" Land asked. She had squared herself up to him, her chin lifted, tight, catching his shirt sleeve as he passed her. She had smart, dark eyes that picked at him.

Bekker, his voice straining, nodded and said, "I think so. . . . I get them from a friend of hers. I'm afraid to ask what they are."

"What are you . . ." Land began, but Bekker was climbing the stairs away from her. At the top of the stairs, he glanced back, and Land was turning away, toward the door.

"Please don't tell," Bekker said. "She's in pain. . . ."

"Did you see Bridget?" Mrs. Lacey asked.

"Yes, down below. . . ." He got a glass of water and carried the pills to Mrs. Lacey. She gulped them greedily, hands trembling, smacking her lips in the water.

"Bridget asked me if these were illegal drugs. I'm afraid she might call the police," Bekker said.

Mrs. Lacey was horrified. "You mean . . ."

"They *are* illegal," Bekker said. "You could never get these in a nursing home."

"Oh no, oh no . . ." The old woman rocked, twisting her gnarled, knobby fingers.

"You should call her. Give her time to get home, and talk to her," Bekker said.

"Yes, yes, I'll call her. . . ."

"Her number's on the emergency pad, by the telephone," Bekker said.

"Yes, yes . . ." She looked up at him, her thin skin papery and creased in the moody light.

"Don't forget . . ."

"No . . ." And then: "I can't find my glasses."

He found them near the kitchen sink; handed them to her without a word. She bobbed her head in thanks and said, "My glasses, my glasses," and shuffled toward the TV. "Have you seen . . . No, you don't watch. I saw Arnold on the news."

Arnold Schwarzenegger. She expected him any day to clean the crooks out of New York.

"I've got to go."

"Yes, yes . . ." She waved him away.

"Call Bridget," Bekker said.

"Yes . . ." From the side, her face glowed blue in the light from the television screen, like a black-light painting. Like the face of the dying Chinese . . .

Ultraviolet.

The idea came from nowhere, but with a force that stopped him at the head of the stairs. Could the illumination of the dying man be related to a shifted spectrum? A light phenomenon that occurred in infrared or ultraviolet, that occasionally strayed into visible light? Was that why some people glowed and others didn't? Was that how an old camera caught it, with the poor, wide-spectrum film of the nineteenth century? He'd seen both ultraviolet and infrared photography as a medical student. Ultraviolet could actually increase the resolution of a microscope, and highlight aspects of a specimen not visible in ordinary light. And infrared could pick up temperature variations, even from dark objects.

But that was all he knew. Could he use his ordinary cameras? How to check?

Excited, excited, the science pounded in his brain. He hurried down the stairs, remembering Bridget Land only at the last minute. He slowed, looked ahead apprehensively, but she was gone.

He hurried out the back, got in the Volkswagen, drove it to the fence, hopped out, unlocked the fence, drove through, checked for intruders, climbed back out, locked the gate behind him. He was flapping, frantic, eager to get on his way, to sustain the insights of the evening.

North across Prince, east across Broadway, keeping to the side streets, the buildings pressing against him, working his way north and east. There. First Avenue. And Bellevue, an aging pile of brick.

Bekker looked at his watch. He was a minute or so early; no problem. He took it slowly, slowly. . . . And there he was, walking toward the bus stop. Bekker leaned across the car and rolled the passenger-side window halfway down, pulled to the curb.

Whitechurch saw him, looked once around, stepped to the window. "Three of the white, thirty crosses, all commercial. Two of the angels, good stuff . . ."

"Only two?" Bekker felt the control slipping, fought to retain it. "Okay. But I'll be calling you in a couple of days."

"I'll have more by then. How many could you handle?"

"Thirty? Could you get me thirty? And thirty more of the crosses?"

"Yeah, I think so," Whitechurch said. "My guy's bringing out a new line. Call me . . . and I'll need twenty-one hundred for tonight."

Bekker nodded, peeled twenty-one one-hundred-dollar bills from the roll in his pocket and handed them to Whitechurch. Whitechurch knew Bekker carried a pistol; in fact, he had sold it to him. Bekker wasn't worried about a rip-off. Whitechurch stuffed the bills in his pocket and dropped a bag onto the front seat.

"Come again," he said, and turned toward the hospital.

Bekker rolled the window up and started back, the sack shoved under the seat; but he knew he wouldn't make it without a sample. He *deserved* a sample. He'd had a revolutionary idea this night, the recording of the human aura. . . .

He stopped at a traffic light, checked the streets, turned on the dome light and opened the bag. Three fat twists of coke and two small Zip-Loc bags. Thirty small commercial tabs in one, two larger tabs in the other. His hands shook as he kept watch and unrolled one of the twists. Just enough to get home.

The coke jumped him and his head rolled backward with the force of it roaring through his brain like a freight train. After a moment, he started out again, slowly, everything preternaturally clear. If he could hold this . . . His hand groped for the PCP bag, found it; only two. But the coke had him, and he popped them both: the angels would hold the coke in place, build on it. . . . He could see for miles now, through the dark. No problem. His mouth worked, fathering a wad of saliva, and he popped a hit of speed, crunched it in his teeth. Only one, just a sample, a treat . . .

A red light. The light made him angry, and he cursed, drove through it. Another. Even more angry, but he held it this time, rolled to a stop. One more pinch of the white: sure. He *deserved* one more. One more hit . . .

He hadn't taken an experimental subject in more than a week. Instead, he'd huddled in the basement, typing his papers. He had a backlog now, data that had to be collated, rationalized. But tonight, with the angels in his blood . . . And Davenport in town, looking for him.

In taking the other subjects, he worked out a system: hit them with the stun gun, use the anesthetic. And more important, he'd begun looking for safe hunting grounds. Bellevue was one. There were women around Bellevue all the time, day and night, small enough to handle, healthy, good subjects. And the parking ramp there was virtually open. . . . But Bellevue wasn't for tonight, not after he'd just come from there.

In fact, he shouldn't even think of taking one tonight. He

hadn't planned it, hadn't done the reconnaissance that provided his margin of safety. But with the angels in his blood, anything was possible.

A picture popped into his head. Another parking ramp, not Bellevue. A ramp attached to a city government building of some kind.

Parking ramps were good, because they were easy to hide in, people came and went at all hours, many of them were alone. Transportation was easily at hand. . . .

And this one was particularly good: each level of the parking ramp had an entrance into the government building, the doors guarded by combination lockpad. A person entering the ramp in a car would not necessarily walk out past the attendants in the ticket booth. So Bekker could go in, and wait. . . .

The ramp itself had a single elevator that would take patrons to the street. In his mind's eye, he could see himself in the elevator with the selected subject, getting off at the same floor, hitting her with the stun gun as they came out of the elevator, using the gas, hiding her body between a couple of cars, then simply driving around to make the pickup. . . . Simple.

And the ramp was close by, on the edge of Chinatown. . . .

The rational Bekker, trapped in the back of his mind, warned him: *no no no no . . .*

But Gumball-Bekker cranked the wheel around and headed south, the PCP angels burning in his blood.

Chinatown.

There were people in the street, more than Bekker would have thought likely. He ignored them, the PCP-cocaine cocktail gripping his mind, focusing it: he drove straight into the parking garage, hunched over the wheel, got his ticket, and started around the sequence of up-slanting ramps. Each floor was lit, but he saw no cameras. The sequence had him now, his heart beating like a hammer, his face hot. . . .

He went all the way to the top, parked, opened the cocaine twist, cupped some in his hand, snorted it, licked up the remnant.

And went away . . .

When he came back, he climbed out of the car, taking his collection bag from the backseat. A stairwell wrapped around the elevator shaft and he took the stairs down, quietly, the stairs darker than the main ramp area. Bekker was on his toes, his collecting bag around his shoulder, hand on the stun gun. . . .

At the second floor, he stopped, checked the anesthetic tank and mask. Okay. He rehearsed the sequence in his mind: get behind her, hit her with the stun gun, cover her mouth against screams, ride her down, get the gas. He stepped out of the stairwell, glanced into the tiny elevator lobby. Excellent.

Back to the stairwell.

He waited.

And waited.

Twenty minutes, tension rising. Fished in his pocket, did another cross, chewing it, relishing the bite. He heard a steel door close somewhere overhead, echoing through the ramp, and a few minutes later, a car went down. Then silence again. Five more minutes, ten.

A car came in, stopped on the second floor, high heels on concrete . . . Bekker tensed, his hand going quickly to the tank, flicking the switch once on the stun gun.

Then . . . nothing. The sound of high heels receding. The woman, whoever it was, was walking down the ramp to get out, rather than entering the stairwell or going to the elevator.

Damn. It wasn't working. He glanced at his watch: another ten minutes. No more . . . His mind flashed back to the Twin Cities, to an actress. He'd fooled her by dressing as a gas company employee looking for leaks, had killed her with a hammer. He remembered the impact and the flush. . . . Bekker went away.

And came back, sometime later, with the telltale sigh. At the sound of feet below, and a woman's voice.

The elevator doors opening, one floor below . . .

He picked up his bag, hurried around, went into the lobby, pushed the up button: the Bekker at the back of his mind saying *no no no no,* the foreground Bekker hot with anticipation . . .

The elevator came up, lurched to a stop, and the doors opened.

Inside was a dark-haired woman with an oversized purse, eyes large, one hand in her purse. She hadn't expected the stop at the second floor. She saw Bekker, relaxed. Bekker nodded, stepped inside, waited for the doors to close. The woman had punched six, and Bekker reached for it, then stopped, as if he were also going to six. He stepped against the back of the elevator, looking up at the numbers flashing down at them. . . .

She had a gun in her purse, Bekker thought, a gun or tear gas. He thought about that, thought about that . . . got caught in a loop, thinking about thinking about it . . . and when he came back, groping in his collection bag for the stun gun, they were already at six.

He glanced sideways at the woman, caught her staring at him; he looked away. Eye contact might tell her too much. . . . He glanced again, and the woman seemed to be shrinking away, had her hand in her purse again. A tone sounded, a sharp *bing,* and the doors slid open. For a moment, neither of them moved, then the woman was out. Bekker followed a few feet behind, turned toward her, slipping his shoes off, expecting to pad after her, catch her unexpectedly. . . .

But the woman suddenly stepped out of her own shoes and began running, and at the same time, looking back at him, screaming, a long, shrill, piercing cry.

She knew. . . .

Bekker, frozen for an instant by the scream, went after her, the woman screaming, her purse skidding across the floor, spilling out lipsticks and date books and a bottle of some kind, rolling on the rough concrete. . . . She dodged between two cars, backing toward the outer wall, a can in her hand, screaming. . . .

Tear gas.

Bekker was right behind her, losing his bag, going after her bare-handed, the urgency gripping him, the need to shut her up: *She knows knows knows . . .*

The woman had braced herself between the cars, her hand extended with the tear gas, her mouth open, her nostrils flexing. No way to get her but straight ahead . . .

Bekker charged, stooping at the last moment, one hand up to block the tear-gas spray. She pressed the can toward him, but nothing happened, just a hiss and the faint smell of apple blossoms. . . .

She'd backed all the way to the ramp wall, the lights of the city behind her, the wall waist-high, her shrill scream in his ears, piercing, wailing.

He went straight in, hit her in the throat with one hand, caught her between the legs with the other, heaved, flipped . . .

And the woman went over the waist-high wall.

Simply went over, as though he'd flipped a sack of fertilizer over the wall.

She dropped, without a sound.

Bekker, astonished at what he'd done, panting like a dog, looked down over the wall as she went. She fell faceup, arms reaching up, and hit on the back of her head and neck.

And she died, like that: like a match going out. From six floors up, Bekker could see she was dead. He turned, looking for someone coming after her, a response to the scream.

Heard nothing but a faraway police siren. Panicked, he ran back to the stairs, up two flights, climbed in the Volkswagen, started it, and rolled down through the ramp. Where were they? On the stairs?

Nobody.

At the exit booth, the woman ticket-taker was standing on the street, looking down at the corner. She came back and entered the booth. She was chewing gum, a frown on her face.

"One-fifty," she said.

He paid. "What's going on?"

"Fight, maybe," she said laconically. "A couple of guys were running . . ."

Twelve hours later, Bekker hunched over an IBM typewriter, a dark figure, intent, humming to himself "You Light Up My Life," poking the keys with rigid fingers. Overhead, a flock of his spiders floated through the air, dangling from black thread attached to a wire grill. A mobile of spiders . . .

The PCP made the world perfectly clear, and he marveled over the crystal quality of the prose as it poured forth from the machine onto the white paper.

. . . refuted claims that cerebral-spinal pressure obfuscated reliable intercranial measurements during terminal brain activity as per Delano in TRS Notes [Sept. 86]; Delano overlooked the manifest and indisputable evidence of . . .

It simply sang—and that cockroach Delano would undoubtedly lose his job at Stanford when the world saw his professional negligence. . . .

Bekker leaned back, looking up at his spiders, and cackled at the thought. A gumball dropped, and he leaned forward, thoughtful now, Bekker the Thinker. He'd made a mistake this night. The worst he'd made yet. His time was probably coming to an end: he needed more work, he needed another specimen, but he had to be very, very careful.

Mmmm. He turned off the typewriter and laid his manuscript aside, carefully squaring the corners of the paper. Went to the bathroom, washed his face again, stared at the scars. The drugs were still with him, but he was also running down. Might even catch some sleep. When had he last slept? Couldn't remember.

He dropped his clothing on the floor, looked at the clock. Midmorning. Maybe a couple of hours, though . .

He lay down, listened to his heart.

Closed his eyes.

Almost slept.

But then, just on the edge of oblivion, something stirred. Bekker knew what it was. He felt his heart accelerate, felt the adrenaline spurting into his blood.

He hadn't done her eyes. It had been impossible, of course, but that made no difference. She could see him, the dark-haired woman.

She was coming.

Bekker stuffed a handful of sheet in his mouth, and screamed.

CHAPTER

9

The car slowed and the window between the front seat and the backseat dropped an inch. The early-morning traffic was light, and they were moving quickly, but O'Dell was grumpy about the early hour. Lily hadn't slept at all.

"You want a *Times*?" Copland asked over his shoulder.

"Yes." O'Dell nodded, and Copland eased the car toward the curb, where a vendor waved newspapers at passing cars. A talk show babbled from the front-seat radio: Bekker and more Bekker. When Copland rolled his window down, they could hear the same show from the vendor's radio. The vendor handed Copland a paper, took a five-dollar bill, and dug for change.

"I'm worried," Lily said. "They could try again."

"Won't happen. They didn't mean to kill him, and coming after him again, that way, would be too risky. Especially if he's this tough guy you keep telling me about. . . ."

"We thought they wouldn't go after him the first time. . . ."

"We never thought they'd try to mug him. . . ."

Copland handed a copy of the *Times* into the backseat. A headline just below the fold said "Army Suspects Bekker of Vietnam Murders."

"This has gotta be bullshit," O'Dell grumbled, scanning the story. "Anything from Minneapolis?"

"No."

"Dammit. Why don't these assholes check on him? For all they know, the Minneapolis story could be a cover for an Internal Affairs geek."

"Not a thing, so far. And the people in Minneapolis are looking for it."

Silence, the car rolling like an armored ghost through Manhattan.

Then: "It must be Fell. It has to be."

Lily shook her head: "Nothing on her line. She got one call, from an automated computer place saying that she'd won a prize if she'd go out to some Jersey condominium complex to pick it up. Nothing on the office phone."

"Dammit. She must be calling from a public phone. We might need some surveillance here."

"I'd wait on that. She's been on the street for a while. She'd pick it up, sooner or later."

"Had to be Fell, though. Unless it really was muggers."

"It wasn't muggers. Lucas thinks they were cops. He says one of them was carrying a black leather-wrapped keychain sap; about the only place you can buy them is a commercial police-supply house. And he says they never went for his billfold."

"But they weren't trying to kill him."

"No. But he thinks they were trying to put him out of commission. Maybe break a few bones . . ."

"Huh." O'Dell grunted through a thin smile. "You know, there was once a gang on the Lower East Side, they'd contract to bite a guy's ear off for ten bucks?"

"I didn't know that," said Lily.

"It's true, though. . . . All right. Well. With Davenport. String him along. . . ."

"I still feel like I'm betraying him," Lily said, looking away from O'Dell, out the window. A kid was pushing a bike with a flat tire down the sidewalk. He turned as the big black car passed, and looked straight at Lily with the flat gray serpent's eyes of a ten-year-old psychopath.

"He knew what he was getting into."

"Not really," she said, turning away from the kid's trailing eyes. She looked at O'Dell. "He thought he did, but he's basically from a small town. He's not from here. He really doesn't know, not the way we do. . . ."

"What'd you tell Kennett, about why Davenport was at your place?"

"I . . . prevaricated," Lily said. "And I could use a little backup from you."

"Ah."

Lucas hadn't been badly hurt, so Lily flagged a cab, took him to Beth Israel, then reported the attack. Because she'd fired her weapon, there had been forms to fill out. She'd started that night, and called Kennett to tell him about it.

"Should I ask why he was at your place at two in the morning?" Kennett had asked. He'd sounded amused, but he wasn't.

"Um, you don't want to know," Lily had said. "But it was strictly business, not pleasure."

"And I don't want to know."

"That's right."

After a moment: "Okay. Are you all right? I mean, really all right."

"Sure. I've got a busted window I've gotta get fixed. . . ."

"Good. Get some sleep. I'll talk to you tonight."

"That's all? I mean . . . ?"

"Do I trust you? Of course. See you tonight."

Lily looked out the car window, at the city rolling past. Maybe she was betraying Lucas. Maybe she was betraying Kennett. She wasn't sure anymore.

O'Dell said, "Cretins," and his paper shook with anger.

CHAPTER

10

The reporters came and went, the naive ones swallowing Lucas' story that he had been mugged, others not so sure. A reporter from *Newsday* said flatly that something else was going on: that Bekker had a gang, or that somebody else was trying to stop Lucas' investigation.

"I don't know about muggers in Minneapolis, but in New York they don't work in professional tag teams. Unless you're lying, you were done by professionals. . . ."

After they were gone, Lucas took a few more Tylenol, wandered down to the bathroom and got back in time to see Lily coming down the hall.

"You look . . . pretty rough," she said.

"It's my cheek. My cheek hurts like hell," he said. He touched a swollen magenta bruise with his middle finger. "At least the headache's going away. They're letting me out after lunch."

"I heard," Lily said.

"Thanks for sending the jeans over. The other pants . . ."

"Are shot." Lily said.

"Yeah."

"O'Dell's fixed the Mengele speech—there'll be a notice in all the papers this afternoon, the *Times* tomorrow morning, and we're asking everybody to do a note about it. TV, too. We found a guy, a legit guy, who already lectures on Mengele."

"Terrific," Lucas said. "When?"

"Monday."

"Jesus, that quick?"

"We gotta do everything quick. Maybe we can get him before he does another one. . . ." Lily backed into a hospital chair, dropped her purse by her foot. "Listen, about last night. Are you absolutely sure they were cops?"

"Fairly sure. They could have been professional bone-breakers, but it didn't feel that way. They felt like cops. Why?"

"I was thinking about another possibility."

"Smith?"

"Yeah. After you chopped up his putting green . . ."

Lucas pulled his lip. "Maybe," he said. "But I doubt it. One thing you learn as a sleazoid businessman is to roll with the punches."

"Have you talked to Fell this morning?"

"She's on her way over. We have a line on a couple of people who might know something about Bellevue. She's been talking to Kennett, to make sure we don't step on any toes. . . ."

"Okay. I've got Bobby Rich coming over. He's the guy who took the tip about the witness."

"The witness Petty found . . ."

"Yeah, the day he got killed. And there's still some more paper to look at."

"That's pointless, I think," Lucas said. "With these guys, the dead guys, we won't find anything in their lives that'll point to the killers. It has to be bureaucratic: who pulled their files, and when . . ."

"That's impossible."

"Yeah, I know."

"So we're stuck?"

"Not quite, but it's getting sparse. Maybe Rich'll have something. We've still got Fell. I want to take a look at Petty's apartment, his personal stuff. And I wouldn't mind seeing the place where he was shot."

"That's about a half-mile from my apartment—we could walk. His apartment's sealed. I'll get some new seals and take you over. When?"

"Tonight? After we talk to Rich?"

"Fine."

"What'd you tell Kennett . . . ?"

"About you being at my apartment? I said you came over to visit. I told him that sex was not a consideration, last night or in the future. I told him that you weren't making any moves on me and I wasn't making any moves on you, but that we had things to talk about."

"Sounds pretty awful," Lucas said, grinning.

"It could have been, but I just came out with it. I also told him O'Dell was there part of the time. John will back that up."

A few minutes later, Kennett and Fell arrived together, and Lily blew up: "For Christ's sakes, Dick, what're you doing here? Did you walk all the way in?" Hands on hips, she turned to Fell, angry. "Barbara, did you let him . . . ?"

"Shut up, Lily," Kennett said. He touched her cheek with an index finger. To Lucas, he said, "Well, you look like shit."

"What do you think, Barb?" Lucas asked.

Fell had taken cover behind Kennett, and she peered out and said, "He's right. You look like shit."

"Then it's unanimous," Lucas said. "That's what Lily said when she came in. The only one who didn't was a twenty-four-year-old *Times* reporter with a great ass, who thought I looked pretty good and would probably like to hear more about this case from the hero of it. . . ."

"Gotta be a concussion," Fell said to Lily.

"He's always been like this," Lily said. "I think it's native stupidity."

Kennett, shaking his head, said, "Goddamn women, they're

always impressed by a beat-up face. I used to get beat up whenever I needed to get laid. Worked like a charm . . ." He stopped,
and frowned at Lucas: "Are you trying to get laid?" and his eyes
flicked sideways at Lily.

Fell said, "Not very hard."

Lucas and Kennett laughed; Lily didn't.

Kennett said, "Listen, I wanted to tell you. Go ahead with
those names you got. Barb's run them down. . . ."

"One good address and one probable," Fell said.

"Junkies?"

"Nope. Neither one of them. Not the last anybody heard,
anyway."

"All right." Lucas eased down from the hospital bed. "Let's
go down to the nursing station. Maybe I can talk my way out
before lunch."

The charge nurse said the attending physician wanted another
look at him: she'd send him down as soon as he arrived, which
should be within the next few minutes. "We'll see you first," she
said.

"All right, but pretty quick?"

"Soon as he gets here."

Lily said, "I've gotta go. Take it easy today."

"Yeah."

He walked gingerly back to the room with Fell, trying not to
move his head too quickly. At the door, he looked back toward
the elevators. Kennett and Lily were waiting, looking up at the
numbers above the door, then Kennett leaned toward Lily, and
she went up on her toes, a kiss that wasn't taken lightly by either
of them. Lucas turned away, and caught Fell watching him
watch Lily and Kennett.

"True love," he said wryly.

The hot, hazy sun left him feeling faintly nauseous, and the
headache lurked at the back of his skull.

"You look pale and wan," Fell said.

"I'm all right." He looked up at the storefront: Arnold's TV and Appliance, Parts & Repair. "C'mon, let's do her."

A bell tingled when they went through the door; a heavyset woman looked up from a ledger, slapped it shut, and moved ponderously to the counter. "Can I help ya?" She had a cheerfully yellow smile and an improbable West Virginia hills accent. To Lucas: "Whoa, you look like you've been in a dustup."

"We're police officers," Fell said. She lifted the flap of her purse, flashed the badge. "Are you Rose Arnold?"

The woman's smile sagged into a frown. "Yeah. What'd you want?"

"We're looking for a guy," Lucas said. "We thought you could help."

"I ain't been here all that long. . . ."

Lucas dug in his pocket, took out his money clip, freed his driver's license and handed it to Arnold. "Barbara here"—he nodded at Fell—"is a New York cop. I'm not. I'm from Minneapolis. They brought me in to help look for this Bekker dude who's chopping people up."

"Yeh?" Arnold was giving nothing away, watching him with her small wandering eyes like a pullet who suspects the axe.

"Yeah. He killed my woman out there. Maybe you read about it. I'm gonna catch him and I'm gonna do him."

Arnold nodded and asked, "So what's that got to do with me?"

"We think he's getting stuff—drugs and medical equipment—from Bellevue. We know that you handle stuff out of Bellevue."

"That's bullshit, I never touch nothing. . . ."

"You moved five hundred cases of white Hammermill Bond copy paper out of there two weeks ago, paid a dollar a case, and sold it to a computer supply place for three dollars a case," Fell said. "We could bust you if we wanted to, but we don't want to. We just want some help."

She looked at them, quietly, a gleam of strong intelligence in her eyes. Calculating. Lucas had a quick vision of her jerking some crappy piece of hillbilly iron out of a drawer, something like a rusty Iver Johnson .32, and popping him in the chest. But nothing happened, except the sound of flies bumping against the front window.

"Killed your woman?" she asked. She tipped her head, looking at him from the corner of her eyes.

"Yeah," he said. "It's real personal."

She mulled it over for another few seconds, then asked, "What do you want?"

"I need the name of a guy who rips stuff out of there on a regular basis."

"Will this come back on me?"

"No way."

She thought about it, then mumbled: "Lew Whitechurch."

"Lew . . ."

"Whitechurch," she said.

"Who else?"

"He's the only one, right out of Bellevue. . . ."

"Any chance he might be peddling pills, too?"

"I think he might. I never touch them, but Lew . . . he's got a problem. He takes a little nose."

"Thanks," Lucas said. He took a personal business card from his pocket, turned it over, wrote his hotel phone number on it. "Have you handled, or know anybody who has handled, a load of emergency-room monitoring equipment?"

"No." Her voice was positive.

"Ask around. If you find somebody, have them call me. It'll never get past us, I swear it on a Bible. I'm only in this because Bekker cut my woman's throat."

"Cut her throat?" The fat woman touched her neck.

"With a bread knife," Lucas said. He let the bitterness flow into his voice. "Listen: anybody dealing with Bekker is liable to find himself strapped to an operating table, eyelids cut off, getting his heart sliced out while he's still alive. . . . You read the papers."

"Watch TV." She nodded.

"Then you know."

"Fuckin' lunatic, is what he is," Arnold said.

"So ask around. Call me."

Outside, Fell said, "You're a scary sonofabitch sometimes. You sorta used your friend . . ."

"My friend's dead, she doesn't care," he said. And he shrugged. "But hillbillies understand that revenge shit."

"What's the name?"

"Lew Whitechurch. And she thinks he might deal pills."

"Let's get him," Fell said. As they were flagging the cab, she said, "If I bust Bekker myself, I'll make detective first before I get out."

"That'd be nice." A cab zigged through the traffic toward them.

"More pension. I could probably afford a straight waitress job. I wouldn't have to dance topless," Fell said.

"Aw," he said. "I was planning to come down for your first night."

"Maybe we could work something out," she said, and climbed into the cab before he could think of a comeback.

They caught Lewis Whitechurch pushing a tool cart through a basement hallway at Bellevue. His supervisor pointed him out, the hospital's assistant administrator hovering anxiously in the background. Kennett's people had been there earlier, had talked to two employees, she said, but not Whitechurch.

"What?" Whitechurch said.

Fell flashed her badge, while Lucas blocked the hall. "We need to talk to you, privately."

Whitechurch shook his head. "I don't want to talk to anyone."

"We can talk here or I can call a squad and we can go over to Midtown South."

"Talk about what?" Whitechurch shot a glance at the supervisor.

"Let's find a place," Lucas suggested.

They found a place in the hospital workshop, sitting on battered office chairs, Whitechurch spinning himself in quarter-turns with the heel of one foot. "I honest to God don't know. . . ."

Five hundred cases of paper, they said.

"I ain't gonna talk about nothing like that," he said, his Jersey accent as thick as mayonnaise. "You want to talk about this other guy, Bekker, I'd help you any way I can. But I don't know nothing about him, or any medical gear. I wouldn't touch that shit. . . ." He caught himself. "Listen, I don't take nothing out of here, but if I did, I wouldn't take that stuff. I mean, people might die because of it."

"If we catch the guy who's helping Bekker . . . that guy's going down as an accessory. Attica, and I'll tell you what, man: there'd be no fuckin' parole, not for somebody who helped this asshole. . . ."

"Jesus Christ, I'd tell you," Whitechurch said. He was sweating. "Listen, I know a couple of people who might know something about this. . . ."

"What do you think?" Fell asked.

"He covered himself pretty well. I don't know. We got names, anyway. We'll come back to him. Let him stew. . . ." Whitechurch had given them two more names. Both men were working.

"Jakes is an orderly—he oughta be around," the assistant administrator said. She was getting into the hunt, falling into Fell's laconic speech pattern. "Williams—I'll have to look him up."

They found Harvey Jakes moving sheets out of the laundry.

"I don't know about this shit," he said. He was worried. "Listen, I don't know why you'd come looking to me. I never been up on anything, never took anything, where'd you get my name . . ."

Williams was worse. Williams worked in the laundry, and was stupid. "Said what?"

"Said you boosted stuff out of here and . . ."

"Said what?"

Lucas looked at him closely, then at Fell, and shook his head. "He's not faking."

"What?" Williams looked slowly from one to the other, and they sent him back to his laundry.

"We're into a black market—pretty casual, hard to pin down, picking up the occasional opportunity," Fell said as they ambled down the hall. Like the rest of New York, the Bellevue interior was mostly a patch, painted white with black trim. "Doesn't feel like a real tight ring. Whitechurch might be bigger, if he really organized a truck to haul that paper out of there. Jakes and Williams are small-time, if they're stealing anything at all."

"That's about right," Lucas said. "Whitechurch might be something, though."

"Want to go back on him?"

"We should," he said, sticking his hands in his pockets. "But I fuckin' hurt. . . ."

"You keep poking at your cheek," she said. She reached out and touched the bruise, and her light hand didn't hurt at all. "So what are we doing?"

"I'm going back to the hotel. I need a nap, I feel like shit," Lucas said.

"We're stuck?"

"Except for Whitechurch, I don't know where we go," Lucas said. "Let's think about it. I'll call you tomorrow."

CHAPTER

11

At the Lakota, Lucas examined his swollen cheek in the mirror. The color of the bruise was deepening, a purple blotch that dominated the side of his face, shiny in the middle, rougher toward the edges. He touched the abraded skin and winced. He'd been hit before, and knew what would happen: the abrasions would scab over while the skin around them turned yellow-green, and in a week, he'd look even worse; he'd look like Frankenstein. He shook his head at himself, tried a tentative grin, ate a half-dozen aspirin and slept for two hours. When he woke, the headache had faded, but his stomach was queasy. He gobbled four more aspirin, showered, brushed his teeth, fished an oversize Bienfang art pad from under the bed and got a wide-tipped Magic Marker from his briefcase. He wrote:

> *Bekker.*
> Needs money.
> Needs drugs.
> Lives Midtown w/friend?
> Has vehicle.
> Hasn't been seen. Disguise?
> Chemist skills.

Medical skills.
Contact at Bellevue.
Night.

He tacked the chart to a wall and lay on his bed, studying it. Bekker needed money if he was buying drugs, and he almost certainly would be. In the Hennepin County Jail he'd begged for them, for chemical relief.

Therefore: he had to be talking to dealers, or at least one dealer. Could he be working for one? Not likely as a salesman: even the dumbest of the dumb would recognize him as a time bomb, if they knew who he was. But if he was working as a chemist—methedrine was simple to synthesize, with the right training and access to the raw materials. If he were running a crank line, that would explain where he'd get money, and drugs, and maybe even a place to stay.

The car was another problem. He was dumping the bodies, obviously from a vehicle. How would he get access? How would he license it? Everything pointed to an accomplice. . . .

He stood, wandered into the bathroom and looked in the mirror. The abrasion was stiffening. He probed it with a finger-nail, lifting a flake of skin, and blood trickled down his cheek. Damn. He knew better. He got a wad of toilet paper, held it to his cheek, and went back to the bed.

He looked at the chart again, but his mind drifted away from Bekker, toward the other case. Why had they jumped him? And had they really gone after him, or was something else happening? They could have taken him with guns: they had him cold. If they hadn't wanted to kill him, they still could have gotten to him more quickly, with baseball bats. Why had they risked resistance? If he'd had a gun in his hand, he would have killed them. . . .

Why had Lily looked out the window when she did?

But the major puzzle was more subtle. He wasn't getting any-where, and Lily and O'Dell must see that. All he could do was look at paper, and listen to people talk. He had none of the insider information, the history, that could point him in the right direction. And yet . . . he was surrounded by people who might be involved: Fell, Kennett, O'Dell himself, even Lily. And not coincidentally.

At eight-thirty he got up; he dressed, went out to the street, flagged a cab, and rode ten minutes to Lily's apartment. She was waiting.

"You still look rough," she said as she opened the door. She touched his cheek. "Feels hot. Are you sure you want to do this? It's a lot of running around."

"Yeah," he said, nodding. "Rich is set for nine?"

"Yes. He's nervous, but he's coming."

"I don't want him to see me," Lucas said.

"Okay. You can sit in the kitchen with the lights out, talk to him down the hall."

"Fine." Lucas, hands in his pockets, wandered down toward the kitchen.

"Anything new on Bekker?" she asked, trailing behind.

"No. I was thinking, though, he must be out only at night." Lucas perched on a tall oak stool and leaned on the breakfast bar. A handicraft ceramic bowl full of apples sat on the bar, and he picked one of them up and turned it in his fingers. "Even with stage makeup, his face would be too noticeable in daylight."

"So?"

"Would it be possible to make random stops of single men driving inexpensive cars, after midnight, Midtown?"

"Jesus, Lucas. The chance of picking him up that way would be nil—and we'd probably get three cops shot by freaks in the meantime."

"I'm trying to figure out ways to press him," Lucas said. He dropped the apple back in the bowl.

"Do we really want to chase him out of here? He'd just go somewhere else, start again. . . ."

"I don't know if he can. Somehow, I don't know how, he's got a unique situation here. He can hide, somehow," Lucas said. "If he travels, he loses that—I mean, look, right now Bekker's one of the most famous people in the country. He can't go to motels or gas stations, he can't take any kind of public transportation. He can't really ride in a car without a lot of tension—if he gets pulled over by a cop, he's done. And he needs his dope, he needs his money. If we pushed him out, if he tried to run, he'd be finished."

She thought about it, then nodded. "I suppose we could do something. I wouldn't want to make a lot of stops, but we could *announce* that we are, and ask for cooperation from the public. Maybe make a couple of stops for the TV crews . . ."

"That'd be good."

"I'll talk to Kennett tomorrow," she said. She perched on a stool opposite from him, crossed her legs and wrapped her hands around the top knee.

"How'd he get on this case? Kennett?" Lucas asked.

"O'Dell pulled some strings. Kennett's one of the best we've got on this kind of thing, organizing and running it."

"He and O'Dell don't like each other."

"No. No, they don't. I don't know why O'Dell pulled him, exactly, but I can tell you one thing: he wouldn't have done it unless he thought Kennett would find Bekker. Back in Minneapolis, you can control the bureaucratic fallout, because the department's small and everybody knows everybody else. But here . . . We've got to find Bekker, or heads'll start rolling. People are pissed off."

Lucas nodded, thought about it for a second, and said, "Kennett's an intelligence guy: are you sure he's not involved with Robin Hood?"

Lily looked down at her hands. "In my heart, I'm sure. I couldn't prove it, though. Whoever's running this thing must have a fair amount of charisma, to hold it together, and good organizational skills . . . and certain political opinions. Kennett fits."

"But . . . ?"

"He has too much sense," Lily said. "He's a believer in, what? Goodness, maybe. That's what I feel about him, anyway. We talk about things."

"Okay."

"That's not exactly proof," Lily said. She was tight, unhappy with the question, chewing at it.

"I wasn't asking for proof, I was asking for an opinion," Lucas said. "What about O'Dell? He seems to be running everything. He runs you, he runs Kennett. He's running me, or thinks he is. He picked Fell out of the hat. . . ."

"I don't know, I just don't know. Even the way he picked Fell, it seems more like magic than anything. We may be on a complete wild-goose chase." She was about to go on, but chimes sounded from the door. She hopped off her stool and walked down the hall and pushed her intercom button. A man's voice said, "Bobby Rich, Lieutenant."

"I'll buzz you in," Lily said. To Lucas, she said, "Get the lights."

Lucas turned off the lights and sat on the floor, legs crossed. Sitting in the dark, he watched Lily as she waited by the door, a tall woman, less heavy than she once was, with a long, aristocratic neck. *Charisma. Good organizational skills. Certain political opinions.*

"How did you talk O'Dell into bringing me here?" he asked abruptly. "Was he reluctant? How hard did you have to press?"

"Bringing you here was more his idea than mine," Lily said. "I'd told him about you and he said you sounded perfect."

Rich knocked on the door as Lucas thought, *Really?*

Rich was a tall black man, balding, athletic, hair cropped so closely that his head looked shaven. He wore a green athletic jacket with tan sleeves, and blue jeans. He said, "Hello," and edged inside the apartment. Lily pointed him at a chair where Lucas could see his face, and then said, "There's another guy in the apartment, in the kitchen."

"What?" Rich, just settling on the chair, half rose and looked down the hall.

"Don't get up," Lily snapped. She pointed him back into the chair.

"What's going on here?" Rich asked, still peering toward the kitchen.

"We have a guy who's getting close to Robin Hood. Maybe. He doesn't want you to see his face. He doesn't know who to trust. . . . If you don't want to talk about it, with him back there, we can cut it off right here. You can go back into the bedroom while he leaves. Then it'll be just you and me . . . but I wanted you to know."

Rich's tongue slid over his lower lip, his hands gripping the arms of the chair. After a minute, he relaxed. "I don't see how he can hurt me," he said.

"He can't," Lily said. "He's mostly going to listen, maybe ask a couple of questions. Why don't you just tell me what you told Walt? If either of us has questions, we'll break in."

Rich thought about it for another moment, looked into the dark, trying to penetrate it, then nodded. "Okay," he said.

He'd been at home when he got a call from an ex-burglar he'd busted a couple of times, a man named Lowell Jackson. Jackson was trying to go straight, as a sign painter, and was doing okay.

"He said an acquaintance of his had called, a kid named Cornell, nicknamed Red. Cornell had said he'd seen Jimmy King go down and that it wasn't no gang-bangers—that one of the guys in the car was an old white guy and Cornell thought he was a cop. Jackson gave me an address."

Old white guy?

"Did you go after Cornell?" asked Lily.

"Yeah. Couldn't find him. So I went and talked to Jackson."

"What he say?"

"He said right after he talked to me, that same day, he saw Cornell at this playground on 118th—this is all in my report. . . ."

"Go ahead," Lily said.

"Cornell came down to a playground on 118th and said he was going home. Getting out of town. Nobody knew where he went. His last name is Reed. Cornell Reed. He's got a sheet. He's a doper, into crack. But he used to be some kind of college kid. Not a regular asshole."

"How old is he?" Lily asked.

"Middle twenties, like that."

"New York guy?"

"No. Supposedly he came from down south somewhere, Atlanta maybe. Been here a few years, though—Jackson said he didn't talk about where he came from. There was something . . . wrong. He just wouldn't talk about it. Used to cry about it, though, when he was drunk."

"How many times was he busted?"

"Half-dozen, nothing big. Theft, shoplifting, minor possession. We looked for background on him, NCIC, but there's nothing—his first busts were here in New York, addresses up in Harlem."

"And he's gone."

"Nowhere to be found. We checked Atlanta, but they don't know him."

"Dead?"

Rich frowned. "Don't think so. When he took off from the playground, he had some new shoes and a big nylon suitcase. That's what the guys at the playground say. He came up to 118th to say good-bye, they were sitting around. Then he jumped a cab and that's the last they saw of him."

"You wrote a report on all of this?"

"Yeah. And we're still looking for him. To tell you the truth, he's about the only thing we ever got on the case."

"What were you doing for Petty?" Lucas asked.

"Just looking at guys, mostly," Rich said. "Made me a little nervous, tell you the truth. I tried to get off it. I don't like looking at our own people."

"How'd you get assigned to the case?" Lucas asked.

"I don't know. Someone downtown, I guess," Rich said, his forehead wrinkling as he thought about it. "My lieutenant just said to report down to City Hall for a special assignment. He didn't know what was going on either."

"All right," said Lucas. Then, "How did Cornell know the white guy was old?"

"Don't know; if I find him, I'll ask him. Maybe just because he knows him from somewhere . . ."

They talked for another half hour, but Rich had almost nothing that wasn't in the reports. Lily thanked him and let him go.

"Waste of time," Lily said to Lucas.

"Had to try. What do you know about him? Rich?"

"Not much, really," she said.

"Good detective?"

"He's okay. Competent. Nothing spectacular."

"Hmp." Lucas touched the sore cheek, head down, considering.

"Why?"

"Just wondering," he said, looking back up. "You ready to go?"

"Want to walk? Down to the restaurant?"

"How far?" Lucas asked.

"Ten, fifteen minutes, taking it easy."

"Are we gonna get shot, going out the door?"

"No. O'Dell had a couple of people talk to the supers all along the block," Lily said. "They're looking for strange people wandering around their apartments."

The street outside the apartment was clear, but before they went out through the lobby door, Lucas scanned the windows across the street.

"Nervous?"

"No. I'm trying to figure it," he said.

She studied his face. "What?"

"Nothing." He shook his head. Rich had seemed straight enough.

"C'mon . . ."

"Nothing, really . . ."

"All right," Lily said, annoyed, still watching him.

The Village was pretty, quiet, well-tended brick townhouses with flowers in window boxes, touches of wrought iron, the image wounded here and there by a curl of concertina, a touch of razor wire. And the people looked different, Lucas thought, from the people farther uptown; a deliberate touch of the Bohemian: sandals and canvas shorts, beards and waist-length hair, old-fashioned bikes and wooden necklaces.

The Manhattan Caballero was buried in a street of red stone buildings, a small place, its name and logo painted on one window, a beer sign in the other.

"They shot from up there, the third window in, second floor," Lily said, standing on the sidewalk outside the Caballero door, pointing across the street.

"Couldn't miss with a laser sight," Lucas said, looking up at the window, then down at the sidewalk. "He must've been about right here, you see the chip marks."

Caught by the geometry and technicalities of the killing, he'd paid no attention to her. Now he looked up and she had one hand on the restaurant window, as if for support, her face pale, waxen.

"Jesus, I'm sorry. . . ."

"I'm okay," she said.

"I thought you were gonna faint."

"It's anger now," she said. "When I think about Walt, I want to kill somebody."

"That bad?"

"So bad I can't believe it. It's like I lost a kid."

They flagged a cab to go to Petty's apartment. Crossing the Brooklyn Bridge, Lily asked, "Have you ever been here? Brooklyn Heights?"

"No."

"Great place for an apartment. I thought about it, I would've come, except, you know, once you live in the Village, you don't want to leave."

"This looks okay . . ." Lucas said, peering out the window as they rolled off the end of the bridge. "The woman at Petty's apartment building . . ."

"Logan."

"She says somebody was in his apartment when he was already dead, and before the cops arrived?"

"Yes. Absolutely. She remembers that she thought he'd come home and then gone out again. She was watching television, remembered the show, and what part of the show. We checked— he'd been dead for ten minutes."

"Somebody was moving fast."

"Very fast. Had to know the minute Walt went down. Had to be *waiting* for it. There's a question about how he got into Walt's apartment. Whoever it was must have had a key."

"That's simple enough, if you're talking about an intelligence operation."

"You should know," she said.

Petty's apartment was in a brown brick building stuck on the side of a low hill, in a cul-de-sac, the area long faded but pleasant. Marcy Logan's door was the first one to the left, inside the tiny lobby.

"Very late," Logan said, peering over the door chain at Lily's badge. She was an older woman, in her middle sixties, gray hair and matching eyes. "You said ten o'clock."

"I'm sorry, but something else came up," Lily said. "We just need to talk for a minute."

"Well, come in." Her tone was severe, but Lucas got the impression that Logan was happy for the company. "I'll have to warm up the coffee. . . ."

She had made cookies and coffee, the cookies laid out on a silver tray. She stuck a carafe of coffee in a microwave, fussed with cups and saucers.

"Such a nice apartment," Lily said.

"Thank you. They filmed *Moonstruck* just down the way, you know. Cher was right down by the Promenade, I saw her . . ."

When the coffee was hot, Logan poked the tray of cookies in Lucas' face. Lucas tried one: oatmeal. He took another, with a cup of coffee.

"It wasn't a woman," Logan said, positively, when Lily asked. "The footsteps were too heavy. I didn't see him, but it was a man."

"You're sure?"

"I hear people come and go all day," Logan said. "That's something I'd know. I thought it was Walter coming back—I wouldn't have thought that if it was a woman."

"He went up, was there for a few minutes, then came right back down?" Lily asked.

"That's right. Couldn't have been more than a half-hour, because my show was a half-hour, and he came after the show started and left before it ended."

"You told the investigators that it occurred to you that it wasn't Petty," Lily said. "But not seriously enough that you actually looked. Why did you think it might not be him?"

"Whoever it was, stopped in the lobby. Like he was looking at my apartment door or maybe listening for anybody inside. Then he went up. Walter was always very forthright. Walked right in, went right up. Especially on his Fridays. He'd always have two or three beers, and he couldn't hold it at all, and by the time he got here, he'd . . . you know: he had to go. You could hear the water running from the toilet, right after he went up. That night, though, whoever it was stopped inside. He did the same thing on the way back out. Stopped in the lobby. It gives me the shivers. Maybe he was thinking about rubbing out witnesses."

"I don't think that's much of a threat," Lily said, smiling at the "rubbing out."

"Why don't you say something, young man?" Logan asked Lucas, who was eating his sixth cookie. He couldn't seem to stop.

"Too busy eating cookies," he said. "These things are great. You could make a fortune selling them."

"Oh, that's nice," she said, smiling. "What happened to your face?"

"I was mugged."

"Isn't that just like New York? Even the cops . . ."

"How do you know this guy went to Petty's apartment?" Lucas asked.

"Well, I heard him come in, and then the elevator dinged, so he was going up. Then just a second later, I heard another ding, like it was coming from the kitchen. That's the second floor. If it goes to the third floor, I can barely hear it. If it goes to the fourth, I can't hear it at all."

"Okay," Lucas said, nodding. "So you heard it ding on the second floor."

"Yes. And the Lynns and Golds were already in and the Schumachers were at Fire Island that whole weekend. So it had to be Walter, and it was about the time he always came in. I didn't hear him flush, though. Then I heard the elevator ding on the second floor again, and it came down. Then whoever it was, I thought was looking at apartments again, because it was a minute before the outside door opened. . . . I should have looked, but I was watching my show."

"That's fine," said Lucas, nodding. "And it wasn't a visitor to one of the other apartments?"

"No," Logan said, shaking her head. "When the cops got here and I found out what happened, I told them about somebody coming, and they talked to everybody up there. Nobody came in at that time, and nobody had any visitors."

When they finished with Logan, they rode up in the elevator and Lily cut the seals off Petty's door. The apartment had been neatly kept but had been pulled apart by investigators. The refrigerator had been unplugged, and the door stood open. Cupboard doors were open and paper was stacked everywhere. Lucas went to Petty's desk, which was set in a tiny alcove, and thumbed through financial records. . . . No personal phone book.

"No phone book."

"The Homicide guys probably have it. I'll ask."

Ten minutes later, Lily said, "This is like the interview with Rich. There isn't anything here."

On the way out, Mrs. Logan met them in the hallway with a brown paper bag, which she handed to Lucas. "More cookies," she said.

"Thanks," he said, and then, "When I finish them, I may come back for more."

The old lady giggled, and Lucas and Lily went looking for a cab.

Cornell Reed. Cornell Reed had seen the killer, an old white guy, and recognized him as a cop.

Lucas lay on the hotel bed and thought about it, sighed, rolled off the bed, found his pocket address book, and picked out Harmon Anderson's home phone number. As he dialed the number, he glanced at his watch. It would be midnight, Minneapolis time.

Anderson was in bed.

"Jesus, Lucas, what's going on?"

"I'm in New York. . . ."

"I know, I heard. I wish I was there. . . ." Lucas heard him turn away from the phone and say to someone in the background, "Lucas." Then to Lucas, he said, "My wife's here, she says hello."

"Look, I'm sorry I woke you up . . ."

"No, no . . ."

"And I don't want to cause you any problems, but would you be available to do a little computer work? I'd pay you a consultant's fee."

"Ah, fuck that, what do you need?"

"I'm in a snakepit, man. Could you find out what airlines fly out of New York, all the big airports, including Newark, and check from the beginning of the month, see if there's a ticket for a Cornell Reed? Or any first name Cornell, if you can do that? Or Red Reed? I don't think it'd be overseas, except maybe the Caribbean. Check domestic first, like Atlanta, L.A. or Chicago. I need to know where he went and I need to know who paid for the ticket, if we can find that out."

"Could take a couple of days."

"Get back to me—and I'm serious about a fee, man. A few bucks."

"We can work that out. . . ."

"Get back to me, man."

When he hung up, Lucas dropped back on the bed, thinking back to the interview with Rich. Rich didn't know why he'd been picked for Petty's team. Neither did Lily. His only qualification seemed to be that he'd later get a call from a burglar he knew, producing the only lead in the case. Good luck of a rare and peculiar variety.

Rich said that Cornell Reed was heavy into the crack. If that was right, Reed shouldn't be flying out of town. If he had enough cash to fly, he'd buy dope with the cash and take the bus. Or hitchhike. Or just not go. With enough crack, you didn't have to go anywhere. . . . He certainly wouldn't take several hundred dollars out to La Guardia and push it across the ticket counter.

On the other hand, a doper doesn't take a cab to the bus depot, not when the A train would have him there quicker and leave him enough change for a rock or two. La Guardia was another story. There was no easy way to get there, except by cab. . . .

So maybe he was flying. And maybe he was flying on an unrefundable ticket. And that sounded like a ticket issued by a government.

Or a police department.

And then there was Mrs. Logan's story.

That was very interesting; interesting and disturbing. Had Lily not understood it? Or had she hoped that Lucas hadn't?

CHAPTER

12

Thirty hits of speed, two days; Bekker hadn't slept forever. He was carried along on the chemicals like a leaf in a river, the flow of time and thought rolling about him. And he was avoiding the woman with the eyes, the woman watching him. She terrified him: but the chemicals had defeated her after two days, and she was losing her grip.

But other things were happening.

Late in the afternoon of the second day, the bugs came. He could feel them, lines of them, inching through his veins. All of his veins, but in particular, a vein on the forearm; he could feel them, little bumps, rattling along, doing their filthy work. Eating him.

Eating the blood cells. He could remember, as a child, kicking open ant nests and seeing the ants running for cover, their mealy white eggs in their jaws. And this was the image that came to him: ants running, but with blood cells caught in their pincers. Thousands of them, running through his veins. If he could let them out . . .

A voice in his head: *No no no, hallucination, no no no . . .*

He stood up, his knees and feet aching. He'd walked for miles in the basement, back and forth, back and forth. How far? A few errant brain cells wandered away and did the calculation . . . say five thousand round trips, twenty feet each way . . . thirty-seven point eight seven eight miles. Thirty-seven point eight seven eight seven eight seven eight seven eight seven . . .

He was snared in the eight-seven loop, captivated by the sheer infinity of it, a loop that would last longer than the sun, would last longer than the universe, would go on for . . . what?

He shook himself out of the loop, felt the bugs raging through his veins, took his forearm to the bathroom, turned on the light, looked for bumps, where the bugs scuttled along. . . .

A voice: *formication* . . .

He pushed it away. Had to let them out, squeeze them out somehow. He walked into the operating theater, went to the instruments pan, found a scalpel, let them out. . . .

He began to walk, the bugs draining away, began to pace again—what was that smell? So clean and coppery, like the sea. Blood?

He looked down at himself. Blood was running from his arm. Not heavily, now slowing, but his hand and forearm looked as though they had been flayed. Where he'd been pacing, blood splattered the floor, an oval line marking his pattern, as though someone had been swinging a decapitated chicken.

The voice: *stereotypy*.

What? He stared at the arm and a bug zipped down the vein. Like Charlie Victor on the Ho Chi Minh Trail, like Charlie Victor at the Hotel Oscar, Charlie Hotel India Mike November Lima Tango Romeo . . .

Another loop—where had that come from? 'Nam? He shook himself out. The bugs were waiting, in all their ranks.

Medication. He went to his medicine table, found a half-dozen pills. That was all. He popped one, then another. And a third.

He picked up the phone, struggled with himself, put it back down. No telephone from here, not to a dealer. Cops bugged dealers, bugged . . . He looked down at his arm, at the sticky blood. . . .

Calmed himself. Washed. Dressed. Put a bandage on the cut on his forearm. Cut? How did that . . .

He lost the thought and fixed himself in the mirror, preparing for his public, the *need* always there, looking over his shoulder. The *need* brought up the street personality. Changed his voice. Changed his manner. When he finished dressing, he went out to the corner, to a pay phone.

"Yes?" Woman's voice.

"May I speak to Dr. West?"

Whitechurch was there a second later. "Jesus Christ, we gotta talk. Like now. The cops have been here and they're looking for your buddy—or whoever you sold that shit to, the monitoring gear."

"What?"

"The guy you sold it to," Whitechurch said insistently. "He's this fruitcake killer, Bekker. Jesus Christ, the cops were all over me."

"New York cops?"

"Yeah, some cooze and this mean-looking asshole from Minneapolis."

"Are they on your phone?"

"This is not my phone. Don't worry about that. Just worry about the dude who bought that shit. . . ."

"I can handle that," Bekker squeaked. The effort hurt. "But I need some product."

"Jesus Christ . . ."

"A lot of it."

"How much?"

"How much do you have?"

There was a moment's silence, then Whitechurch said, "You're not with this Bekker dude, are you?"

"It wasn't Bekker. I sold it to a high school kid out on Staten Island. He's using it for his science project."

That clicked with Whitechurch: Schoolteacher . . .

Whitechurch had decided to take a vacation to Miami, could

use the extra cash. "I could get you two hundred of the crosses, thirty of the angels and ten of the white, if you can handle it."

"I can handle it."

"Twenty minutes?"

"No . . . I've got to come over. . . ." Let him think Bekker lived on Staten Island. "I need a couple of hours."

"Two hours? All right. Two hours. See you at nine. Usual place."

Bekker left the Volkswagen in a staff parking ramp off First Avenue; the ramp was open to the public from six until midnight. He nodded to the guard in the booth and rolled all the way up to the top floor. He'd watched Whitechurch before. He believed in taking care and knew that drug dealers routinely sold friends and customers to the cops. He'd learned a lot in jail; another side of life.

Whitechurch insisted on punctuality. "That way, I only have the stuff on me, on the street, for a minute. Safer that way, you know?"

Usually, Whitechurch would be walking out of the hospital, or down the sidewalk toward a bus bench, when Bekker came by. Once Bekker, arriving early, had watched him from the ramp. Whitechurch had come out, walked down the sidewalk toward the bus bench, had waited for two or three minutes, then had gone back inside, using the same door he'd used on the way out. Bekker had called to apologize, and made the pickup a few minutes later.

Bekker walked down to the first floor, past the pay booth, and down the street to an alleylike passage to the emergency room. Night was settling in, the streetlights coming on. He was early, slowed down. Several people around. Not good. He turned down the alley to the emergency room, walked up to the door that Whitechurch usually came through. Pulled on the handle. Locked. Glanced at his watch. Still two minutes early. Whitechurch should be coming, just any moment. . . .

He'd done an angel before he came, part of his emergency stash. Strong stuff; it freed his power. . . .

The derringer was in his hand.

The door opened and Whitechurch stepped out, and jumped, startled, when he saw Bekker.

"What . . ."

"We've got to talk," Bekker whispered. "There's more to this than I thought. . . ."

He looked past Whitechurch to an empty tile-walled corridor. "Back inside, just a few minutes. I feel obligated to tell you about this."

Whitechurch nodded and turned, leading the way. "Did you bring the cash?"

"Yes." He held out the cash envelope and Whitechurch took it. "Have you got the product?"

"Yeah." Whitechurch turned as the metal fire door closed behind them. The corridor lights weren't strong, but they were unforgiving blue fluorescents.

Whitechurch had a plastic baggie in his hand and half stepped toward Bekker when he said, "You're . . ." He stopped, catching his tongue, and began to back away.

"The fruitcake killer," Bekker said, smiling. "Just like on *I've Got a Secret*. You remember that show? Garry Moore, I think."

Whitechurch's head snapped around, looking for room, then turned back to Bekker, but already his body was moving, trying to run.

"Listen," he said, half over his shoulder.

"No." Bekker leveled the gun at Whitechurch's broad back and Whitechurch shouted, "No way," and Bekker shot him in the spine between the shoulder blades. The muzzle blast was deafening, and Whitechurch pitched forward, tried to catch himself on the slick tile walls, bounced and turned. Bekker pointed the pistol at him, from two feet.

"No way . . ."

Bekker pulled the trigger again, firing into Whitechurch's forehead. Then he pushed the gun into his pocket, hurrying, took out a scalpel, stooped, and ruined Whitechurch's dead eyes. Good.

Down the hall, a door banged open. "Hey." Somebody yelling.

Bekker looked down the corridor: empty. He grabbed the baggie full of pills, stood, remembered the money, saw it half trapped under Whitechurch. Down the hall, the door banged open again and Bekker jerked at the money envelope. The envelope ripped, but he got most of it, just a bill or two still trapped under the body.

"Hey . . ." He looked back as he went through the door, but there was nothing in the corridor but the voice. Outside, he gathered himself and hurried, but didn't run, down the alley, turning left on the sidewalk to the parking ramp. He went inside to the stairs, heard footsteps behind, and half turned.

A young woman was hurrying after him. He started up the steps and she caught up with him, a few steps behind. "Wait up . . ." Breathless. "I hate to go up here alone. If there were somebody . . . You know."

"Yes." The woman was worried about being attacked. There was only one open entrance to the ramp, but anyone could get in over the low walls. Judging from the graffiti spray-painted on the concrete walls, several people had.

"God, what a day," the woman said. "I hate to work when it's so nice outside, I never see anything but computer terminals."

Bekker nodded again, not trusting his voice. If he'd had the time, he could have taken her. She'd have been perfect: young, apparently intelligent. A natural observer. Might possibly understand the privilege she was being given. He could take her, he thought. Right now. Hit her in the head . . .

Behind her, he balled his hand into a fist, and he thought, *Or the gun. I could use the gun.* He felt the weight of the gun in his pocket. Empty now, but a threat . . .

But if he hurt her, struck her, had to fight, if she was less than a perfect specimen . . . his results would be impeachable. People were watching him, people who hated him, who would do any-thing to impeach his results. He fell back a step, his heart beating like a drum.

"See you," she said, one half-level below his car. She looked out on the open floor before she went through the door. "No-body here . . . makes you feel a little stupid, doesn't it?"

He could, but . . . wait. No improvisation. *Remember the last time . . . Easy, easy, there are plenty of them.*

Bekker lifted a hand and risked it: "Good-bye," he said, in his careful voice.

He had to get one. Had to. He didn't realize, until he saw the woman get in the car and lock the doors, how strong the need was now.

He rolled out of the ramp, straight down the street; there was some commotion in the emergency entrance alley, but he didn't stop to look. Instead, he went straight back to his apartment, almost frantic now, and got out his collector's bag: the stun gun and the anesthetic tank and mask. He flicked the stun gun once, checked the discharge level. Fine. And dug through the bag he'd taken from Whitechurch: just a taste. He snapped one of the angels between his teeth, thinking to take a half, but a half wouldn't do, and he took a whole, waiting for the power to come.

Cruising, thinking: *Infrared. Ultraviolet. Breakthrough.*

He knew this bar. . . .

Later. He saw the woman slouch out of the back of the bar, lean against the brick exterior, and light a cigarette with what looked like an old-fashioned Zippo. Not many men around, lots of women coming and going, many of them alone. Easy targets.

The woman was leaning against the outside wall, wearing jeans and a sleeveless T-shirt, with a wide leather belt. She had short black hair, with gold hoop earrings.

Bekker came up, stepping carefully around the Volkswagen as though he didn't own it. Not too aggressive. Stun gun in his hand, tank under his arm, hand on mask.

"Terrific night," he said to the woman.

She smiled. "You're looking pretty good," she said.

Bekker smiled back and stopped next to the nose of the Volks-wagen.

Come to the gingerbread house, little girl . . .

CHAPTER
13

"What's wrong?" Lily asked.

Kennett rolled toward her and put an arm under her head. "I feel like an invalid when we do that. I mean, nothing *but* that."

The forward double berth was wedge-shaped, shoved into the bow of the boat. Kennett was lying on his side. He reached toward her face in the near-darkness, touched her at the hairline with the pad of his index finger, drew it down her nose, gently over her lips, between her breasts, then up to gently tap each nipple, then down around her navel, over her hipbone and down the inside of her thigh to her knee. She was still warm, sweating.

"We're not . . . compelled . . . to do it," Lily said.

"Maybe you're not, but I am," Kennett grumbled. "If I couldn't make love anymore, I'd feel like a goddamn vegetable."

"You just wanna be on top," she said, trying to make a joke out of it. When he didn't respond, she said, "You've got to listen to Fermut."

"Fuckin' doctors . . ." Fermut, the cardiologist, had reluctantly agreed that Kennett could resume his sex life "as long as your partner does the hard work."

"Listen to him," Lily said, gently but urgently. "He's trying to save your life, you dope."

"Yeah." Kennett turned his head away from her, his hand scratching at his chest."

"You want a cigarette, right?"

"No, that's not it. I was just thinking . . . it's not the doctors. It's me. When I get turned on and my heart starts thumping, I start listening to it. . . ."

"Then we oughta quit. Maybe only for a few weeks . . ." Lily said.

"No. That'd be worse. It's just . . . Christ, I wish one thing— just one goddamn thing in this world—was simple. Just one thing. I gotta get laid, but if I get laid, I can't help thinking about my heart, and that can mess up getting laid. Then with you on top all the time, and me just laying there like a dead man with a hard-on, I start thinking, what's it like for her? It must be like necrophilia, screwing me."

"Richard, you idiot . . ."

"Christ, I'm glad I met you," he said after a while. "I couldn't believe you were in there, working for O'Dell. I kept thinking, she can't be just working for him, a woman like that, there's gotta be something else going on here."

"Oh, God . . ." Lily giggled, an odd, pleasant sound with her husky voice.

"Sorry 'bout that," Kennett said, touching her again. "I wonder what O'Dell does for sex? Fly out to Vegas and get a couple-three fat ones in the sack? I wonder how long it's been since he's seen his dick? He's so fat I don't think he can even reach it anymore. . . ."

"C'mon . . ." Lily said, but she giggled again, a big woman giggling, and that set Kennett off, laughing.

And then: " 'Course, things must've been different with Davenport."

Lily cut him off: "Shut up. I don't want to hear it."

"Probably hung like a Shetland pony . . ."

"You wanna get bit?"

"Is that a clear offer?"

"Dick . . ."

"Hey. I'm not jealous. Well, maybe a little. But I really like the guy. This whole business of bringing him to dance with the media, that's pretty bizarre, and it's working. You think he'll get in the sack with Barbara Fell?"

"I don't know," she said, crisply.

"He seems like the kind of guy who'd be looking around," he offered.

"Pot and kettle."

"Hey—I didn't say it was bad. I just wondered about him and Fell. That's a match made in hell."

"She's very attractive."

"I guess, if you like the type," Kennett said. "She looks like a biker chick who fell off the Harley one too many times. Why'd you put him with her? Some kind of psychological compulsion to bury your sexual history?"

"No, no, no. We just needed somebody who knew Midtown fences. . . ."

"Yeah, but Davenport's supposed to be a talking head."

"He's never a talking head. Even when he's talking. The guy has more moves than you do, and you're the sneakiest, shifti-est . . ."

". . . crookedest . . ."

". . . most underhanded asshole on the force. Besides, he had to do something to get the media to talk to him."

"I suppose." Kennett's fingertips slipped along her thigh again, her skin soft and slightly cool from evaporating sweat. "We'll either have to get a sheet to cover up or figure out some way to warm up the place again."

Lily groped for his groin and said, "Oh, Jesus. Are you sure? Dick . . ."

He rolled into her, his arm around her, pulling her tight. "That's the word, all right. Dick."

"Be serious."

"All right. How's this: I really do need you; it's the thing that keeps my heart going. . . ."

Much later, when he was sleeping, she thought: *They can all make you feel guilty; it's what they do best.* . . .

CHAPTER

14

The phone rang early and Lucas rolled out of the blankets, dropped his feet to the floor and sat a moment before he picked up the receiver. "Yeah?"

"How's your head?" Kennett sounded wide awake and almost chipper.

"Better," Lucas said. He couldn't seem to focus and noticed that the window shade was bright with low-angle sunshine. "What time is it?"

"Seven o'clock."

"Ah, Jesus, man, I don't get up at seven. . . ." His face hurt again, and when he turned toward the bed, he noticed a spot of blood on the pillowcase.

"Hey, it's a great day, but it's gonna be hot," Kennett said cheerfully.

"Thanks. If you hadn't called, I woulda had to look out the window. . . ." *What's going on?*

"I understand that you and Fell talked to a guy named Whitechurch yesterday, at Bellevue?"

"Yeah?"

"Bekker took him off last night."

"What?" Lucas stood up, trying to understand.

"Shot him in a hallway. Cut his eyes," Kennett said. "The morgue guys said it's gotta be Bekker, 'cause it was done too well to be a copycat. And with you talking to him about Bekker, there's no way it's a coincidence. When they called me, a couple of hours ago now, I shipped Carter over to the hospital. Somebody there finally figured out that cops were talking to Whitechurch yesterday. . . ."

"Ah, Jesus," Lucas said. "Whitechurch was wrong, too. We knew it. We knew he was bullshitting us."

"How'd you get onto him?"

"A fence," Lucas said. "Down on the Lower East Side."

"Smith?"

"No, a small-timer, a woman named Arnold. We'll go back and talk to her, but I don't think she has any connection with Whitechurch except to handle occasional shipments from him. But why was Bekker talking to Whitechurch again? More equipment?"

"Whitechurch was dealing dope," Kennett said.

"Ah. For sure?"

"Yeah, we got it from a couple of places. And I'd bet that's where the halothane is from."

"Telephones?"

"We sent a subpoena over, and the phone company's mopping up their computers right now. They'll run back all the calls that came into Whitechurch's apartment and his office phone, both, and where they came from, for the last two months."

"That should do it," Lucas said. "Fell's got a beeper: if you find him, call us. I'd like to see the end of it."

"Mmm. It doesn't feel that easy," Kennett said.

"All right. Well: I'll get Fell and get back to the fence. Goddammit, why'd Whitechurch cover for him? That'd be something to figure out."

Lucas called Fell and told her.

"Did we mess it up?" she asked anxiously.

"No. We barely touched the guy—there was no way to know.

But Kennett's people are all over him now. Everybody who knew him. We've got to talk to what's-her-name, the fence."

"Arnold. Rose."

"Yeah . . . So what's your status? Are you ready?" Lucas asked.

"Hey, I'm just sitting here on my bed, buck naked, half asleep."

"Jesus, if you had a warm croissant and a cup of coffee, I'd come right over," Lucas said. The nude photo of Fell and the other cop popped up in his head.

"Fuck you, Davenport," Fell said, laughing. "If you're ready, why don't you get a cab? I'll be out front by the time you get here."

"You come get me," Lucas said. "I'm barely awake, and I gotta shave." He touched his raw cheek.

"Be ready," she said.

Fell, when she arrived, was wearing a black tailored cotton dress with small flowers—the kind of dress women wore in Moline, Illinois—black low heels and nylons.

"Jesus, you look terrific," Lucas said, climbing into the cab behind her.

She blushed and said, "We just gonna walk in on Arnold?"

"You don't want to talk about how terrific you look?"

"Hey, just shut the fuck up, okay, Davenport?" she said.

"Anything you want . . ." Under his breath, he added, "Toots."

"What? What'd you just say?"

"Nothing," Lucas said innocently.

She closed one eye and said, "You're walking on the edge, buddy."

Arnold was scared. "He maybe got done because he talked to you," she said, sucking her heavy lips in and out.

"No. He got done because he called this asshole Bekker, who he was protecting, and told him that we'd interviewed him,"

Lucas said. "Bekker knows me. He didn't want to take any chances."

"So what do you want from me? I gave you everything."

"How'd you get in touch with Whitechurch when you needed to?" Lucas asked.

"I never needed to. When he had something good, he'd bring it over. Otherwise—shit, I don't handle hospital stuff. I handle shit you can sell, cheap. Suits. Neckties. Telephones. I wouldn't know what to do with no hospital stuff."

Fell pointed a finger at her: "You took down Simpson-McCall, what, two months ago . . . ?"

Arnold looked away. "No. I don't know nothing about that."

Fell studied her for a moment, then looked at Lucas. "Brokerage moves to a new building, one of those over-the-weekend moves. Trucks coming and going all night with files, computers, telephones, furniture, putting it in. The only thing is, not all of the trucks were hired by the brokerage. Some assholes rented trucks, drove them up to the loading docks, and disappeared over the horizon. . . . One of them took off six hundred brand-new beige two-button phones. Somebody else got fifty Northgate IBM compatibles, still in the boxes."

"Really?" said Arnold, faintly distressed. "Computers?"

Fell nodded, and Lucas looked back at Arnold. "If you *had* to get to Whitechurch, what'd you do?"

Arnold shrugged. "Call him at the hospital. Wasn't no big secret where he worked. Nights only, though."

"Did he have a special number?"

"I don't know, man, I never called him."

"Did . . ."

Fell's beeper went off. She took it out of her purse, glanced at the readout. "Where's the phone?" she asked Arnold. To Lucas, she said, "I bet they got him."

"Over there, at the end of the counter, underneath . . ." Arnold said, pointing.

As Fell punched the number into the telephone, Lucas went back to Arnold. "Did he work with anybody?"

"Man, I bought telephones from him, four dollars apiece," Arnold said impatiently. "Boxes of pens and pencils. Notepads. Cartons of Xerox paper. Cleaning supplies. He once came in with two hundred bottles of ERA, you know, the laundry soap. I don't know where he got it, I didn't ask any questions. And that's all I know about him."

"Yeah, this is Fell, you beeped?" Fell said into the phone. And then, voice hushed, "Jesus. What's the address. Huh? Okay." She hung up and looked at Lucas. "Bekker did another one, another woman. Ten minutes from here, walking."

Lucas pointed a finger at Arnold: "Did you hear that? Think about Whitechurch. Anything you think of, call us. Anything."

"Man, there's nothin' . . ."

But Lucas and Fell were out the door.

The body was in a dead-end alley off Prince. Uniforms blocked the mouth of the alley, kept back the curious. Fell and Lucas flashed their badges and went through. Kennett and two other plainclothesmen were there, staring into a window well. Kennett's hands, gripping the rail around the well, were white with tension.

"Goddamn maniac," he said as Lucas and Fell walked up. The crime-scene techs had dropped a ladder into the well. Lucas looked over the railing and saw a small woman's body at the bottom of the well, nude, crumpled like a doll, the techs working over her.

"No question it was Bekker?" Lucas asked.

"No, but it's different. This doesn't look so scientific. She's pretty slashed up, like he . . . I don't know. It looks like he was having fun."

"Eyes?"

"Yeah, the eyes are cut and the doc says it looks like his work. The eyelids gone, very neat and surgical. The sonofabitch has a signature."

"How long has she been down there?" Fell asked.

"Not long. A few hours at the most. Probably went in before dawn, this morning."

"Got an ID?" asked Lucas.

"No." Kennett looked at Fell, who was lighting a Lucky. "Could I bum one, I . . ."

"No." Fell shook her head, carefully not looking at him.

"God damn it," Kennett said. He stuck one hand in his jacket pocket, put two fingers of the other between his shirt buttons, over his heart. He caught himself, pulled them out, looked at his hand and finally stuck it in the other jacket pocket. "Fuckin' do-gooders."

"Anything on the Bellevue phones?" Lucas asked, watching the techs get ready to roll the woman's body.

Kennett's forehead wrinkled. "Think about this, Davenport: We got a guy who deals drugs, but he gets no phone calls. I mean, like, almost none. He got six calls at his apartment last month. There was a phone in the maintenance office he could use, but he didn't, much. At least, that's what his supervisor says."

"Did he carry a beeper? Maybe a cellular?" Fell asked.

"Not that we can find," said Kennett.

"That's bullshit," Lucas said flatly. "He was dealing, right? We know that for sure?"

"Yeah."

"Then he's got a phone. We've just got to find it. . . ."

"Carter's guys are interviewing people over there right now, at Bellevue. Maybe you could listen in for a while?" Kennett said. He looked at Fell. "You're the only guys who've come up with anything."

At the bottom of the window well, the crime-scene techs rolled the body. The woman's head flopped over, and her wide white eyes suddenly looked up at them.

"Aw, shit," Fell gagged. She turned away, hunched over the alley cobblestones, and a stream of saliva poured from her mouth.

"You okay?" Lucas asked, his hand on her back.

"Yes," she said, straightening. "Sorry. That just caught me, the eyes . . ."

Five minutes later, the body was out of the window well. The removal crew had wrapped it in a blanket, but Kennett ordered the wrapper peeled away. "I want to look," he said evenly. "I wish the fuck I could have gotten down there. . . ."

Kennett and Lucas squatted next to the collapsible gurney as the blanket was lifted. The woman's face was like marble, white, solid, her dying pain and fear still graven on her face. The gag was like the earlier ones, carved from hard rubber, held in place with a wire that had been twisted tight behind her ear.

"Pliers," Kennett said absently.

"Treats them like . . . lumber," Lucas said, groping for the right concept.

"Or lab animals," Kennett said.

"Sonofabitch." Lucas leaned to one side, almost toppled, caught himself with his hand, then knelt over the body until his face was only inches from the body's left ear. He looked up at one of the techs and said, "Roll her a little to the left, will you?" He took a pen from his shirt pocket and, to Kennett, said, "Look at this."

Kennett knelt beside him and Fell squatted behind the two of them, the other detectives crowding in. Lucas used the pen to point at two oval marks on the dead woman's neck muscle.

"Have you ever seen anything like that?" Lucas asked.

Kennett shook his head. "Looks like a burn," he said. "Looks like a fuckin' snakebite."

"Not exactly. It looks like a discharge wound from one of those electroshock self-defense gizmos, stun guns. The St. Paul cops carry them. I went over to see a demonstration. If you keep the discharge points on bare skin for more than a second or two, you can get this kind of injury."

"That's why there's no fight," Fell said, looking at him.

Lucas nodded. "He hits them with the shocker. When you get hit, you go down, like right now. Then he comes with the gas."

"Couldn't be too many places around that sell those things," Kennett said.

"Police-supply places, but I've seen them in gun magazines, too, mail order," Lucas said.

Kennett stood and rubbed alley sand from his hands and tipped his head back, as though looking up to heaven. "Please, God, let me find a Midtown address on an order form."

Lucas and Fell took a cab to Bellevue, windows open, the hot popcorn smell of the city roaring in as they dodged through traffic, and got trapped for five minutes in a narrow one-lane crosstown street. Fell's jaw was working with anger.

"Thinking about Bekker?"

"About the body . . . Jesus. I hope Robin Hood gets him," she said. "Bekker."

"What? Robin Hood?" He looked at her curiously.

"Nothing," she said, looking away.

"No, c'mon, who's Robin Hood?"

"Ah, it's bullshit," she said, digging in her purse for a cigarette. "Supposedly somebody is knocking off assholes."

"You mean, a vigilante?"

She grinned. "How else you gonna run this place?" she asked, gesturing out the window. "It's supposed to be cops, but I think it's just bullshit. Wishful thinking."

"Huh."

She lit the cigarette, coughed, and looked out the window.

Whitechurch had been a maintenance foreman. A changing roll of a dozen people worked under his loose supervision, doing minor repairs all over the hospital on the three-to-eleven shift.

"A great goddamn job if you're stealing stuff," Fell said as they joined Carter in an employees' lounge. Three detectives were interviewing hospital employees, with Carter supervising.

"Or if you're dealing," said Carter. He looked at his list. "Next one is Jimmy Beale. Goddamn, I got little faith in this."

"I know what you mean," Lucas said, watching the scared employees trooping through the lounge.

Beale knew nothing. Neither did any of the rest. Fell burned through a pack of Luckys, left to get another, came back and leaned in the door.

"God damn it, Mark . . . it's Mark?" Carter was saying. "God damn it, Mark, we're not getting anywhere and it's hard to believe that a guy could be stealing the place blind and nobody'd know about it. Or dealing dope, and nobody'd know. . . ."

Mark, tall, narrow, acned, nodded nervously, his Adam's apple working convulsively, sliding up and down his thin neck. "Man, you never seen the dude, you know? I mean, I'd come in and he'd say, Mark, g'wan up to 441D and put on a new door-knob and then see if there's a leak on the drinking fountain up on six, and that's what I'd do. He'd come by, but like, I never hung out with him or nothing."

When he was gone, Lucas said, "Nobody knew. How many do you believe?"

"Most of them," Carter said. "I don't think he was dealing here. And if you're stealing stuff, you don't talk about it. Somebody'll try to cut in—or somebody'll try to do the same thing, then feed you to the cops on plea bargain."

"Somebody must've known," Fell objected. "That was the last of them?"

"That was the last . . ." said Carter.

A woman knocked on the edge of the door and stuck her face in. She had curly white hair and held her hands in front of her as though she were knitting.

"Are you the police?" she asked timorously.

"Yeah. C'mon in," Lucas said. He yawned and stretched. "What can we do for you?"

She stepped inside the room and looked nervously around. "Some of the others were saying you were asking if Lew had a beeper or a walkie-talkie?"

"Yes. Who are you?"

"My name is Dotty, um, Bedrick, I work in housekeeping?" She made her sentences into questions. "Last week, Lew split out his pants, right down by housekeeping? There was some kind of pipe thing he was working on and he bent over and they went, split, right up the back?"

"Uh-huh," Lucas said.

"Anyway, I was right there? And everybody knows I sew, so he came in and asked if I could do anything? He slipped right out of his pants—he was wearing boxer shorts, of course—he slipped right out and I sewed them up. He was just wearing a T-shirt on top, and the boxer shorts, and I had his pants. There was nothing in there but his wallet and his keys and his pocket change. There wasn't any beeper or anything like that."

"Hey. Thank you," Lucas said, nodding. "That was a problem for us."

"Why did you have to know?" Bedrick asked. Lucas thought, *Miss Marple.*

"We think that—I'm sure you've heard this from the others— we think he was dealing drugs. If he was, he needed access to a telephone."

"Well, there was something odd about the man. . . ."

She wanted to be led: Lucas put his hands on his waist, pushing his sport coat back on both sides, like a cop on television, let a hip pop out and said, "Yeah?"

She approved: "Sometimes when the calls came over the speakers for doctors, I've seen him look up at the speakers. And the next thing, *he'd* be calling in. I saw him do it two or three times. Like he was a *doctor.*"

"Sonofagun," Carter said. "There'd be a call for a doctor?"

"That's right."

"Jesus," he said, turning to Lucas and Fell, dumbfounded. "That's it."

"That's it?" chirped Bedrick.

"That's it," Carter said. He smiled at the old lady and shook his head. "I never had a civilian do that before."

* * *

Fell decided to stay at Bellevue and work the lead. Lucas, shaking his head, decided to head back to Midtown South.

"You don't think it'll be anything?" Fell asked.

"It might be—but with Whitechurch dead, I don't know how you'd find out," he said.

"I want to stay anyway," she said. "It's all we've got."

All we've got, Lucas thought. *Yeah. We find Bekker's supplier, the best damned lead all week, and Bekker kills him right under our noses.* Some hotshot cops they were. There had to be another way to approach this situation, to find a way in. . . .

At Midtown South, Lucas could hear Kennett all the way out to the reception desk.

". . . know it's hot, but I don't give a shit," he was saying. "I don't want people around here reading the goddamn reports, I want everybody out on the street. I want the fuckin' junkies to know there's a war going on. Instead of coming in here, I want you out on the street with your people, rousting these assholes. Somebody knows where he's at. . . ."

Lucas leaned in the door. Seven or eight detectives were sitting uncomfortably around the conference room, while Kennett sat on a folding chair at the front, his fingers over his heart, an angry flush on his face. He looked over the cops to Lucas and snapped, "Tell me something good."

"Did you talk to Carter?"

"I'm supposed to call him back," Kennett said, looking at a phone slip. "What happened?"

"An old lady maybe told us how Whitechurch got his calls."

"Well, goddamn," somebody said.

Lucas shook his head: "But it might not be good. He may have had doctor code names for his clients. When a buyer needed to call in, the switchboard—or somebody—would page the doctor. Whitechurch would pick up a phone and answer the page. There are thousands of doctors in there every day, thousands of phone calls. Hundreds of pages."

"Sonofabitch," Kennett said. He ran his hand through his

hair, and a swatch of it stood up straight, in a peak. "Carter's pushing it?"

"Yeah. Six guys and Fell stayed to help."

Kennett thought about it for a second, then exhaled in exasperation and asked, "Anything else?"

"No. I'm still reading paper on him, but I think . . . Look, I had an idea on the way over. Entirely different direction. Carter's taking the phone angle, you got guys on everything else. I was thinking again about how hard Bekker is to find, about where he's getting his money, about all the things we don't know about him. So I was thinking, maybe I should talk to the guys who *did* know Bekker."

"Like who?"

"Like the guys who were in jail with him. Maybe I ought to go back to the Cities. I could run down the people who were in the next cells to his. Maybe he said something to somebody, or somebody gave him an idea of how to hole up. . . ."

"That's not bad," said Kennett, scratching his breastbone. "Kind of a long shot, though, and it takes you out of the action here." He thought about it some more. "I'll tell you what. Read paper for the rest of the day, think about the phones. Day after tomorrow's the lecture. If we've got nothing by then, let's talk about it. . . . You see the art?"

"Art?"

Kennett said, "Jim . . ."

One of the detectives handed Lucas a brown envelope. Lucas opened it and found a sheath of eight-by-ten color photos. Fell stood at his elbow as he flipped through them. Whitechurch, dead in the hallway, flat on his back. Blood on the tile behind his head, and on the wall. A twenty-dollar bill half pinned under the body.

"What's the money?" Lucas said.

"They must have been hassling over the cash when Bekker shot him," said the cop named Jim. "One of the janitors heard the shots. Not being stupid, he hollered before he went to look. Then he kind of carefully stuck his head through a fire door and saw Whitechurch on the ground. The outside door was just closing. Bekker must've grabbed what he could and run for it.''

"He didn't take the eyelids," Lucas said. Except for the blood, Whitechurch might have been a sleeping drunk.

"Nope. Just poked him in the eyes and grabbed the dope, if there was any. They got a print, by the way, off a bill. It was Bekker.''

"All right, let's get out there," Kennett said to the cops. There was an unhappy silence, all of them on their feet and moving through the door, shaking heads. "Hey. Everybody. Tell your people to put on the vests, huh? They're gonna be talking to some pissed-off people.''

Huerta, bumping past Kennett, stopped to pat him on the head, pushing his hair down.

Kennett said, "What?" and Huerta, grinning, said, "Just knocking down your mohawk. With all that white hair stickin' up you looked like Steve Martin in *The Jerk,* except skinny and old.''

"Yeah, old, kiss my ass, Huerta," Kennett said, laughing, straightening his hair.

Lucas, astonished, watched Huerta walk away, then looked back at Kennett.

"What?" Kennett asked, puzzled, raking at his hair again.

"Steve Martin?" Lucas asked.

"Asshole," Kennett grumbled.

"They're probably calling you the same thing, you putting them on the street like that," Lucas said. Switching the topic away from Steve Martin, covering, covering . . .

"I know," Kennett said soberly, looking after the detectives. "Jesus, roustin' junkies in this heat . . . it's gonna stink and the junkies'll be pissed and the cops are gonna be pissed and somebody's gonna get hurt.''

"Not a hell of a lot of choice," Lucas said. "Keep pushing everywhere. With Whitechurch dead, Bekker's gotta find a new source.''

* * *

An hour later, Lucas lay on his bed at the Lakota and thought about what Huerta had said. That he looked like Steve Martin, with all that white hair . . .

All right. You're on the street. There's been a killing. A car speeds by and inside is an old white guy. That's what Cornell Reed told Bobby Rich's snitch. An old white guy. How would you know he was old, when he was in a moving car? If he had white hair . . .

And then there was Mrs. Logan, and what she'd said, in the apartment beneath Petty's. . . .

Kennett fit. He was a longtime intelligence operative. He was high up, with good access to inside information. He was tough but apparently well liked; he had charisma. He had white hair.

Kennett was sleeping with Lily. How did that cut across it? How did she wind up in the sack with a guy who might be a suspect? And the biggest question: with several hundred possible suspects, how did Kennett wind up in Lucas' lap, available for daily inspection?

O'Dell was one answer. Lily was another. Or both together.

He lay on the bed with the Magic Marker and his art pad, trying to put together a list. Finally he came up with:

1. Cornell Reed.

CHAPTER

15

Lucas was flat on his back, half asleep, when Fell called. The room was semidark; he'd turned out all the lights but the one in the bathroom, and then half closed the door.

"I'm downstairs," she said. "If you're awake, let's get something to eat."

"Anything at Bellevue?" Lucas asked.

"I'll tell you about it."

"Ten minutes," he said.

He was fifteen minutes. He shaved, going easy over the bruises, brushed his teeth and took a quick shower, put on a fresh shirt, dabbed on after-shave. When he got down to the lobby, Fell looked him over and said, "Great. You make me feel like a rag."

"You look fine," he said, but she didn't. She looked worn, dirty around the eyes. The dress that had been crisp that morning hung slackly from her shoulders. "There's an Italian place a couple of blocks down that's friendly."

"Good. I couldn't handle anything complicated." As they were going out the door, she said, "I'm sorry about ditching you and going with Kennett, but this case really could mean a lot for me. And Mrs. Bedrick, she was mine . . . ours . . . and I wanted to be there to get the credit."

Lucas nodded and said, "No problem." On the sidewalk, he added, "You don't sound happy."

"I'm not. Bellevue's a rat's nest. They have a dial-in paging system, so now we're trying to figure out if we can match up the calls. And we're looking for people who might have been paging doctors who shouldn't have, that somebody else might have noticed. There are about two thousand suspects."

"Can you thin them out?"

"Maybe. We're trying extortion. Kennett worked out a routine with an assistant D.A. Everybody we talk to, we tell them the same thing: if we find out who Whitechurch's phone contact is before she comes forward, we'll charge her as an accomplice in the Bekker murders. If she comes forward and cooperates, we'll give her immunity on Bekker. And she can bring a lawyer and refuse to cooperate on anything else. . . . So there's a chance. If we can scare her enough."

"How do you know it's a *her*?"

Fell grinned up at him: "That's Kennett. He said, 'Have you ever heard a male voice on a hospital intercom?' We all thought about it, and decided, Not very often. If a male voice kept calling out the names of nonexistent doctors—that's what we think she was doing, whoever she is, calling out code names—he'd be noticed. So we're pretty sure it's a her."

"What if it's just the switchboard?"

"Then we're fucked . . . although Carter thinks it probably isn't. A switchboard might start recognizing names and voices. . . ."

The Whetstone had an old-fashioned knife-grinding wheel in the window, a dozen tables in front, a few booths in back. Between the booths was a wooden floor, worn smooth and soft by a century of sliding feet. A couple turned slowly in the middle of it, dancing to a slow, sleepy jazz tune from an aging jukebox.

"Booth?" asked Lucas.

"Sure," said the waitress. "One left, in the no-smoking area."

Fell smiled ruefully at Lucas, and said, "We'll take it."

They ate spaghetti and garlic bread around a bottle of rosé, talking about Bekker. Lucas recounted the Minneapolis killings:

". . . started killing them to establish their alibis. They apparently picked out the woman at the shopping mall at random. She was killed to confuse things."

"Like a bug. Stepped on," Fell said.

"Yeah. I once dealt with a sexual psychopath who killed a series of women, and I could understand him, in a way. He was nuts. He was *made* nuts. If he'd had a choice, I'd bet that he'd have chosen not to be nuts. It was like, it wasn't his fault, his wires were bad. But with Bekker . . ."

"Still nuts," Fell said. "They might look cold and rational, but to be that cold, you've got to be goofy. And look what he's doing now. If we take him alive, there's a good chance that he'll be sent to a mental hospital, instead of a prison."

"I'd rather go to prison," Lucas said.

"Me, too, but there are people who don't think that way. Like doctors."

A heavyset man in work pants and a gray Charlie Chaplin mustache stepped across to the jukebox and stared into it. The waitress came by and said, "More wine?"

Lucas looked at Fell and then up at the waitress and said, "Mmmm," and the waitress took the glasses.

Behind her, the heavy man in work pants dropped a single quarter in the jukebox, carefully pressed two buttons, went back to his table and bent over the woman he had been sitting with. As she got up, the "Blue Skirt Waltz" began bubbling from the jukebox speakers.

"Jesus. *Blue Skirt.* And it's Frankie Yankovich, too," Lucas said. "C'mon, let's dance."

"You gotta be kidding. . . ."

"You don't want . . . ?"

"Of course I want," she said. "I just can't believe that you do."

They began turning around the floor, Fell light and delicate, a good dancer, Lucas denser, unskilled. They turned around the heavy man and his partner, the two couples caught by the same rhythm, weaving around the dance floor. The waitress, who'd taken menus to another table, lingered to watch them dance.

"One more time," the heavy man said to Lucas, in a heavy German accent, as the song ended. He bowed, gestured to the jukebox. Lucas dropped a quarter, punched "Blue Skirt," and they started again, turning around the tiny dance floor. Fell fit nicely just below his jaw, and her soft hair stroked his cheek. When the song ended, they both sighed and wandered back to the booth, holding hands.

"Sooner or later, I'd like to spend some time in your shorts, as we say around the Ninth," Fell said across the table as she sat down. "But not tonight. I'm too fuckin' dirty and miserable and tired and I've got too many bad movies in my head."

"Well," he said.

"Well, what? You don't want to?"

"I was thinking, well, I've got a shower."

She cocked her head, looking at him steadily, unsmiling. "You think it'll wash away that woman rolling over this morning, with those eyes?" she asked somberly.

After a moment, he said, "No. I guess not. But listen . . . you interest me. I think you knew that."

"I didn't really," she said, almost shyly. "I've got no self-confidence."

"Well." He laughed.

"You keep saying that. Well."

"Well. Have some more wine," he said.

Halfway through the second bottle of wine, Fell made Lucas play it again and they turned around the room, close, her face tipped up this time, breathing against his neck, warm, steamy. He began to react and was relieved to get her back to the booth.

She was drunk, laughing, and Lucas asked about the cop she used to date.

"Ah, God," she said, staring up at the ceiling, where a large wooden fan slowly turned its endless circles. "He was *so* good-looking, and he was *such* a snake. He used to be like this *Pope of Greenwich Village* guy with these great suits and great shoes, and he hung out, you know? I mean, he was cool. His socks had clocks on them."

"How cool can a Traffic guy be?" Lucas cracked.

She frowned. "Were we talking about him? I don't . . ."

"Sure, at your place," he said, thinking, *As a matter of fact, you didn't, Lily did, Davenport, you asshole.* "I remember, mm, important details. . . ."

"Why's that important?" she asked, but she knew, and she was flattered.

"You're the fuckin' detective," Lucas said, grinning at her. "Have another drop of wine."

"Trying to get me drunk?"

"Maybe."

Fell put her wineglass on the table and poked a finger at him. "What the fuck are you doing, Davenport? *Are* you Internal Affairs?"

"Jesus Christ—I told you, I'm not. Look, if you're really serious, my goddamn publisher's not far from here and my face is on the game boxes. There's a biography and everything, we could go over . . ."

"Okay. But why are you pumping me?"

"I'm not pumping you. . . ."

"Bullshit," she said. Her voice rose. "You're a goddamn trouser snake just like he was, and just like Kennett. I knew that as soon as you asked me to dance. I mean, I could feel myself *melting*. Now, what the fuck are you doing?"

Lucas leaned forward and said, trying to quiet her, trying not to laugh, "I'm not . . ."

"Jesus," she said, pulling back. She went back to the table and picked up her purse. "I'm really loaded."

"Where're we going?"

"Up to your room. I've changed my mind."

"Barbara . . ." Lucas threw three twenties at the tabletop, and hurried after her. "You're a little drunk . . ."

"Fuckin' trouser snake," Fell said as she led the way through the door.

He woke in the half-lit room, a thin arrow of light from the bathroom falling across the bed. He was confused, a feeling of déjà vu. Didn't Fell just call, didn't she say . . . ? He stopped, feeling the weight. She'd fallen asleep cradled beneath his arm, head on his chest, her leg across his right. He tried to ease out from beneath her, and she woke and said, "Hmmm?"

"Just trying to rearrange," he said, whispering, catching up with the night. She'd been almost timid. Not passive, but . . . wary.

"Um . . ." She propped herself up, her small breast peeking at him over the top of the blanket. "What time is it?"

Lucas found his travel clock, peered at it. "Ten minutes of three," he said.

"Oh, God." She pushed herself up, her back to him, and the sheet fell off. She had a wonderful back, he decided, smooth, slender, but with nice muscles. He drew a finger down her spine and she arched away from him. "Oooo. Stop that," she said over her shoulder.

"Come lay down," he said.

"Time to go."

"What?"

She turned to look at him, but her eyes were in shadow and he couldn't see them. "I really . . ."

"Bullshit. Come on and sleep with me."

"I really need some *sleep.*"

"So do I. Fuckin' Bekker."

"Forget Bekker for a few hours," she said.

"All right. But lay down."

She dropped back on the bed, beside him. "You're not still with Rothenburg?"

"No."

"It's over?"

"It's weird, is what it is," he said.

"You're not saying the right thing," said Fell. She propped herself up again, and he drew three fingers across the soft skin on the bottom of her breast.

"That's because Lily and I are seriously tangled up," Lucas said. "You know she's sleeping with Kennett."

"I figured. The first time I saw them together, she was dropping him off at Midtown South, and she kissed him good-bye and I had to go inside and put a cool wet rag on my forehead. I mean, hot. But then I saw you two talking to each other, you and Rothenburg, and it looked like unfinished business."

"Nah. But I was there when her marriage came apart and she helped kill off the last of my relationship with a woman I had a kid with. We were kind of . . . pivotal . . . for each other," Lucas said.

"All right," Fell said.

"Lily was driving?"

"What?"

"You said she dropped off Kennett."

"Well, yeah, Kennett can't drive. That'd kill him, the Manhattan traffic would." She sat up again, half turned, and this time he could see her eyes. "Davenport, what the *fuck* are you up to?"

"Jesus . . ." He laughed, and caught her around the waist, and she let him pull her down.

"The one thing I want to know—if you're up to something, you're not screwing me to get it, are you?"

"Barbara . . ." Lucas rolled his eyes.

"All right. You'd lie to me anyway, so why do I ask?" Then she frowned and answered her own question: "I'll tell you why. Because I'm an idiot and I always ask. And the guys always lie to me. Jesus, I need a shrink. A shrink and a cigarette."

"So smoke, I don't mind," Lucas said. "Just don't dribble ashes on my chest."

"Really?" She scratched him on the breastbone.

"I mean, it's killing you, slowly but surely, but if you need one . . ."

"Thanks." She got out of bed—a wonderful back—found her purse, got her cigarettes, an ashtray and the TV remote. "I gotta get some nicotine into my bloodstream," she said. Ingenuously, genuinely, she added, "I didn't have a cigarette because I was afraid my mouth would taste like an ashtray."

"I thought you'd decided not to sleep with me, and changed your mind."

She shook her head. "Dummy," she said. She lit the cigarette and pointed the remote control at the TV, popped it on, thumbed through the channels until she got to the weather. "Hot and more hot," she said, after a minute.

"It's like Los Angeles, 'cept more humid," Lucas said.

"Shoulda been here last year. . . ."

They talked and she smoked, finished the cigarette, and then lit up another and went around the room and stole all his hotel matches. "I never have enough matches. I always steal them," she said. "When I'm working I've got two rules: pee whenever you can, and steal matches. No. Three rules . . ."

"Never eat at a place called Mom's?"

"No, but that's a good one," she said. "Nope: it's never sleep with a goddamn cop. Cops are so goddamn treacherous. . . ."

CHAPTER
16

Sunday morning.

Sunlight poured like milk through the venetian blinds. Fell woke at nine o'clock, stirred, then half-sat, looking down at Lucas' dark head on the pillow. After a moment, she got up and stumbled around, picking up clothes. Lucas opened an eye and said, "Have I mentioned your ass?"

"Several times, and I appreciate all of them," she said. She offered a smile, but weakly. "My head . . . that goddamn cheap wine."

"That wine wasn't cheap." Lucas sat up, still sleepy, dropped his feet to the floor, rubbed the back of his neck. "I'll call Kennett, see if we can figure something out."

She nodded, still groggy. "I gotta go home to change clothes, then back to Bellevue. There'll be people around we wouldn't see during the week."

Lucas said, "This is really important to you, isn't it?"

"It's the biggest case I've ever been on," she said. "God, I'd love to get him. I mean, me, personally."

"You won't get him at Bellevue," Lucas said. "Even if you find Whitechurch's helper, and she talks, I wouldn't be surprised if Bekker's using a pay phone. Then where are you?"

"So if we find the phone, we can stake it out. Or maybe he uses one on the block where he lives, we can look at the apartments."

"Mmm."

"Maybe we'll get him tomorrow night, at the speech."

"Maybe . . . C'mon. I'll make sure you get clean in the shower."

"That's something I've always needed," she said. "Help in the shower."

"Well, you said your head feels weird. What you need is a hot shower and a neck massage. Really. I say this in a spirit of fraternity and sorority."

"Good, I don't think I could handle another sexual impulse," Fell said. But the shower took them back to the bed, and that took them back to the shower, and Fell was leaning against the wall, Lucas standing between her legs, drying her back with a rough terry-cloth towel, when Anderson called from Minneapolis.

"Cornell Reed. United to Atlanta out of La Guardia, transfer to Southeast to Charleston. No return. Paid for by the City of New York."

"No shit . . . Charleston?"

"Charleston."

"I owe you some bucks, Harmon," Lucas said. "I'll get back to you."

"No problem . . ."

Lucas hung up, turning it over in his head.

"What's Charleston?" Fell asked from the bathroom door-way.

"It's both a dance and a city. . . . Sorry, that was a personal call. I was trying to get through to my kid's mother. She's gone to Charleston with the Probe Team."

"Oh." Fell tossed the towel back into the bathroom. "You're still pretty tight with her?"

"No. We're done. Completely. But Sarah's my kid. I call her."

Fell shrugged and grinned. "Just checking the oil level," she said. "Are you going to call Kennett?"

"Yeah."

* * *

They ate a quick breakfast in the hotel coffee shop, then Lucas put Fell in a cab back to her apartment. He called Kennett from his room and got switched from Midtown South to a second phone. Kennett picked it up on the first ring.

"If we don't get him tomorrow, at the speech, I'm heading back to the Twin Cities, see what I can find," Lucas said.

"Good. I think we've got all the routine stuff pinned down here," Kennett said. "Lily's here, and we were about to call you. We're thinking about a boat ride."

"Where's here?" Lucas asked.

"Her place."

"So come and get me," Lucas said.

After talking to Kennett, Lucas sat with his hand on the phone, thinking about it, then picked it up again, dialed the operator, and got the area code for Charleston. He had no idea how big the city was, but had the impression that it was fairly small. If they knew assholes in Charleston the way they knew them in the Twin Cities . . .

The information service got him the phone number for the Charleston police headquarters, and two minutes later, he had the weekend duty officer on the line.

"My name is Lucas Davenport. I'm a cop working out of Midtown South in Manhattan. I'm looking for a guy down your way, and I was wondering about the prospects of finding him."

"What's the problem?" A dry southern drawl, closer to Texan than the mush-mouth of Alabama.

"He saw a guy get shot. He didn't do it, just saw it. I need to talk to him."

"What's his name?"

"Cornell Reed, nickname Red. About twenty-two, twenty-three . . ."

"Black guy." It was barely a question.

"Yeah."

"And you're from Midtown South."

"Yeah."

"Hang on . . ."

Lucas was put on hold, waited for a minute, then two. Always like this with cops. Always. Then a couple of clicks, and the line was live again. "I got Darius Pike on the line, he's one of our detectives. . . . Darius, go ahead . . ."

"Yeah?" Pike's voice was deep, cool. Children were laughing in the background. Lucas identified himself again.

"Am I getting you at home? I'm sorry about that. . . ."

" 'S okay. You're looking for Red Reed?"

"Yeah. He supposedly witnessed a killing up here, and I'm pretty hot to talk to him."

"He came back to town a month ago, the sorry-ass fool. You need to bust him?"

"No, just talk."

"Want to come down, or on the phone?"

"Face-to-face, if I can."

"Give me a call a day ahead. I can put my hands on him about any time."

Now he had to make a decision: Minneapolis, Charleston. Two different cases, two different leads. Which first? He thought about it. He wouldn't be able to get down to Charleston and back in time. The New School trap was the next night; if they didn't get Bekker, then the trip to Minneapolis was critical. Bekker was killing people, after all. Charleston might shed some light on Robin Hood, and Robin Hood was killing people, too— but those were mostly *bad* people, weren't they? He shook his head wryly. It wasn't supposed to matter, was it? But it did.

Lucas made one more call, to Northwest Airlines, and got a seat to Minneapolis–St. Paul, then a triple play, Minneapolis– St. Paul to Charleston to New York. There, that was all he could do for now. It all hinged on tomorrow night.

When Lily called from the front desk, he'd changed to jeans and blue T-shirt. He went down, found her waiting, eyes tired but relaxed. She was wearing jeans and a horizontally striped French fisherman's shirt that might have cost two hundred dollars on Fifth Avenue, and an aqua-colored billed hat.

"You look like a model," he said.

"Maybe I oughta call *Cruising World.*"

"Yeah, you look kinda gay," he said.

"That's a sailboat magazine, you dope," she said, taking a mock swipe at him.

Kennett was waiting in the passenger seat of a double-parked Mazda Navaho, wearing comfortable old khakis and a SoHo Surplus T-shirt.

"Nice truck," Lucas said to Lily as he crawled in back.

"Kennett's. Four-wheel drive must help testosterone production," Lily said, walking around to the driver's side and climbing in. "You've got one, don't you?"

"Not like this: this is sort of a *Manhattan* four-wheel drive," he said, tongue in cheek. To Kennett he said, "I didn't think you could drive."

"Got it before the last attack," Kennett said. "I think the price is what brought the attack on. And don't give me any shit about Manhattan four-by-fours, this is a fuckin' workhorse. . . ."

"Yeah, yeah . . ."

They left Manhattan through the Lincoln Tunnel, emerging in Jersey, took a right and then followed a bewildering zigzag path back to the waterfront. The marina was a modest affair, filling a dent in the riverbank, a few dozen boats separated from a parking lot by a ten-foot chain-link fence topped with razor wire. Most of the boats were in concrete slips, halyards clinking softly against the aluminum masts like a forest of one-note wind chimes; a few more boats were anchored just offshore.

"Look at this guy, putting up his 'chute," Kennett said, climbing down from the truck. Lucas squeezed out behind him as Lily climbed out of the driver's seat. Kennett pointed out toward the river, where two sailboats were tacking side-by-side down the Hudson, running in front of a steady northwest breeze, their sails tight with the wind. A man was standing on the foredeck of one of them, freeing a garish crimson-and-yellow sail. It filled like a parachute, and the boat leapt ahead.

"You ever sailed?" Kennett asked.

"A couple times, on Superior," Lucas said, shading his eyes. "You feel like you're on a runaway locomotive. It's hard to believe they're barely going as fast as a man can jog."

"A man doesn't weigh twenty thousand pounds like that thing," Kennett said, watching the lead boat. "That *is* a locomotive. . . ."

They unloaded a cooler from the back of the truck and Lucas carried it across the parking lot, past a suntanned woman in a string bikini with a string of little girls behind her, like ducklings. The smallest of the kids, a tiny redheaded girl with a sandy butt and bare feet, squealed and danced on the hot tarmac while carrying a pair of flip-flops in her hands.

Lily led the way through a narrow gate in the chain-link fence, Lucas right behind her, Kennett taking it slow, down to the water. Here and there, people were working on their boats, listening to radios as they worked. Most of the radios were tuned to rock stations, but not the same ones, and an aural rock-'n'-roll fest played pleasantly through the marina. Few of the boats actually seemed ready to go out, and the work was slow and social.

"There she blows, so to speak," Kennett said. The *Lestrade* was fat and graceful at the same time, like an overweight ballerina.

"Nice," Lucas said, uncertainly. He knew open fishing boats, but almost nothing about sailboats.

"Island Packet 28—it *is* a nice boat," Kennett said. "I got it instead of kids."

"Not too late for kids," Lucas said. "I just had one myself."

"Wait, wait, wait." Lily laughed. "I should have a say in this."

"Not necessarily," Lucas said. He stepped carefully into the cockpit, balancing the cooler. "The goddamned town is overrun with nubile prospects. Find somebody with a nice set of knockers, you know, not too smart so you wouldn't have to worry about the competition. Maybe with a fetish for housework . . ."

"Fuck the sailing, let's go back into town," Kennett said.

"God, I'm looking forward to this," Lily said. "The flashing wit, the literary talk . . ."

Lily and Lucas rigged the sails, with Kennett impatiently supervising. When he was bringing the sails up, Lucas took a moment to look through the boat: a big berth at the bow, a tidy, efficient galley, a lot of obviously custom-built bookshelves jammed with books. Even a portable phone.

"You could live here," Lucas said to Kennett.

"I do, a lot of the time," Kennett said. "I probably spend a hundred nights a year on the boat. Even when I can't sail it, I just come over here and sit and read and sleep. Sleep like a baby."

Kennett took the boat out on the motor, his fine white hair standing up like a sail, his eyes shaded by dark oval sunglasses. A smile grew on his tanned face as he maneuvered out along the jetty, then swung into the open river. "Jesus, I love it," he said.

"You gotta be careful," Lily said anxiously, watching him.

"Yeah, yeah, this takes two fingers. . . ." To Lucas he said, "Don't have a heart attack—it just unbelievably fucks you up. I can run the engine and steer, but I can't do anything with the sails, or the anchor. I can't go out alone."

"I don't want to talk about it," Lucas said.

"Yeah, fuck it," Kennett agreed.

"What does it feel like?" Lucas asked.

"You weren't gonna talk about it," Lily protested.

"It feels like a pro wrestler is trying to crush your chest. It hurts, but I don't remember that so much. I just remember feeling like I was stuck in a car-crusher and my chest was caving in. And I was sweating, I remember being down on the ground, on the floor, sweating like a sonofabitch. . . ." He said it quietly, calmly enough, but with a measure of hate in his voice, like a man swearing revenge. After another second, he said, "Let's get the sails up."

"Yeah," Lucas said, slightly shaken. "I gotta pull on a rope, right?"

Kennett looked at the sky. "God, if you heard the man, forgive him, the poor fucker's from Minnesota or Missouri or Montana, some dry-ass place like that."

Lucas got the mainsail up. The jib was on a roller, with the lines led back to the cockpit. Lily worked it from there, sometimes on her own, sometimes with prodding from Kennett.

"How long have you been sailing?" Lucas asked her.

"I did it when I was a kid, at summer camp. And then Dick's been teaching me the big boat."

"She learns quick," Kennett said. "She's got a natural sense for the wind."

They slid lazily back and forth across the river, water rushing beneath the bow, wind in their faces. A hatch of flies was coming off the water, their lacy wings delicately floating around them. "Now what?" Lucas asked.

Kennett laughed. "Now we sail up and then we turn around, and sail back."

"That's what I thought," Lucas said. "You're not even trolling anything."

"You're obviously not into the great roundness of the universe," Kennett said. "You need a beer."

Kennett and Lily gave him a sailing lesson, taught him the names of the lines and the wire rigging, pointed out the buoys marking the channel.

"You've got a cabin on a lake, right? Don't you have buoys?"

"On my lake? If I peed off the end of the dock, I'd hit the other side. If we put in a buoy, we wouldn't have room for a boat."

"I thought the great North Woods . . ." Kennett prompted, seriously.

"There's some big water," Lucas admitted. "Superior: Superior'll show you things the Atlantic can't. . . ."

"I *seriously* doubt that," Lily said skeptically.

"Yeah? Well, once every few years it freezes over—and you look out there, a horizon like a knife and it's ice all the way out. You can walk out to the horizon and never get there. . . ."

"All right," she said.

They talked about ice-boating and para-skiing, and always came back to sailing. "I was planning to take a year off and single-hand around the world, maybe . . . unless I got stuck in the Islands," Kennett said. "Maybe I would have got stuck, maybe not. I took Spanish lessons, took some French . . ."

"French?"

"Yeah . . . you run down the Atlantic, see, to the Islands, then across to the Canaries, maybe zip into the Med for a look at the Riviera—that's French—then come back out and down along the African coast to Cape Town, then Australia, then Polynesia. Tahiti: they speak French. Then back up to the Galápagos, Colombia and Panama, and the Islands again . . ."

"Islands—I like the idea," Lucas said.

"You like it?" asked Kennett, seriously.

"Yeah, I do," Lucas said, looking out across the water. His cheekbones and lips were tingling from the sun, and he could feel the muscles relax in his neck and back. "I had a bad time a year ago, a depression. The medical kind. I'm out now, but I never want to do that again. I'd rather . . . run. Like to the Islands. I don't think you'd get depressed in the Islands."

"Exactly what islands are we talking about?" Lily asked.

"I don't know," Kennett said vaguely. "The Windwards, or the Leewards, or some shit . . ."

"What difference would it make?" Lucas asked Lily.

She shrugged: "Don't ask me, they're your islands."

After a moment of silence, Kennett said, "A unipolar depression. Did you hear your guns calling you?"

Lucas, startled, looked at him. "You've had one?"

"Right after the second heart attack," Kennett said. "The second heart attack wasn't so bad. The depression goddamned near killed me."

They turned and started back downriver. Kennett fished in his pocket and pulled out a pack of cigarettes.

"Dick. Throw those fuckin' cigarettes . . ."

"Lily . . . I'm smoking one. Just one. That's all for today."

"God damn it, Dick . . ." Lily looked as though she were going to cry.

"Lily . . . aw, fuck it," Kennett said, and he flipped the pack of Marlboros over the side, where they floated away on the river.

"That's better," Lily said, but tears ran down her cheeks.

"I tried to bum one from Fell the other day, but she wouldn't give it to me," Kennett said.

"Good for her," said Lily, still teary-eyed.

"Look at the city," Lucas said, embarrassed. Kennett and Lily both turned to look at the sunlight breaking over the towers in Midtown. The stone buildings glowed like butter, the modern glass towers flickering like knives.

"What a place," Kennett said. Lily wiped her cheeks with the heels of her hands and tried to smile.

"Can't see the patches from here," Lucas said. "That's what New York is, you know. About a billion patches. Patches on patches. I was walking to Midtown South from the hotel, crossing Broadway there at Thirty-fifth, and there was a pothole, and in the bottom of the pothole was another pothole, but somebody had patched the bottom pothole. Not the big one, just the little one in the bottom."

"Fuckin' rube," Kennett muttered.

They brought the boat back late in the afternoon, their faces flushed with the sun. And after Lucas dropped the mainsail, Lily ran it into the marina with a soft, skillful touch.

"This has been the best day of my month," Kennett said. He looked at Lucas. "I'd like to do it again before you go."

"So would I," Lucas said. "We oughta go down to the Islands sometime. . . ."

Lucas hauled the cooler back to the truck and Lily brought along an armload of bedding that Kennett wanted to wash at home.

"Shame that he can't drive the truck," Lucas said as Lily popped up the back lid.

"He does," she said in a confidential voice. "He tells me he doesn't, but I know goddamn well that he sneaks out at night and drives. A couple of months ago I drove back to his place, and when we parked I noticed that the mileage was something like 1-2-3-4-4, and I was thinking that if I only drove one more mile, I'd have a straight line of numbers: 1-2-3-4-5. When I came over the next day, the mileage was like 1-2-4-1-0, or something like that. So he'd been out driving. I check it now, and lots of times the mileage is up. He doesn't know. . . . I haven't mentioned it, because he gets so pissed. I'm afraid he'll get so pissed he'll have another attack. As long as it has power steering and brakes . . ."

"It'll drive a guy nuts, being penned up," Lucas said. "You oughta stay off his case."

"I try," she said. "But sometimes I just can't help it. Men can be so fucking stupid, it gives me a headache."

They went back to the boat and found Kennett below, digging around. "Hey, Lucas, a little help? I need to pull this marine battery, but it's too heavy for Lily."

"Dick, are you messing around with that wrench again . . . ?" Lily started, but Lucas put an index finger over his lips and she stopped.

"I'll be down," Lucas said.

Ten minutes later, while Kennett and Lily did the last of the buttoning-up, Lucas humped the battery back to the car. In the parking lot, he propped one end of it on the truck bumper while he sorted out the keys, then turned and looked back through the fence. Lily and Kennett were on the dock, Lily leaning into him, his arms around her waist. She was talking to him, then leaned forward and kissed him on the mouth. Lucas felt a pang, but only a small one.

Kennett was okay.

CHAPTER
17

The New School auditorium was compact, with a narrow lobby between the interior auditorium doors and the doors to the street.

"Perfect," Lucas told Fell. They'd taken the tour with a half-dozen other cops, and now, waiting, wandered outside to Twelfth Street. Fell lit a cigarette. "Once he comes around the corner, he'll be inside the net. And the lobby's small enough that we can check everyone coming through before they realize there are cops all over the place."

"You still think he'll show?" Fell asked skeptically.

"Hope so."

"It'd be too easy," she said.

"He's a nut case," Lucas said. "If he's seen the announcement, he'll be here."

A car dropped Kennett at the curb. "Opening night," he said as he climbed out. He looked up and down the fashionable residential street, bikes chained to wrought-iron fences, well-kept brick townhouses climbing up from the street. "It feels like something's gonna happen."

They followed him inside, and Carter came by with radios. They each took one, fitting the earpieces, checking them out.

"Stay off unless it's critical," Carter said. "There are twelve guys here, and if all twelve start yelling at the same time . . ."

"Where do you want me?" Lucas asked.

"Where do you think?" Carter asked. "Ticket booth?"

"Mmm, I'd be looking at too many people's backs," Lucas said. He glanced around. A short hall led from the auditorium lobby to the main entrance lobby of the New School. "How about if I stood back there in the hall?"

"All right," Carter said. To Fell, he said, "We've got you handing out programs. You'll be right there in the lobby."

"Terrific . . ."

"What's the setup?" Kennett asked.

"Well, we're supposed to start in twenty minutes. We've got you just inside the auditorium entrance, where you can see everyone, or get back out to the lobby in a hurry," Carter said. "It's right down here. . . ."

Bekker tottered down Twelfth Street ten minutes before the lecture was scheduled to begin, past a guy working on a car in the failing daylight. Bekker was nervous as a cat, excited, checking the scattering of people walking along the street with him, and toward him, converging on the auditorium. This was dangerous. He could feel it. They'd be talking about him. There might be cops in the crowd. But still: worth it. Worth some risk.

Most of the people were going through a series of theater-style doors farther up the street. That would be the auditorium. There was another door, closer. On impulse he entered there, turned toward the auditorium.

Almost stumbled.

Davenport.

Trap.

The fear almost choked him, and he caught at his throat. Davenport and another man, their backs to Bekker, were in the hallway between the separate entries. Not ten feet away. Watching the crowd come through the other door.

Davenport was to the left, half turned toward the second man, his back directly to Bekker. The second man, half turned toward Davenport, glanced toward Bekker as simple momentum took Bekker inside. Couldn't stop. He went straight through the school lobby, past the entrance to the auditorium. An empty guard desk was to the right, with a phone behind it. Ahead of him, another hallway that seemed to lead back outside.

Bekker unconsciously touched his face, felt the hard scars under the special makeup. That night in the funeral home, Davenport hacking at him . . .

Bekker wrenched himself back, forced himself to walk down the stairs, through the next door, outside. He was sweating, almost gasping for breath.

He found himself in a sculpture garden, facing another door like the one he'd come through. On the other side of the door was a hallway, and beyond that, maybe a hundred feet away, another set of doors and the next street. Nobody ahead. He strode quickly across the courtyard, caught the door, pulled.

Locked. Stricken, he gave it a tug. It didn't budge. The glass was too thick to break, even if he had something to break it with. He turned and looked back, toward the way he'd come. If he tried to get out that way, he'd be face to face with Davenport for several seconds, just as he'd been with the cop Davenport had been talking to.

He stood, frozen, unable to sort the possibilities. He had to get out of sight. He went to his left, found a short hallway with a door marked with a B and the word "Stair." He jerked at the door, hoping . . .

Locked. Damn. He huddled in the doorway, temporarily out of sight. But he couldn't stay: if anybody saw him like this, hiding, they'd know.

Another goddamned Davenport trap, pulling him in . . .

Bekker lost it for a moment, his mind going away, dwindling, imploding. . . . He came back with a gasp, found himself pulling at the door, fighting the door handle.

No. There must be something else. He let go of the door, turned back to the courtyard. He needed help, needed to think.

He groped for his pillbox, found it, gulped a half-dozen crosses. The acrid taste on his tongue helped cool him, get him thinking again.

If they caught him—and if they didn't kill him—they'd put him back inside, they'd pull him off his chemicals. Bekker shuddered, a full-body spasm. Take him off: he couldn't live through that again, he couldn't even think about it.

He thought of the funeral home again. Davenport's face, inches from his, screaming, the words unintelligible, then the pistol coming up, the gunsight coming around like a nail on a club, the nail ripping through his face . . .

Had to think. Had to think.

Had to move. But where? Davenport was right there, watching. Had to get past him. Only half aware of what he was doing, he fetched the pill box and gulped the rest of the speed and a single tab of PCP. Think.

"They gotta start pretty soon," Carter said.

"Give him another five minutes," Davenport said. "Fuck around with the slide projector or something."

"The crowd's gonna be pissed when Yonel makes the announcement."

"Maybe not," said Kennett, who'd gotten tired of waiting in the auditorium. "Maybe they'll get a kick out of it."

"Yonel says he'll do a half-hour on Mengele and Bekker anyway, before he says anything," Lucas said. He stood and stepped to the door: "I'm going to take a quick turn through the crowd. There're not many people coming in."

"Fuck it, he's not coming," Carter said.

"Maybe not, but he should have," Lucas said.

Bekker, desperately exploring the courtyard, followed a short flight of steps into an alcove and found another door. Behind the stage? Would there be cops back there? He took the handle in his hand, pulled . . . and the door moved. He eased it open until just a crack of light was visible and pressed his eye to the opening.

Yes. Backstage. A man was there, wearing slacks and a sport coat, peering out at the audience from a dark corner on the opposite side of the stage. As Bekker watched, he lifted a rectangular object to his face. A radio? Must be. Cop.

Just inside the door, in front of Bekker, was a scarred table, and on the table an empty peanut butter jar, a black telephone and what looked like a collapsible umbrella in a nylon case. Bekker let the door close, turned back toward the steps. A finger of despair touched him: no way out. No way. And they'd be checking the building before they left. He knew that. He had to get out. Or hide.

Wait. A radio? The cop had a *radio.*

Bekker turned, went back to the door, peeked inside again. The cop was still in the corner, peering out from behind the curtain, checking the crowd. And on the table, not an umbrella, but a folding music stand, apparently left behind after a concert.

He flashed on Ray Shaltie, and the blood splashing from his head. . . .

The PCP was coming up now, warming him, bringing him confidence. He needed that radio. He let the door close, took a quick, silent turn around the alcove outside the door, thinking. A paper? He dug in his bag, found an envelope, folded it. Thought again for a moment, but there was no other way: he *would not* be beaten. Bekker took a breath, posed for a moment, then stepped to the door, pulled it open, and stepped inside.

The cop saw him immediately and frowned, took a step toward him. Bekker held up the envelope, and in a whisper, called, "Officer. Officer."

The cop glanced out at the crowd, then started across the stage behind the curtain. Radio in his hand. Bekker took a step forward, touched the music stand. It would be flimsy when opened, but when closed, and wrapped in its plastic sheath, a perfect club.

"You're not . . ." the cop started. Deep voice.

"The man out there . . ." Bekker whispered, and thrust the envelope at the cop, dropping it at the same time. The envelope fell to the cop's feet. Without thinking, the cop bent to catch it.

And Bekker hit him.

Hit him behind the ear with the music stand, swinging it like a hatchet. The impact sounded like a hammer striking an over-ripe cantaloupe, and the cop went down, the radio hitting the floor beside him. There'd been little noise, and that was muffled by the curtains, Bekker thought, but he hooked the man by the collar and dragged him into the corner by the door. And waited. Waited for the call, for the shout, that would end it. Nothing.

The cop couldn't be allowed to talk about how he was ambushed. Bekker stood over him for a moment, waiting, waiting, then pushed open the exterior door, dragged the body through it. The courtyard was still empty. Bekker lifted the music stand and hit the unconscious cop again and again, until the head resembled a bloody bag of rice.

Stop . . . no time. But the eyes . . .

Hurrying now, he used his penknife to cut the eyes, then patted down the body and found an identification card: Francis Sowith. The radio. Shit. The radio was still inside. He went to the door, peeked through, saw the radio, stepped quickly inside and retrieved it.

Back out on the porch again, stepping over the dead man. He noticed he had blood on his hands, and wiped them on the cop's coat. Still sticky: he lifted them to his face and sniffed. The smell of the blood was familiar, comforting.

He looked at the radio. Basic thumb switch. Calmed himself, checked his clothing, straightened it, and walked up the steps to the door back inside.

He took a breath, tensing, opened the door, and walked straight ahead. A staff member, he thought. That's what he was: a teacher who worked here. He heard a voice, a man, from around the corner. He slipped up to the guard desk, where he'd seen the telephone, and stepped around behind the desk, the phone to his ear. He could see the shoulder and sleeve of Davenport's jacket now, if that was in fact Davenport, in the same place. He leaned over the desk, head down, put the radio to his mouth, and thumbed the switch.

"This is Frank," he blurted. "He's here, backstage, back-stage. . . ."

He dropped the radio hand, and pressed the phone receiver to his ear, his shoulder turned away: the body language said *making a date.* At the same time, there was a shout, then another. Davenport's shoulder disappeared from the doorway, but another man came through it, running, right past the desk and down into the courtyard.

Moving quickly, Bekker walked from behind the desk, looking straight ahead, out through the school doors into the street. A woman screamed from the auditorium. Bekker kept walking. The man who'd been working on the car hurried past him, heading toward the doors, a pistol in his hand.

And then the night closed around him. Bekker was gone.

18

They wound up in the courtyard, a half-dozen senior police officers shouting at each other. Lights burned in every room of the building and uniformed cops crawled through it inch by inch, but the people in the courtyard knew the search was pointless.

"Silly motherfucker . . . How many got out? How many?"

"I was trying to save his ass. Where the fuck were your guys, huh? Where the fuck . . ." A square guy pushed a tall guy, and for a moment it looked like a fight; but then other cops got between them.

"Jesus Christ, you gotta go out the back, the fuckin' TV is sweeping the streets. . . ."

"Who had the watch on the stairs? Where was . . ."

"Shut up." Kennett had been sitting on a bench, talking to Lily and O'Dell. Now he shouldered through the ring of cops, his voice cutting through the babble like an icicle going through a sponge cake. "Shut the fuck up."

He stood on the sidewalk, pale, two fingers hovering over his heart. He turned to one of the cops: "How many got out?"

"Listen, it wasn't my . . ."

"I don't give a shit whose fault it was," Kennett snarled. "We all fuckin' blew it. What I want to know is, how many got out?"

"I don't know," the cop said. "Twenty or thirty. When everybody stampeded backstage, a bunch of people in the lobby and near the doors just went outside. Nobody was there to stop them. When I came back . . . most of them were gone."

"There were only about fifty people in the auditorium," Kennett said. "So maybe half of them got out."

"But that's not the thing," the cop said.

"What's the thing?" Kennett asked. His voice was like a hangnail, sharp, ragged, painful.

"The thing is, I looked into every one of those faces. Bekker wasn't there. I don't care if you hang me up by my nuts, you ain't gonna get me to say he was, 'cause he wasn't. He wasn't there."

"He had to be somewhere," Carter snapped.

"Nobody came across the stage. Nobody went out through the courtyard. There was only one other door, and that doesn't go anywhere, it just comes back to the lobby. . . ."

There was a long moment of silence, compounded of anger and fear. Heads would roll for this one. Heads would roll. A couple of cops glanced furtively at O'Dell and Lily, deep in private talk. After a moment, Huerta said, "He must've been here all the time. He must've hid out before we got here, saw that he couldn't get out, figured we'd sweep the place before we left, and nailed Frank to get his radio."

Kennett was nodding. "That couldn't have been Frank who called. . . ."

"Sounded like Frank. . . ."

"So Bekker's got a deep voice, big fuckin' deal. We had people back there in five seconds, and Frank was gone. It took a while to mess him up like that."

"Then why'd he call? Bekker? If he was already gone?" Kuhn asked.

"To get us running back there," Lucas said. "Say he goes back there, nails Frank, takes the radio, goes off through the side door around the corner from the lobby, makes the call, then pushes through the door and goes right through the lobby and out."

"Billy said nobody came through the door," Kuhn said.

A young plainclothes cop with his hands in his pockets shook his head. "I swear to God, I don't see how anybody could've got through there. Lieutenant Carter told me to stay there, and even when Frank called, I stayed there. I saw everybody running . . ."

"But your back was to the door?" Kennett asked.

"Yeah, but I was right *there,*" the young cop said. He could feel the goat horns being fitted for his head.

Kennett turned to Lucas: "You're sure he didn't come past you?"

"I don't see how. It's like this guy said . . ." Lucas pointed at the cop who looked at the faces. "I looked at every goddamn face coming through the door; he just wasn't there."

"All right, so he was inside," Kennett said. "We assume he made the radio call as a diversion to get out. . . ."

"Or to hide," somebody said. "If he had a bolthole during the day . . ."

"We'll find out," Kennett said, peering up at the brightly lighted windows. He glanced sideways at Lucas, who shook his head. Bekker was gone. "The other possibility is that he went out a window somewhere and made the radio call to pull the guys off the street. . . ."

"What if he had keys and was already outside, and was just taunting us?" one of the cops asked.

They talked for twenty minutes before drifting away to specific assignments, or simply drifting away, afraid that their names and faces might become associated with the disaster. In the alcove outside the stage door, a crime-scene crew worked under heavy lights, picking up what they could. But there was no real question: it was Bekker. But Bekker, how?

"Okay, now we're out of cop work: now we're down to politics," Kennett said to Lucas as they stood together in the courtyard.

"You gonna hang?" Lucas asked.

"I could," Kennett nodded. "I gotta start calling people, gotta get some spin on the thing, fuzz it up."

"Gonna be tough, with you right here," Lucas said.

"So what would you do?" Kennett asked.

"Lie," Lucas said.

Kennett was interested. "How?"

"Blame Frank. Unlock the back door," Lucas said, nodding to the opposite side of the courtyard. "Tell them that Bekker hid in the building during the day and that he must've stolen keys from somewhere. That when he came out and got down here, cutting through the courtyard, using his keys—where we only had one man, because we'd secured the place ahead of time—and he ran head-on into Frank. There was a fight, but Bekker's a PCP freak and he killed Frank and escaped back out the other side of the building. If anybody gets blamed, the blame goes on Frank. But nobody'll say anything, because Frank's dead. You could even do a little off-the-record action. *Tell* them that Frank fucked up, but we can't say it publicly. He was a good guy and now he's dead. . . ."

"Hmph." Kennett pulled at his lip. "What about the radio call?"

"Somebody's already suggested that he was taunting us: go with that," Lucas suggested. "That he was already outside. That fits Bekker's character, as far as the media's concerned."

"Do you think . . . ?"

"No, I think he suckered us."

"So do I." Kennett stared at his feet for a moment, then glanced at Lily and O'Dell. "The story might not hold up for long."

"If we get him before it breaks, nobody'll care."

Kennett nodded. "I better go talk to O'Dell. We'll need a ferocious off-the-record media massage."

"You think he'll help?"

Kennett permitted himself a very thin grin. "He was here too," Kennett said. "They'd just pulled up outside . . ."

Kennett started toward Lily and O'Dell, then stopped and turned, hands in his pockets, no longer grinning. "Get your ass back to Minneapolis. Find something for us, God damn it."

CHAPTER

19

Lucas sat alone in the worst row of seats on the plane, in tourist class behind the bulkhead, no good place to put his feet except in the aisle. The stewardess was watching him before they crossed Niagara Falls.

"Are you all right?" she asked finally, touching his shoulder. He'd dropped the seat all the way back, tense, his eyes closed, like a patient waiting for a root canal.

"Are the wheels off the ground?" he grated.

"Uh-oh," she said, fighting a smile. "How about a scotch? Double scotch?"

"Doesn't work," Lucas said. "Unless you've got about nine phenobarbitals to put in it."

"Sorry," she said. Her face was professionally straight, but she was amused. "It's only two more hours. . . ."

"Wonderful . . ."

He could see it so clearly in his mind's eye: ripped chunks of aluminum skin and pieces of engine nacelle scattered around a Canadian cornfield, heads and arms and fingers like bits of trash, fires guttering just out of sight, putting out gouts of oily black smoke; women in stretch pants wandering through the wreckage, picking up money. A Raggedy Ann doll, cut in half, smiling senselessly; all images from movies, he thought. He'd never actually seen a plane crash, but you had to be a complete idiot not to be able to imagine it.

He sat and sweated, sat and sweated, until the stewardess came back and said, "Almost there."

"How long?" he croaked.

"Less than an hour . . ."

"Sweet bleedin' Jesus . . ." He'd been praying that it was only a minute or two; he'd been sure of it.

The plane came in over the grid of orange sodium-vapor lights and blue mercury lights, banking, Lucas holding on to the seat. The window was filled with the streaming cars, the black holes of the lakes stretching down from just west of the Minneapolis Loop. He looked at the floor. Jumped when the wheels came down. Made the mistake of glancing across the empty seat next to him and out the window, and saw the ground coming and closed his eyes again, braced for the impact.

The landing was routine. The bored pilot said the usual goodbyes, the voice of a Tennessee hay-shaker, which he undoubtedly was, not qualified to fly a '52 Chevy much less a jetliner. . . .

Lucas stunk with fear, he thought as he bolted from the plane, carrying his overnight bag. *My God, that ride was the worst.* He'd read that La Guardia was overcrowded, that in a plane you could get cut in half in an instant, right on the ground. And he'd have to do it again in a day or two.

He caught a cab, gave directions, collapsed in the backseat. The driver took his time, loafing along the river, north past the Ford plant. Lucas' house had a light in the window. The timer.

"Nice to get home, huh?" the cabdriver asked, making a notation in a trip log.

"You don't know how good," Lucas said. He thrust a ten at the driver and hopped out. A couple strolled by on the river walk, across the street.

"Hey, Lucas," the man called.

"Hey, Rick, Stephanie." Neighbors: he could see her blond hair, his chrome-rimmed glasses.

"You left your backyard sprinkler on. We turned it off and put the hose behind the garage."

"Thanks . . ."

He picked up the mail inside the door, sorted out the ads and catalogs and dumped them in a wastebasket, showered to get the fear-stink off his body and fell into bed. In thirty seconds, he was gone.

"Lucas?" Quentin Daniel stuck his head out of his office. He had dark circles under his eyes and he'd lost weight. He'd been the Minneapolis chief of police for two terms, but that wasn't what was eating him. Innocent people had died because of Quentin Daniel: Daniel was a criminal, but nobody knew except Daniel and Lucas. Lucas had resolved it in his mind, had forgiven him. Daniel never could. . . . "C'mon in. What happened to your face?"

"Got mugged, more or less . . . I need some help," Lucas said briefly, settling into the visitor's chair. "You know I'm working in New York."

"Yeah, they called me. I told them you were Mr. Wunnerful."

"I need to find the guys who were in the jail cells next to Bekker—or anybody he talked to while he was in there."

"Sounds like you're scraping the bottom of the bucket," Daniel said, playing with a humidor on his desk.

"That's why I'm here," Lucas said. "The cocksucker's dug in, and we can't get him out."

"All right." Daniel picked up his phone, punched a number. "Is Sloan there? Get him down to my office, will you? Thanks."

There was a moment of awkward silence, then Lucas said, "You look like shit."

"I feel like shit," Daniel said. He turned the humidor around, squared it with the edge of the desk.

"Your wife . . . ?"

"Gone. Thought it'd be a lift, seeing her go, but it wasn't. I'd get up every morning and look down at her and wish she was gone, and now I get up and look at the bed and there's a hole in it."

"Want her back?"

"No. But I want something, and I can't have it. I'll tell you one thing, between you and me and the wall—I'm getting out of here. Two months and I hit a crick in the retirement scale. Maybe go up north, get a place on a lake. I've got the bucks."

There was a knock on the door, and Daniel's secretary stuck her head in and said, "Sloan . . ."

Lucas stood up. "I do wish you luck," he said. "I'm serious."

"Thanks, but I'm cursed," Daniel said.

Sloan was lounging in the outer office, a cotton sport coat over a tennis shirt, chinos, walking shoes. He saw Lucas and a grin spread across his thin face.

"Are you back?" he asked, sticking out his hand.

Lucas, laughing: "Just for the day. I gotta find some assholes and I need somebody with a badge."

"You're working in the Big Apple. . . ."

"Yeah. I'll tell you about it, but we gotta go talk to the sheriff."

Three names, a deputy sheriff said. He'd looked at the records, checked with the other guards. They all agreed.

Bekker had been next to Clyde Payton, who was now at Stillwater, doing twenty-four months on a drugstore burglary, third offense. A doper.

"Motherfucker's gonna come out and kill people," the deputy said. "He thought Bekker was like some rock idol, or something. You could see Payton thinking: *Killing people. Far out.*"

Tommy Krey, car theft, had been on the other side. He was still out on bail; Krey's attorney was dragging his feet on the trial. "The car owner's gonna move to California, I hear. Tommy's lawyer's looking for a plea," the deputy said.

Burrell Thomas had been across the aisle, and pled to simple assault, paid a fine. He was gone.

"I know Tommy, but I don't know the other two," Lucas said. Out of touch.

"Payton's from St. Paul, Rice Street. Basically a doper, sells real estate when he's straight," Sloan said. "I don't know Thomas either."

"Burrell's a head case," the deputy said. "They call him Rayon. Y'all know Becky Ann, the cardplayer with the huge hooters, see her down on Lake sometimes?"

"Sure." Lucas nodded.

"She was going with this super-tall black dude. . . ."

"Manny," said Sloan, and Lucas added, "Manfred Johnson."

"Yeah, that's him—he's a friend of Burrell's. Like from high school and maybe even when they were kids . . ."

"How's New York?" Sloan asked. They were in Sloan's unmarked car, poking into the south side of Minneapolis.

"Hot. Like Alabama."

"Mmm. I never been there. I mean New York. I understand it's a dump."

"It's different," Lucas said, watching the beat-up houses slide by. Kids on bikes, rolling through the summer. They'd called Krey's attorney, a guy who worked out of a neighborhood storefront. He could have Krey there in a half-hour, he said.

"How different? I mean, like, Fort Apache?"

"Nah, not that," Lucas said. "The main thing is, there's an infinite number of assholes. You never know where the shit is coming from. You can't get an edge on anything. You can't know about the place. Here, if somebody hijacks a goddamn Best Buy truck and takes off fifty Sonys, we got an idea where they're going. Out there . . . Shit, you could make a list of suspects longer than your dick, and that'd only be the guys that you personally *know* might handle it. And then there are probably a hundred times that many guys that you don't know. I mean, a list longer than *my* dick."

"We're talking long lists here," Sloan said.

"It's strange," said Lucas. "It's like being up at the top of the

IDS Building and looking out a window where you can't see the ground. You get disoriented and you feel like you're falling."

"How 'bout that Bekker, though?" Sloan said enthusiastically. "He's a fuckin' star, and we knew him back when."

Tommy Krey was sitting on a wooden chair in his attorney's office. His attorney wore a yellow-brown double-knit suit and a heavily waxed hairdo the precise shade of the suit. He shook hands with Sloan and Lucas; his hands were damp, and Lucas smothered a grin when he saw Sloan surreptitiously wipe his hand on his pant leg.

"What can Tommy do for yuz?" the lawyer asked, folding his hands on his desk, trying to look bright and businesslike. Krey looked half bored, skeptical, picked his teeth.

"He can tell us what he and Michael Bekker talked about in jail," Lucas said.

"What are the chances of knocking down this car-theft . . ."

"You're gonna have to do that on your own," Lucas said, looking from the lawyer to Krey and back again. "Maybe Sloan goes in and tells the judge you helped on a big case, but there's no guarantees."

The lawyer looked at Krey and lifted his eyebrows. "What d'you think?"

"Yeah, fuck, I don't care," Krey said. He flipped his toothpick at the basket, rimmed it out, and it fell on the carpet. The lawyer frowned at it. "We talked about every fuckin' thing," Krey said. "And I'll tell you what: I been beatin' my brains out ever since he went out to New York, trying to figure out if he gave me, like, any *clues*. And he didn't. All we did was bullshit."

"Nothing about friends in New York, about disguises . . . ?"

"Naw, nothing. I mean, if I knew something, I'd a been downtown trying to deal. I know that his buddy, the guy who did the other kills, was an actor . . . so maybe it is disguises."

"What was he like in there? I mean, was he freaked out . . . ?"

"He cried all the time. He couldn't live without his shit, you know? It hurt him. I thought it was bullshit when I first went in, but it wasn't bullshit. He used to cry for hours, sometimes. He's totally fuckin' nuts, man."

"How about this Clyde Payton? He was in for some kind of dope deal, he was around Bekker."

"Yeah, he came in the day before I made bail. I don't know; I think he was a wacko like Bekker. Square, but wacko, you know? Kind of scary. He was some kind of businessman, and he gets onto the dope. The next thing he knows, he's busting into drugstores trying to steal prescription shit. He mostly sat around and cursed people out while I was there, but sometimes he'd get like a stone. He figured he was going to Stillwater."

"He did," said Sloan.

"Dumb fuck," said Krey.

"How about Burrell Thomas?"

"Now, there's something," Krey said, brightening. "Bekker and Burrell talked a lot. Rayon's one smart nigger."

Burrell's address was a vacant house, the doors pulled down, the floor littered with Zip-Loc plastic bags. They crunched across broken glass up an open stairway, found a burned mattress in one room, nothing in the other, and a bathtub that'd been used as a toilet. Flies swarmed in an open window as Sloan reeled back from the bathroom door.

"We gotta find Manny Johnson," Sloan said.

"He used to work at Dos Auto Glass," Lucas said. "Not a bad guy. I don't think he's got a sheet, but that woman of his . . ."

"Yeah." Manny's girlfriend called herself Rock Hudson. "She took twenty-five grand out of a high-stakes game down at the Loin last month. That's going around."

"She's a piece of work," Lucas agreed.

They found both Manny and Rock at the auto glass. The woman was sitting in a plastic chair with a box full of scratch-off lottery tickets, scratching off the silver with a jacknife blade, dropping the bad ones on the floor.

"Cops," she said, barely looking up when they came in.

"How are you?" Lucas asked. "Doing any good?"

"What d'ya want?"

"We need to talk to Manny," Lucas said. She started to heave herself to her feet, but Lucas put a hand in front of her head. "Go ahead with the tickets. We can get him."

Sloan had moved to the door between the waiting area and the workroom. "He's here," he said to Lucas.

They went back together. Johnson saw them, picked up a rag, wiped his hands. He was at least seven feet tall, Lucas thought. "Manny? We need to talk to you about Burrell Thomas."

"What's he done?" Johnson's voice was deep and roiled, like oil drums rolling off a truck.

"Nothing, far as we know. But he was bunked down at the jail next to Michael Bekker, the nut case."

"Yeah, Rayon told me," the tall man said.

"You know where we can reach him?"

"No, I don't know where he's living, but I could probably find him, tonight, if I walked around the neighborhood for a while. He usually goes down to Hennepin after nine."

"Bekker's chopping people up," Sloan said. "I mean chopping them up. I don't know if Burrell's got trouble with the cops, but if there's any way he could help us . . ."

"What?"

Sloan shrugged, picked up a can of WD-40, turned it in his hand, and shrugged. "We might be able to take a little pressure off, if he has another run-in with the cops. Or if your friend out there, if she . . ."

Johnson looked them over for a minute, then said, "You got a phone number?"

"Yeah," Sloan said. He fished a card out of his pocket. "Call me there."

"Like tonight," Lucas said. "This guy Bekker . . ."

"Yeah, I know," Johnson said. He slipped Sloan's card in his shirt pocket. "I'll call you, one way or another."

The drive to Stillwater cut another hour out of the day; the interview took ten minutes. Payton looked like an ex–college lineman, square, running to fat. He wasn't interested in talking. "What the fuck'd the cops ever do for me? I'm a sick man, and here I am in this cage. You guys can fuck yourselves."

They left him talking to himself, muttering curses at the floor.

"How're you gonna threaten him? Tell him you're gonna put him in jail?" Sloan asked as they walked back through the parking lot.

Lucas glanced back at the penitentiary. It looked like an old Catholic high school, he decided, inside and out, until you heard the steel doors open and shut. Then you knew it couldn't be anything but the joint. . . .

Johnson called Sloan's number a little after six o'clock. Burrell would talk and he'd meet Lucas at Penn's Bar, on Hennepin. Johnson would come down, to introduce them.

"Um, I got some shit to do at home," Sloan said.

"Hey, take off," Lucas said. "And thanks."

They shook hands, and Sloan said, "Don't take no wooden women."

Penn's bar had a sagging wooden floor and a thin mustachioed bartender who poured drinks, washed glasses, ran the cash register and kept one eye on the door. A solitary black hooker leaned on the bar, smoking a cigarette and reading a comic book, ignoring a half-drunk, pale-green daiquiri. The hooker picked up Lucas' eyes for a second, saw something she didn't like, and went back to her comic.

Farther toward the back, four men and two women stood around a coin-op pool table. Layers of cigarette smoke floated around them like the ghosts of autumn leaves. Lucas walked past the bar to the back, past the pool table, past a beat-up pay phone hung in an alcove next to a cigarette machine. He looked in the men's john, came back, walked around the crowd at the pool table. The men wore jeans and vests, with big wallets chained to their belts, and looked at him sideways as he went through. Johnson wasn't there. Neither was anyone who might be Burrell.

"What can I do you for?" the bartender asked, drying his hands on a mustard-stained towel.

"Bottle of Leinie's," Lucas said.

The bartender fished it out of a cooler and dropped it wet on the bar: "Two bucks." And then, tipping his head toward the back, "Looking for someone?"

"Yeah." Lucas paid and sat on a stool. The back-bar mirror ended before it got that far down, and Lucas stared into the fake walnut paneling opposite his stool, hitting on the beer, trying to straighten his schedule out.

If he didn't find Burrell quick, he'd have to stay over a day. Then he'd miss the early flight to Atlanta. Instead of getting into Charleston in the morning, he wouldn't make it until the afternoon and probably wouldn't get out until the next day. Then he'd have to think of an excuse for the New York people.

The hooker rapped on the bar with her knuckles, nodded at the daiquiri, got a new one. She wore a pale-green party dress, almost the color of the drink. She caught his eyes again, let her gaze linger this time. Lucas didn't remember her. He'd known most of the regulars when he was working, but he'd been off the streets for months now. A week is forever, on the streets. A whole new class of thirteen-year-old girls would be giving doorway blow jobs to suburban insurance agents who would later be described in court documents as good fathers. . . .

Lucas was halfway through the beer when Johnson walked in, out of breath, as though he'd been running.

"Jesus, Davenport," he said. "Missed the bus." He looked down the bar at the hooker as Lucas swiveled on the stool.

"Where is he?" Lucas said.

Johnson's face lit up. "What'd you mean, where is he? He's right there."

Lucas looked past the hooker to the back of the bar; all the pool players were white.

"Where?"

Johnson started to laugh, lifted a leg and slapped a thigh. "You sittin' next to him, man."

The hooker looked at Lucas and said, in a voice an octave too low, "Hi, there."

Lucas looked at the hooker for a second, rereading the features, and closed his eyes. Transvestite. In a half-second, it all fell into place. Goddamn Bekker. This was how he got close to the women and the tourist males. As a woman. With the right makeup, at night, with his small, narrow-shouldered body. That was how he got out of the New School. . . .

God damn it.

"Did you tell Bekker how to . . . do this?" Lucas asked, gesturing at the dress. "The dress, the makeup."

"We talked about it," Thomas said. "But he was a sick motherfucker and I didn't like talking to him."

"But when you talked about it . . . was he real interested, or did you just talk?"

Thomas tipped his head back, looked up at the ceiling, remembering. "Well . . . he tried it. A couple of things." He hopped off the bar stool and walked away from Lucas and Johnson, moving his hips, turned and posed. "It ain't that easy to get just the right walk. If you forget halfway through the block, it ruins your whole image."

The bartender, watching, said, "Are you guys gay?"

"Cop," said Lucas. "This is official."

"Forget I asked . . ."

"I won't forget, honey," Thomas said, licking his lower lip.

"You fuckin' . . ."

"Shut up," Lucas snapped, poking a finger at the bartender. He looked back at Thomas. "But did he do it? The walk?"

"Couple times, a few times, I guess. You know, we *did* talk about it, when I think back. Not so much about how good it feels, but how to do it. You know, gettin' the prosthetic bras and like that. He'd make a good-lookin' girl, too, 'cept for the scars."

"You think so?" Lucas asked. "Is that a professional opinion?"

"Don't dick me around, man," Thomas said, flaring.

"I'm not. That's a real question. Would he make a good woman?"

Thomas stared at him for a minute, decided the question was real: "Yeah, he would. He'd be real good at it. 'Cept for the scars."

Lucas hopped off the bar stool, said thanks, and nodded to Johnson: "We owe you. You need something, talk to Sloan."

"That's all?" asked Thomas.

"That's all," Lucas said.

Lucas called Fell from the pay phone at the back of the bar. When she answered, he could hear the television going in the background, a baseball game. "Can you get to Kennett? Right now?"

"Sure."

"Tell him we've figured out how Bekker is doing it," Lucas said. "How he's staying out of sight on the streets, getting out of the New School."

"We have?"

"Yeah. I just talked to his former next-door neighbor at the Hennepin County Jail, name of Rayon Thomas. Nice-looking guy. Good makeup. Great legs. He's wearing a daiquiri-green party dress. He gave Bekker lessons. . . ."

After a moment of silence, she breathed, "Sonofabitch, Bekker's a woman. We're so fuckin' stupid."

"Call Kennett," Lucas said.

"You haven't talked to anyone?" she asked.

"I thought you'd like to break it."

"Thanks, man," Fell said. "I . . . thanks."

CHAPTER

20

Bekker could count the drops, each and every one, as the shower played off his body. The ecstasy did that: two tiny pills. Gave him the power to imagine and count, to multiply outrageous feelings by ineffable emotions and come up with numbers. . . .

He turned in the shower, letting jets of water burn into him. He no longer used the cold water at all, and the stall was choked with heat and steam, his body turning cherry red as the old skin scalded away. And as he turned, his eyes closed, his head tipped back, his hands beneath his chin, his elbows close together, on his belly, he could count all the drops, each and every one. . . .

He stayed in the shower until the water ran cold, then, shivering, blue, annoyed, he leaped out. What time was it? He walked to the end of the room where he'd fitted a black plastic garbage bag over a barred basement window, and peeled back a corner of the plastic. Dark. Midnight. That was good. He needed the night.

Bekker walked back toward the bed, felt the stickiness on the soles of his feet and looked down. He needed to wash the floor. The sight of the dried blood on the floor reminded him of the cut. He looked at his arm, rolled it between his thumb and forefinger. The cut was painful, but the ants were gone.

He caught sight of himself in a wall mirror, his furrowed face. He went into the bathroom and washed his face, grimacing at the sight of the scars. They were in long jagged rows, raised above the soft skin around them. The gunsight cuts had been sewn closed by an emergency-room butcher, instead of a qualified plastic surgeon.

He thought of Davenport, Davenport's teeth, the eyeteeth showing, his eyes, the gun swinging, battering . . .

He sighed, came back, shaken, staring at his face in the mirror. He put the makeup on mechanically, but carefully. Cover Mark to hide the scars, then straight, civilian makeup. Max Factor New Definition. Cover Girl nail polish. Suave styling spritz, to pull his blond hair down to cover his jawline, which was a bit too masculine.

The lipstick was last. Lipstick the color of a prairie rose. Just a touch. He didn't want to be mistaken for a harlot. . . . He made kisses at the mirror, smoothed the lipstick with his tongue, blotted it with toilet paper. Just right.

Satisfied, finally, he went to the chest, picked out underwear, got the prosthetic bra and sat on the bed. He'd shaved his legs the night before, and they were just getting prickly. Bekker was fair-haired, fine-haired: even if he hadn't shaved, his legs wouldn't have been a problem. But he did shave, to capture the feel. Rayon had said that was important, and Bekker understood—or he'd understood at the time. You had to live the part, feel the part. He flashed. A woman hurrying behind him, afraid of the dark parking ramp. Live the part . . .

The panty hose slid smoothly up his leg; he'd discovered the technique of gathering them, slipping them up piece by bit-bit-bit. When the hose were on, he stood and looked at himself in the dressing mirror; he looked like a fencer, he thought, bare chest and tights. He posed, turning sideways. A little full in the front. He reached into the panty hose and arranged his penis, pushing it down and under, tight, pulling the hose up to hold it in place. Posed again. Good.

The bra was next. He disliked it: it was cold and awkward, and cut into the muscles of his shoulders. But it gave him the right look and even the right feel. He snapped it in back, and again checked the mirror. With his soft blond hair, falling naturally now to his shoulders—no more wigs—he *was* a woman. White-church had certainly been convinced. Bekker flashed: the look on Whitechurch's face as the *realization* came to him, and the gun came up . . .

He picked out a medium-blue blouse with a high collar and the remnants of shoulder padding, a conservative, midcalf-length pleated skirt, and dark gym shoes with thick walking soles. With the breast prosthetics and his narrow shoulders, he had the figure of a woman, but his hands and feet might yet give him away.

They were simply too big, too square: he wore size ten men's shoe. But when he wore dark women's gym shoes, the size was not so obvious. As a woman he was taller than average, but not awkwardly so. And people expected blondes to be tall. Hiding his hands was a bigger problem. . . .

When he'd finished dressing, he looked in the mirror. Fine. Excellent. The big shoulder bag was something he might keep dressier shoes in, wearing the gym shoes to walk back and forth to the parking ramp. Yuppie. He added a necklace of synthetic pearls, picked up a bottle of Poison by Christian Dior, dabbed it along his throat, on the inside of his wrists. The perfume was too flowery, and he deliberately used too much. Perfume, Rayon told him, was a feminine, psychological thing. The odor of per-fume alone might subliminally convince, in close quarters. . . .

There. Ready. He touched himself at the pit of his throat, and remembered that he'd seen his late wife do that, touch herself there, a sort of completion. He stepped to the mirror again, to take in the whole ensemble, and spontaneously laughed with the joy of it.

Beauty was back.

Beauty stepped carefully through the weeds to the lean-to garage, careful to not to snag the hose. He left the car lights out, drove it to the gate, looked up and down the street, unlocked the gate, drove through, relocked it behind himself. He sat in the car for a moment, trying to think.

The parking garage at Bellevue was locked in his brain. Bellevue. He reached across the floor to his purse, found the bag, shook out a greenie: PCP. Popped one, two. Folded the bag and dropped it back in the purse, turned left. Careful. Bellevue? The hands on the steering wheel took him there, rolling through the dimly lit streets, precisely, evenly. A woman? Yes. Women were smaller and handled more easily, after they'd been taken. He recalled the struggle with Cortese, wedging the deadweight into the backseat of the Bug.

And women, he thought with sudden clarity and some curiosity, lasted longer. . . .

The guard nodded. He recognized the attractive blonde in the old Volkswagen Bug. She'd been there before. . . .

Bekker took the car to the top floor, which was virtually deserted. A red Volvo sat in a corner and looked like it might have been there for a couple of days. Two other cars were widely spaced. The garage was silent. He got his bag from the passenger-side floor, with the tank of anesthetic and the stun gun.

Bekker flashed: Cortese, the first one. Bekker'd hit him with the stun gun, had ridden him like a . . . No image came for a moment, then a hog. A heavy, midwestern boar, a mean brute. Bekker had ridden him down in the alley behind the Plaza, then used the mask. The power . . .

A car door slammed somewhere else in the garage; a hollow, booming sound. An engine started. Bekker went to the elevator, pushed the down button, waited. A sign on the wall said: "RE-MOVE VALUABLES FROM CAR: Although this ramp is patrolled, even locked cars are easily entered. Remove all valuables."

The first hit of PCP was coming on, controlling, toughening him, giving his brain the edge of craft it needed. He glanced around. No camera. He walked slowly down the stairs past the cashier, around the corner toward the main entrance of the hospital. The sidewalk that led to the entrance was actually built as a ramp, slanting down between the parking ramp and a small hospital park. Bekker walked down the ramp, paused, then went left into the park, sat at a bench under a light.

Outside, the night was warm and humid, the smell of dirty rain and cooling bubble gum. A couple on the street were walking away from him, the man wearing a straw hat; the hat looked like an angel's halo at that distance, a golden-white oval encircling his head.

Then: A main hospital door opened and a woman walked out. Headed toward the ramp, digging in a purse for keys. Bekker got up, started after her. She paused, still digging. Bekker closed. The woman was big, he realized. As he got closer, he saw she was too big. A hundred and eighty or two hundred pounds, he thought. Moving her would be difficult.

He stopped, turned, lifted a foot so he could look at the sole of his left shoe. Watch women, Rayon had told him. Watch what they do. Bekker had seen this, the stop, the check, the look of anger or disgust, depending on whether a heel was broken or she'd simply stepped in something, and then a turn. . . .

He turned, as though he might be going somewhere to fix whatever he was looking at, walked away from the heavy woman, back down into the park. He might be waiting for someone inside, might even be grieving. There were cops around, nobody would bother him. . . .

Shelley Carson was a graduate nurse. She ran an operating suite, took no crap from anyone.

And she was just the right size.

Bite-size, Bekker's brain said when he saw her.

At five-two, she barely reached a hundred pounds when she was fully dressed. Aware of her inviting size, she was careful about the ramp. Tonight she walked out with Michaela Clemson, tall, rangy, blonde and tough; a lifelong tennis player, both a nurse and a surgical tech. They were still in uniform, tired from the day.

"Then you heard what he said? He said 'Pick it up and put it

where I told you to in the first place,' like I was some kind of
child. I am definitely going to complain . . ." Clemson was saying.

Bite-sized Shelley Carson encouraged her: nurses were not less
than doctors, they were members of a different profession. They
should take no shit. "I'd certainly go in. . . ."

"I just can't ignore it this time," the blonde said, building
her courage. "The asshole is a bad surgeon, and if he'd spend
more time working on his surgery and less time trying to pull
rank . . ."

Bekker slid in behind them. They saw him, peripherally, but
neither really looked at him until they started into the ramp
together, and then up the stairs.

"I definitely would," the small one was saying. Her dark hair
was cut close to the head, like a helmet, with little elfin points
over her ears.

"Tomorrow afternoon at three o'clock I'm going to march
in . . ." The blonde looked down at Bekker, then back up at her
friend. Bekker climbed behind them, one hand on the stun gun.

Halfway up, the blonde said, "Tomorrow, I go for it."

"Do it," said the elf. "See you tomorrow."

The blonde broke away, stepping into the main part of the
ramp, peering out. "All clear," she said. The blonde started
toward a Toyota. Bekker and the dark-haired woman continued
up, Bekker's heels rapping on the stairs.

"We have an arrangement," the elf said, looking down at
Bekker. "If one of us has to go out alone, we watch each other."

"Good idea," Bekker squeaked. The voice was the hard part.
Rayon had said it would be. Bekker put a hand to his mouth and
faked a cough, as though his voice might be roughed by a cold,
rather than forty years of testosterone.

"This parking garage, somebody's going to get attacked here
someday," the woman said. "It really isn't safe. . . ."

Bekker nodded and went back to the purse. The elf looked at
him, a puzzled look, something not quite right. But what? She
turned away. Turn away from trouble. Bekker followed her out

at the top floor, heard the Toyota's engine start below. Brought the stun gun out, got the tank ready in the bag. Heard the hiss. Felt the action in his feet . . .

The woman saw him moving. A fraction of a second before he was on her, she took in the violence of his motion and started to turn, her eyes widening in reflex.

Then he had her. One hand over her mouth, the other pressing the stun gun against her neck. She went down, trying to scream, and he rode her, pressing the stun gun home, holding it. . . .

She flapped her arms like the wings of a tethered bird. He dropped the stun gun, groped for the tank, found it, flipped the valve and clapped the mask over her face. He had her now, his hair a bush around his head, his eyes wide, feral, like a jackal over a rabbit, breathing hard, mouth open, saliva gleaming on his teeth.

He heard the sound of the Toyota going down the ramp as the bite-sized woman's struggles weakened and finally stopped. He stood up, listening. Nothing. Then a voice, far away. The little woman was curled at his feet. So sweet, the power . . .

Bekker worked all night. Preparing the specimen—wiring the gag, immobilizing her. Taking her eyelids; he held them in the palms of his hands, marveling; they were so . . . interesting. Fragile. He carried them to a metal tray, where he'd collected the others. The others were drying now, but kept their form, the lashes still shiny and strong . . .

Shelley Carson died just before seven o'clock, as silently as all the rest, the gag wired around her skull, her eyes permanently open. Bekker had crouched over her with the camera as she died, shooting straight into her eyes.

And now he sat in his stainless-steel chair and gazed at the proof of his passion, eight ultraviolet photos that clearly showed something—a radiance, a presence—flowing from Carson as she died. No question, he exulted. No question at all.

Dink.

The intercom bell. It cut through the sense of jubilation, brought him down. Old bitch. Mrs. Lacey got up early, but habitually slumped in front of the television until noon, watching her morning shows.

Dink.

He went to the intercom: "Yes?"

"Come quick," she squawked. "You have to see, you're on the television."

What? Bekker stared at the intercom, then went quickly to the bed, picked up his robe, wrapped himself, put fluffy slippers on his feet. The old lady didn't see very well, didn't hear very well, he could pass . . . and he still had on his makeup. On television? As he passed the dresser he slipped two tabs off the tray, popped them, as brighteners. What could she mean?

The first floor was dark, musty, a thin orangish morning light filtering through the parchmentlike window shades. The second floor was worse, the odor of marijuana hanging in the curtains, a stench of decaying cat shit, the smell of old vegetables and carpet mold. And it was dark, except for the phosphorescent glow of the tube.

Mrs. Lacey was standing, staring at the television, a remote control in her hand. Bekker was there on the screen, all right. One of the photos that had plagued him, had kept him off the street. But in this photo, he was a woman and a blonde. The details were perfect:

". . . credited to Detective Barbara Fell and former Minneapolis detective lieutenant Lucas Davenport, who had been brought to New York as a consultant . . ."

Davenport. Bekker was struck by a sudden dizziness, a wave of nausea. Davenport was coming; Davenport would kill him.

"But . . ." said Mrs. Lacey, looking from the screen to Bekker.

Bekker steadied himself, nodded. "That's right, it is me," he said. He sighed. He hadn't expected the old woman to last this long. He stepped carefully across the carpet to her.

She turned and tried to run, a shuffling struggle against age and infirmity, gargling in terror. Bekker giggled, and the cats, hissing, bounded across the overstuffed furniture to the highest shelves. Bekker caught the old woman at the edge of the parlor.

He put the heel of his left hand against the back of her skull, the cup of his right under her chin.

"But . . ." she said again.

A quick snap. Her spine was like a stick of rotten wood, cracked, and she collapsed. Bekker stared down at her, swaying, the brightener tab coming on.

"It is me," he said again.

CHAPTER

21

Most visitors came through O'Dell's office; when the knock came at Lily's unmarked office door, she looked over the top of her *Wall Street Journal* and frowned.

There was another light knock and she took off her half-moon reading glasses—she hadn't let anyone see them yet —and said, "Yes?"

Kennett stuck his head in. "Got a minute?"

"What're you doing down here?" she asked, folding the paper and putting it aside.

"Talking to you," he said. He stepped inside the door, peeked through a half-open side door into O'Dell's office, and saw an empty desk.

"He's at staff," Lily said. "What's going on?"

"We've papered the town with the female Bekker picture," Kennett said, dropping into her visitor's chair. Small talk. He tried a smile, but it didn't work. "You know Lucas got it, the cross-dressing thing. It wasn't Fell."

"I thought maybe he did," Lily said. "He wants Fell to do well."

"Nice," he said, his voice trailing off. He was looking at her as though he were trying to see inside her head.

"Let's have it," she said finally.

"All right," he said. "What do you know about this Robin Hood shit that O'Dell is peddling?"

Lily was surprised—and a small voice at the back of her head said, that was good, that look of surprise. "What? What's he peddling?"

Kennett looked at her, eyes blinking skeptically, as though he were reevaluating something. Then he said, "He's been putting out shit about Robin Hood, the so-called vigilantes. I've got the feeling that the fickle finger is pointed at my ass."

"Well, Jesus," Lily said.

"Exactly. There aren't any vigilantes. It's all bullshit, this Robin Hood business. But that doesn't mean he can't fuck me up. If they think they've got a problem . . ." He pointed a thumb at the ceiling, meaning the people upstairs, "And they can't find anybody, they might just want to hang somebody anyway, to cover their asses."

"Boy . . ." Lily shook her head. "I've got a pretty good line on what O'Dell's doing, but I don't know anything like that. And I'm not holding out on you, Richard. I'm really not."

"And I'm telling you, he's behind it."

Lily leaned forward. "Give me a few days. I'll find out. Let me ask some questions. If he's doing it, I'll tell you."

"You will?"

"Of course I will."

"All right." He grinned at her. "It's, like, when you're a lieutenant and down, you've got friends and lovers. When you're a captain or above, you've got allies. You're my first ally-lover."

She didn't smile back. She said: "Richard."

The smile died on his face. "Mmm?"

"Before I risk my ass—you're not Robin Hood?"

"No."

"Swear it," she said, looking into his eyes.

"I swear it," he said, without flinching, looking straight back at her. "I don't believe there is such a guy. Robin Hood is a goddamn computer artifact."

"How?"

He shrugged. "Flip a nickel five hundred times. The events are random, but you'll find patterns. Flip it another five hundred times, you'll still find patterns. Different ones. But the pattern doesn't mean anything. Same thing with these computer searches—you can always find patterns if you look at enough numbers. But the pattern's in your head; it's not real. Robin Hood is a figment of O'Dell's little tiny imagination."

Her eyes narrowed: "How'd you find out so much about what he's doing?"

"Hey, I'm in intelligence," he said, mildly insulted by the question. "The word gets around. I thought his little game was pretty harmless until my name started popping up."

She thought about it a minute, then nodded. "All right. Let me do some sneaking around."

CHAPTER

22

Lucas called Darius Pike in Charleston and gave him the plane's arrival time, then met Sloan and Del downtown. They hit a sports bar, talking, remembering. Lucas was long out of the departmental gossip—who was kissing whose ass, who was shagging who. Sloan went home at one o'clock and Lucas and Del wound up in an all-night diner on West Seventh in St. Paul.

"... shit, I said, gettin' married was okay," Del said. "But then she started talking about a kid. She's, like, forty."

"Ain't the end of the world," Lucas said.

"Do I look like *Life with Father*?" Del asked. He spread his arms: he was wearing a jeans jacket with a black sleeveless tank top. An orange and black insignia on the sleeve of the jacket said, *"Harley-Davidson*—Live to Ride, Ride to Live." He had a five-day beard, but his eyes were as relaxed and clear as Lucas had ever seen them.

"You're looking pretty good, actually," Lucas said. "A year ago, man, you were ready for the junk heap."

"Yeah, yeah . . ."

"So why not have a kid?"

"Jesus." Del looked out the window. "I kinda been asking myself that."

Del peeled off at three o'clock and Lucas went home, opened all the windows in the house, and began writing checks to cover the bills that had arrived with the mail. At five, finished with the bills, and tired, he closed and locked all the windows, went back to the bedroom and repacked his overnight bag. He called a cab, had the driver stop at a SuperAmerica all-night store, bought two jelly doughnuts and a cup of coffee, and rode out to the airport.

The plane taxied away from the terminal at six-thirty. The stewardess asked if he wanted juice and eggs.

"I'm gonna try to go to sleep," he said. "Please, please don't wake me up. . . ."

The fear got him as the takeoff run began, the sense of helplessness, the lack of control. He closed his eyes, fists clenched. Got off the ground with body English. Held his breath until the engine noise changed and the climb rate slowed. Cranked back the seat. Tried to sleep. A while later, he didn't know how long, he realized that his mouth tasted like chicken feathers, and his neck hurt. The stewardess was shaking his shoulder: "Could you bring your seat upright, please?"

He opened his eyes, disoriented. "I was sleeping," he groaned.

"Yes," she said in her most neutral voice. "But we're approaching Atlanta, and your seat . . ."

"Atlanta?" He couldn't believe it. He never slept on airplanes. The plane's left wing dipped, and they turned on it, and, looking down, he could see the city of Atlanta, like a gritty gray rug. Ten minutes later, they were down.

The Atlanta airport was straight from *RoboCop,* with feminine machine voices issuing a variety of warnings just below the level of consciousness, and steel escalators dropping into sterile tile hallways. He was glad to get out, though the flight to Charleston was bad. He fought the fear and managed to compose himself by the time the plane was on the ground.

Pike was waiting inside the small terminal, a stolid black man wearing a green cotton jacket over a white shirt and khaki pants. When his jacket moved, Lucas could see a half-dozen ballpoint pens clipped to his shirt pocket and a small revolver on his belt.

"Lucas Davenport," Lucas said, shaking hands.

"I gotta car," Pike said, leading the way. "How's New York?"

"Hotter'n here," Lucas said.

"This is nothin'," Pike said. "You ought to be here in August."

"That's what they say in New York. . . ."

They left the airport at speed. Lucas, disoriented, asked, "Where's the ocean?"

"Straight ahead, but the city's not really on the ocean. It's kind of like . . . Manhattan, actually," Pike said. "There's a river coming in on both sides, and they meet, and that's the harbor, and then you gotta go on out past the Fort to get into the ocean."

"Fort Sumter?"

"That's it," Pike said.

"I'd like to see it sometime. I've been going to battlefields. Tell me about Reed."

Pike whipped past a gray Maxima, took an off-ramp, then turned left at the bottom. The street was cracked, the borders overgrown with weeds and scrub. "Reed is a stupid mother-fucker," he said matter-of-factly. "I get mad talking about it. His old man has lived here all his life, runs a garage and gas station, does the best body work in town, and makes a ton of money. And Red did good in high school. Did good on his tests and got into Columbia University on a scholarship. The silly fuck goes up to New York and starts putting junk up his nose, the cocaine. Hanging out in Harlem, coming back here and talking shit. Then he didn't come back anymore. The word was, he was putting it up his nose full-time."

"Huh. How long's he been back?"

"Few weeks," Pike said. "I feel bad for his folks."

"Is he staying?"

"I don't know. When he first got back, there were a couple of rumbles from Narcotics that he was hanging out with the wrong people. But I haven't heard that lately. Maybe something changed."

Lucas hadn't thought about what Charleston might look like, but as they drove through, he decided it was just right: Old South. Clapboard houses with peeling paint, and weird trees; bushes with plants that had leaves like leather, and spikes. A few palms. A lot of dirt. Hot.

The Reed garage was a gray concrete-block building sitting side by side with a Mobil gas station and convenience store. All but one set of the gas pumps had a car parked next to them, and uniformed attendants moved around cleaning windshields and checking oil. "You come in here, they wipe your windshield, check your oil, put air in your tires. The only place you'll find it," Pike said. "That's why Don Reed makes the money he does."

He killed the engine in the body shop's parking lot and Lucas followed him into the shop office. The office smelled of motor oil, but was neatly kept, with plastic customer chairs facing a round table stacked with magazines. Behind a counter, a large man was hunched over a yellow-screen computer, poking at a keyboard one finger at a time. He looked up when they came in and said, "Hey, Darius."

"Hey, Don. Is Red around?"

Reed straightened up, his smile slipping off his face. "He done somethin'?"

Pike shook his head and Lucas said, "No. I'm from New York. Your son witnessed a shooting. He was a passerby. I just need to talk to him for a couple of minutes."

"You sure?" Reed asked, a hostile tone scratching through. "I got a lawyer . . ."

"Look: You don't know me, so . . . But I'm telling you, with a witness standing here, that all I want to do is talk. There's no warrant, no anything. He's not a suspect."

Reed regarded Lucas coolly, then finally nodded. "All right, come on. He's out back."

Red Reed was coming out of a paint room when they found him, a plastic mask and hat covering his head. When he saw his father and the two cops, he pulled off the protective gear and waited uncertainly by the paint room door. He was tall, too thin, with prominent white teeth.

"Police to talk to you. One from New York," his father said. "I'm gonna listen." Red Reed looked apprehensive, but nodded.

"Can we find a place to sit?" Lucas asked.

The elder Reed nodded: "Nobody in the waiting room. . . ."

Lucas took Bobby Rich's report from his pocket, unfolded it, and led Red Reed through it, confirming it bit by bit.

"White-haired guy," Lucas said. "Thin, fat?"

"Yeah. Skinny, like."

"Dark? Pale? What?"

"Tan. He was, like, tan."

"What was the scene like, when Fred Waites was shot?"

"Well, man, I wasn't right there. I saw the car go by and I thought I saw a gun and I headed the other way. I heard the shooting, saw the car."

"What kind of car?"

"I don't know, man, I wasn't paying attention to that," Reed said. He was looking at his hands. Pike moved impatiently, and Reed's father looked out the door but didn't say anything. Reed's eyes wandered to his father, then back to Lucas.

"What time was it?" Lucas asked.

"I didn't have a watch. . . ."

"I mean, afternoon, evening, night?"

Reed nervously licked his lips, then seemed to pick one: "Evening."

"It was three o'clock in the afternoon, Red," Lucas said. "Bright daylight."

"Man, I was fucked up . . ."

"You don't know what kind of car it was, but you could see inside that the guy was white-haired, skinny and tanned? But you didn't see anything about the other guys? Red . . ." Lucas glanced at Don Reed. "Red, you're lying to us. This is an important case. We think the same guys shot a cop and, before that, a lawyer."

"I don't know nothing about that," Reed said, now avoiding everyone's eyes.

"Okay, I don't think you do. But you're lying to me . . ."

"I'm not lying," Reed said.

Don Reed turned to face his son and in a harsh, cutting voice said, "You remember what I told you? No bullshit, no lies, no dope, no stealing, and we'll try to keep you alive. And you're lying, boy. There never was a time, from when you were a little baby, that you didn't know what kind of car was what—and you see a man and know he's got white hair and a tan, and you don't know what car he was in? Horseshit. You're lying. You stop, now."

Lucas said, "I want to know how much John O'Dell had to do with it."

Reed had been staring miserably at his feet, but now his head popped up.

"You know Mr. O'Dell?"

"Aw, shit," Lucas said. He stood up, walked once around the tiny room, whacked the spherical Lions Club gum machine with the palm of his hand, then pinched the bridge of his nose, closing his eyes. "You're fuckin' working for O'Dell."

"Man . . ." said Reed.

"O'Dell a dope pusher?" Don Reed asked, voice dark, angry.

"No," Lucas said. "He's about the fifth most important cop in New York."

The two Reeds exchanged glances, and Pike asked, "What's going on?"

"A goddamned game, pin the tail on the donkey," Lucas said. "And I'm the jackass."

He said to Reed, "So now I know. I need some detail. Where'd you meet him, how'd you get pulled in on this . . ."

Reed blurted it out. He'd met O'Dell at a Columbia seminar. O'Dell spoke three times, and each time, Reed talked to him after class. Harlem was different than an Irish cop could know, Reed said. The fat cop and skinny southerner argued about life on the streets; went with a few other students and the professor to a coffee shop, talked late. He saw O'Dell again, in the spring, but he was into the dope by then. Busted in a sweep of a crack house, called O'Dell. The arrest disappeared, but he was warned: never again. But there *was* another time. He was arrested twice more for possession, went to court. Then a third time, and this time he had a little too much crack on him. The cops were talking about charging him as a dealer, and he called O'Dell. He got simple possession, and was out again.

Then O'Dell called. Did he know anybody, a crook, with a connection to a cop? To a detective? Well, yes . . .

"Sonofabitch. It was too neat, it had to be," Lucas said.

"What the fuck is going on?" Pike asked again.

"I don't know, man," Lucas said. To Reed, he said, "Don't call O'Dell. You're out of this and you want to stay out. Whatever's going on here, and it's pretty rough, doesn't have anything to do with you. You'd best lay low."

"He's out," Don Reed said, looking at his son.

Reed's head bobbed. "I don't want nothing more to do with New York."

On the way back to the airport, Pike said, "I don't think I'd like New York."

"It's got some low points," Lucas said. He took a card from his pocket diary, scribbled his home phone number on the back of it. "Listen, thanks for the help. If you ever need anything from New York or Minneapolis, call me."

The flight to Atlanta was bad, but on the way to New York, the fear seemed to slip away. Lucas had reached a tolerance level: his fifth flight in three days. He'd never flown that much in his life. More or less relaxed, he found a notepad in his overnight case and doodled on it, working it out.

Bobby Rich hadn't been assigned to work the case because he had the best qualifications—he'd been assigned simply because he knew a guy who knew Red Reed. So that Red Reed could call his friend and insist that the friend pass information to the cops about the shooting of Fred Waites.

Except that Reed hadn't been there at all. The man with white hair and the deep tan was an O'Dell invention. Lucas grinned despite himself. In a crooked way, it was very nice: lots of layers.

He closed his eyes, avoiding the next question: Did Lily know?

At La Guardia he saw a copy of the *Times* with Bekker as a blonde woman. He bought a copy, queued for a cab, got a buck-toothed driver who wanted to talk.

"Bekker, huh?" buck-tooth said, his eyes on the rearview mirror. He could see the picture on the front of the paper as Lucas read the copy inside. "There's a goofball for ya. Dressed up like a woman."

"Yeah."

"This last one, man, took her right out of a parking garage. Girlfriend says Bekker was right there with them, could've took them both."

Lucas folded the paper down and looked at the back of the driver's head. "There's another one? Today?"

"Yeah, this morning. They found her in a parking lot with the wire gag and the cut-off eyelids and the whole works. I say, when they get him, they ought to hang him off a street sign by his nuts. Be an example."

Lucas nodded and said, "Listen, forget about the hotel. Take me to Midtown South."

CHAPTER

23

Carter, Huerta and James were huddled together over a tabloid newspaper in the coordinating office, all three of them with Styrofoam coffee cups in their hands. Lucas looked in and James said, "Kennett's down in the corner office, he wants to see you."

"Have you seen Barbara Fell?" Lucas asked.

"Gone home." There was a rapid-fire exchange of glances among the three cops, a vein of thin amusement. They knew he was sleeping with Fell.

"Anything happening?"

"About a thousand sightings on Bekker, including three good ones," Carter said. "He's driving a Volkswagen Bug. . . ."

"Jesus, that's terrific," Lucas said. "Who saw him? How'd you get the car?"

"Two witnesses last night at the parking ramp. The Carson woman's girlfriend and the cashier. The girlfriend is a sure thing—she even told us he was wearing too much Poison. That's a perfume . . ."

"Yeah."

". . . And the cashier remembers the blonde part, and says she—he—was driving an old Volkswagen. He remembers because it looked like it was in pretty good shape and he wondered if Bekker was an artist or something. He thinks it was dark green or dark blue. We're running it through the License Bureau right now, but the Volkswagen part isn't public yet. If he goes outside now, he's gonna have to go in a car. And we're stopping every Bug in Midtown."

"You said three people. . . ."

"The third's a maybe, but pretty definite. The night clerk in a bookstore down in the Village says he remembers the face very clearly, says it was Bekker. He says he was buying some weird book about torture."

"Huh."

"We're getting close," Carter said. "We'll have him in two or three days, at the outside."

"I hope," Lucas said. "Any returns on that stun-gun business?"

"Three. Nothing."

"Phones?"

"Nope. Goddamn rat's nest."

"Okay . . ."

Lucas started to turn away, and Carter said, "You've seen the papers?"

"With Bekker? Yeah . . ."

"No, that was this morning; the afternoon paper . . ." Huerta picked up the paper they'd been looking at, closed it, and handed it to Lucas. On the cover was a woman's face, eyes staring; before the headlines reached the brain, the terror of the face came through, then the words: *"Kill #8—Bekker Death Pix."*

"This legit?" Lucas asked.

"That's Carson," Carter said grimly. "He sent notes and photos to three newspapers and two TV stations. They're using them."

"Jesus . . ."

From down the hall, he heard a woman's voice.

Lily.

He walked down to the corner, found the room in semidarkness, the door open. He knocked, standing back, and Kennett said, "Yeah?"

Lucas stuck his head in. "Davenport," he said.

"Come on in. We were just talking about you," Kennett said. He was sitting in a visitor's chair in front of a standard-issue metal desk, his feet up. His shirt collar was open, and his bright Polynesian Gauguin tie was draped across a stack of phone books at the front edge of the desk. Lily sat in another chair at the side of the desk, facing him.

"Fuckin' photographs," Lucas said.

"The shit is hitting the fan," Kennett said grimly. "First the New School thing and now the pictures. The mayor had the commissioner on the carpet. You could hear the screaming in Jersey."

Lucas dragged a third chair around, bumped Kennett. "Move your ass over so I can get my feet up."

"And me with a fuckin' bad heart," Kennett mumbled as he moved.

"You told Fell about the transvestite thing," Lily said. She pushed the phone books out of the way, picked up the necktie.

Lucas shrugged, sat down, put his feet up. "We talked it over and decided it was likely."

"That came at a good time. We told everybody that Carson'll probably be the last, that we've pretty much got him pinned down," she said.

"Should have thought of it sooner, the cross-dressing," Kennett said glumly. "The one before was a lesbian, we knew that. We should have seen that she wouldn't let a strange guy get too close, not outside a lesbian bar."

"Hell, you did everything right . . ." Lily began.

Kennett interrupted: "Everything but catch him . . ."

"He's pinned."

"We fuckin' hope," Kennett said.

Lily had been rolling the tie in her fingers, and now she looked down at the bare-breasted Polynesian woman, shook her head and said, "This is the craziest tie."

"Don't knocker it," said Kennett, then slapped his leg and laughed at the pun, while Lily rolled her eyes.

"You were jerking me around, Gauguin and Christian Dior," Lucas said to Kennett. He looked at Lily. "He told me this Gauguin dude was Christian Dior's necktie partner."

Lily laughed again, and Kennett said, "How do you know he wasn't?"

"Looked him up," Lucas said. "He died in 1903. He was associated with the symbolists."

"Now if you knew what a symbolist was, you'd be in fat city," Lily said.

"It was the use of color specifically for its symbolic impact, the emotional and intellectual impact," Lucas said. "Which makes sense. Some holding cells are painted bubble-gum pink for the same reason. The color cools people out."

Kennett, staring, said, "I never fuckin' thought of that."

"Carter tells me you'll have Bekker in three days at the outside," Lucas said.

"That fuckhead. That's the kind of talk that gets us in trouble," Kennett grumbled. "We'll get him soon, but I wouldn't bet on the three days. If he's got food and water, he could hole up."

"Still . . ."

"I figure no more than a week," Kennett said. "He'll break. I just hope I'm still working for the goddamn police department when it happens. I mean, people are *pissed.* These fuckin' pictures, man: the mess at the New School was nothing, compared to this."

"People think cops . . ." Lucas started.

But Lily was shaking her head. "It's not the people, it's the politicians. People understand you can't always catch a guy immediately; most of them do, anyway. But the politicians think *they've* got to do something, so what they do is run around and scream and threaten to fire people."

"Mmmm. A week," Lucas said. "That's a long time, in ward-heeler years."

"Anxious to get home?" Kennett asked.

"Nah. I'm enjoying myself. I want be there for the bust."

"Or the kill," said Kennett.

"Whatever . . ."

Lily pushed herself out of the chair, stretched, and tousled Kennett's hair. "Let's go look at the river," she said.

"Jesus Christ, the woman's indefatigable, and me with this heart," Kennett complained.

Lucas, vaguely embarrassed, stood and drifted toward the door. "See you guys tomorrow. . . ."

A message from Fell was waiting at the hotel: "Call when you get in, until one o'clock." He held the slip in his hand as he rode the elevator to his floor, dropped it on the bedstand, went into the bathroom, doused his face with hot water, and looked up in the mirror, the water trickling down his face.

He'd had a long relationship with a woman, the mother of his daughter, that now, when he looked back, seemed to have been based on a shared cynicism. Jennifer was a reporter, with too much time on the street, edging toward burnout. A baby, for her, had been a run at salvation.

He'd had a shorter, intense relationship with Lily, who had been struggling with the end of her own marriage; that might have been something, if they'd been in the same town, from the same emotional places. But they hadn't been, and some of the guilt of their affair still stuck to their relationship.

He'd had any number of other relationships, long and short, happy and unhappy. Most of the women he'd gone with still liked him well enough, in a wary, once-burned way; but he tended to think of them as *others,* not Jennifer, not Lily.

Fell was one of the others. A wistful, lovely, finally lonely woman. In a permanent relationship, they would drive each other crazy. He wiped his face with one of the rough hotel towels and wandered back to the bed. He sat down, picked up the phone, looked at the receiver for a moment, then smiled. He'd felt for a year as though he were under water: quiet, placid, out of it. The New York cops were bringing him up, and Fell was fixing him in other ways. He tapped out her number. She picked it up on the second ring.

"This is Lucas," he said.

"Kennett knew it was you, but I got good mileage out of the cross-dressing thing," Fell said, without preamble. "My name was on the TV news, and it's in the *Times* and the *Post*. That never hurts."

"I saw it. . . ."

"I'd like to find a way to thank you. Oral sex comes to mind, if I get my share," Fell said.

"Women are so *forward* these days," Lucas said. "How quick can you get here?"

Fell brought a change of clothes with her, and they spent the evening laughing and making love. The next morning, when they were dressed, Lucas asked, "How would we find Jackie Smith?"

"Call his office," she said.

"That easy?"

"He's a hustler," Fell said. "Getting found is part of his business."

"So call him."

Smith called back in five minutes. "Aren't you guys ever going away? Can't you find out anything on your own?" he complained. "I've done everything you wanted. . . ."

"All we want to do is talk," Lucas said.

"I gave you what you wanted," Smith said again. He was angry.

"Jackie . . . ten minutes, please? Have breakfast with us or something. We'll buy."

Smith would meet them at a café outside the St. Moritz hotel, he said. They caught a cab, struggling north through the midmorning traffic, the driver with his arm out the window, whistling. The day would be hot again; already the sky was showing a whitish haze, and when they got out of the cab across from Central Park, Lucas could see the leaves on the park trees were curling their leaves against the heat.

Smith was sitting at a metal table, eating a cream cheese croissant and drinking coffee. He didn't get up when they arrived.

"Now what?" he asked, a sullen look on his face.

"We wanted to thank you—those names you gave us started
a chain reaction. We've maybe got the asshole pinned down."

"No shit?" Smith looked surprised. "When'll you get him?"

"Some of the guys are betting a couple-three days. Nobody
gives him more than a week," Lucas said. "But we do have
something we need from you. All the small-time fences who buy
from the junkies—they need to tell the dopers that Bekker'll be
out looking for angel dust, ecstasy, speed. Maybe acid. And he'll
kill. The guy we got to, with your help, was boosting stuff out of
Bellevue, but he was also dealing dope. Bekker killed him. Cold
blood. Walked up and *bam.* Killed him."

"I saw that on TV. I wondered . . ."

"That was him," said Lucas.

Smith nodded. "Okay. No skin off my butt. I'll tell everybody
I know and ask them to pass the word."

"He's probably around the Village, but could be anywhere
between the civic center and Central Park. That's about all we
know. That's where the word's got to be," Lucas said.

"That's my territory," Smith said. "Is that all?"

Lucas glanced at Fell, then said, "No. I gotta ask you something else. You might not want to talk about it with another
witness here." He tipped his head at Fell. "But if you don't mind
if she stayed . . ."

Fell frowned at him, and Smith said, "What's the deal?"

"Back when I first got here, I banged up your place. Tried to
get your attention . . ."

"Well, that worked," Smith said ruefully.

"Yeah. A couple of days later, I got the snot beat out of me
when I was coming out of a friend's place. I need to know if that
was you. Off the record. If it was, it's no problem, I swear it."

Smith dropped his croissant on the plate and laughed. "Jesus
Christ, it wasn't me. I read about it, though—but it wasn't me."

"Yeah?"

"Yeah. And if you don't mind me saying so, you're the kind of guy that shit happens to, getting beat up," Smith said.

Lucas looked at Fell. "Could you hike down to the end of the block for a minute?"

"I don't know," she said, studying him.

"C'mon," Lucas said.

"Are you Internal Affairs?"

"Fuck no, I told you," Lucas said impatiently. "C'mon, take a hike."

Fell pushed back her chair, picked up her purse and stalked away.

"She's pissed," Smith said, looking from Fell to Lucas and back to Fell. "Are you screwing her?"

Lucas ignored the question: "There's a big-dog shoot-out going on. Inside the department. And I'm tangled up in it. Now. The people who jumped me might be one set of those big dogs. That's why I really need to know."

"Listen . . ."

"Just a minute," Lucas said, putting up a hand. "I want to put it to you as simple as I can. If you tell me no, it wasn't you, and I find out that it was, I'll come back and hurt you. All right? I really will, because I've gotta know the truth of this. Not knowing the truth could get me killed. On the other hand, if you say yes, it was you, there's no problem. I'll take the lumps."

Smith shook his head in disbelief, a half-smile fixed on his face. "The answer is still no. I didn't do it. I wasn't even particularly happy to see the story in the paper, because I thought you might come back on me."

Lucas nodded, and Smith spread his hands, lifted his shoulders: "I'm a businessman. I don't want any shit. I don't want any muscle around. I hate people with guns. Everybody's got a fuckin' gun." He stared off across Sixth Avenue, the traffic waiting for the light at Central Park South, then looked back at Lucas. "No. Wasn't me."

"All right," Lucas said. "So get the word out to the junkies on Bekker. You might also point out that there's a twenty-five-thousand-dollar crime-stoppers award for his capture."

Lucas turned away from Smith and walked down the street to Fell. "I wish I could read lips," she said. "I'd give a lot to know what you just told him."

"I told him why I wanted to know if those were his guys who came after me," Lucas said.

"Tell me," she said.

"No. And I'm not Internal Affairs."

They spent the day walking through the Village and SoHo, drifting in and out of shops, talking to Fell's contacts on the street, chatting with uniform cops in Washington Square, watching the street action on Broadway. They found the bookstore where Bekker had been spotted, a long, narrow shop with a narrow front window and a weathered, paint-peeled door three steps up. A sign in the door said "Open All Night, 365 Nights a Year."

The clerk who had talked to Bekker wasn't working, but happened by on his bike a few seconds after they asked for him. A thin man with a goatee and a book of poetry, he looked like a latter-day Beat, his face animated as he told them about the encounter.

"He's a good-looking woman, I'll tell you that," the clerk said. "But you can look at somebody and know what kind of book they're going to buy, and I never picked her—him—out for the one he found. Torture and shit. I thought maybe he was, like, an NYU professor or something, and that's why he bought it. . . ."

Down the sidewalk, Fell said, "I think he's real."

"So do I," said Lucas. "He saw him." He looked up at the red-brick buildings around him, with their iron stoops and window boxes full of petunias. "And he's somewhere close, Bekker is. He didn't drive any distance to get to a small bookstore. I can smell the sonofabitch."

He took her to the restaurant where Petty had been killed, sat and had Cokes, and almost told her about it.

"Not too bad a place," he said, looking around.

"It's all right," she said.

"You ever been here? Your regular precinct is around here, right?"

"Ten blocks," Fell said, poking a straw in her Coke. "Too far. Besides, this is sort of a sit-down place, not the kind of place you come to for lunch if you're a cop."

"Yeah, I know what you mean."

Late in the afternoon, while Fell browsed a magazine rack, Lucas stopped at a pay phone, dropped a quarter, and got Lily in O'Dell's car.

"Where are you?"

"Morningside Heights."

"Where's that?"

"Up by Columbia."

"I need to see you. Tonight. By yourself. Won't take too long."

"All right. How about nine, at my place?"

"Good."

When he hung up, Fell looked up from a copy of *Country Home* and said, "So. Are you up for dinner?"

"I'm talking to Lily tonight," he said. "I'd like to come around later, though."

"I hate to see you hanging around with that woman," Fell said, dropping the magazine back on the rack.

"This is purely business," Lucas said. "And look, could you stop by Midtown and pick up those file summaries? We've been floating around all day, listening to bullshit . . . maybe something'll come out of the files."

"All right. I'll haul them over to my place. . . ."

Lily was sitting in a living room chair, her high heels in the middle of the carpet, her bare feet up on a hassock. The hassock was covered with a brocaded throw that seemed to Lucas to be vaguely Russian, or Old World. She was sipping a Diet Coke, tired smudges under her eyes.

"Sit down. You sounded tense," she said. "What happened?" Her head was back, her dark hair a perfect frame around her pale oval face.

"Nothing happened, not today, anyway. I just need to talk to you," he said. He perched on the edge of her other overstuffed chair. "I need to know about you and Walter Petty—your relationship."

She leaned farther back in the chair, wiggled once to settle in, laid her head back, and closed her eyes. "Can I ask why you need to know?"

"Not yet."

She opened her eyes and looked at him carefully and said, "Robin Hood?"

"I'm not sure. What about Petty?"

"Walt and I went back as far as you can go," Lily said, her eyes unfocusing. "We were born on the same block in Brooklyn, sort of middle-class brownstones. I was exactly one month older, to the day. June first and July first. His mother and mine were friends, so I suppose I first laid eyes on him when I was five or six weeks old. We grew up together. Went to kindergarten together. We were both in the smart group. Someplace along the way, sixth or seventh grade, he got interested in math and science and ham radio in that geeky way boys do, and I got interested in social things. After that we didn't talk so much."

"Still friends, though . . ."

She nodded. "Sure. I'd talk to him when I saw him around the block, but not at school. He was in love with me for most of his life. And I guess I loved him, you know, but not sexually. Like a handicapped brother, or something."

"Handicapped?"

She carefully set the glass on the table and said, "Yeah, he was socially handicapped. Walked around with a slide rule on his belt, his table manners went from bad to worse, he got weird around girls. You know the type. Sort of ineffectual, nonphysical. Really nice, though. Eager . . . too eager."

"Yeah. A dork. A nerd. The kind of kid that gets shredded by girls."

"Yes. Exactly. The kind that gets shredded," she said. "But we were friends. . . . And whenever I needed something done—you know, get an apartment painted, or help fixing something—I could call him up and he'd drop everything and be there. I took him for granted. He was always there, and I assumed he always would be."

"Why'd he become a cop?"

" 'Cause he could. It was a job you could get with a test and with family connections. He was brilliant on tests and had the connections."

"Was he a good cop?"

"He was terrible in uniform," she said. "He didn't have that . . . that . . . cold spot. Or hot spot. Or whatever it is. He couldn't get on top of people—you ought to know about that."

"Yeah." Lucas grinned. "I don't know if it's hot or cold, though. Anyway, Petty . . ."

"So he was terrible on the street and they moved him inside. He was working guard details and so on. Then they tried him on dope. And Jesus, he was something else. I mean nobody, *nobody* would believe he was a cop. He'd make a buy and the backup would drop on the dealer, and they still wouldn't believe it. This *dork* couldn't be an undercover cop. Sometimes even the judges didn't believe it. Anyway, that's about the first job he ever did really well at; he was a bit of an actor. Then he got interested in investigation, in crime-scene processing. He was good at that, too. The best. He'd go into a crime scene and he'd see *everything.* And he could put it together, too. Then computers came along, and he was great with computers." She laughed, remembering. "Suddenly, the guy who fucked up everything, the nerd as big as the moon, was a hot item. And he was still good old Walt. When you needed your apartment painted, there he was. He had this great open smile, completely . . . geeky, but honest. When he looked happy to see you, he was happy to see you; he'd just light up. And if he got angry, he'd go off and start yelling, and then he'd maybe start crying or something; or you thought he would. . . ."

Lily's lip was trembling, and she dropped her feet off the hassock and dropped her head.

"How'd he get the job looking for Robin Hood?"

"He knew computers and he'd worked with O'Dell, and we swung it for him. He could help us, and it was a chance for him to break out. And maybe I had something to do with it—he'd be working with me. Like I said . . ."

"Yeah. I know exactly what you mean."

"Sounds like arrogance, or vanity."

Lucas shook his head. "Not really. Just life . . . You think he got close to Robin Hood?"

"He must have. Jesus, when he was killed, I couldn't stop crying for a week. I really . . . I don't know. There was no sexual impulse at all, but when I thought of him over all those years, that puppy-dog quality, that he loved me . . . It was like . . . I don't know. I loved him. That's what it came to."

"Huh." He was watching her, his elbow on the arm of the chair, one finger at his chin.

"So what's this all about?" she asked. The weariness had slipped from her voice, and she looked up, intent.

"You and O'Dell are running me as some kind of lure," Lucas said. "You're dragging me out in front of whoever your targets are. I need to know who you think they are."

After a long moment of silence, she said, "Fell. As far as I know, that's it."

"Bullshit."

"It's not bullshit," she said. "She's all we've got."

"That can't be right."

"It is."

"You know everything that O'Dell is doing?"

"Well, yes, I mean I schedule for him . . . I suppose he could run something on the side. . . ."

There was another moment of silence, then Lucas said, "I'm afraid you're betraying me."

She was offended, angry. "God damn it."

"I know you are—or somebody is. O'Dell for sure, and you're with O'Dell. . . ."

"Tell me about it," she said, sitting back again.

Lucas looked her over and said, "First of all, Fell's not involved."

"Why not?"

"I just know, and I'm not wrong," Lucas said.

"Lucas, instincts or no instincts, the goddamn records aren't lying about this," Lily said. "She's all over the place."

"I know. She's an alarm."

"What?"

"She's a trip wire," Lucas said. "Working the jobs she has, in Burglary, and as a decoy, she knows half the assholes in Midtown. So Robin Hood used her as a reference and picked on assholes that she knew. Then they watched her. If anybody got close, they'd get close to her first. . . ."

"I don't know." Lily was shaking her head. She didn't believe it.

"It'd have to be a tough sonofabitch to set that up," Lucas continued. "As soon as you pulled her off her regular job and put me next to her, the alarm went off. Petty's been killed, the official investigation seems to be dead in the water—and here comes Lily Rothenburg and the department's Svengali, towing me along behind. And you stick me next to Fell. They never bought the Bekker thing: they've been reading us like a book."

"Who?"

Lucas hesitated. "I'm tempted to say Kennett."

"Bullshit." Lily shook her head. "I'd know. In fact, I asked him. He doesn't even think there is such a group."

"But we know there is. And I'm still tempted to say Kennett.

O'Dell put me right up against Fell and he put me right up against Kennett. It's possible that O'Dell *knows* it's Kennett, but doesn't have the proof."

Lily thought it over, staring at him. "That's . . ."

"Bizarre. I agree. And of course, there're other possibilities, too."

"That it's me?" She smiled a small and frosty smile.

"Yeah." Lucas nodded. "That's one of them."

"And what do you think?"

He shook his head. "It's not you, so . . ."

"How do you know it's not me?" she asked.

"Same way I know it's not Fell—I've seen you operate."

"Thanks for that," Lily said.

"Yeah . . . which brings us to the last possibility."

"O'Dell?"

"O'Dell. He has access to everything he needs to organize the group. He knows everybody on the force, and he probably could pick out likely candidates for his hit teams. He has the computer files to pick out the assholes, and to set up Fell as an alarm. . . ."

"There's a hole," Lily said quickly. "He's so high up he wouldn't need an alarm. . . ."

"Internal Affairs—he might not know about Internal Affairs investigations."

She bit her lip. "Okay. Go ahead."

"Since Petty was a computer maven too, maybe computers led him to O'Dell. Whatever it was, for whatever reason Petty got hit, O'Dell was right there to manage the investigation. Kept it out of Internal Affairs . . ."

"Said it was too political," Lily said thoughtfully.

"Yeah. Then he pulls me into it, produces Fell, and he puts me up against Kennett. And you know what? Fell and Kennett are all I've got—all that paper you gave me, the regular investigation, the reports. It's all bullshit. It's all a stone wall. It looks impressive, but there's nothing in it."

"Why would O'Dell pick on Kennett?"

"Because Kennett's going to die," Lucas said bluntly. "Suppose he gets everything pointed at Kennett, and then Kennett . . . dies. Natural causes, a heart attack. If there was an agreement that Kennett was it, the investigation would die and the real organizer would be clear."

Lily, pale as notebook paper: "He couldn't have . . . I don't think."

"Why not?"

"I don't think . . . I don't think he's brave enough. Physically. He'd be thinking about prison."

"That all depends on how he's set it up. Maybe his shooters don't know him."

"Yeah, but remember—if O'Dell is it, he wouldn't have to give you Fell. If Fell's an alarm, I mean, he'd know what you were here for."

"Yeah. And he'd know that Fell would get me exactly where she has: nowhere. And at the same time, lend a touch of truth to the whole business. Fell did know all those dead guys. Besides, with Petty talking to both of you, and Fell popping out of the computer, there was no way to get her back inside. . . ."

"Maybe," she said.

"How'd you meet Kennett?" Lucas asked abruptly.

"In the intraconference meetings."

"As O'Dell's assistant?"

"Yes."

"Did O'Dell feed you to him?" Lucas asked.

"Jesus, Lucas," she said.

"Did he? I mean, he knows both of you. Could he have figured . . ."

"I don't know. They don't like each other, you know." Lily stood and turned in place, like a dog trying to make a bed more comfortable. "You know, you've put this whole tissue together without a single goddamned fact. . . ."

"I've got one interesting, surprising, generally unknown fact," he said; and it was his turn to produce a wintry smile.

"What?"

"I know that O'Dell's trying to frame Kennett. I know *that* for sure. The question is, is he doing it because Kennett's guilty and it's the only way to get him? Or because he's looking for a scapegoat?"

"Bullshit," she said, but he could see the shock in her eyes.

"I found Red Reed in Charleston, South Carolina," he said. "He's a friend of O'Dell's, from Columbia. . . ."

And then he told her most of the rest of it, except for the curious thing Mrs. Logan had said, when they interviewed her in the apartment below Petty's.

CHAPTER
24

Lily listened as Lucas called Fell, watched his face, watched him smiling, turning away, setting up a date. Lucas left, hurrying, and she stood at the window with her purse, watching him. He flagged a cab, and just before he got in, looked up and saw, pointed at her purse, waved.

Then he was gone.

She walked through the apartment, touching things, with the sense of something ending, with a sense of dread.

Kennett? No. But O'Dell was unthinkable too. Could O'Dell have coldly executed his own man . . .

Finally, she picked up the phone and punched in the number for Kennett's boat. He picked it up and said, "Lily."

Pleased, she said, "How'd you know it was me?"

"I think it might be love," he said. "Are you feeling lonely?"

"You're reading my mind."

"The river's beautiful tonight. . . ."

The river was quiet, smelling of mud and oil and salt. Halyard hardware tinkled against the aluminum masts. A late-night squall was rolling off the coast far to the northeast, and they could see the lightning in the sky far beyond the lights of Manhattan.

As Lily and Kennett made love, she had a moment of absolute clarity, could hear the Crash Test Dummies' song "Superman" roll mournfully out of a nearby boat, muted by the ten thousand unidentifiable cheeps and knocks of the marina.

Later, in the cockpit . . .

"Jesus, I'm sitting here bullshitting and you're sitting there crying," Kennett said quietly. He reached across and thumbed a tear off her cheek. "What's all this about?"

"I was just looking across the river, thinking how pretty it was, how good it feels. Then I thought about Walt, about how he'd never see it again."

"Petty?"

"Yeah. God damn it."

"The guy has a strange hold on you, m'dear," Kennett said, trying to keep his voice light: an invitation to talk.

"You know why?" she asked, taking up the invitation.

"Why?"

"Because we were so goddamn mean to him, that's why. Us girls, in school. Lucas got me thinking about it. . . ."

"It's hard to see you as mean," Kennett said.

"I didn't think about it at the time. The thing about Walt was, he'd do anything for you. He was always so *eager.* And when we were in school—and even after that, on the force—we paid him back by laughing about the way he dressed, and the way he acted, and all those pens he used to carry around. We made him be a clown and he wasn't a clown; but whenever he tried to be serious, we wouldn't let him. We hurt him. That's what I was thinking about, the times I know we hurt him—girls, in high school—that hurt look on his face when he'd try to do something, try an approach and we'd laugh in his face. He never really understood. . . . Oh, God."

Suddenly, she was sobbing and Kennett patted her on the back, helplessly. "Jesus, Lily . . ."

A moment later she said, her voice clearing, "You're a Catholic. Do you believe in visions? You know, like the Virgin Mary and all of that, talking to shepherds?"

"I'd want to see it myself," Kennett said wryly.

"The thing is, I keep seeing Petty. . . ." She laughed, a short, sad laugh, and poked him. "No, no, no, I don't see him floating around my room, I see him in my mind. . . ."

"Whew."

"But the thing is, it's so clear. Walt running down the street, and his hair plastered down and his ears sticking out . . . Jesus Christ. Walt was the only guy who ever loved me and didn't want anything from me. No sex, no kids, no favors, just me being there and he was happy."

Kennett found nothing to say, and they sat there, their feet up, watching the dark river. After a while, Lily began to cry again.

CHAPTER

25

Lucas called Fell from Lily's, apologizing for the late hour.

"I was going down to the tavern," she said. "Why don't you meet me. . . ."

He flagged a cab, Lily watching from her window, smiling down at him. He waved, and she lifted her purse in her left hand, slipped her right inside the gun tote. *Remember the last time?*

At the tavern, Lucas pulled a twenty out of his Muskies Inc. money clip and tipped the driver two dollars for the eight-dollar ride. Fell was in the back booth, a beer on the table with a bowl of peanuts. She was reading a free newspaper.

"Hey," he said, slipping into the booth.

"Hi. Any developments at Rothenburg's?"

"No . . ."

"Good," she said.

Lucas shook his head. "Jesus." And then: "I gotta get a beer." He waved at a waitress, pointed at Fell's glass and gave her a victory/two sign. While they waited, a swarthy man in a light-blue sport coat and khaki slacks, a glass of dark beer in his hand, wandered up to the table and said to Fell in a bad imitation Bogart, "Howdy, shweet-heart. Sheen your name in the public prints."

"Hey, Tommy. Sit down." Fell patted the seat beside her, then pointed her trigger finger at Lucas. "That's Lucas Davenport, who's a cop."

"I know who he is," Kantor said, dropping into the booth. "But somehow I got left off the invitation list for the Welcome to New York interviews."

"And Lucas," Fell continued, "this is Tommy Kantor, who's a columnist for the *Village Voice. . . ."*

They talked about the case for a while, and Kantor attracted the attention of a free-lance magazine writer and his girlfriend. They pulled up a chair and ordered a pitcher of beer. Then a TV producer stopped by and began talking to Fell.

"You'd make a good piece," she told Fell.

"I'd certainly agree with that," Lucas said, straight-faced.

"Fuckin' Davenport . . ." Fell said.

They got back to Fell's apartment at two o'clock, spent ten soapy minutes in the shower, dropped into her bed.

"That was fun, talking to those people," Lucas said. "As long as your friend Kantor doesn't get us in trouble."

"He takes care of sources," Fell said. "It'll be okay. I'm surprised you get along so well with media people. . . ."

"I like them, mostly," he said. "Some are a little stupid and half of them would kill for two dollars, but the good ones I like."

"You like *this?"* she asked.

"Ooo, I think I do," he said. Then: "I'm sure of it."

He came out of the shower the next morning, rubbing his hair dry with a terry-cloth towel, and heard Fell's voice from the living room. She came down the hall to the bedroom as he was pulling on his underwear. She was still naked and stood on her tiptoes to kiss him.

"I just talked to Carter. Not a thing, nada."

"All right. Did you bring those files?"

"In the front room, on the floor," she said.

"I'd like to sit around and read for a while, then maybe go back and change clothes. I don't know, I'd like to be there when they get him. . . ."

"Bullshit. You'd give your left nut to get him yourself. So would I."

"You'd give my left nut?" he asked, appalled.

"Well . . . you want a bagel with chive cream cheese and some juice?"

"Yeah, as a matter of fact."

They read the files and talked, and sometime after one o'clock Lucas chased her back into the bedroom, and they didn't make it back out until two.

"I'm going back to the hotel to change," he said, pulling on his jacket. "Why don't we get together at Midtown. Like four-thirty, for the daily roundup."

"All right . . ."

He looked at the floor by his feet, at a Xerox copy of the crime-scene photograph of Whitechurch, dead in the hospital. The few pitiful twenties stuck out from under his body like a comment on greed.

"Change oxen in midstream and you'll come to a bad end," he said.

"What?"

"An old English proverb my mom used to tell me," Lucas said.

"Bullshit," she said.

"You're calling my mom a liar?"

"Get out of here, Davenport. See you at four-thirty."

He took the elevator to the lobby, nodded at a guard who knew a one-night stand when he saw one, spotted a cab pulling up to the curb to drop a passenger, stopped and slapped his coat pocket where his wallet was.

"Dammit," he said.

"Huh?" The guard looked up from his desk.

"Sorry. Not you . . . I forgot something upstairs."

He went back up, knocked on the door. Fell, wrapped in a robe, let him in. "You got twenty bucks you can loan me?" he asked. "I got like two dollars left after last night. All the traveler's checks are at the hotel."

"Oh, jeez . . ." She went to her purse, opened it, took out a billfold. "I've got six bucks," she announced. Then she brightened and dug further. "And a cash card. There's a machine down the block. I'll trust you with my code and change it when you skip on me."

He looked at the cash card, looked down past it to the floor, at the Xerox of Whitechurch, the twenties under his body. The money, the money. Bekker.

"Get dressed," Lucas snapped. "Hurry the fuck up."

Three twenty-dollar bills had been found around and under Whitechurch's body. They drew the money from the evidence locker, under the watchful eye of the custodian.

"Consecutive?" Fell whispered. She was excited, barely controlled.

Lucas scanned the numbers, rearranged the bills on the countertop. "Two of them," he said. He took the numbers down on a notepad. "Let's go talk to the feds."

Terrell Scopes of the Federal Reserve had a procedure for everything, including the dispensing of information about serial numbers. "I can't just have people come in here . . ." He waved, a wave that seemed to suggest that they didn't quite meet a standard. Lucas was rumpled. Fell's hair was beginning to go haywire, standing around her head in a halo.

"If we take several hours to get the data and Bekker cuts the heart out of somebody, your picture'll be on the front page of the *New York Times* right along with his," Fell snarled, leaning across his desk.

Scopes, naturally pale, went a shade paler. "Just a minute," he said. "I'll have to make some inquiries."

After a while he came back and said, "Citibank . . ."

Citibank was more cooperative, but the process was a long one. "The money came out of a machine on Prince, all right, but exactly when, or where it went, that'll take a while to figure out," said a round-faced banker named Alice Buonocare.

"We need it in a hurry," said Lucas.

"We're running it as fast as we can," Buonocare said cheerfully. "There's a lot of subtraction to do—we have to go back to a known number and then start working through the returns, and there's a lot of stuff we have to do by hand. We're not set up for this kind of sorting . . . and there are something like twenty thousand items. . . ."

"How about the pictures?"

"They're not really very good," Buonocare confessed. "If all you know is that he's got blond hair, there are probably a thousand blondes on the tape. . . . It'd be easier to do the numbers, then confirm with the pictures."

"All right," Lucas said. "How long?"

"I don't know: an hour, or maybe two. Of course, that's almost quitting time."

"Hey . . ." Lucas, ready to get angry.

"Just kidding," Buonocare said, winking at Fell.

Three hours. A mistake was found halfway through the first run, a question of which numbers went where, and another machine on Houston Street.

"All right," one of the computer operators said at six o'clock. "Give us another twenty minutes and we'll have it down to one person. If you want to look right now, I can give you a group of eight or ten and it's ninety percent that he's in that group."

"How about the photos?"

"We'll get the tape up now."

"Let's see the ten accounts," Buonocare said.

The programmer's fingers danced across the keyboard and an account came up on the green screen. Then another, and another and more. Ten altogether, six men, four women. Two accounts, one man, one woman, showed non-Manhattan addresses, and they eliminated them.

"Can we get account activity on the other eight? For the last two months?" Buonocare asked over the shoulder of the computer operator.

"No problemo," he said. He rattled through some keys, and the first account came up.

"Looks routine . . ." Buonocare said after a minute. "Get the next one."

"Better find it in a hurry," Fell said. "I'm about to pee my pants."

Edith Lacey's account was the fifth one they looked at. "Oh-oh," Buonocare said. To the computer operator: "Get the rest of this up, go back as far as you can."

"No problemo . . ."

When the full account came up, Buonocare reached past the computer operator and pressed a series of keys, then paged down through an extensive account listing. After a moment, she ran it back to the top and turned to Lucas and Fell.

"Look at this: she started with a balance of $100,000 six weeks ago, and then started pulling out the max on her bankcard, five hundred a day, just about every day for a while. Even now, it's three or four times a week."

"That could be him," Lucas said, nodding, excited. "Let's get a picture up. You've got a name and address?"

"Edith Lacey . . ."

"In SoHo. That's good, that's right," Fell said, tapping the screen.

"How about the video . . . ?"

"Let's get the reference numbers on those withdrawals . . ." Buonocare said. She wrote the number on a scratch pad and they carried it to the storage. The right cassette was already in the machine, and Buonocare ran it through, looking at the numbers. . . .

"Here," she said.

The screen showed a blonde, her face down.

"Can't tell," Fell said. "I swear to God, I'm gonna pee my pants."

"Let's try another withdrawal in that sequence," Buonocare said.

She ran the tape, stopped, started, searched. Found another blonde.

"Motherfucker," Lucas said, looking at the screen. "Nice to see you again, Mike."

"That's him?" Fell asked, peering at the screen. "He's so pretty."

"That's him," Lucas said.

Bekker was smiling at the lens, his blond hair pulled demurely away from his forehead.

CHAPTER

26

Bekker awoke at noon. He wandered about the apartment, went to the bathroom, and stared at himself. Pretty. Pretty blonde. Too late for pretty blonde.

He cried, sitting on the edge of the tub, but he had to do it. He shaved his head. Hacked his fine silken hair to stubble with a pair of orange-handled scissors from Mrs. Lacey's sewing box, lathered it with shampoo, scraped off the stubble with a safety razor. Cut himself twice, the blood pink in the lather . . .

Sigh.

He found himself in front of the mirror, dried soap around his ears, hair. Gone. The tears came again, in a rush. His head was far too small, and sickly white, like a marble. Where was Beauty?

He examined himself with the eye of an overseer, the Simon Legree of inspections. Bald. Pale. No good. Even in the Village, the scalp pallor would attract the eye, and the facial makeup would be obvious.

The scars—the scars would give him away. He touched his face, felt the furrowed, marbled flesh. A new role, that's what he needed. He'd thought to cut his hair, shift back to a male role, but that wouldn't work. Besides, women were allowed a greater latitude of disguise. He'd go back to the wigs he'd worn before his own hair grew out.

Bekker strode through the apartment, headed for the stairs, stopped to touch the cloud of spiders that hung over his desk in the outer apartment. So fine, so pretty . . .

Go. Get the wig, get dressed—he hadn't bothered to dress. Clothes seemed inconvenient and restrictive. He marched now, directed by the PCP, upright and dignified, then he was suddenly aware of his penis, bobbling along like an inconveniently large and flaccid nose, doing a color commentary on his dignity. Bekker pressed his penis to his thigh, but the rhythm of the march was broken. . . .

A new gumball dropped. From when? The fifties? A comedian on *The Ed Sullivan Show*? Yes. A small man looking into a cigar box, talking to a voice inside . . . *Okay? Okay.* Was that the line? Yes.

Bekker, passing the kitchen, swerved, went in. Opened the refrigerator and peeked inside: Have a Coke, Mr. Bekker. Thank you. I will. *Okay? Okay.* He slammed the refrigerator door like the comedian and howled with laughter. *Okay? Okay.*

Really funny . . . He howled. . . .

Coke in hand, he staggered back to the television, turned to CNN, and watched for a few minutes. He'd been on one of the news shows in the morning, with the pictures of the Carson woman; they'd ridiculed him, said the halos from Carson had been finger-press points on the photo paper. What did that mean? Was that methodology? He had a hard time remembering anymore. . . .

He watched, hoping to see the report again, but they'd cut him out of the news cycle.

He went downstairs, naked and barefoot, stepped carefully through the shambles of the first-floor shop, and down into the basement. Found the dark wig, with the pixie cut. Carried it back up, to the bathroom, put it on. It was warm on his head, like a fur piece, and scratchy. But it looked good. He'd have to do something about his eyebrows, shade them, and his lashes. Maybe something to tone his face . . .

Mrs. Lacey had been too old for sophisticated makeup, had been satisfied with a pinkish mascara to make two little pink spots on her cheeks, like Ronald Reagan's. But she had an eyebrow pencil. He found the pencil, came back to the mirror, wet it with his tongue and began feathering it through the lashes. A new face began to form in the mirror. . . .

He ventured out at five-thirty, tentative, wary, the day still bright, and turned toward Washington Square. He was unused to the sunlight, and squinted against it, his speed-hyped vision dazzled by the color and intensity. He carried his handbag and an old newsprint drawing pad he had found in one of Mrs. Lacey's cupboards.

Not much foot traffic, not north and south. He stayed on the shadier side of the narrower streets, head down. Dark hair, dark eyebrows, dark blouse, jeans, gym shoes. A little dykey. A little too tough for a woman. An attitude.

During his early reconnaissance of the city, he'd seen some action around the square. Dealers drifting through. Baggies and cash. He felt the plastic box in his jeans pocket, the tabs rattling inside. Six left, six between himself and . . . He couldn't think about it. He had five thousand in cash in his purse, and the pistol, just in case.

He needed some luck.

Oliveo Diaz had ten hits of ex and another ten of speed, and maybe a couple of hours to sell it. Party that night; he could use the cash to pick up some coke for himself. Coke was a mellower high than the speed. With enough speed, Oliveo felt that he could go anywhere. With cocaine, he'd already arrived.

Oliveo crossed the south side of the square, saw Bekker sitting on a concrete retaining wall, sketching. Looked nice, from a distance, with the inky black hair, like maybe a PR. Closer, and he thought, maybe Irish, black Irish with the pale skin.

Bekker paid no attention to him, his face down in the sketch pad, a pencil busy in his hand. But watching . . .

"Hey, Oliveo, doood . . ."

Oliveo turned, flashed the automatic smile. Some guy named Shell. Young white guy with a battered forehead, hazy blue eyes and a Mets hat with the bill turned backward. Oliveo had a theory that a guy's intelligence could be determined by how far around his head the bill was turned. Backward was a complete fool, unless he was a baseball catcher. Shell's hat was backward, and he said again, "Hey, doood," and he lifted a hand for a cool five.

"Shell, my man, what's happenin' . . . ?" Oliveo said. Shell worked in a tire-recap place, had cash sometimes.

"You servin'?" A quick look left and right.

"Man, what you need?" The smile clickin' on again. Oliveo thought of himself as a pro, a street Mick Jagger, smile every ten seconds, part of the act.

"Gotta get up, man . . ."

"I got ten hits of really smooth shit straight from Miami, man. . . ."

Bekker sat on the wall and drew the fire hydrant; drew it well, he thought. He'd learned drawing techniques in medical school, found them useful as a pathologist. They made structure clear, simple. He struggled to keep the drawing going as he watched Oliveo chatting with the white kid, watched them circle each other, checking for cops, and finally a flash of plastic.

Bekker looked around. There *were* cops in the square, but on the other side, near the arch. Three blue Plymouths parked side by side, the cops sitting on the hoods or leaning on the fenders, talking. Bekker picked up his purse and, as the white guy peeled away from Oliveo, sauntered over.

"Servin'?" he squeaked.

Oliveo jumped. The woman with the art pad, her head down. He couldn't see her face very well, but he knew he'd never dealt to her. She was wrong, something wrong. A cop?

"Get the fuck off me, man," he said.

"I've got a lot of cash," Bekker said, still squeaking. He sounded like a mouse in his own ears. "And I'm desperate. I'm not a cop. . . ."

The word "cash" stopped Oliveo. He *knew* he should walk away. He knew it, had told himself, don't sell to no strangers. But he said, "How much?"

"A lot. I'm looking for speed or angels or both. . . ."

"Fuckin' cop . . ."

"Not a cop . . ." Bekker glanced up the street, over at the cop cars, then put his hand in the bag and lifted out an envelope full of cash. "I can pay. Right here."

Oliveo looked around, licked his lips, then said, "What you look like, mama?" He reached out, grabbed Bekker under the chin and tried to lift his face. Bekker grabbed his arm at the wrist and twisted. There was muscle there, testosterone muscle. As he pushed Oliveo away, his head came up, his teeth bared, eyes wide.

"Motherfucker . . ." Oliveo said, backing away, sputtering. "You're that dude."

Bekker turned away, started across the street, half running, mind twisting, searching for help, for an answer, for anything.

Behind him, Oliveo had turned toward the cop cars across the square. "Hey," he screamed. He looked from the cops to Bekker, then at the cops again, then dashed toward them, yelling, waving his arms. "Hey, hey, that's him, that's him. . . ."

Bekker ran. He could run in the gym shoes, but there were a lot of cops, and if they came quickly enough, and if they asked about a woman running . . .

A bum stood at the mouth of an alley, picking through a garbage can. He wore a crumbled hat and a stained army coat, ankle length.

A half-brick sat on the sidewalk, a remnant of concrete lapped over it like frosting on a piece of carrot cake.

It was a narrow street, the closest people a block away, not looking.

Bekker snatched the brick off the street, still running. The bum looked up, straightened, leaned away, astonished when Bekker hit him squarely in the chest. The bum pitched over the garbage can and went down into the alley, on his back. "Hey," he groaned.

Bekker hit him between the eyes with the brick, then hit him again. Hovered over him, growling like a pit bull, feeling his blood rising . . .

A siren, and another.

He stripped the hat and trench coat from the bum, pulled the trench coat over the purse, stripped off the wig, pulled the hat down low on his head. The bum blew a bubble of blood. Still alive. Bekker lurched back to the mouth of the alley, trying on the new persona, the mask of beggary. . . .

Behind him, a gargling sound. He half turned; the bum was looking at him, one good eye peering brightly out of a ruined face. The bum was dying. Bekker recognized the gargle. Something cold, distant and academic spoke into his mind: cerebral hemorrhage, massive parietal fracture. And that eye, looking at him. The bum would die, and then he'd be back, watching. . . . Bekker looked both ways, then hurried back to the bum. Pocketknife out, quick jabs; eyes gone. The bum moaned, but he was going anyway.

The brick was by the bum's head, and Bekker picked it up and jammed it in his pocket. Good weapon. A gun was too noisy. But he groped for the gun inside the bag and transferred it to the pocket.

Into the street. Six blocks. He saw a cop car go by, screech to a stop at the intersection, the cops looking both ways out the windows, then go on. The coat stunk: dried urine. The smell clogged his throat, and he imagined fleas crawling onto him. More sirens, cops flooding the neighborhood. Bekker hurried . . .

Turned onto Greene, tottering, a drunk, his shabby coat dragging on the pavement. A woman coming. Closer, same side. Bekker changed to the other side of the street. His vision wavered, changed tenses: Approaching Lacey building. Sirens in the distance, but fading. Woman goes to Lacey building door . . .

What . . .

The panic gripped him for a moment. Confused. What did she want? Blank-faced buildings looking down. Gumball drops. Red one, loading anger. They would do this to him, a man of talent. The woman was half turned toward him, head cocked.

A distant voice, in the back of his head: Bridget. Bridget Land. Come to visit . . .

He straightened, walked back across the street, away from her, and she put a key in the front-door lock and turned it, pushing the door open. Bridget Land, he'd forgotten about her. . . . She must not know.

She pushed the door open, her shoulders rounded, aged, straining with the effort, then stepped up and inside. Bekker, caught by anger and opportunity, began moving. There was no space or time, it seemed, and he hit the door, smashed inside, and hit her.

He was fast, angel-dust fast, quicker than a linebacker, smacking her with the brick full in the face. She went down with a strange, harsh croak, like a wing-shot raven.

Bekker, indiscreet, beyond caring, slammed the door, grabbed her by the hair and dragged her to the stairs, and down.

He forgot the bum's clothes, and paid no attention to the woman, yipping like a chihuahua with a bone in its throat. He dragged her to the room, strapped her down. Her legs started to work now, twitching. He wired the silencer into her mouth, working like a dervish, hovering. . . .

27

Buonocare, the banker, ran the photo tape through two more withdrawals. Bekker posed in all three, a startling feminine beauty coming through despite the rough quality of the tape.

"Jesus, I wish I looked that good," Buonocare said. "I wonder who does his hair."

"Gotta call Kennett," Fell said, reaching across the desk to pick up a phone.

"No." Lucas looked into her eyes, shook his head. "No."

"We've gotta . . ."

"Talk to me outside," Lucas said, voice low.

"What?"

"Outside." Lucas looked at Buonocare and said, "There's a security thing here, I'm sorry I can't tell you. . . ."

Fell got her purse, Lucas his coat, and they half ran to the door. "Will I see it on the news?" Buonocare asked as she escorted them past a security guard to the front door.

"You'll probably be *on* the news, if this is him," Fell said as the guard let them out.

"Good luck, then. And see you on TV," Buonocare said. "I wish I could come . . ."

Outside, it had begun to rain, a warm, nasty mist. Lucas waved at a taxi, but it rolled by. Another ignored him.

Fell grabbed his elbow and said urgently, "What're you doing, Lucas? We've gotta call now. . . ."

"No."

"Look: I want to be there too, but we don't have time. With this traffic . . ."

"What? Fifteen minutes? Fuck it, I want him," Lucas said.

"Lucas . . ." she wailed.

A cab pulled to the curb and Lucas hurried over, three seconds ahead of a woman who sprinted from a door farther up the street. He hopped in, leaving the door open. Fell was behind him, still in the street. "Get in."

"We gotta call . . ."

"There's more going on here than you know about," Lucas said. "I'm *not* Internal Affairs, but there's more going on."

Fell looked at him for a long beat, then said, "I knew it," and climbed in the cab. As the cab pulled away, the woman who'd run for it, back in the doorway, gave them the finger.

They inched silently uptown through the nightmare traffic, the rain growing heavier. Fell was tight-lipped, agitated. The cab dropped them on Houston, Lucas paid. A squad car rolled by, the cops looking carefully at Lucas before going on. They dodged into a convenience store, damp from the misty summer rain.

"All right," said Fell, fists on her hips. "Let's have it."

"I don't know what's going to happen, but it could be weird," he said. "I'm trying to catch Robin Hood. That's why they brought me here, from Minneapolis."

Her mouth dropped open. "Are you nuts?"

"No. You can either come along or you can take a hike, but I don't want you fuckin' this up," Lucas said.

"Well, I'll come," she said. "But Robin Hood? Tell me."

"Some other time. I gotta make a call of my own. . . ."

Lily was with O'Dell, just coming off the Brooklyn Bridge into Manhattan, ten minutes from Police Plaza.

"Have you heard?" she asked.

"What?"

"Bekker was spotted at Washington Square, but took off. This was around three o'clock. We've got people all over the place, but nothing since. . . ."

"That sounds right, because I think we know where he is. Fell and me. And it's up in SoHo."

"What?" And he heard her say, "Lucas says he's got Bekker."

O'Dell's voice replaced Lily's. "Where are you?"

"We're at Citibank and we're stuck here. I think Bekker's holed up with an old lady in SoHo, but I'm not sure. I'm going up there to take a quick informal look around before I call in the troops. I just wanted Lily to know, in case something misfires. . . ."

"Besides, if you called now and you're stuck downtown, Kennett would get all the credit for the bust," O'Dell said with his wet chuckle. "Is there any possibility that what you've done, whatever it is, has tipped off Bekker?"

"No. But it'll take us a while to get up there; it's raining here, and cabs are impossible."

"Yeah, it's raining here, too. . . . Okay, go ahead. But take care. Just in case there's a problem, why don't you give me the address, and I'll get Lily to start a search warrant. That'll help explain the delay, why you didn't call it in."

"All right . . ." Lucas gave him the address, and Lily came on the line. "Careful," she said. "After your . . . look around . . . give us a ring. We'll have the backup waiting."

Lucas hung up, and Fell asked, "All right—what's going on?"

"We're gonna surveil for a while. . . ."

"Surveil what?" Another cop car rolled by, and again they got the look.

"This Lacey woman's building, for a start. Bekker knows me, I don't want to go right up front . . ."

"I know where we can get a hat," Fell said. "And it's on the way. . . ."

* * *

They dodged from doorway to canopy, staying out of the rain as much as they could. Fell finally led Lucas into a clothing store that apparently hadn't changed either stock or customers since '69. Every male customer other than Lucas was bearded, and three of the four women customers wore tie-dye. Lucas bought an ill-fitting leather porkpie hat. In the mirror, he looked like a hippie designer's idea of an Amazon explorer.

"Quit grumbling, you'd look cute in the right light," Fell said, hurrying him along.

"I look like an asshole," Lucas said. "In any light."

"What can I tell you?" she said. "You ain't posing for *Esquire.*"

The rain had slowed further, but the streets were wet and slick, stinking of two centuries of grime emulsified by the quick shower. They found Lacey's building, cruised it front and back. The back wall was windowless brick. A weathered shed, or lean-to, folded against the lower wall. The gate in the chain-link fence had been recently opened, and car tracks cut through the low spotty weeds to the shed.

Lucas walked to the edge of the lot, where he had the sharpest angle on the shed. "Look at this," he said.

Fell peered through the fence. The back end of a rounded chrome bumper was just visible inside the shed. "Sonofabitch, it's a Bug," she breathed. She grabbed his arm. "Lucas, we gotta call."

"Lily and O'Dell are taking care of it," he said.

"I mean Kennett. He's our supervisor. Christ, we're cutting out the boss. . . ."

"Soon," Lucas promised. "I want to sit and watch for a few more minutes."

They walked around front, and Lucas picked out a store a hundred feet up the street from Lacey's, on the opposite side, an African rug-and-artifact gallery. The owner was a deep-breasted Lebanese woman in a black turtlenecked silk dress. She nodded, nervous, and said, "Of course," when they showed their badges.

She brought chairs and they sat at an angle to the window, among draperies and wicker bookcases, watching the street.

"What if he goes out the back?" asked Fell.

"He won't. There're cops all over the place. He's holed up."

"Then what are we waiting for?"

"For some guys. Robin Hood and his merry men. If nothing happens in a half-hour, we go in. . . ."

"Would you like some cookies?" the Lebanese store owner asked, a touch of anxiety in her voice. She was twisting her hands, and looked, Lucas thought, remarkably like the wicked-witch stepmother in *Snow White,* if he had his Disney movies right. "Baklava, maybe . . . ?"

"No, thanks, really," Lucas said. "We're fine. We might want to use your phone."

"Yes, surely . . ." The woman gestured at a black telephone next to the cash register and retired to the rear of the shop, where she perched on a high stool and continued to rub her hands.

"Eat her goddamn baklava and your nuts'd probably wind up sealed in a bottle with a genie," Lucas muttered.

Fell glanced back and said, "Shh," but smiled and shook her head. "Fuckin' midwestern white guys, it must be something out there, wall-to-wall Wasps. . . ."

"Look," Lucas said.

Two men in sport coats and slacks were walking up the street, not looking at Lacey's building. One was beefy, the other rail-thin. Their sport coats were too heavy for a New York summer, the kind of coat called "year-round" by the department stores, too hot in summer, not warm enough in winter. The beefy one walked stiffly, as though something were wrong with his back; the thin one showed a cast on his left arm.

"Cops," Fell said. She stood up. "They look like cops."

"The sonofabitch with the cast is the guy who whacked me, I think," Lucas said. Fell took a step toward the door, but Lucas caught her by the arm and said, "Wait, wait, wait . . ." and backed toward the counter and picked up the phone, still watching the two cops. They passed Lacey's building, strolling, talking too animatedly, phony, walked on until they were in front of the next building, then stopped.

Lucas punched Lily's office number into the telephone. She picked it up on the second ring. "I'm at Lacey's place. . . ."

"How'd you get . . . ?"

"I lied. And the Robin Hoods just walked in, we're watching them across the street. So it's O'Dell. . . ."

"Can't be. He hasn't touched a phone."

"What?"

"I'm with him now. In his office."

"Shit . . ."

Across the street, the Robin Hoods had turned and had started back toward Lacey's. One drew a pistol while the other dropped a long-handled sledge from beneath his jacket.

"Get me backup . . ." Lucas said. "Jesus—they're going in. Get me backup *now.*"

Lucas dropped the phone back on the hook. "Let's go," he said. "Get on my arm, really drag on it, like we had a few too many."

They went out the door and Lucas, hat tipped down, wrapped an arm around Fell's shoulder and put his face close to hers. The two cops paused just before they passed the windows in front of Lacey's, looked around one more time, saw Lucas and Fell fifty feet away. Lucas pushed Fell into a building front with one hip, groped at a breast with his free hand. She pushed him away, and the two cops went to the door.

They were running now.

The cop with the hammer stopped, pivoted, swinging his hip like a golfer. Backswing and drive, the hammer flashing overhead.

The hammerhead hit the door just at the handle and it exploded inward, glass breaking, wood splintering.

The cop with the gun and the cast went through; the other dropped the hammer and drew his pistol. Then he went in, crouched, focused, straight ahead.

"Go," said Lucas. His .45 was in his hand, and he was at the door in three seconds. Through the door. The two cops were inside, their pistols pointing up an open stairway, and Lucas dropped in the doorway, screaming, "Police, freeze."

"We're cops, we're cops. . . ." The cop nearest Lucas kept his gun pointed at the stairs.

"Drop the piece, drop, drop it, God damn it, or I'll blow your fuckin' ass off, drop it. . . ."

"We're cops, you asshole. . . ." The heavyset cop was half turned toward him, his gun still pointed up the stairs. The pistol was black with a smooth, plastic look about it, a high-capacity Glock 9mm. This guy wasn't using the issue crap from the department.

"Drop it . . ."

Fell came in behind, her gun out, searching for a target, Lucas feeling the black barrel of the cut-off Colt .38 next to his ear.

"Drop it," Lucas screamed again.

The slat-thin cop, who was closest to the door, dropped his weapon, and Lucas focused on the other, who was still looking uncertainly up the stairs. The disarmed cop said, "Jesus, you asshole, we're plainclothes for Bekker. . . ."

Lucas ignored him, focused on the other gun: "Said drop the fuckin' weapon, jerkweed; you assholes beat the shit out of me, and I'm not in the mood to argue. I'll fuckin' pull the trigger on you right now. . . ."

The cop stooped and laid his gun on the floor, glanced at his partner. "Listen . . ."

"Shut up." Lucas looked at Fell. "Keep your gun up, Bekker's here somewhere."

"Lucas, Jesus . . ." Fell said, but she kept the gun up.

Lucas motioned the two cops to a steam radiator, tossed them a set of handcuffs. "I want to hear them click," he said.

"You motherfucker, I oughta fuckin' pull your face off," the heavy one said.

"I'd kill you if you tried," Lucas said simply. "Cuffs."

"Motherfucker . . ." But the two cuffed themselves to the radiator pipe. Lucas looked up the stairs.

"Now what?" asked Fell.

"Backup's on the way, should be here." He kept the .45 pointed at the chained cops.

"You're fuckin' up," said the thick cop.

"Tell that to O'Dell," Lucas said.

"What?" the cop said. He frowned, puzzled.

Lucas shifted around behind him, his .45 pointed at the guy's ear. "I'm going for your ID, don't fuckin' move. . . ." He slipped his hand inside the cop's coat pocket and came out with a badge case. "Now you," he said to the other one.

When he had both IDs, he stepped back and flipped them open. "Clemson," he said. "A sergeant, and Jeese . . ." Lucas looked at the man with the cast, Clemson, and said, "That's what you yelled—you yelled 'Jeese.' You thought he left you behind, running off like that. I thought you yelled 'Jesus'. . ."

"Here comes the cavalry," Fell said. A blue Plymouth jerked to a stop at the door, and they heard screeching tires from up the block. A uniform came through the door, his gun out.

"Davenport and Fell," Lucas said to them, holding up his badge case. "Working for Kennett with the Bekker team. These guys are cops too, but they're cuffed for a good reason. I want them left like that, okay?"

"What's going on?" the uniform asked. He was a sergeant, older, a little too heavy, uneasy about what he'd walked into. Another car screeched to a stop outside.

"Politics," Lucas said. "Somebody's got their tit in a wringer and the top guys are going to have to sort it out later. But these guys will shoot you if they have a chance. They already shot one cop . . ."

"Bullshit, motherfucker," said one of the cuffed cops.

". . . So stay cool. Their weapons are on the floor, but I haven't checked them for backup pieces, which they've probably got."

"I don't know . . ."

Two more uniforms squeezed in, their pistols in their hands.

"Look, half the goddamn department will be here in five minutes," Lucas said. "If we're fucked up, we can always apologize to each other later. For now, just freeze the place."

"What about you guys . . . ?" the uniform asked.

"We're going upstairs. You stay here, don't let anybody or anything in or out. Just freeze the scene and be careful. Bekker might be down below, for all we know, and he's armed."

"This is Bekker?"

"This is Bekker," Lucas confirmed. To Fell, he said, "Come on. Let's get him."

CHAPTER

28

Lily called the patrol lieutenant at the Fifth Precinct and ordered backup squads to Lacey's building: "It's Bekker," she said. "Get them there *now.*"

She dropped the phone back on its cradle and sat down, heavily, in O'Dell's visitor's chair, sorting it out.

They were in the car . . .

O'Dell peered at her across his expansive desk. "What was that all about?" he asked. "The call from Davenport? I believe I was mentioned." His voice was ugly, peremptory. Cold.

Lily shook her head.

"I want to know what he said, Lieutenant," O'Dell barked.

"Shut up, I'm thinking," she said.

O'Dell's eyes narrowed and he sat back. He'd been a politician for five decades, and he instinctively reacted to the warning tone in her voice. Balances had changed somewhere, and he didn't know exactly where. He tried a probe.

"I won't be maneuvered, Lieutenant," he said, emphasizing the rank. "Perhaps a precinct-level job would be more your style after all."

Lily had been peering at the wall above his head, her lips moving slightly. Now she dropped her eyes to his face: "You should have wiped out the ticket requisition for Red Reed before you sent him to South Carolina, John. I've got the ticket vouchers with your signature, I've got the reports on his alleged statements, I've even got the Columbia University transcripts showing that he took classes you lectured at. I also know you fixed at least one drug arrest for him. So don't give me any shit about precinct-level jobs, okay?"

O'Dell nodded and settled in his chair. This could be handled. Everything can be handled by he who waits. He sat silently as she stared at the wall above his head. Finally, a tear trickled down her cheek and she said, "I need your help with the computer."

"What about the Red Reed stuff?" O'Dell asked.

"I'm not going to *use* it, for Christ's sakes. I mean, I can't conceive of any circumstances that I'd use it. It was just something . . . I found out."

O'Dell grinned in spite of himself. This could be handled, all right. The question now was, who would do the handling? "Davenport," he said. "You *told* me not to underestimate him. But he looks like a fuckin' brawler with that scar on his face, and what he did to Bekker . . ."

"Two Robin Hoods just showed up at Bekker's hideout. Lucas is going to take them."

"What?" Now O'Dell was confused.

"The computer?"

"Tell me what's going on. . . ."

"I want you to run Copland against Kennett."

O'Dell stared, his thick lips going in and out as he did the calculations, a nursing motion, wet and unpleasant. "Oh, no," he said. He turned, pulled himself across to the computer terminal, flicked a switch, waited until the computer booted up, entered a user name and password, and began the process.

The matching run took ten minutes. A double column of dates and times marched down the screen.

"All so many years ago," O'Dell said tonelessly, reading down the list. "They must've been like father and son. Copland broke him in on the beat. Copland was a tough old bird. He busted more than a few heads in his day."

"Kennett planted him on you. How long ago?"

O'Dell shrugged. "Five years now. He's been driving me for five years. He must have a microphone arrangement in the car, or a bug—or maybe he just pulled out some sound insulation, so he could hear us talk. Every damn thing we said." He looked at Lily. "How?"

"Lucas looked at everything, figured that Robin Hood was either you or Kennett. . . . He trusted my judgment that it wasn't Kennett. At least, he said he trusted my judgment. And he likes Kennett."

"I'm mildly flattered that he thought I could do it," O'Dell said. "So you and Davenport set me up?"

"He suggested that I cover your phones, then plant some information with you and see what happened. Watch where it went. We hadn't agreed on exactly what to do, we were going to talk about it tonight. Then this came up. When he called us with the Bekker thing, he wasn't at Citibank. He was already watching Bekker's place. He expected you to call somebody and maybe send somebody down, some Robin Hoods. And some showed up. But I've been with you. . . ."

O'Dell said, "Now what?"

The tears had started down her face again, but she seemed unaware of them. "What do you mean?"

He made a questioning gesture with his hands, palms up. At the same time, an oddly satisfied expression had settled on his face. "You seem to be running things for the time being. So what do we do?"

She looked at him for a moment, then said, "Call Carter, with Kennett's group."

"Yeah?"

"Tell him what's happening with Bekker, but tell him to cut Kennett out of the loop."

"What about you?"

"Don't ask," she said. She stood and wobbled toward the door of her own office. "Don't fuckin' ask, 'cause I don't know."

CHAPTER
29

Bekker crouched over Bridget Land, his scalpel in hand, frozen, humming. . . .

When the front door came down, he snapped back, looked down at himself, as though to make sure he was still there, and then at the woman on the table, the scalpel, the monitoring equipment. He heard the footsteps, then the shouts.

Too soon, they'd come too soon, when he was so close.

A tear ran down his cheek. His life had been like this, misunderstood, tormented, unappreciated. Bridget Land, still alive, but hurt, strained away from him, silently. . . .

To do one more would only take minutes, he thought. If he could hold himself together, if they didn't come down too soon.

But Davenport was coming. The gun. He turned, the scalpel in front of his face. The gun was in the other room.

Two impulses fought for control. One propelled him toward the gun, for Davenport; the other told him to finish with Land. Maybe Land would be the transcendent one. . . .

"Don't shoot me in the ass," Lucas said.

He edged up the stairs, Fell two steps behind. Her face was pale, determined, her pistol at Lucas' waist and to the left.

"Just don't roll left," she said.

"Uh-uh . . ."

The smell of marijuana was steeping from the walls, and something else. Lucas sniffed, frowned. Cat urine? And the marijuana odor was years old, not Bekker. In any case, Bekker wasn't much interested in the weed.

At the corner, the first landing, Lucas could see the second-floor door standing partly open, hear Fell breathing below and beside him, smell her faint scent under the odors of the grass and cat piss. . . .

He moved up slowly, across a landing, back against the wall. With the tip of his .45, he pushed the door open. A hall led away, past a closet door, into a living room; he could see the left edge of a television screen. There was no movement, no sound. And the room lacked the peculiar spatial tension of a person in hiding. It *felt* clear.

"Going in," he whispered.

He stepped past the open doorway to another flight of stairs, the second flight stacked with cardboard cartons, the cartons grimy with years of dust and flaking paint.

"Move," he whispered to Fell. She nodded and eased past him, leveled her gun through the door.

"Go," she whispered back. Lucas crouched, took a breath, then scuttled through the open door on his hands and knees, one hand pushing, his gun extended toward the living room arch, searching for movement, for an anomaly. . . . Nothing.

He stood, held up a hand cautioning her, did a quick head-juke to scan the living room again, then went in. When he was sure it was clear, he waved her in. They checked a sitting room and a dining room; found a pair of glasses lying beside the couch, thick lenses, bifocals. Old-lady glasses. Checked the closets, groped through them. Nothing.

The kitchen was small, smelled of boiled beets, boiled cabbage, boiled carrots, porridge. A pool of water shimmered below the refrigerator. Fell squatted next to it, then looked up at the refrigerator. The main door wasn't quite closed, and water dripped from the bottom of it. She pointed, then put her finger to her lips.

Lucas, standing beside her, reached out, took the door handle. Nodded. Jerked it open.

"Aw, shit," Fell said, lurching away from the refrigerator.

Mrs. Lacey hadn't fit that well, but Bekker had managed to crush her into the limited space. Her head lay at right angles across her shoulders, and the light behind her head glowed like a perverse advertisement. Her eyes were bloody holes. A dozen cans of Coke were carefully stacked around her body, one jammed between her twisted arms and her chest. Two dead cats were stuffed in a plastic meat compartment, their tails trailing out.

"Jesus. Jesus." Lucas backed away. "Let's go up the next one, but make it quick."

"You think he's up there?" Fell asked doubtfully. She was staring at the refrigerator, her throat working.

"No. If he's in the building, he's down—I don't feel anything up here."

"Air's too quiet," Fell said. "C'mon, you cover me. . . ."

She went ahead for the next flight, climbing past the cartons, through the dust. At the top, they found three bedrooms and an old-fashioned bath. They checked the closets, the shower, under the beds. Nobody home.

"Down," Lucas said.

"How about the roof?"

"We'll send a couple of guys up—but Bekker would look for a hole, not a perch."

Six cops were spread through the first floor, all looking up apprehensively when Lucas and Fell hurried down the stairs.

"He killed an old woman and stuffed her body in the refrigerator," Lucas told the partrol sergeant, flicking a thumb at the stairs. The two Robin Hoods watched silently from the radiator, their hands still looped through the cuffs. "We went through both floors, nobody home. Send a couple of good people up, see if they can find the roof access. We didn't check that. Tell them to be careful. He's got a gun."

"I'll go myself. . . ."

"No. You stay here. You've got enough rank to keep these assholes cuffed up," Lucas said, nodding at Clemson and Jeese. "There'll be more people coming soon, just hang on. We're gonna do the basement. . . ."

"Take it easy, then," the sergeant said, still uneasy, looking at the two sullen cops chained to the radiator.

The stairs were clean; they looked used. Lucas edged down, taking it easy, leading with the .45, while Fell crouched at the top, focused on the corner at the bottom. If Bekker came around, she would see him before Lucas. But as Lucas reached the corner, her firing line was cut off and he held up a hand to caution her.

Crouching on the bottom step, he did a head-juke around the corner, a one-eyed peek at waist level. A short concrete-floored hallway ended at a green wooden door. A bare bulb hung in the hall above the door. He groped around the corner for the switch, found it, flicked it on.

He stood and crooked two fingers at Fell and she padded down the stairs. "Get that sledgehammer and bring back somebody who knows how to throw it."

Fell nodded. "Be right back," she whispered.

Lucas waited by the door, the gun pointed at the knob. If Bekker was in the basement, and alive, he'd know the cops had arrived. But if he was waiting with a gun, it was critical that he not know the instant that the door would come down. . . .

Fell came back down the stairs with the sergeant and the sledge.

"We got an entry team coming," the sergeant whispered urgently. "They got the armor. . . ."

Lucas shook his head. "Fuck it. I'm taking him. . . ."

"Listen, these guys can take him, no problem. . . ."

"I'm going," Lucas said. He looked at Fell. "What about you?"

"I'll cover, or go in, whatever. . . ."

"God damn it, you're gonna get our asses shot," the sergeant whispered.

"Give me the sledge," Lucas said.

"Listen to me."

"Give me the fuckin' sledge. . . ."

"Ahhh, shit . . ." The sergeant shook his head and hefted the hammer. "I'll swing it, you assholes back me up. I'm going to hit that fucker once, and then I'm on the floor."

"Let's do it," said Fell.

Bekker wandered through the murky basement, trying to remember why he was going to the couch. A song went through his head:

Jesus loves me this I know, for the Bible tells me so. . . .

Sung at a funeral, sometime, way back, he could remember a bronze coffin that sat higher than his head and the choir singing. It was all very sharp, as though he'd just stepped into the picture. . . .

A spider brushed his cheek, tickling, and Bekker snapped out of the funeral picture. Something thumped overhead. That was it. The noise. He had to go to the couch because of the noise overhead.

The couch had been pushed out from the wall, and he stepped behind it and sat down on the rug. The gun was waiting, cheap chrome steel. Loaded. Two shots. He picked it up. Said, Hello, put it in his mouth, sat, like a man with his pipe, then took it out and looked down the barrel.

Hello . . .

His finger tightened, he felt the pressure of the trigger, took up the slack . . . and his mind cleared. Clear as a lake. He saw himself, huddled in the corner of the basement. Saw Davenport come in. Saw himself, hands crossed over his chest, shoulders pulled in, head down.

Saw Davenport coming closer, screaming at him; saw himself rocking back and forth on his heels. Felt the pistol in the bottom hand on his chest, concealed. Saw Davenport reaching out to

him, ordering him to turn; Davenport unaware, unknow-
ing, unthinking. Saw himself reach out with the derringer, press
it to Davenport's heart, and the explosion and Davenport's
face . . .

The sergeant looked at Lucas, raised an eyebrow. Ready?
Lucas nodded. The sergeant took a breath, raised the hammer
overhead, paused, then brought it crashing down. The door flew
inward, and the sergeant hit the ground. There was no immediate
fire from the dark room, and he scrambled back past Fell to the
stairs, groping for his gun.

"Too fuckin' old for this shit," he said.

Lucas, focused on the room, said, "Flashlights."

"What?"

"Get some flashlights. . . ."

With quick peeks around the corner, they established that the
interior of the basement wasn't quite dark. A light was on somewhere, but seemed to be partially blocked, as though the thin
illumination were seeping through a crack in the door, or coming
from a child's night-light. Lucas and Fell, looking over the sights
of their weapons, could see the blocky shapes of furniture, a
rectangle that might be a bookcase.

"Got 'em," the sergeant said.

"Poke them around the corner, hit the interior, about head
high. Keep your hand back if you can. Tell me when you're
going, I'll shoot at a muzzle flash," Lucas said. He looked at Fell,
saw that she was sweating, and grinned at her. "Life in the big
city."

The cop nodded. "Ready?"

"Anytime."

"Now."

The cop thrust the light around the corner, and Lucas, four
feet below, followed with the muzzle of his gun, and his arm, and
one eye. No movement. The sergeant leaned a bit into the hallway, played the light around the interior.

"I'm going," said Lucas.

"Go," said Fell.

Lucas scrambled across the floor to the apartment door, then, flat on the floor, eased his head and shoulders through the door, reached up, flicked a light switch. A single bulb came on. Nothing moving. He crouched, and Fell eased down the hall.

"What's that?" she whispered.

Lucas listened.

Jesus loves me . . .

Not a child's voice. But not an adult's, either—nothing human, he thought. Something from a movie, a special effect, weird, chilling.

For the Bible tells me so. . . .

"Bekker," Lucas whispered. "Over there, I think . . ."

He was inside the apartment, duckwalking, the .45 in a double-handed grip, following his eye-track around the apartment. Fell, behind him, said, "Covered to the right."

"I got the right, you watch that dark door. . . ." The sergeant's voice. Lucas glanced back, quickly, saw the older man easing inside with his piece-of-shit .38.

"Got it," Fell agreed.

"He's in the corner," Lucas said. He half stood, looking at a velour couch. The couch was pushed away from the wall, and the unearthly voice was coming from behind it.

"Bekker," he called.

Jesus loves me . . .

"Stand up, Bekker. . . ."

This I know . . .

Lucas focused on the couch, crept up on it, the gun fully extended. Up close, he could see the top of Bekker's head, shaven, smooth, bobbing up and down with the simple rhythms of the song.

"Up, motherfucker," he yelled. And to Fell and the cop: "He's here, got him . . ."

"Watch a gun, watch a gun . . ."

Lucas, pointing his weapon at the top of Bekker's head, slid around the side of the couch and looked down at him. Bekker looked up, then stood, hands across his chest, rocking, humming. . . .

"Turn around," Lucas shouted.

Fell moved up beside him. . . .

"Nuttier 'n shit," she whispered.

"Watch him, watch him . . ."

She stepped around to get a better angle, then batted at her face and batted again, then waved her hand overhead.

Lucas, glancing sideways: "What?"

"I'm tangled . . ."

Bekker's head turned, like a ball bearing rotating in a socket. "Spiders . . ." he said.

The sergeant, near the kitchen door, coming up slowly, punched a light switch, and Fell groaned, weakly, thrashing at the objects that hung around her head.

"Get away," she choked. "Get away from me. . . ."

They hung on individual black threads from a bundle of crossed wire coat hangers, floating in their separate orbits around Fell's head, wrinkled now, drying, the varicolored lashes as sleek as the day the eyelids were cut from their owners. . . .

Fell staggered away from them, appalled, her mouth open.

"Get him," Lucas said, his pistol three feet from Bekker's vacant eyes. The sergeant took a step forward. Behind Fell, a thin shaft of light cut through a crack in a door. The light was hard, sharp, blue, professional. As the sergeant stepped forward, Fell pushed the door open.

Bekker took a step toward Lucas, his hands crossed on his chest. "Spi . . ."

An old woman lay there, bound and wired silent, her eyes permanently open now, staring, white eyeballs, the skin removed from her chest. . . .

Alive . . .

"Aw, fuck," Fell screamed. She pivoted, the gun coming up, her mouth open, working, her hands clutching.

Lucas had time to say "No."

Bekker said, ". . . ders." And one hand dropped and the other swung up, a glint of steel. He thrust the derringer at Lucas' chest . . .

. . . and Fell fired a single .357 round through the bridge of Michael's Bekker's nose and blew out the back of Michael Bekker's sleek, shaven head.

CHAPTER
30

The walls of Lily's office seemed to melt, and Petty was there, the adult face superimposed on the child's face, both of them together.

And then Kennett's face.

Kennett's face in the dark, in Lily's bedroom. Must've been in winter: she'd bought a Christmas tree, shipped into a lot on Sixth Avenue from somewhere in Maine, and she could remember the scent of pine needles in the apartment as they talked.

No sex, just sleeping together. Kennett laughing about it, but unhappy, too. His heart attack not that far past . . .

"Hanging out with a geek," he said. "I can't believe it. I'm not enough, she's got a geek on the side."

"Not a geek," she said.

"All right. A dork. A nerd. Revenge of the Nerds, visited on Richard X. Kennett personally. A nerd may be dorking my woman. Or wait, maybe it's a dork is nerding my woman. Or wait . . ."

"Shut up," she said, mock-severely. "Or I will fondle your delicate parts and then leave you hanging—in good health, of course."

"Lily . . ." A change of tone. Sex on the mind.

"No. I'm sorry I said it. Kennett . . ."

"All right. Back to the dork . . ."

"He's not a dork. He's really a nice guy, and if he cracks this thing, he could go somewhere. . . ."

She'd talked, Lily had, about the Robin Hood case. She'd talked in bed. She'd talked about the intelligence guys who'd stumbled over it, she'd talked about Petty being assigned to it, she'd talked about computers.

Not all at once. Not formally. But bits and pieces. Pillow talk. But Kennett got most of it. With what Copland overheard, and what Kennett got in bed, they must've known it all.

Petty's image floated in her mind's eye, his hair slicked down, his red ears sticking out, running down the Brooklyn sidewalk with the paper overhead, so happy to see her. . . .

"I killed you," she said to his image, speaking aloud. Her voice was stark as a winter crow. "I killed you, Walt."

CHAPTER

31

The river was black as ink, but thick, oily, roiled, as it pushed the last few miles toward the sea. A full moon had come up in the east, red, huge, shrouded by smog over the city. Lily waited until the elderly night guard and his dog were at the far end of the marina, then used her key at the member's gate.

The docks were cluttered, as always, badly lit by widely spaced yellow bug lights. Out in the water, anchor lights shone off the masts of a half-dozen anchored boats. Here and there, lights showed at portholes, and a light breeze banged halyards against aluminum masts, a pleasant whipping tinkle like wind chimes. The smell of marijuana hovered around a small Capri daysailer and a man was giggling inside the tiny cabin. She walked out of the marijuana stink into the river smell, compounded of mud and decaying fish.

"Lily." Kennett's voice came out of the dark as she approached the *Lestrade*. He was sitting behind the wheel, smoking a cigarette. "I was wondering if you'd come."

"You know about Bekker?"

"Yeah. And that I've been cut out of the loop."

Lily stepped into the cockpit, sat down, staring at him. His face was flat, solemn; he was looking steadily back. "You're Robin Hood," she said.

"Robin Hood, bullshit," he said wearily. He flicked the cigarette into the water.

"I'm not wearing a wire," she said.

"Stand up, turn around." She stood up and Kennett ran his hands down her, between her legs. "Gimme the purse."

He opened the purse, clicked on an electric light that hung from the backstay, looked inside. After poking inside, he took the .45 out of its holder, dropped the magazine and shucked the shells out into the water. Then he jacked the slide, to eject the shell in the chamber. The chamber was empty, and he shook his head. "You oughta carry one under the hammer."

"I'm not here to talk about guns," she said. "I'm here to talk about you being Robin Hood. About using me as a dummy to spy on O'Dell. About killing Walt Petty."

"I didn't use you as a dummy," he said flatly. "I got with you because I liked you and I'm falling in love with you. You're beautiful and you're smart and you're a cop, and there aren't many women around I can talk to."

"I don't doubt that you like me," she said, squaring off with him. "But that didn't keep you from running me. On the way up here, I was remembering when we'd lie down below there, in the berth, and you running those goddamn fantasies about what O'Dell did for sex. Do you remember that? You must've scripted those things, to get me talking about O'Dell. And before that, talking about Walt. When I think of the things I told you, because I felt secure. Because you were a lover and a brother cop. Jesus Christ, every time we got into bed, you were pumping me for information."

"Christ, Lily . . . Lily, if you told me anything about O'Dell or Petty . . . it was by-product. I wasn't sleeping with you to get information. Jesus, Lily . . ."

"Shut up," Lily said. She reached overhead and pulled the chain on the backstay light and they were plunged into the dark again. "I want to know some shit. We've got Jeese and Clemson, Davenport got them, and we know about Copland. . . ."

"I knew Davenport was dangerous," Kennett said quietly. "I really didn't underestimate him. I knew he was a *really* dangerous sonofabitch when he looked up Gauguin, about the necktie. And I couldn't help liking him."

"Is that why your guys tried to beat him up, instead of just whacking him?"

Kennett grinned: she could see his teeth. Not a happy smile, a rueful one. "Another mistake," he said. "You start feeling that everything in New York is *more*. That a small-town guy could never hold off a couple of real New York pros. So we were just gonna break a few ribs, maybe. Something that'd take him off the street for a month. They said he was quick as a pro fighter. They were pissed, said that if they'd been a half-inch slower, he'd of blown them up, he'd of had his .45 out. . . ."

"They were lucky," Lily said. "Why didn't you try again?"

Kennett shrugged. "At that point, we figured it was either kill him or forget him. He didn't seem . . . close enough . . . to kill. And I don't know if the guys would've done it anyway. Petty was already hard to stomach. Davenport's message to O'Dell, the one Copland picked up. That was fake?"

"Not completely. It was Davenport who found Bekker, all right. He was feeding the message to O'Dell to see if any hitters showed up. They did, but I was with O'Dell the whole time. He didn't make any calls. So I started thinking about it."

"God damn it. I thought about skipping Bekker."

"You should have."

"Couldn't. Didn't know what he'd say about . . ." He stopped, remembering.

"About the guys he saw hit Walt. Jeese and Clemson. Thick and Thin."

"No," Kennett said evenly. "It wasn't them."

"Bullshit," she flared. "They fit."

"No. It wasn't."

"Who, then?"

"I won't tell you, but Jeese and Clemson, no." He pulled at his lip. "Old Copland. A good guy. What happens to him?"

"O'Dell will think of something. . . . How many of you are there? And how many people have you done?"

Kennett shook his head. "There are . . . several. Some singles, some two-man teams. None of them knows the others, and I won't tell you who they are."

"We can put Jeese and Clemson in Attica if we want—assault on a police officer with a firearm. And if O'Dell wants to fix it, I'm sure we can find a problem with Copland's pension. He'll spend his last twenty years sitting on a park bench. Or rolled in an army blanket on a sidewalk."

"Don't fuckin' do that," Kennett whispered.

"That's what happens when you lose," Lily said, her voice like ice.

"We were doing right," Kennett said. "I'll call it off. Walk away, and I'll call it off. I'll quit the force, if you want."

"What, so you can write for the *Times*? You'd be a bigger danger there than where you are now," Lily said.

"So what do you want from me?"

"I want the goddamned names."

Kennett shook his head. "No. Never happen. If I gave you the names, only two things could happen: a lot of good guys would get ripped off, or O'Dell would set up his *own* little force of stormtroopers. I'm not going to let any fat, puling, alcoholic fixer do that, I won't. . . ." His voice grew cold as he said it. He bared his teeth and added, "I really like you. But the worst thing you do is, the worst thing about you, is that you associate with that . . . that . . . cunt O'Dell."

"I'm the cunt," Lily said. "I'm the one you rolled for information."

"Fuck you, then," Kennett said, and turned away. "You want to make something out of it, make it in court. I'll tear you up. Now take your ass off my boat."

"I've got another question before I go."

"What?"

"Why Walt?"

Kennett stared at her a moment, then dug in his shirt, found a pack of cigarettes, shook one out, lit it with a match. Tossed the match overboard: they heard it hit, the hiss hanging in the damp air.

"Had to," he said. "Him and his fucking computers. When I started this, nobody really knew about computers and what they could do. They were like electric filing cabinets. Looking in a computer was like snooping through papers on somebody's desk. We didn't know that every time we went into a file, we left tracks. Petty nailed us down. We had to have time to get into the machines, to fix things. We did that. The information's gone now." He looked downriver, at the Manhattan glittering along the river, the arcs of the bridges. "Listen, Lily. If you could take five hundred or a thousand people out of Manhattan, you could make it eighty percent safer. You could make it a paradise."

"Not a thousand," she said. "Maybe ten thousand."

"No. No, not really. A thousand would do it. We couldn't take down a thousand people, probably, but we could make a difference. Arvin Davies. You look at him? Was he one of the people . . ."

"Yes."

"We think . . . intelligence estimates . . . that he committed up to a hundred crimes, all sorts: assaults, burglaries, rapes, murder. He could have done a hundred more. Now he won't."

"You can't make that decision."

"Sure I can. And somebody has to," Kennett said, looking at her. "Your average junkie does fifty or a hundred burglaries for every time he gets caught, and for small burglaries, chances are he'll be right back out on the street. Plea-bargains out, or he'll do thirty days or six months or something. Not enough. If we let all the one-time passion killers out of prison and put all the junkies inside, Manhattan would be a garden spot. Even the ones we took off . . . Christ, we knocked down a thousand violent crimes a year, just the ones we took down."

"How many were there?"

He shook his head. "You don't need to know. But that's why."

"That's why you shot Petty? So we'd have a garden spot?"

Kennett turned away. "We didn't like doing that. But we had no choice. . . . O'Dell is trying to frame me, by the way. Supposedly had a witness who saw me when Waites was gunned down."

"I know."

His eyebrows went up. "You know?"

"Davenport found the kid who supposedly saw you. Found him in Charleston and broke him down. He knows it was phony."

Kennett smiled. "When he went to Minneapolis, he went to Charleston the next day. I thought it was weird that he took the day off—weird for a guy like Davenport."

"How about the others? Waites was a loudmouth, but . . ."

"They nurtured it, the festering. My God, look over there, look at that city, think what it could be. . . ."

She looked across the water at the twinkling lights, like the lights of the Milky Way, seen large. "And you sold it out. And used me like a fucking Kleenex."

"Bullshit," he said. His face was getting red.

"When Walt was killed, I came over here and cried on your shoulder, and you took care of all the arrangements and patted me on the head and took me down below and made love to me, comforting me. I can't believe I did it."

"Yeah, well . . ."

"Well, what?"

"That's life." His teeth were clenched. "Now, go on, Lily, get the hell out of here."

Lily stood, took a step toward the dock. Then another step, toward Kennett.

"What . . ." Kennett began.

She hit him, open-handed, hard: a slap that almost knocked

him down. He took a step toward her, hand on his face, and caught her arm. "Lily, dammit!"

"Let go of me," she said. She tried to pull away, but he held on, and for a moment, they struggled together, his face getting redder; then suddenly, he pinched his shoulders and let his hand drop away.

He turned, seeming to crouch, then went to his knees. "Oh, Jesus," he gasped. "Lily . . . in my bag, down below . . ."

His pills. His pills were in the bag. She started to turn toward the cabin.

A spasm hit him and he went flat in the cockpit, his face straining, the tendons standing out in his neck. "Lily . . ."

She stopped. Looked at the cabin and then back at him. And then carefully, as if in slow motion, she climbed out of the boat, stood on the dock a second, looked at the city and then back down at Kennett. His face was chalky, his mouth open, straining, his eyes large and staring. His hand scrabbled along the deck, as though he were trying to get hold of it. "Lily . . ."

"Say hello to Bekker," she said.

CHAPTER

32

O'Dell sat in his semidarkened office, an air of satisfaction about him, like a bullfrog who'd snapped up a particularly tasty fly. "I really don't give a fuck what you think," he told Lucas.

"Which makes me want to come across the desk and slap the shit out of you," Lucas snarled.

"The New York jails aren't pretty," O'Dell said, mildly. "I could guarantee you a tour. . . ."

Lucas shook his head. "Nah. You wouldn't do that. I spent too much time with Red Reed. We had witnesses. So I slap the shit out of you, you put me in jail, and I tell the papers about Reed, and tell them that you hid a key witness in the murder of a well-known black politician. You'd be right in there with me."

O'Dell seemed to think about it for a minute, then sighed and half closed his heavy-lidded eyes. "All right. But look, if you're gonna slap the shit out me, why don't we get it over with? I need some sleep."

They sat quietly for a minute, then Lucas said, "You know I won't. But you owe me, God damn it. You got me whacked by Kennett's hoods. What I want to know is, how much was set up? Did you know it was Kennett? Is Lily in it? How about Fell? And who else?"

"Lily's okay—she never had anything to do with it. And Lily

says you believe Fell was an alarm. I don't know if I believe it, but I can see the possibility. . . ."

"Kennett?"

"Yeah, I knew about Kennett and a couple more—and frankly, you and Lily should have known that," O'Dell said. "Petty's investigation wasn't a TV show. He didn't sneak off and do all the work and keep all of his conclusions to himself. He came up and sat here every day and told me what he thought. We had Kennett and a couple more people spotted—not Copland, unfortunately. We *didn't* know that Kennett had his own computer people. We figured we could go into the system anytime, print out our evidence. Then Petty got killed and his printouts were lifted. When I went back into the system, the files had been trashed. All I had were a few names and no way to push."

"So you set us up."

O'Dell smiled, still pleased with himself. "Yes. Lily had talked about you. Said you were smart. And I saw one of your simulations. So I put Kennett on Bekker, and you on Kennett, and brought Fell to work with you, and had Lily running you on the side. With all that pressure, something had to blow. Anyway, I had nothing to lose."

Lucas thought about it, stood, stretched, yawned, wandered to O'Dell's window, pulled back the heavy plush drapes and looked out at the twinkling city. "This goddamn place is one big patch, you know? Have I given you my rap on how the place is one big patch?"

"Yeah."

"And I was another one."

"Yeah."

Lucas stretched again, then wandered across the room toward the door. "Nice game," he said.

O'Dell looked at him, then laughed, low and long, genuinely delighted. "It was, wasn't it?"

Lucas sat behind a round, simulated-wood table the size of a manhole cover, in a plastic bar full of plastic pictures of old airplanes. Through the clear Plexiglas walls, he could watch the people streaming out toward the departure gates. He glanced at his watch: three twenty-seven in the afternoon, more or less. With a Rolex, he'd discovered, more or less had to be good enough. He sipped at his Budweiser, not interested, just holding his seat.

Fell showed up at three-thirty, thin, bird-gawky, tough. And maybe angry or something else. She stopped near the end of a long queue for the security gates, looked both ways, and spotted the bar. She paused again at the door, and Lucas raised a hand. She saw him and threaded her way through the tables. When she saw his suitcase by his leg, she looked from the case to Lucas and said, "So I was a three-night stand, or whatever it was."

"Not exactly," Lucas said. "Sit down."

She didn't sit down. Instead she said, "I thought we might go someplace for a while." Tears rimmed her eyes.

"Sit down," Lucas said.

"You fuck," she said, but she sat down, dropping heavily into the chair across from him, hands dangling dispiritedly between her legs. "You said we . . ."

"I thought about asking you to come down to the Islands with me," Lucas said. "I even called out to Kennedy, out to United, to find out what islands we could go to."

She looked down at the tabletop. "Tell me," she said.

"Well, I . . . couldn't." He dug in his pocket and tossed a red matchbook on the table in front of her. The matchbook had a horsehead on it. She picked it up and put it in her purse.

"So you were in the restaurant where Walter Petty got killed," he said. "You told me you weren't."

"Yeah?"

"Yeah. I saw the matches in your apartment."

"When?"

"Well, when we were up there. . . ."

"Bullshit, I got rid of them. When I thought you might be coming over, I saw them, and I thought, 'I got to get rid of these.' I threw them out. So when did you see them?"

He looked levelly across the table at her. "The first day we worked together, I copped your purse, made molds of your keys. The next day I went in."

"You sonofabitch," she said. Then a realization came to her eyes. "You're wearing a wire?"

"No. I like you too much. But the thing is, I can't trust you. Not completely. I thought about going down to the Islands with you and decided I couldn't. I'd eventually talk to you about this, and then . . ." He let the thought dangle, and so did she. He went on: "I tried to think up a lie that would get me back to Minnesota. But I couldn't think of one. And I wanted to tell you why."

"Well. I appreciate it. But you'd have been safe enough. A matchbook is pretty thin . . ."

"There was more than a matchbook. This whole goddamned episode was a game set up by O'Dell. It was so beautiful it makes me laugh. He used every one of us. But anyway—he did a computer run on the victims. You come up way too often. That was a big piece."

She frowned. "Will they get me?"

"No, I don't think so. They think you're an alarm." He explained, and she listened quietly, staring at the floor.

"And you won't tell them different?" she asked, when he finished.

"No. I'm the one who sold them the alarm idea."

"Why?"

He shrugged. "You're a friend."

She looked him over for a moment and then nodded. "Okay."

"If Lily ever found out, though, she very well might kill you. That's another reason I wanted to talk. . . ."

"Did she kill Kennett?" Fell blurted.

"Kennett? No, no, she was downtown with O'Dell all evening."

"Goddamn," Fell said, gnawing a thumbnail. "When I shot Bekker . . ."

"Bekker knew you," Lucas said. "And that's why, in his letter, he wouldn't say anything about Thin. He didn't want people thinking about women killers. . . ."

"Yeah," Fell said. "But that's not why I shot him. I shot him because of their eyelashes, and that woman . . . and everything."

"I know. I mean, I believe it. But why Petty?"

"I didn't want to do Petty," Fell said, voice low, out of gas. "I was there, but I tried to stop it."

"You didn't have to be there. . . ."

"Well . . . I was. If I'd had a couple of more minutes, I think I would've talked . . . the other guy out of it. But Petty came through the door a minute too soon. A minute later and nothing would've happened. At least, not then. Petty had something on us. . . . I'll burn in hell for Petty."

"I doubt it," Lucas said wryly.

"Well, so do I," she said. Then: "I would've liked the Islands, though. Going down with you."

"Yeah, it would have been nice. But I'm the only one who knows about you. You're quick with that gun . . . and you might start thinking about it, if I'm there, laying around."

"I wouldn't," she said, but she couldn't suppress a small grin. "It's interesting that you're scared of me, though."

"Yeah, well . . ."

She sighed. "Fucking trouser-snake cops. So goddamned treacherous."

"And I wanted to tell you about Lily," he said.

"What?"

"She's got a line on a half-dozen of Kennett's shooters. She's gonna be tough, one way or another. But I want you to know two things: they've got no proof of anything. They just want it to stop."

"What's the other thing?"

"The other thing is, if anybody takes Lily, I'll be coming back to town," he said. He'd been watching her, and his eyes had gone hard as granite.

"You oughta be one of us," she said.

"Pass the word on," he said.

"I don't know anybody, except my . . . pal . . . and one other guy. But I'll tell them. Maybe they know more. We don't talk about it. That was one of Kennett's rules. Nobody talks about nothin', he'd say."

"Good rule," Lucas said. He looked at his watch again. "Lily's coming pretty soon."

"Here?"

"Yeah, I've got to talk to her too."

"Then I better get going," Fell said, picking up her purse. She stood and stepped away from the table, then turned back. "Remember when you said something like, 'This place is the armpit of the universe,' the first day we were together?"

"Yeah?"

"Kennett's people . . . we were just trying to make it something else."

"Okay."

"Were we wrong?"

He thought about it for a while. "I don't know," he said finally.

Fell went away and Lucas stared at his beer bottle, making wet O's on the table. After the shooting in the basement, after the dictated statements and interrogations, after the press conference, he'd gone back to the team office. Most of the office staff had gone, but he'd found a computer adept, and said that he needed to look up some information on a couple of cops: Jeese and Clemson.

The computer operator had put him at a vacant terminal, showed him how to call up the files. He'd done it, read through them quickly, then punched in Fell's name. When he'd gotten the file, he'd scanned through to the bottom, found the next of kin: Roy Fell, at an address in Brooklyn. He'd punched in Roy Fell. A file had come up. *Retired,* it said. Then: *Retrieve Retired File? (Y/N).*

Lucas had pushed the Y key. A photoscan was a simple matter of selecting the right option on a short menu, and Fell's father's face had come up. Heavy face, gray hair, gray mustache, a smile that looked almost painful. Six feet, two inches tall. Born 1930. Bekker had had him pegged almost exactly.

"Thick," Lucas had said aloud.

The computer operator said, "What?"

"Nothing," said Lucas, and he'd shut the terminal down.

Sitting at the airport now, drawing circles with the bottom of his beer bottle, Lucas thought, *You can't walk away from family. . . .*

Lily arrived ten minutes later. Like Fell, she stopped by the security queue, looking for the bar. She saw him as she came in, her face ashen, tired, but controlled.

"You talked to O'Dell," she said as she sat down.

"Yeah."

"He fixed the whole thing."

"Yup."

"When did you know?" she asked.

"In Charleston. I suspected before that—everybody was too close together, everything was too convenient. But I didn't know for sure that he wasn't Robin Hood."

"Do you still think Fell was an alarm?"

"Yeah, I'm pretty sure. Not positive. But I think she was simply set up by Kennett. I mean, she *took* those Robin Hoods at Bekker's place. She didn't have to: her piece was right in my ear."

"The word is going around that Robin Hood *did* get Bekker."

"What'd you expect? He got shot to death."

Lily sat for a moment, staring at the fake grain on the tabletop. "When did you know about Dick?" she asked.

"O'Dell tried to set him up—that thing about a white-haired guy killing the politician. I didn't know it was a setup, so even then, I was thinking about him."

"But when . . . ?"

"When we went to Petty's apartment and that Logan wo-man said whoever came to Petty's apartment seemed to stop before he got to the elevator, and after he got off the elevator, and to take a long time getting to the door. . . ."

"Sure," she said, avoiding his eyes. "Dick."

"Yeah, but I couldn't figure it. I assumed he couldn't drive— that's what everybody assumed—and saw a driver dropping him off at Midtown South. And if he couldn't drive, it wasn't him. If he'd been driven, by Copland or one of his other buddies, he wouldn't have had to walk up all those steps himself. He could have sent the driver in for the stuff. So that pushed me off him for a while. Until the day on the river and you told me that he *could* drive. That he sometimes drove the four-by-four, and it pissed you off . . ."

"So," she said. "I not only betrayed Petty, I betrayed Dick."

"Ah, come on, Lily, stop sniveling. You were doing the best you could in a goddamned rat's nest," Lucas said.

"And everybody winds up dead," she said.

"Hey." There wasn't much else to say. Lucas looked at his Rolex. "I gotta go. They're probably boarding the plane now," he said.

At the end of the security queue, Lucas faced her, hands in his pockets, and said, "If this was a movie, there'd be a big hot kiss right here and everything'd be all right."

She had eyes that Rembrandt would have painted. "But there's never anything after a movie," she said. "It ends with a hot kiss and you never see the going-back-to-work part."

"The getting-to-be-important part . . ."

"Yeah. And to tell you the truth, if there was going to be a big hot kiss, I thought Fell'd be getting it. I thought you'd be going out to the Islands with her."

"Nah. She's New York, I'm not. Besides . . ."

"What?"

"There really aren't any Islands, are there?"

She looked away from him, thinking of Petty and Kennett. "No," she said after a minute, "I guess not."

There was another moment, and she stuck out her hand.

"Give me a fuckin' break, Rothenburg," Lucas said, and leaned into her and kissed her on the lips, almost, but not quite, chastely. He turned and started through the security check. "If you get another Bekker, give me a whistle. You know . . . ?"

"Yeah, yeah. Jesus," she said, not quite believing him. A tiny smile crinkled the corner of her mouth. "I do know how to whistle."